Dark Side
of the Moon

Dark Side
of the Moon

Les Wood

**FREIGHT
BOOKS**

First published 2016
This edition published in 2017

Freight Books
49–53 Virginia Street
Glasgow, G1 1TS
www.freightbooks.co.uk

A CIP catalogue reference for this book is available from the British
Library.

All the characters in this book are fictitious and any resemblance to
actual persons, living or dead, is purely coincidental.

ISBN 978-1-911332-00-8
eISBN 978-1-911332-01-5

Typeset by Freight in Plantin
Printed and bound by Bell and Bain, Glasgow

the publisher acknowledges investment from
Creative Scotland toward the publication of this book

Les Wood lives in Barrhead with Marie, his better half, and Skye, the staffie dug. He has had several short stories and poetry published in various anthologies and magazines. He has previously been a winner of the Canongate Prize for New Writing and a prizewinner in the McCash Scots Poetry Competition.

leswoodwriting.com

For Marie, the luvama…

There is no dark side of the moon really...
...matter of fact, it's all dark.

(Gerry O'Driscoll)

Prologue: A Little Night Music

Foreigners.

First it was the Russians and Italians, and they were bad enough. But containable, willing to negotiate.

Now, it was Albanians and Romanians, shady characters with their too-black moustaches and thick eyebrows, hands always stuffed in the pockets of their leather coats, permanently looking into the middle distance, half smirking, never meeting your eye.

They thought they could just waltz in and take over. In bloody Glasgow.

Aye, that'll be right, Boddice had once thought. This is *my* territory; *I* run the show around these streets. Nobody gets to piss in my porridge and expect to get away with it.

Except they did. These bastards didn't give a toss. They were blatant, nonchalant, unruffled. They had the drugs, the contacts, the distribution, the confidence and the will. And now they were starting to muscle in. Without as much as a by-your-fucking-leave. Boddice had found his patch shrinking, his circle of fear and intimidation pulling away from him like a receding tide. Not that the others could ever know this. Oh no.

It was late. He sat in his darkened living room trying to listen to Mozart. All that Classic FM Snoozy-Sounds-At-Seven, Notes-To-Nod-Off-To rubbish. It was all shite – an effort just to listen to it, never mind try to understand it.

But it was necessary. He had an image to cultivate: refinement, pedigree, taste.

His cigar had long ago gone out, and his whisky glass was empty; the central heating had clicked off and the room was chilling rapidly. He sat on the sofa staring into the blackness. Thinking.

And this evening had given him a lot to contemplate. The message. The offer. A bolt from the blue. A blast from the past.

After all these years.

It was certainly different. Difficult. Yet tempting. Very tempting.

And exciting. Oh, yes, definitely that. It would make him rich. More money than he would know what to do with. If he pulled this off, the Albanians, Russians, Italians, all the Glasgow fucktards who were jostling for position, establishing their own wee gangster empires, all those pricks would be eclipsed by the enormity of what he had done. He would become a legend. And he liked the sound of that.

If he could pull it off.

He found the remote and switched the music off, letting the sound of the rain thrown against the window take over.

A smile spread across his face.

It was time to tell the others.

PART 1: THE PALACE

Prentice:
What is and What Should Never Be

For Davie Prentice, a shitey day was just about to get shitier.

Boddice had him doing the rounds, collecting money from assorted schemie-scum, noising up the chancers in graffiti-scrawled, rubbish-strewn tenement blocks; the kind of places where a tattered old bed sheet Sellotaped to the window served as a curtain, and carpets that didn't squelch under your feet were a Grand Designs luxury. Pale, wasted faces answering the door. Barely conscious. Eyes hooded, crack-riddled. Some of the bastards still in their underwear or jammies.

Desperate.

Most of them had a couple of quid to hand over, but not enough to pay off the full whack of what they owed. Which, Boddice had told Prentice, was all fine as far as he was concerned. Just add another two hundred percent onto the interest rate and come back the next day with the baseball bat. That was usually enough to get them to cough up the readies.

But Prentice was weary of the whole thing. He wasn't exactly a coffin-dodger at thirty-five, but he felt old beyond his years. Here he was, trudging around on foot, taking the bus, forgetting to dress for the weather – losing his driving licence had fucked him up good-style – dealing with the dregs of the city. Christ, it was only early afternoon and already Prentice felt ready for his bed. He should be getting out of this line of work. Think about settling down into something sensible. A wife. Weans. A real job.

He'd come to Rosco's place to collect the three hundred Rosco owed. It was the top flat in a manky, scunnersome close, the doors to the other flats boarded up by graffiti-covered metal sheets. No answer when Prentice rapped on Rosco's door, he tried the handle and found it open.

The first thing that hit him was the stench. It nearly knocked him off his feet: a combination of piss, shite and something else, some bass note of unpleasantness humming underneath it all. He fought back the urge to gag and moved through the dimness of the hall to the living room. The smell was worse in here. A plate with the congealed remains of a fish supper sat on a cushionless sofa beside what looked like a weeks-old vomit stain. It was the only furniture in the room. Prentice covered his mouth. Did people really have so little dignity that they could live like this? To pricks like Rosco though, dignity was just the name of a boat in a Deacon Blue song.

There was no sign of him. 'Rosco, are you here ya clatty bastard?' Prentice shouted.

No reply.

He made his way back to the hallway and found the door to the bedroom. The smell was almost overpowering now. His gorge was rising. 'Rosco! You in there?'

Prentice turned the handle and opened the door. A blast of heat hit him, along with the stupefying stink of decay. He dry-heaved a couple of times, his eyes watering. The orange glow from a four-bar heater lit the room. It must have been on for days to heat the room like this.

Out of the corner of his eye Prentice spotted a shapeless shadow on the floor at the far side of the bed. He flipped the light switch and forced himself to move further into the room.

It was Rosco. Or rather, what used to be Rosco. He was naked, lying half under the bed. His face was a bloated, purple balloon, his fingers and hands blackened and puffy. A yellow, jelly-like fluid oozed on the floor beside his body.

'Holy fuck, what happened to you?' Prentice said aloud. As if in reply, a soft mewing sound came from behind him. Prentice spun round. There, in the corner, was a baby. It lay on its back on the floor, gurgling and kicking its feet, oblivious to its surroundings. Prentice's jaw dropped. 'Jesus…'

He knelt beside the baby. It was dressed in a white jumpsuit with miniature trainers on its feet. As far as Prentice could tell, the baby was unharmed. What the hell was it doing in here? He picked it up and took it into the hallway. The air felt fresher here, but he knew it was only relative compared to the reek of putrefaction in the bedroom. The baby looked up at him, its little eyes blinking, searching. Its mouth moved forming unknown baby-words.

Prentice was at a loss. Rosco was gone, and whatever had happened to him was bound to have happened sooner or later. The guy was a loser, had always existed barely half an inch this side of the Great Divide. It was no big surprise. But this baby? Where had it come from? Whose was it?

Another thought came to him. What was he going to do with it? Call the police, let them deal with it? That was the obvious move. But there was the risk they'd manage to trace something back to him. Snooping, curtain-twitching neighbours could have spotted him entering Rosco's close. Unlikely, but not improbable.

Or, he could just leave the baby where it was. Surely the mother would come back for it? Or would it be the father? Prentice went through to the living room, checked the kitchen, the bathroom. No pram, no infant formula, no nappies. No sign of any baby paraphernalia. No sign any parent had ever been here. Christ, what kind of person leaves a baby alone in a flat with a dead junkie? Prentice already knew the answer to that one; it hardly seemed likely someone like that would be coming back any time soon.

Or, there was the third option.

He could take the baby with him. Okay, that was just an insanely stupid idea – he didn't know the first thing about infants, they were an alien species – Jesus Christ, he couldn't even remember holding one before. And what would he do with it once he'd taken it?

What a mess.

Bugger it. Easy decision. He would leave the baby behind. Let fate decide. It wasn't his problem.

He went back to the bedroom and placed the baby on the bed. He switched off the electric fire and surveyed the room before leaving. The baby lay quietly. It turned towards him and in the gloom he could see its little eyes watching his face. It kicked its legs a few times and flapped its arms on its chest. Prentice went out into the hallway and pulled the bedroom door shut.

He stood in the hallway for a full five minutes, staring at the door.

Prentice sighed. *Jesus, Mary and Joseph*, he thought. *Ah can't do it.*

He went back into the bedroom, gathered the baby into his arms and rushed out of the flat before he could change his mind.

Prentice got to the bottom of the stairs and ran out into the street. The air was sweet and cool after the stench of Rosco's flat and he sucked it in, savouring it. The baby lay with its head back, blinking at the sky, as if seeing it for the first time. Prentice scanned the windows of the flats opposite. They stared back, grim, lifeless. At least no-one had seen him.

Prentice turned to walk up the street when his phone buzzed: an incoming text. He fished the mobile from his pocket, glanced at the message: *Boddice at the Palace 4.00.* He frowned, not sure what it meant. Obviously Boddice wanted some sort of meet – and it was to be in private, out of sight. Boddice had a habit of picking obscure places to arrange gatherings – abandoned bus depots, derelict tower blocks, once even a bloody disused mine working in the north of the city. But what was the Palace? Prentice sighed. Why the hell couldn't Boddice be more explicit in his messages? The bastard was so paranoid Prentice thought he would consider holding a meeting up his own arse just so no-one could see what he was up to.

Prentice looked at his watch. Two o'clock. Two hours to work out where he was supposed to be and then actually get there. Two hours to work out what to do with this bloody baby.

It began to stir in his arms. He hoisted it up and felt a soft, squishy heaviness under its backside. God knew how many days had passed since the nappy had been changed. The baby squirmed and began a low whimpering. Prentice sighed and looked up the street. In the distance he could see Marmion Court, a twenty-five-storey tower block which rose from the surrounding scheme like a solitary grave stone.

It gave him an idea.

***

Mark's Market was the only functioning shop in a row of derelict units at the bottom of the high rise. A couple of boys of about eight or nine were kicking a ball against the metal shutters of one of the empty units as Prentice made his way over to the door of the shop. Seagulls wheeled and dived on the icy downdraft from the tower block, swooping onto the overflowing binbags piled outside the entrance to the flats.

'Heh, mister?' one of the boys called. 'Any fags you could give us?'

'You going into Mark's? Gonnae get us a bottle of Buckie when ye're in?' said the other.

'Are youse two fed up with they faces?' said Prentice, turning to them. 'Cos if youse don't fuck off right now, Ah'll rearrange them for ye, alright?'

The two boys looked at each other and laughed. 'Aye, so ye will. Come ahead ya prick,' said the smallest one, giving Prentice the come-on with his hands. Prentice started to walk towards them and they ran off to the end of the row of shops.

'Aye, run, ya wee shites!' he called after them.

Prentice turned back to the shop and pushed through the door.

'*Market*' was hardly the word to describe the place. Pale fluorescent strips lit a couple of bare aisles, disintegrating cardboard boxes placed on the floor to soak up the wet footprints of the customers. A woman in a heavy overcoat and house slippers stood playing the puggy machine next to the door, pulling pound coins from her purse and feeding them into the slot. Prentice walked past the miserable shelves of cut-price tinned vegetables, cans of soup and packets of chocolate biscuits to the checkout at the back of the shop. Boxes of crisps of different flavours surrounded the counter and there was a selection of cheap whiskies and wines stacked on the wall behind the till.

The man at the counter looked up from his Daily Record. 'Aw, wait a minute,' the man said, standing and raising his hands. 'Heh, Prentice what are you here for? Ah'm all squared up with Boddice. He's got what he's owed. Ah paid ye a fortnight ago, remember?'

'Settle yourself Mark,' said Prentice, smiling. 'Ah'm not here for collectin.' He looked around him, making a show of scanning the shop, glancing up at the fake CCTV camera in the corner. 'How's business? Gettin any more trouble from anybody?'

'No, not really,' said Mark. 'Just the usual. Stupid boys wantin to noise me up. Coupla bags of crisps an sweeties nicked. No real trouble... no... not really.' He kept his gaze on the counter in front of him, never meeting Prentice's eyes.

'See?' said Prentice. 'Told ye Mr Boddice would look after ye, didn't Ah?'

'Aye, ye did.'

Prentice continued inspecting the shop. 'Tell ye what Ah'm here for, Marky boy. Do ye sell they disposable nappy things in here?'

'Eh?' Mark looked up, noticing the baby for the first time. 'Oh, right, Ah see. Aye... aye we've got somethin like that.' He pointed to the aisle behind Prentice. 'Bottom shelf on the left there.' He came round from behind the counter. 'Here, let me get them.' Mark picked up a packet of *Snuggies* from the shelf and laid them on the counter. 'Anythin else?'

'Not just now,' said Prentice, looking over Mark's shoulder to the stockroom at the back of the shop. 'But have ye got anywhere Ah can get this wean changed? It's mingin.'

Mark leaned over and stuck his finger into the baby's hand. Its fingers curled round his own, grasping tightly. 'Ah didn't know ye had a wean Prentice,' he said, pulling his hand away. 'Takin it out on yer rounds now, eh?'

Prentice glared at him. 'It's no mine. It's… eh, it's… my sister's.' He raised his eyebrows. 'Ah'm looking after it, right?'

'What's its name?'

Ah wish Ah fuckin knew, thought Prentice. He said the first thing that came into his head. 'Jack… name's Jack.'

'Hiya Jack,' said Mark, tickling the baby under the chin. Mark screwed up his face. 'Man alive, yer right, it *is* stinkin.' He stepped back behind the counter and went to the till to ring up the nappies. He noticed Prentice staring at him and his hand froze above the keyboard. He gave a nervous laugh. 'Aye, right enough, right enough. Have them on the house Prentice.'

Prentice held up the nappies. 'Well?' he said. 'Where can Ah go?'

'Listen,' said Mark. 'Ah've got a better idea.' He stuck his head into the stockroom. 'Moira! C'mere a minute will ye?' He smiled at Prentice and rolled his eyes. 'Better to get somebody that knows what they're doing, eh?'

A woman dressed in a black shell suit, her blonde hair scraped back in a tight pony tail, came through from the stockroom. Her face was pale, her eyes puffed from lack of sleep. Mark put his arm around her shoulder. 'This is my wife, Moira,' he said. 'Listen, will ye take this wean through the back and change its nappy for me?'

Moira pulled away and looked at him. '*What?*' she said. 'Do Ah look as if Ah'm runnin a bloody nursery here? Is there somethin Ah've missed while Ah've been through the back? Have ye changed the name of the shop to Mark's Mugs when Ah've no been looking? Cos Ah tell ye, Ah'll be a bloody mug before Ah'll change some other bastard's wean's nappy.' She glanced at Prentice. 'No offence.'

She turned to go back through to the stockroom and Mark grabbed her arm. 'Moira. Ye don't understand.' He gave a little jerk of his head to indicate Prentice. 'This here's Mr Prentice. He works for Mr Boddice.' He widened his eyes at her. 'Mr *Boddice*.' He paused to let it sink in. 'And Mr Prentice here has done us a few favours in the past, so Ah think we owe him one back. Do ye not think?'

Moira turned to Prentice and looked him up and down. 'Favours is it?' She snorted. 'Oh aye, Ah know what kind of favours you do *Mister* Prentice.'

'Call me Davie,' said Prentice.

'No, mister'll do fine for me,' said Moira. 'Funny isn't it? The favours, as he calls them, that you do for us cost us a hundred pound a week. And what do we get for that? We pay *you*, so that *you* don't come round and fuck up our business. Our shop.'

'Moira,' said Mark.

She ignored him. 'We work all the hours of the bloody day to break even, *just to break even*, not even a profit mind ye, and you come round here and—'

'Moira!'

'What? What is it?' She pointed at Prentice. 'Do ye think he doesn't need tellin? You've said it often enough yourself. We can't afford this. We're gonnae go under. We're—'

This was getting out of hand. 'Wait!' Prentice shouted. The baby gave a startled kick. 'Just wait a fuckin minute!' He shook his head and grinned. 'Mark, my man, you'd better learn to keep this one under control, or ye might find yourself with a wee increase in yer weekly outgoings.'

'Don't you threaten us,' said Moira. 'We can—'

'You can what?' said Prentice. 'Go to the polis?' He laughed. 'Go a-fuckin-head. It'll no get ye anywhere.' Prentice could see tears start in Moira's eyes. He could see the despair, the helplessness. He hated himself for it. But this was what he did. This was his fucking job. 'They're scared.' He leaned across the counter and whispered into Moira's face. 'Aye, even the polis. Scared of Boddice. They wouldn't touch him.'

Moira stood, arms folded in silent defiance, blinking back her tears and Mark put his arm around her. She shrugged it off. 'Piss off,' she said. 'Leave me alone.'

'And now,' said Prentice. 'If ye don't fuckin mind, Ah've had a bastard of a day and you two are just makin it worse. So Missus, or rather... Moira.' He forced himself to smirk. 'Moira. If you please.' He held up the pack of Snuggies. She looked at him and scowled.

'You prick,' she said, and snatched the nappies. She took the baby from him and went through to the stockroom.

Prentice sighed. He picked up Mark's newspaper from the counter and took it into a corner. 'Tell me when she's finished,' he said.

He opened the paper and pretended to read. He could feel Mark staring at him, could feel the suppressed hatred. He couldn't blame him. These people were trying their level best to get by, and here he was, someone who hadn't made an honest penny in his life, fucking them over. Prentice hated himself. He had been the hardman for too long. Folk crossed the street to avoid him. Looked at him sideways in pubs, nudging their pals and whispering behind their pints. His reputation went before him. Always would.

He turned the page and stared, without seeing, at the words and the pictures. He felt his chest tightening, a feeling of claustrophobia coiling around him. Was there really no way out? Would Boddice even *let* him get out?

That was something else. Prentice knew things. Lots of things. Boddice might not be too happy if one of his team were to decide to up sticks and go back into the real world. What if Boddice thought Prentice might be the kind of guy to pass on a wee detail here or there to the police or to some rival?

These fucking thoughts and questions going round in his head – he felt like screaming.

'Right ya waster, that's her done,' said Moira in his ear. How long had he been daydreaming? He hadn't even heard her come up. 'You should be ashamed of yourself,' she said. 'That wee lassie was in a right mess, shite all up her back and everything. Dried-in shite. Nappy rash all over the wee soul. Ah had to put extra cream on her bum and thighs. How long since she was changed? Eh?'

Prentice gathered himself, switched the hardman back on. 'Haven't a scooby missus, don't care, don't want to care.' He grinned at her.

'Wait a minute,' said Mark. '*Wee lassie?* Ah thought ye said its name was Jack?' Moira frowned at him.

'Ah did. Jack… Short for… Jackie,' said Prentice, thinking on his feet.

'Aye… aye, Ah suppose,' said Mark.

'Well, anyway,' said Moira, handing the baby back. 'She's cleaned up now. An Ah fed her too. She was starvin.' She looked Prentice up and down, making no effort to conceal her contempt. 'Anythin else ye want from us, or can we get on with our work?'

'No, that's it Ah think,' said Prentice.

'Ye sure? Don't want any ironing done while you're here? Want me to come round to yer house and do some hoovering?'

Mark shot her a look. 'Moira, don't.'

Prentice laughed. 'Don't worry about it Marky boy. She could do more than that for me if she came round my house, eh Moira?'

'Hey, Ah don't think that's called for,' said Mark. 'It's not fu—'

'Don't bother defendin me to the likes of him Mark,' said Moira. 'He looks the type that wouldn't know what to do with a woman.'

Prentice knew he had gone too far. The right thing to do

14

would be to back down. But there was that little niggle at the back of his mind. The one that told him what he should do is break this woman's fucking teeth.

'Alright Mark, calm down. It's not a problem,' he said, walking to the front door. 'What *will* be a problem, will be the hundred and fifty pound ye'll owe Mr Boddice, startin from next week. Like Ah said, you've got to start thinkin of keepin that wee bitch under a bit more control.'

'*What?*' Moira shouted. '*A hundred and fifty?* You're joking, please say you're joking.' She burst into tears.

Prentice paused beside the old woman who was still playing the puggy and pushed open the door. 'No joke Moira,' he said. 'See you next week.' He went out into the cold.

***

A slurry of sleet swirled around him as he leaned against the wall of the shop and closed his eyes. Another notch on the bad-ass bedpost.

He had to hand it to Moira though. She'd shown she was more than simply another spineless no-mark.

Which was why she had to be crushed.

Reputation. That's what it was all about. He had to keep them scared. He had to be a boot-in-the balls of a man, a bone-crunching head-butt of a man, a Stanley knife of a man. A total cunt of a man.

Reputation.

People like Mark and Moira – got to let them know where they stood in the great hierarchy of things, and that was right down at the bottom of the pile. More important, they had to know that the bottom of the pile was as good as it was going to get for the likes of them.

Aye, fucking reputation.

Except, he didn't believe in it any more. He was nothing more than a lackey for someone bigger. He had no real reputation at all. All he had was a persona, and a persona built on the back of people's fear of someone else – Boddice. Prentice was tired of it all.

He blew out a long sigh and set off from Mark's. One thing about his visit had been worthwhile though. He knew now what the Palace was. It was the old dear playing the puggy that had brought it into his head.

Mindless gambling. Women. Bingo.

Of course. The Palace was the old bingo hall on Cardenhall Road. Typical Boddice venue – disused for years – if he cut through the bottom end of the Cardenhall scheme he could maybe catch a bus that would all but take him to the front door. He pulled his coat around the baby, looked at his watch. He should make it in time.

He crossed the road to the Cardenhall estate. The streets were empty, the sleet and rain driving the kids who would normally be hanging around back to their homes and Xboxes. The wind whipped around him, and he shivered as he walked. The light was fading and he knew he had to pick up the pace if he was going to get to the Palace in time. He remembered a short-cut at the next street that would take him out at Cardenhall Road, a lane that ran for about a hundred yards between two sets of tenements and emerged at the service alley behind the shops on the main road. It would save him ten minutes at least.

When he reached the lane, the street lights were just coming on, powering up from the dull red switch-on glow but not yet reaching the full-blown orange sodium glare. High walls lined with overgrown shrubs and brambles ran into the distance towards the neon lights of the shop stockrooms at the far end.

He walked quickly, anxious to get to the main road as soon as possible. When he saw the figure enter the lane ahead of him, he gave a sigh. Young lad. Red and yellow Berghaus jacket. Waist drawstring pulled tight. Collar fastened high.

Baseball cap tugged low on his forehead. All the ingredients. Prentice guessed what was coming.

Prentice cradled the baby against his shoulder and kept up his pace, but the figure walked towards him slowly, slinking against the right-hand wall. As he approached, Prentice could see the boy was avoiding eye contact.

As they drew level, the boy stepped in front of him.

'Alright pal?' the boy said. 'Got the time on ye?'

Prentice laughed. The wee tube actually used that line. 'Fuck off son,' he said. 'Ah'm in a hurry.'

'No, honest pal, have ye got the right time?' the boy said, still blocking Prentice's path.

'No, honest son, fuck off. *Alright?*'

Prentice moved past him, deliberately bumping him with his shoulder as he did so.

'Hey, ya bastard,' the boy said. 'Ye want to come back and try that again?'

Prentice stopped in his tracks, stared straight ahead, his back to the boy.

He waited.

Could hear the boy breathing behind him.

'You thinking you're hard enough son?' Prentice said quietly without turning around.

The boy sniffed. 'Naw mister.'

'Good,' said Prentice and carried on walking.

***

For the first time that day he was in luck. When he got to the main road, a bus was already waiting at the stop in front of the shops. He paid his fare and went up to the top deck. It was deserted apart from two women sitting near the front, deep in an animated conversation. He went to the back row and slumped into the seat. He was surprised to see his hands trembling. The boy in the lane had been lucky. If he hadn't backed down Prentice might have had to do some serious damage.

And he still had this bloody baby to deal with. She was asleep in his arms, her mouth open, revealing gums but no teeth. A small scratch, like a Nike tick, marked the skin on her cheek. She was young. She had no idea what was happening to her, where she was, where she had been. Fuck, she had no idea *who* she was. Prentice wished he could be like her – a blank canvas, untainted.

The December dark had already descended and the sleet had turned to a cold, relentless rain. The bus lurched through the grim, desolate streets and Prentice had to wipe the condensation from the window to glimpse the rows of tenements which passed by, gardens littered with burger wrappers, broken bottles and plastic bags. The two women got off at the next stop, leaving Prentice alone with the baby at the back of the bus.

The Palace was three stops further on. He would get off at the next stop and walk the rest. It was an automatic precaution. He didn't want to draw attention to where he was going. He was becoming fed up with all this pretence at subterfuge, all this underhand, secret crap.

He made up his mind. Things were going to change. He had to extricate himself from this life, try to make a new start, Boddice or no Boddice. He had no idea yet how he was going to do it, but he knew it was time.

He had also made up his mind about something else. He could see his stop in the distance. There was a small queue waiting. One of them surely would be coming onto the top deck. He took the baby and laid her securely in the corner of the seat against the rear wall. He made sure she was well-wrapped, and she stirred in her sleep. 'Good luck, wee Jackie,' he said. He bent down and kissed her forehead.

He kept his head down as he got off the bus, brushing past the group huddled against the rain at the bus stop. He stood in a close-mouth as the bus drove off. No-one went up to the top deck. Maybe that was a good thing. When someone did eventually find her there would be no association with his hunched figure stepping down at the bus stop. He kept watching the bus as it rumbled into the distance. As it rounded the corner at the far end of the street he set off.

The Palace was less than three hundred yards away.

Boag:
The Song of the Clyde

Alistair Boag had been sleeping rough.

Very rough.

Things had been getting bad for weeks, money running out, forcing him to beg spare change in the pishy stairwell of a multi-storey car park. And now he didn't even have enough cash to get into one of those shit-hole hostels-for-the-permanently-fucked-up. He'd had to face the reality of sleeping in a bloody skip. It had taken the whole day to find a decent one at the foot of a block of flats near the city centre and, even then, it had been bad. Cold rain pissing down through the night and only a few soggy cardboard boxes to give him any semblance of shelter among the nail-studded planks and twisted metal bars that lay in a tangled nest at the clinkered bottom of the skip. To crown it all, a woman, out of her face with the drink or the drugs, had been wailing some tuneless song from the open window of one of the flats above:

She's just a bare-fitted loaby dancer,
Waitin for someone tae romance her.
To sweep her aff her feet,
No' give her cause tae greet,
Is there a man who'll gie her an answer?

He had no idea what the hell that was supposed to have been about, but she kept at it, singing it over and over, keeping him awake into the wee hours.

When morning finally came, Boag slunk out from the skip with the first sounds of life from the high-rise and made his way into town. He wandered down to Buchanan Bus Station; maybe there'd be the chance of picking up a few coins from the commuters on their way to work. A clock, set on a pair of giant burnished steel legs outside the station looked as if it was about to sprint across the street. It read quarter to nine.

His coat hung with clingy, damp weight and the smirry rain plastered his hair against his head. Secretaries with sombre black umbrellas, half-awake students, men in suits, men in paint-stained overalls, women with shopping bags struggling with novelty brollies, women with briefcases, pensioners dragging wheeled suitcases behind them like strange pets. They all bustled past him, on their way to wherever the hell they were headed. No-one met his gaze.

He carried on, crossing the road to the *Grande Bouffe* restaurant which sat on the corner of the busy junction. He shivered as he watched his reflection in the plate-glass windows move like a ghost through the early breakfasters in the dining room. They were warm and satisfied, cosseted and pampered. Tucking in to bacon and eggs, beans and mushrooms, crisp toast and steaming mugs of dark coffee or tea. Reading the morning papers, talking into their mobiles, scanning the busy street.

They looked right through him.

The window was etched with various signs and slogans – *La Grande Bouffe Restaurant, Fusion Menu, Late Night Jazz, Pre-Theatre Menu, Mediterranean Brasserie.*

Fusion Menu, Boag thought, what the fuck was that supposed to mean?

A man in a dark suit sat at a table near the window, typing into a fancy mobile phone and reading a pink newspaper. He was middle-aged, but his hair was gel-slicked and his sideburns were shaved into small dagger-points on his cheek. He leant back in his chair and turned to see Boag staring in at him. The man looked Boag up and down, considered him for a few moments, and motioned for one of the waiters to come over. Boag watched him say something to the waiter, gesturing towards Boag standing in the rain. The waiter moved off and the man tilted his head back and continued to look along the length of his nose at Boag.

'Alright pal?' It was the waiter, standing beside him, linen towel draped over one arm, squinting against the rain. 'How's about moving on, eh? Give the customers a bit of peace?'

Boag blinked at him. 'What do ye mean? Ah'm just standing here mindin my own business.'

'I know that, pal,' said the waiter. 'But you're putting people off their breakfast.'

'What? That guy in there?' Boag jerked his thumb at the man in the dark suit who was studying them with a slight smile on his face.

'Aye,' said the waiter. 'He doesn't want to see your scraggy face looking in at him. So, if you could just be on your way, that would be great.'

Boag laughed. 'He doesn't want to see my face lookin at him? Go back in and tell him to turn his fuckin chair round then. It's a free country, as far as Ah know, and Ah can stand where Ah bloody well like.'

'Of course you can,' said the waiter. 'But if you don't move your arse, I'm going to get the police. Either that, or you'll get my toe up your backside.' One of the doormen from the hotel next door wandered over to join the waiter.

'Any problems here, Tommy?' said the doorman, folding his arms.

The waiter turned to Boag. 'Well?' he said.

Boag looked from the waiter to the doorman. It wasn't worth making any fuss, not with the two of them now. 'No, you're alright,' he said. 'Ah'll move myself. Just tell that character in there that he doesn't own the pavement. He's no any better than me, just cos he's got a smart suit and a shirt and tie. He still shites broon the same as me.'

The waiter smiled. 'Thanks pal, I'll be sure to use those very words.'

Boag drifted off towards the pedestrian crossing, shuffling slowly and drawing sidelong looks from the commuters making their way from the bus station. He glanced back to make sure the waiter and the doorman had gone back inside and he sprinted back to the window. He drummed hard against it with his fists, making the glass shake and boom. The man in the dark suit jumped, startled by the noise, spilling his coffee onto his trousers. 'Get it right up ye!' Boag shouted, and turned and ran, laughing, through the crowd down towards West Nile Street.

***

Anderson's Amusements at the bottom of West Nile Street was one of the better arcades, mainly because it opened early – eight or half-past – catering for the seriously addicted, or those coming off night shifts. It also served food and hot drinks first thing. For Boag, it provided him with warmth and a place to dry off a bit, and he was grateful to get in out of the cold.

Even at this early hour there were a couple of people sitting at the bingo consoles, and a dreary, monotonous voice calling the numbers – *one and eight, eighteen, three and five, thirty five, on its own, number six...* Boag used the last of his money to buy a dry roll and a cup of tea and found the little group of tables hidden amongst the clacking puggy machines. He made sure he sat at a table with one of the gaudy, pink table lamps. He leant under the table and unplugged the lamp from the socket in the wall and plugged in his mobile charger.

His mobile was his lifeline, his link with Boddice. He'd waited for weeks now without so much as a peep from the phone. No voicemail, no texts. Had Boddice forgotten him? There was a time when he'd get a call, maybe even two, every week. Wee jobs, driving stuff around the city – 'couriering' Boddice called it – or keeping watch overnight at a warehouse. Sometimes he was asked to come along with Prentice and Kyle on more complicated jobs. But he wasn't so keen on those – Prentice scared him, and Kyle was just plain weird. But Boddice always paid well.

Recently though, there'd been nothing. Maybe he'd fallen out of favour. He tried to remember if there was anything in his last couple of jobs that had pissed Boddice off. Something he hadn't done properly. But he was sure there was nothing.

Maybe Boddice had just lost interest. After all, the only reason Boddice bothered with Boag at all was because of Gerry, his Da.

Gerry Boag was doing six years in the Bar-L for Boddice. Incarcerated at Her Majesty's Pleasure for storing fifty grand's worth of heroin in the shed in the back green. It was Boddice's heroin, of course, although Gerry never blabbed that wee bit of valuable information to the police. He didn't want to end up rolled in an old carpet and set on fire in some remote quarry. He'd rather take the six years, maybe only four if he was a good boy. All things considered, old Gerry could have been a lot worse off.

Gerry's time on the inside meant he had lost the flat of course, and, with that, Boag was out on his arse on the street. Boag had been living with the old man since he came out of the army. Gerry had given him the use of the back bedroom as long as he kept out of the way of whatever 'business' deals took place in the flat. The arrangement suited Boag. He'd never really got on with the old man anyway, and as soon as he found his feet he intended moving on. It never worked out that way though. Boag found himself settling into a routine, a comfortable familiarity in which he and the old man largely ignored each other and led their separate lives.

Of course, Boag knew what was going on with his old man and Boddice, and he knew the men who came round to the flat by sight and by reputation – the men who would gruffly nod to him if he passed them on the stairs, or who watched him warily if he happened to wander by accident into some deep conversation that was happening around the smoke-shrouded kitchen table late at night. He mostly stayed out of their way and they seemed to tolerate him for that.

It was the old man's habits that Boag found the hardest to deal with – the drinking and the women and the drugs. Often, he'd lain awake at night listening to the old man humping some tart he'd brought back from the pub; the headboard banging against the adjoining wall, and the desperate, wheezing grunts and moans of his Da (*his Da!*) finally building up to a phlegm-choked convulsion as he shot his load. It made Boag bury deep under the bedclothes, his face burning with shame. Sometimes he met these women in the lobby the next morning. They ranged from blank-faced girls, younger than himself, to haggard women in tight leather mini-skirts and too much make-up who were old enough to be his grandmother. His Da would just look at him and flash a smug smile as they passed.

When they had finally come for the old man, Boag had been out. He'd returned later in the afternoon to see the flashing blue lights and the crowds of police in the street, black shirts and stab-vests making them look like extras from a science fiction film. He wondered who had done the dirty on his old man. Who'd had the balls to run the risk of crossing Boddice? Boag reached the close mouth and kept walking, pushing through the crowd, his eyes fixed firmly in front of him. He knew then that things were changed. He was on his own now.

To his surprise, he found that not to be the case. Out of some warped sense of loyalty or gratitude, Boddice had assured Gerry that he would see the boy was alright, send him on a couple of wee jobs here and there, make sure he didn't go without the bare necessities. In reality, all that meant was that Boag had slowly become in thrall to Boddice, same as his old man.

At first, the jobs Boddice threw his way gave him sufficient cash to pay the rent on a wee place in a crummy, gang-ridden scheme south of the river, and enough food to send him to sleep at night with a full belly.

Then, things began to dry up.

It had been more than a month now since he'd had any kind of contact.

He felt a sickening chill in his stomach as he realised that maybe Boddice would never call again.

Nevertheless, Boag was taking no chances. He made sure that he charged the mobile at every opportunity. As it had done for the last three or four weeks, the thought burrowed into his mind: *maybe today would be the day.*

He took a bite from the roll and slurped his tea. It felt good, and he let out a low sigh. He thought of the man in the hotel and the way he had jumped when Boag banged on the window. He smiled. *Lucky bastard*, he thought. *Wonder if he had any fusions for breakfast.*

Boag looked up and saw the guy in the change booth counting out piles of ten, twenty and fifty pence pieces, but all the while watching Boag, wondering what a low-life piece of shite like him had to smile about. Boag shifted the phone to the seat, made sure the guy couldn't see it.

The door from the street banged open and an old woman reeled in, bouncing off the slot machines like a ball against the bumpers in one of the pinball games at the back of the arcade. She looked as derelict and destitute as Boag did. A skinny Jack Russell terrier followed her, never taking its eyes off the opened can of dog food the woman held in one hand. Her hair sagged like broken grey springs as she navigated her way through the puggy machines. She sang softly to herself, but none of the customers lifted a head as she waltzed by. She stopped when she noticed Boag sitting by himself with his roll and cup of tea.

He lowered his head and stared at the table, but he knew she would come over anyway. It was as inevitable as a bad smell after a fart. She shuffled over, singing now in a low soft voice and giggling to herself. *Oh, the River Clyde, the River Clyde, Ah love the Clyde, a rum-ti-tum-tum-ti somethin somethin inside…*

'Y'alright son?' she asked as she slid into the seat opposite him. The dog jumped onto her knee and stared at him. 'Nice and warm in here isn't it?'

Boag didn't answer.

'Ye know, Ah just love that song,' she went on. 'Ah used to love that Kenneth McKellar singin it. Or Andy Stewart. Great voices. Just like myself,' she laughed.

Boag continued to look at the table.

'Aw c'mon son, Ah'm only makin a wee bit conversation. Ah hardly ever get to talk to anybody, except wee Jess here,' she said, indicating the dog. 'Here, do ye want to know somethin?' she asked, as she picked up Boag's saucer from the table. 'Do ye know how many bridges there are over the Clyde?' She rummaged in some dark cavern inside her coat and produced a fork which she used to empty the contents of the tin of dog food onto the saucer. Boag turned his face away from the smell, and shifted his roll and tea to the corner of the table. The dog plunged its snout into the saucer and began eating the gluey brown food. 'Eh?' she went on, 'The number of bridges over the Clyde?'

Boag finally looked at her, but said nothing. One of her eyes was obscured by the milky pearl of a cataract.

'Ah know them all,' she said with defiant pride. 'Oh aye. There's the Albert Bridge, the Suspension Bridge, the Erskine Bridge, the Kingston Bridge, Glasgow Bridge, King George the Fifth Bridge, the Bell's—'

'Shut up, will ye?' snapped Boag.

She laughed. 'Aha! Knew Ah could get ye to talk.'

'Ah'm no talkin,' he said. 'Ah'm tellin.'

'No, no, no,' she said. 'Ye've started. This is a conversation now.' She laughed again. The dog, already finished with the food, went back to staring at him. 'Ye can talk to me, son. Ah'm no drunk or anything, if that's what ye're wonderin. Just happy to be livin.'

Boag sniffed, avoiding her gaze.

'Do ye no want to know about the bridges?' she asked. 'Ah could tell ye loads about them.'

'Look missus,' he said. 'Just gonnae leave us in peace?

Ah'm no in the mood.'

'Ach, ye don't need to be in any sort of mood to have a wee talk with an auld wumman, do ye?'

'Aye ye do.' He picked up his roll. 'Ah don't know anythin about bridges, and to be honest, Ah couldn't give a toss.'

'Ye look like somebody that needs a wee bit of cheerin up,' she said. 'Ye look as if ye're a wee bit down on yer luck, am Ah right?'

'It's none of yer—'

'When Ah saw ye sittin there Ah thought, he's no happy, that poor boy, his luck looks like it's run out.'

Boag looked at her. 'Ah don't believe in luck,' he said. 'There's no such thing. So it doesn't run out, and it doesn't run in either. We just make do with what's handed down to us.'

'Oh, aye, what's for ye'll no go by ye? That's a loada rubbish son. Ye just don't believe in luck because ye've never had any.'

She scuffled round in her seat and pointed to the puggy machines. 'Take a wee look around this joint. This place is built on the idea of luck. If there wasn't any such thing as luck, these poor bastards wouldn't be in here, day in, day out.'

'Aye, and do they ever win anythin?' Boag asked. 'Ah mean anythin worth having?'

She held the fork to the dog's mouth to let it lick the remains of the food. She considered Boag for a couple of moments. 'Have ye got a fag son?' she asked, eventually.

'No, Ah don't smoke.'

'Are ye sure? Cos ah've got somethin to show ye. Somethin about luck.'

'Ah told ye, Ah've not got any fags. Ah don't smoke, and anyway ye cannae smoke in here.'

She went into an inside pocket of her coat and brought out a crumpled cigarette. 'So ye'll not want half of this then? We don't need to worry about any smoking ban. To hell with that. Naebody'll see us. What do you say, eh?'

He caught her looking at his nicotine-stained fingers, and he moved his hands under the table. He licked his lips. He could do with a good smoke.

She took the cigarette and snapped it in half, handed him one of the pieces. 'Here, take it. Ah know ye want it. And anyway, ye need it for me to show ye something.'

He hesitated for a second, then reached out and took the cigarette from her. It felt damp.

'Now,' she said, fumbling in her coat pocket, 'here's this thing.' She held up something that looked like an oversized brass coin, or an old-fashioned fob watch. She turned it over with fingers that looked so dry and papery that Boag thought he could hear her skin rustle. There was a small knurled wheel at the edge and she brought her thumb up and spun it. A shaky yellow flame stood at the end of a wick of what he now saw was a cigarette lighter. She held it towards him to light his half of the cigarette. She nodded at the lighter. 'Fancy, isn't it?' she asked.

He drew on the fag, pulling hot, bitter smoke into his lungs, the smell of the lighter fuel making his eyes water. She lit her own part of the cigarette and let out a long jet of smoke from her nostrils. She passed the lighter across to him. 'Have a look.'

He took the lighter from her. It was the kind of thing he'd seen before in traders' stalls at the Barras, some artefact that nestled in a dusty tray beside old carburettor components or plastic dials for long-defunct television sets. The kind of useless object you could pick up for fifty pence and later wonder what the hell you were thinking about when you bought it. It was heavier than he expected. On one side there was an engraving of an angel, flying through a cloud-wracked sky using a rope to drag a troop of horses behind her. On the other side was another engraving, this time of a woman's head, her mouth pulled back in a snarl. Boag couldn't decide if her look was one of pain, fear, defiance or a combination of all three. The figure's hair flew out from her head in a tangle of snaking coils. Arching under the woman's head was a vicious-looking scythe and the words *La Guerre*. The images made Boag feel uneasy.

'Interesting, eh?' the old woman said.

'Ah suppose so,' he replied.

'It's from the war, ye know. *The Great War*. Number one.'

Boag looked at the lighter lying in the palm of his hand. 'The first world war?'

'Aye,' she said. 'This belonged to my auld man, and to his father before that.' She lifted the dog, placed it on the floor where it lay down and curled up. 'Ma grandfather fought in that war, Wipers or the Somme or some such place.' The puggy machines continued to whirr and clang in the background and the bingo-caller's voice still sounded mechanically from the far end of the room. The old woman went on, her voice lowering to a splintered, smoky whisper. 'This is a lucky thing,' she told him. 'This thing brings luck with it.' She stared at Boag. 'Ah know ye don't believe me, but listen to my story anyway.'

Boag sighed. He had nothing better to do, and, now that she'd started, he might as well hear her out. 'On ye go,' he said.

She broke into a wide smile, showing teeth the colour of old dominoes. 'Heh, heh. Told ye we could have a conversation didn't Ah? This is rare.' Boag rolled his eyes.

'Ma grandfather was a crabbit auld bastard. Never really liked him that much. Used to hit my granny when he had a good bucket in him. But there were times when he was sober, when he would sit down and tell stories from the war, and what it was like way back in the auld days when he was just a boy himself. He'd gather all the grandweans round about him and hold court. My father and mother would sit on the settee listenin too, even though they'd probably heard the stories a hundred times. One day, no long before he died, he was tellin his stories when he pulled out this auld lighter, the one yer holding now, and gave it to my father. 'Ah've never told ye this story before,' he said. 'But Ah think now's the time.''

'Don't tell me,' said Boag. 'It's not the story about how that lighter stopped a bullet from hittin his heart?'

The old woman fixed him with a hard look. 'No, son. Nuthin like that.'

Boag felt ashamed of his interruption. The old dear seemed genuine enough, and he knew he was just being a bastard by trying to make light of what she was saying. 'Sorry,' he said. 'On ye go. Ah'm listenin.'

She continued staring at him for a moment and then went on.

'It was one of the worst months of the whole war. Hard to imagine in a war where every day must've seemed like the gates of Hell had been opened and the Devil himself had taken control of the world. It was December, and cauld. Nineteen seventeen, the worst winter on record. Cauld enough to freeze the toes off the feet of the men in the trenches. Soldiers were dyin just because they couldn't keep warm enough, never mind what the Germans were tryin to do to them...'

She rambled on, her tale populated with men, long dead; soldiers in the trenches, incompetent captains, men sent to their dooms on a whim, the creeping fog and the constant background of the iron-hard cold seeping into the bones of the men. Men, not much different from himself, living in the very bowels of Hell. Boag felt the story was rehearsed, that she'd told it many times before, but there was something about the rhythm of her words that sucked him in. It all played out in his mind: the terror on the men's faces, the stench of death and destruction, the earth-shuddering intensity of the relentless artillery. He had to concede: she was a fucking good storyteller.

He settled back, submerging himself in the rasping croak of her voice, drifting into the heart of her story, listening to the ebb and flow of the yarn till, finally, her words came fierce and fast as she got to the climax, the part where she was telling how her grandfather had met this young German soldier in a bomb crater in the middle of nowhere and how if the German hadn't offered him a light from this god-awful lighter – the grandfather stooping to take a draw on his fag, suck the flame onto the tobacco – he would have been shot to smithereens by his own men.

As luck would have it, because her grandfather bent forward at that very moment, it was the German who caught the bullet, ended up being blasted.

As luck would have it.

Luck and the lighter. She kept going on about how the lighter was some sort of charm or something. Saved her grandfather's life.

She took the lighter from Boag's hand, laid it on the table and stared at it with a dour intensity. She looked up quickly and grinned. 'It was his lucky lighter,' she said, 'and eventually it got passed on to me, and Ah've always believed it does bring ye luck.'

She sat back in her chair and let out a long sigh. The telling of the story had exhausted her. Boag looked down at his cigarette and saw an inch and a half of flaky ash suspended over the table like a crooked finger. He studied the lighter, the figures sculpted on its surface. The leering face of the woman, the words *La Guerre*, they made his blood run cold. Not for the first time that day he shivered.

'Away and fling shite at the moon,' he said. 'Ye're just makin all that stuff up.' But he wasn't sure. 'Aren't ye?'

'God, son,' the woman said. 'Ye're no a very trustin character, are ye?' Boag let his gaze fall to the table. She went on: 'Every word Ah've told ye is the truth and if ye don't want to believe me, then that's your problem.'

'So, what if it *is* true?' he asked. 'How does that make this lighter a lucky thing? *You've* had it for a while now, and you don't look that lucky to me. It's all just superstitious rubbish.'

She gave a small laugh and leaned over to tickle the dog's ears. It squirmed onto its back, and she rubbed its belly. She looked up at him. 'Ye don't know anything about me son,' she said. 'How do you know Ah'm not lucky? What makes ye think Ah've not got a good life?'

'Well, ye don't look as if—'

She cut him off. 'No, son, don't go on appearances. They count for nuthin. Just cos Ah've not got much money doesn't mean to say Ah've not been lucky in my life. Money means nuthin.' She brought the dog back onto her lap, cuddled it close. The cataract in her eye caught the light and shone like a silver pebble. 'For all you know Ah could be the luckiest woman in the world. And in a way Ah am. Simply because Ah'm alive. And more than that, Ah *know* Ah'm alive.'

Boag frowned. The old woman smiled at him. 'Ye see, son, there's many folk don't even stop to think about the simple fact that they are alive and that they're experiencing the world. That this is the one chance they'll get to be a part of the whole show. Life. They just blunder about without taking any of it in.' She stubbed out the remains of her cigarette on the saucer. 'And then they discover, one day, that they've not got that long to go, the race is nearly finished, and, too late, they begin to wonder what the hell they've done with their time. And that can happen to the wealthiest folk ye can imagine.' She looked down at her dog, smiled and stroked it under the chin. It gave a small groan of contentment. 'Ye know son, we're luckier than any rich man that died yesterday, cos we're here and we're alive the now. Just think of all the folk that won't see out the end of this day. The ones that are gonnae die in an accident on the way home from their work, or the ones that are in their deathbed right this minute. The ones that haven't bothered to enjoy the fact that they've been alive. But here we are, and here we'll be tomorrow. Now, you tell me… who's luckier, us or them?'

'But we all die someday,' said Boag. 'It doesn't make any difference.'

'Aye, we all die right enough. But ye're missin my point. We don't all die knowin that we've ever been alive in the first place. That's why the lighter is lucky. If it hadn't been for that, my grandfather would be dead, but, just as important, after that incident he knew that life was sweet, and to be savoured.'

'The lighter didn't do that though,' he said. 'That's got no more to do with luck than—'

'Of course it didn't,' she interrupted. 'But it's a talisman, it's the thing that started it all off. And ye don't know about all the other things that have happened, to me, to my father, and to my father's father. Things that are hard to explain. But Ah call it luck.' She brushed some crumbs from the table. 'Maybe ye're right son, maybe there's no such thing as luck. Just opportunity, and it's what ye do with that opportunity that makes ye lucky. Ye can think what ye like though, Ah still believe luck exists.'

'Opportunity…,' Boag murmured. 'Chance would be a fine thing.'

The old woman straightened herself, lifting the dog onto the bench beside her and smoothing down her coat. 'Listen,' she said. 'What about another wee cuppa tea? Ah'll pay.'

'No, ye're alright,' he said. 'Ah'm fine.'

'Aww, c'mon,' she said, squeezing out from the table. 'It'll do ye good. When Ah come back Ah'll tell you about the other bits of luck Ah've had, and maybe ye'll even let me tell ye about the bridges over the Clyde?'

He made no answer, but watched her as she waddled across to the tea bar at the far end of the room, the back of her coat smeared with grime and dirt.

He bent under the table and unplugged his mobile, shoving the phone and the charger into his pocket. The dog watched him, its nose twitching. The lighter was sitting on the table, the distorted face of its wild-haired woman scowling at him. Boag thought about what the old woman had said. About luck. About opportunity. She was deluding herself, justifying her own miserable existence on the basis of a fantasy. The lighter glittered in the flashing lights from the one-armed bandits and the figure of the wild woman seemed to wink at him.

He watched the old woman ordering the tea at the other end of the room, her back towards him.

He quickly slid out from the table and edged towards the exit. As he reached the door, he looked back. The dog had climbed up onto the table and was staring at him, its head tilted to one side.

Boag opened the door and quickly slipped out into the swirling wind, feeling the comforting warmth of the lighter against his hand.

The Wilson Twins:
Tattooed Love Boys

Campbell did the drawings, John did the words and the piercings.

Usually.

It had been a slow day for *Two's Tattoos*. In fact, they hadn't had a single customer. Not that it mattered in the long run – the shop, once their livelihood, was now just another of Boddice's money-laundering fronts. Whether they turned a penny or not was neither here nor there.

'Here's one for ye,' said Campbell.

'One what?' said John.

'A thing, a wee interestin thing.'

'On ye go then.'

'Okay – can you think of a sentence that uses the same word three times in a row an still makes sense?'

'Like what? What what?'

'What?'

'No, three times.'

'Wait… wait a minute, that doesn't work. It doesn't make sense.'

'How no?'

'Just because… Uch, now Ah've nearly gave it away.'

'What?'

'The sentence.'

'What sentence?'

'The one with three words that… Bugger it, Ah'll just tell ye.'

'Tell me what?'

'The sentence!'

'Oh, right, on ye go then.'

'Okay, here goes…'

'That's three different words.'

'Ah've not started yet!'

'Oh.'

'Right this is it… *You cannot start a sentence with because, because…*'

'With *because because*?'

'Wait, will ye? Ah'm no finished yet! Jesus Christ!'

'Sorry.'

'*You cannot start a sentence with because, because because is a conjunction.* There.'

'Ye can't start a sentence with because because because? That's shite. What the fuck are ye talkin about?'

'No, no, ye're missin the point.'

'What point?'

'The point is that ye have to *listen* to the sentence!'

'Ah just have!'

'No ye haven't! Listen again… *You cannot start a sentence with…*'

'Hold on. What's a confunction?'

'Conjunction, ye mean.'

'Do Ah?'

'Aye.'

'Well, what is it?'

'Never mind. Christ on a bike!'

'Sorry.'

'Right. Again. *You cannot start a sentence with because, because because is a—*'

'What did ye make that funny wee sign with yer finger for?'

'It was *supposed* to be a comma.'

'A comma?'

'Aye, a comma, ye know – a pause, a—'

'Like a dog's paws?'

'What?'

'Never mind, on ye go…'

'Naw. Fuck it, Ah can't be bothered.'

'Aw c'mon… Ah'm interested, honest.'

'Are ye fuck.'

'C'mon, don't get the hump.'

'No, forget it.'

'Please?'

'No!'

'Ach, fuck off then. You an yer stupid ideas an thinkin. Just because ye 'stuck in at school', like mammy wanted, an ye know all these fancy, high-falutin word thingies.'

'Aye, an what the fuck's wrong with that?'

'An you got that stupid second-name-for-a-first-name thing. *Campbell*. Fuck's sake!'

'Don't fuckin start on that again, right?'

'At least Ah've got a normal name.'

'Look, ye're no gonnae rile me about my name, okay?'

'Ah can't be arsed anyway. Uch, c'mon Campbell, tell me the sentence.'

'Ah already have.'

'Ah'll listen this time. *Because because because*, right what about it?'

'Pay attention then.'

'Ah will. Promise.'

'Okay, now listen. *You cannot start*—'

'Wait a minute… is a comma no one of they things that happens to ye when ye bump yer head, or are in an accident or somethin an ye cannae wake up?'

'Ya wee bastard, ye said—'

'Ah'm no wee, Ah'm the same height as you. We're twins, remember?'

Campbell lunged at John, knocking the newspaper out of his hands and gripping him in a headlock. He wrestled him to the floor. Tattoo design books and photographs skittered across the room.

The bell above the front door jangled as someone entered followed by a swirling flurry of snowflakes. 'Hello? Anybody in?' he called.

Campbell came through from the back room, smiling and smoothing down his overall. 'Alright pal? Helluva day eh?'

The guy nodded. 'Aye, freezin.'

John joined them. He glared at Campbell, but turned to give the guy a toothy grin.

'So, what can we do for ye?' said Campbell.

The guy hesitated, looking from Campbell to John. 'Are youse two…'

'Twins?' said John. 'How could you tell? Not many people notice.'

Campbell shot John a look.

'Really?' said the guy. 'Youse look awfy like each other to me.'

'He's just windin ye up pal,' said Campbell. 'Ignore him. He's the deranged one, Ah'm the sensible one.'

The guy looked unsure.

'No, *he's* windin ye up now,' said John. 'We're both happy as if we're normal.'

'What?' said the guy.

'Don't bother with him,' said Campbell. He clapped his arm around the guy's shoulder. 'So, Ah'm guessin ye're here for a tattoo?'

'Cos if it's a sensual massage ye're after,' added John, 'then Sharon's Sunbed Shack is two doors down.'

The guy frowned. 'Eh, just a tattoo actually,' he said.

'Excellent,' said John. 'Ye've came to the right place. We're just the boys ye need.'

'What kinda thing do ye want?' asked Campbell. 'Celtic knots? Maori Moko designs? Broken heart leakin tears?'

'Nuddy wumman?' said John.

The guy brightened. 'No, Ah've got one of them already,' he said.

'Oh aye?' said Campbell. 'Give us a look'

The guy took off his jacket and rolled up his sleeve. On his arm he had a drawing of a woman with her hair falling down over one eye, and a truly enormous bust thrusting towards the viewer. Her legs looked out of proportion to the rest of her body – too short – and there was something not quite right about the way her arms and hands were angled onto her hips. It was hopeless. Campbell wondered if it was supposed to be Marilyn Monroe. 'Is that…'

'Jessica Rabbit? Aye, crackin isn't it?' said the guy.

'Jessica Rabbit?' John almost choked. 'Christ almighty she's…'

'Perfect,' said Campbell, raising an eyebrow at John. 'Who done it?'

'It was a wee guy who comes into our pub. Does it as a homer kinda thing. Wants to open a tattoo shop of his own sometime. What do youse think? Does he stand a chance?'

John smiled. 'Oh aye… definitely… especially with they new surrealist tattoo designs that are becomin the latest fad now. He's caught that brilliantly there.'

'Do ye think so?' said the guy. 'Wait till Ah tell him.'

'Aye, ye should definitely tell him,' said John.

'Surrealist, eh?' said the guy. 'What's that then?'

Campbell interrupted before things went too far. 'Anyway! We're a wee bit short of time the day. Got to be somewhere by four o'clock.' He nudged his brother.

John grunted.

'It's somethin dead important,' said Campbell. 'Can't get out of it. So, if ye let us know what yer wantin done, we'll get ye sorted out.'

'Eh, right,' said the guy. 'It's no a drawin, it's just some words.'

'*Just* words?' said John. 'How'd ye no just get Salvador Dali down the pub to do it for ye?'

'Ah don't know anybody by that name comes in our pub. Just wee Chris that does the homers.'

Campbell stepped in again. 'So, Ah'm thinkin ye maybe wanted to try out a professional approach, see how the real guys do it?'

'No, not really. It's more a spur of the moment kinda thing. Was just passin, an Ah thought Ah'd maybe get somethin done as a wee Christmas pressie to myself. An Ah'm going up the dancin the night an Ah thought this would be ideal timing for what Ah want.'

'Wee Chris no available the day then?' said John with a sneer.

The guy didn't pick up on it. 'No, haven't seen him for a week or two.'

'Well,' said Campbell before John could get back in. 'Johnny boy here is our lettering man. He'll do yer words for ye, any font ye want.'

'Font?' said the guy.

'Aye ye know,' said John. 'The type of letters. Gothic, Roman, Celtic.' He smiled sweetly at the guy. 'Surrealist, if ye want.'

'No, Ah'm no sure if Ah want anythin sur-thingmy. Ah kinda had in mind they big black letters ye get in German films. Ye know… Where Eagles Dare writing.'

'That'll be Gothic then,' said John.

'An what is it ye're wanting wrote?' asked Campbell.

'And where?' added John.

'Well, Ah don't know if ye do this or no,' said the guy, shuffling his feet. 'But Ah want it above my dick.'

'Yer boaby?' said John.

'Ma dick.'

'Ah think we can do that,' said Campbell.

'An Ah want it to say *Sex Stud*,' said the guy.

John stifled a snigger. 'Are ye sure?'

'Absolutely,' said the guy.

'Ah mean, once it's on it's on. Ye can't really take it off. Are ye sure ye might no regret somethin like that? Ah mean it's—'

'No it's definitely what Ah want. Just *Sex Stud* curving above my dick.'

'But do ye no think it might put the lassies off, seeing something like that?'

41

'Naw,' the guy grinned. 'After all, Ah'm just bein honest, they'll know what they're gettin then.'

'Aye, but…'

'Look, do youse want to do this or not?'

'Of course, pal,' said Campbell. He turned to his brother. 'John, just get on with it right?'

John threw up his hands. 'Alright pal, it's your tattoo, but Ah think ye're makin a mistake.'

'If ye just want to come over to this cubicle, we'll get ye sorted,' said Campbell, ushering the guy to one of the curtained booths at the back of the shop.

'Ye'll have to take yer kegs down,' added John.

'Ah think it's hardly necessary to point *that* out,' said Campbell.

'And yer boxers too,' said John, flashing a humourless smile at Campbell.

'No probs,' said the guy, dropping his trousers and taking off his underwear.

The twins stared at his groin. John smothered another laugh. 'You've—'

'Shaved my pubes, aye,' said the guy. 'Porno trick that one. Makes yer dick look bigger. Not bad, eh?'

'Crackin,' said John, rolling his eyes. 'Might try that one myself.'

The guy settled down on the plinth and lay back. John brought out a sterile needle pack and laid it on the table, while Campbell left them to it and went through to tidy the back room.

'This might hurt a wee bit, being on a sensitive area and that,' said John as he prepared the ink gun.

'Ah think Ah'll be okay,' said the guy. 'It wasn't too bad the last time.'

'Aye, but that was yer arm. This is different. Trust me, Ah've seen folk faint when gettin tattooed or pierced down there.' He went over to a shelf and took down a Walkman.

Old-school technology. He handed the headphones to the guy. 'Here, put these on an listen while Ah'm doing ye. It's heavy metal, Iron Maiden – it'll distract ye from the pain. It works, honest.'

The guy put the headphones on and closed his eyes. John listened to the *tss, tss, tss* of the music, letting it lull him into the dreamlike trance in which he worked best, as he swabbed the guy's skin with methylated spirits and worked out the best way to apply the letters. He made sure they would line up correctly, forming a neat crescent curving across the guy's groin, and then filled the needle gun with deep black ink. He switched the gun on and set to work, skilfully outlining the block letters and filling them in so that they gradually spelled out the words.

He was good. Skilled tattooists were hard to come by and he took pride in his lettering work. Campbell was better at the graphic designs though, and between them they had built up a reasonable little business with *Two's Tattoos*. Return clientele, decent reputation, clean and safe – no hassle from the Environmental Health people.

When Boddice took an interest in the place however, offered to plough in some cash in return for a stake in the business, the twins placed too much value on the integrity of their gonads to knock him back. The tattoo parlour was the ideal cover for Boddice to launder his drug money. No need for stocktaking, since, apart from the batches of ink, latex gloves and the like, they didn't really *have* stock, and any number of clients could be invented to cover the money that was going through the books. Of course, anyone taking a closer look might be surprised to find such a sudden, unexplained burst of public interest in having a tattoo done. But tattoos were more popular than ever now, the numbers wouldn't seem that unreasonable. The twins had been happy to accept kickbacks from Boddice for allowing him to use the business, and had even suggested alternative ways of using the parlour as a front. Before long, they had earned his trust and Boddice had started to include them in other little 'jobs'. It became far more lucrative than inking the pale skin of the great Glasgow public.

Without realising it, they had become part of Boddice's team.

John swabbed the remaining drops of blood from the final *D*, and stepped back to look at his work. The letters stood slightly raised from the reddened, inflamed skin like little black worms. The guy hadn't stirred or flinched once during the whole procedure. Got to give him credit for that, thought John. It looked good, even if John still wasn't sure about that message.

He took the headphones from the guy's head. 'Alright pal. Finished.'

The guy swung his legs out over the plinth and stood up.

'There's a mirror over there in the corner, if ye want a look,' said John. 'But mind, the letters'll be back to front.'

The guy shuffled to the corner and inspected the tattoo. He stood blinking for a moment and then frowned. He turned his head sideways and bit his bottom lip. He stepped back from the mirror and looked down at his groin.

'What the fuckin fuck is *this*!' he shouted.

'It's what...' John began.

'What the hell have ye done to me, ya bastard?' the guy yelled, still staring uncomprehendingly at the tattoo.

Campbell came through from the back room to investigate the commotion. 'Alright pal, is there a problem?' he said.

'A problem?' said the guy. 'A *problem*? Ah'll say there's a fuckin problem.' He was on the verge of screaming now. 'Ah come in here for a straightforward tattoo and Ah end up with fuckin monkey-boy here who's went an done this to me.' He pointed to the tattoo.

Campbell stared wide-eyed at the guy's flaccid penis lying like a newborn hamster against his scrotum, and the two words arcing above it. He looked at John.

'John,' he gasped. 'Did you…'

'What the fuck's the problem?' said John. 'The guy got what he asked for.'

'Got what Ah asked for?' the guy roared. 'Ah wanted two simple words, an all Ah get is fuckin Tweedle-Dee and Tweedle-fuckin'-Dummer makin a right cunt of it.'

'That's what ye fuckin asked for,' John shouted back. 'Ah told ye it wasn't a good idea, but, no, ye wouldn't listen would ye?'

'It's *you* that didn't listen ya prick,' the guy yelled. 'Ah asked for *Sex Stud*, an you've—'

'That's what ye've got, ya bampot, what's wrong with ye?' said John.

'No, no, John you've got it wrong,' said Campbell. 'You've wrote—'

'*Sex Dud*, that's what he wanted!' cried John. 'It's no my fault that he's a fuckin nutter that wants to announce his sexual inadequacies to anybody that wants to look at his prick!'

'*Stud*, John, *Stud*,' said Campbell. 'The second word is *Stud*.'

The room went quiet. A slow realisation dawned on John. His jaw dropped. 'Oh fuck.' He put his hands to his head. 'Oh fuck. Pal, Ah'm sorry. Really, Ah am. Ah thought ye said—'

'Aye, well we all know now what ye fuckin *thought* Ah said,' the guy yelled. 'But it's me that's standing here with the world's worst fuckin possible tattoo scrawled across the top of my cock. Christ Almighty, Ah'm going out clubbin the night… hopin to get my hole or sumhin. Maybe even a blow job…' The guy stopped. His shoulders slumped. 'Aw no. No. For fuck's sake… a blow job. Some lassie kneelin down in front of me, undoes my zipper, all sexy like, pulls down my kegs, an what's she gonnae see starin her in the face? My proud manhood standing tall? Will she fuck! *Sex Dud*. Oh man, Ah'm fucked… Or rather, Ah'm not.'

The guy sank back onto the plinth and started to sob.

Campbell went over and put his arm around him. 'C'mon pal, it's not that bad. Maybe we can salvage it. What do ye say?'

The guy shrugged him away. 'Fuck off! How are ye supposed to salvage a disaster like this?'

'Aye,' John said. 'How are we gonnae…?'

'Shut up,' said Campbell. 'Let me think.'

'Ye could grow yer pubes back,' said John, brightening.

'That's no gonnae bloody well work! Ye'll still see it,' said the guy. 'An, anyway, Ah'll know it's there won't Ah?' He leapt to his feet, knocking over his chair, and swept his hand across one of the shelves at the back of the cubicle, scattering photographs and bottles of different coloured ink across the floor. The bottles smashed, leaving multicoloured ribbons snaking across the floor. 'Every time… every time Ah get myself worked up with some lassie it's gonnae spring into my head isn't it? What's written above my bloody love truncheon. An ye know what's gonnae happen then don't ye?' He kicked over the waste bin. 'Auld John Thomas there is gonnae go into free fall isn't he?'

'Ah know! Maybe we could add a letter,' said John.

'*Add* a letter? What the fuck are ye talkin about?' said the guy. 'Ah'm no lettin you fuckin near me with that needle gun, or whatever ye call it!'

'We could add an *E*,' John went on. 'Add it to the end of *Dud.*'

'Aye,' said Campbell, straightening a bit and nodding. 'That's good thinking. That might work.'

'*Dude?*' said the guy. '*Sex Dude?* Who the fuck in Glasgow calls themselves Dude?' He laughed at the twins. 'Do Ah look like some kinda arsey yank?' He snorted. 'No fuckin way.'

'Wait,' said Campbell. 'Think about it. We could add a *Y* as well. Ye know, make it…' he spread his hands theatrically, '… *Sexy Dude.*' He grinned. 'What about that?'

'*Sexy Dude,*' said John. 'That's even better, is it no?' He nodded at the guy enthusiastically.

The guy stared at them. He started to say something, but stopped. He covered his face with his hands and sighed. 'Wait a minute,' he said, his words muffled. 'That..., that might..., that might actually be okay.' He took his hands down from his face, his gaze darting from one twin to the other. '*Sexy Dude...* Aye, Ah can kinda see that.' He gave a short laugh of relief. 'Aye... *Sexy Dude*, that could be me...'

'That's even better than *Sex Stud* if ye ask me,' said John smiling and turning to his brother. 'What do ye think Campbell? Does this guy no look like one sexy dude to you?'

'Not half,' said Campbell, winking at John. 'One sexxxxy duuuude, man!'

'Lassies would love that, wouldn't they Campbell?' said John.

'Lassies would love it? Hell, *Ah* love it. Might even get ye to do one for me John!' He put on a deep Barry White voice. 'Sexy Dude, that's me baby.'

'Maybe do one to myself as well!' added John, laughing.

'Do youse think so?' said the guy.

'Oh aye,' said John.

'Might even start a fashion,' said Campbell. He noticed John squinting at him questioningly. 'Ye know,' he added, nodding at John. 'Once lassies get to spreading the word and that.'

'You're right!' said John. 'Christ, we'll get inundated!'

The guy smiled crookedly and looked at each of them. He took a big breath. 'Alright, you're on! Let's do it!' He settled himself back onto the plinth. 'Christ, Ah thought Ah was a goner there. Good thinkin guys, good thinkin. Youse've redeemed yourselves.'

'Eh, well... no yet,' said Campbell.

'What do ye mean?' said John and the guy simultaneously.

Campbell tapped his watch. 'It's twenty to four. We've got to be a place by four o'clock. Both of us.'

John grimaced. 'Shite, so we have.' He turned to the guy.

'We'll no have enough time to get it finished the night.'

'No the night?' the guy asked in a small voice. 'What about ma…'

'No, no, don't worry,' said John. 'Come back tomorrow an we'll get it sorted. First thing in the mornin. Promise.'

'Aye, but—,' the guy started to protest.

'Honest, pal,' said Campbell, handing the guy his jacket and motioning for him to do up his trousers. 'We need to leave. Right now.'

'Think we'll be late Campbell?' asked John.

'Ah fuckin hope not.' Campbell replied, showing the guy to the door.

The guy turned back. 'C'mon guys,' he pleaded. 'Ye can't leave me like this! Can ye not finish it the now?'

'Listen pal,' said Campbell. 'This is a kinda life and death matter. An Ah'm not exaggerating.' He pushed the guy out the door. 'Come back tomorrow and we'll fix it for ye. In fact, there'll be no charge.'

'You're bloody right there'll be no charge,' shouted the guy as he stumbled out into a sleety squall.

John went round the shop, quickly shutting off the appliances and the lights, while Campbell gathered their coats. The mess on the floor could wait till later.

'Ye do know we're not open tomorrow,' said John.

'Of course Ah fuckin do,' replied Campbell.

***

They made it to the Palace with five minutes to spare.

As they climbed the back stairs Campbell turned to John. 'Right,' he said. 'This is your last chance. Here's another one for ye. Even better.'

'What?' said John.

'Can ye think of a sentence that uses the same word *eleven* times in a row and that still makes sense?'

John stopped and thought for a moment.

'Naw,' he said. 'But Ah'm sure you're gonnae fuckin tell me.'

Leggett:
The Folsom Prison Blues

It looks like snow, Leggett thought, and giggled. He pushed the white granules around on the plate with the flat edge of a rusted cheese slicer. Snow, just like the weather outside. The similarity comforted him, and he hummed a little tune to himself. All tied together; connectedness. The photograph, the mouse, his uncle Jimmy. All connected. And now the snow and the powder.

He drizzled a little more of the crushed paracetamol tablets onto the plate and mixed the grains with the slicer. Mixed them good and proper, made sure they formed a consistent blend. He'd tried coffee whitener before, but that didn't work so well, it gave a more lumpy appearance and, besides, a faint perfume lingered afterwards. The paracetamol was a better idea. Less chance of detection.

He fought back the urge to giggle again. He was alone in the bedroom, and giggling to yourself was what loonies did wasn't it? He was no fucking loony, no way man. Whoo, no. But this was funny, mixing the two powders. Boddice's gear lay at the side of the table, a freezer bag holding at least a couple of gees worth of finest white. Leggett had spooned half of it onto the plate and he'd gradually added the paracetamol powder, estimating by eye when the amount was back to its original size. When he was finished he would do the same with the other half in the bag. He had a vague suspicion that he should maybe be using scales or something, get a better degree of accuracy, but fuck it, this was good enough. Good enough for junkie wasters. He did giggle then, a little one, which he stifled quickly.

It *was* funny though. Without knowing, Boddice was helping Leggett build his own little empire. Every bag of stuff Boddice supplied for selling on, Leggett was cutting, getting twice the amount. He would sell one half as Boddice's stuff just as usual, but he had used the other half to build his own network of customers among the local schemies, off the books as it were, and he was raking it in. Nineteen years old and he had a couple of grand under the bed. Weehoo! The beauty of it was that Boddice didn't know, didn't need to know. Boddice trusted him.

It was funny.

On the wall above the table Leggett had pinned a photograph cut from a newspaper. According to the writing underneath the photograph, the image had been taken by a man called Eddie Adams, and it showed a South Vietnamese police chief standing in the middle of a Saigon street, holding a gun against the head of another man wearing a crummy lumberjack shirt. The police chief's name was Lieutenant Colonel Nguyen Ngoc Loan. Leggett didn't have a clue how to pronounce it, but he liked the look of the words. It was a gallus kind of name. The picture was grainy on the flaking yellow paper. Leggett knew it had been taken right at the very instant the police chief had pulled the trigger, right at the instant of the guy in the check shirt's death.

Right at the instant.

The picture showed the muscles in the police chief's forearm tensed and contracted, the tendons in his wrist and hand bulging, and the finger on the trigger pulled all the way back. It was right at the instant; no doubt.

The guy in the lumberjack shirt had his hands tied behind his back, and he looked as if he might be crying. His face was screwed up and distorted, his bottom lip petted. One of his eyes was closed against the force of the shot. But his other eye, the left one, looked as if it might be open slightly. Leggett could never be sure. He had studied the picture endlessly, scrutinising every detail of the man's face, and had always come back to the left eye. Was it open? What was he seeing? What was the last image that burned into the man's mind as his life came to an end as suddenly as switching off a light? You'd want it to be something good, fuck aye, something beautiful – a sunset, or a gorgeous woman, or a flower or something. But not this guy, no siree, he was seeing some shitty street in a rundown town, with clapped out cars and guys on bicycles passing down the road. Maybe a dog taking a dump in the middle of the street, or a crowd of yabbering men in cheap shirts, slick with sweat, pushing and shoving to get a good view of his last moment in the universe.

Nice.

It was the instant – that beat of time between existence and oblivion – which fascinated Leggett. One second you're alive; the next, nothing. Would the guy even have time to register he had ceased to exist? Leggett puzzled over that one a lot. If you ceased to exist, could you know anything? Of course you fucking well couldn't. But, then again, there might just be a fleeting microsecond, right at the point where the world closes down around you, when you realise: I'm gone.

He was breathing heavily. A thin string of saliva had inched its way down his chin and he slurped it back. He could feel his prick pushing and pulsing against his jeans. It happened just about every time he studied the picture, and, more times than he liked to admit, he'd locked the bedroom door, taken the picture down from the wall, and wanked over it; all the while scrutinising the look on the guy's face.

Not this time though – he had work to finish. Money to make.

He went back to mixing the powders, working them around the plate, dreaming of when he would be able to set out on his own. When he would be *Mister* Leggett and have his own team around him – guys who would do *his* bidding and be at *his* beck and call. 'Mister Leggett,' he said out loud. '*Mister*, aye that's class, man.' But, first, he would have to get their respect, these guys, whoever they were going to be.

Not arseholes like Kyle or Prentice, that was for sure.

They looked down their noses at him, sneered at everything he did. As far as *they* were concerned he could do nothing right. To the likes of them, Leggett was a snivelling wee snot of a wean. But they were wrong. He was nineteen; he knew things; how to scam off Boddice for a start. They could put that in their fucking pipe.

The pricks.

What was it Kyle had said the other day?

Leggett had been in the car, waiting for Kyle to come out of a house after collecting payments from some druggie or other. Leggett had been bored and started playing a game on his mobile phone. He didn't see the police car draw up and park behind him. Not a problem – the rozzers had gone into a close across the way – but when Kyle came out, he went apeshit, jumping into the car and booting it to the floor down the road.

When they were out of sight at the end of the next street, Kyle stopped the car and grabbed Leggett by the collar, dragging him across the front seat. 'Ya stupid wee shite,' he shouted. 'Ye coulda got us both lifted. Too busy pissing about with yer stupid toys. You know the drill. Somethin like this happens, you get to fuck as quick as ye can, and phone me to let me know, give me a chance to get out the back way. But no, not you. You're spendin yer time fannyin about with this.' He had grabbed the mobile from Leggett's hand and threw it on the back seat. 'Ya wee retard,' he said. 'Your mother should've put you down as soon as you popped out her smelly fanny.'

Leggett had thought about that remark. Oh, aye. Thought about it a lot. Kyle was going to pay for that one. Weehoo, was he going to pay. Once Leggett had his own team, he would make sure Kyle showed some respect. Oh, yes. It wouldn't be long now.

He knew what was required of course. It was all connected. The picture, the mouse and Uncle Jimmy. That guy in the picture, that Nguyen Ngoc Loan, he knew the game as well. He was just standing there, not a shred of emotion as he pumped his gun into the other guy's head. Cool as fuck. Weehoo! That was how to do it.

And Leggett knew *he* could do it too. He'd practiced. Oh, aye. Ever since the time with the mouse. He stopped mixing the powders again and settled back in his chair, closed his eyes and allowed himself to think about it.

***

The washing machine had been on the blink, and his mother was clattering about in the kitchen doing the week's wash in the sink. There was a pile of dirty laundry on the floor and she'd gather up an armful and slunge it around the grey water for a couple of minutes, wring it out, then take it down to the back green and come back to start on the next lot. Leggett sat in the corner, smoking a roll-up and flicking through a copy of *FHM*. He just looked at the pictures, couldn't be arsed to read any of the articles. He glanced up at his mother as she bent to lift another load to the sink. Her arse was getting fatter. It looked like she had a fucking king-size duvet stuffed down there. No wonder the old man had buggered off.

He was just about to get up, maybe go through to the other room and switch on the telly, when his mother screamed and jumped back, throwing the bundle of washing onto the floor. 'Oh, Jesus Christ!' she shouted. 'Get it! Get that thing out of here!'

Leggett stood and went over to her. 'What is it?' he asked.

She put her hands up to her mouth. 'A mouse!' She backed away. 'A bloody mouse!'

'Where?' he asked.

She pointed to the pile of laundry. 'There,' she said. 'In there, wrigglin about. Ah felt it touchin my hand!'

Leggett knelt down and fished through the shirts and underpants. 'There's nothin here,' he said, looking up at her.

'Ye're imaginin things, ya stupid auld cow.'

'Don't you dare call me that,' she said. 'Ah'm imaginin nothin. There's a mouse in there, Ah'm tellin ye.'

He stared at the bundle on the floor. One of the shirtsleeves moved. A tiny ball pushed against the inside and rolled down towards the cuff. 'See!' his mother shouted. 'There it is! Get it. Go on!'

Leggett smiled and put his hand into the sleeve. The mouse was there right enough. He felt it nudge his hand and walk hesitantly onto his palm. Its body was soft and warm, and its paws felt like nail clippings against his skin. He closed his hand around it and brought it out.

'Get that thing away from me!' his mother screamed.

'It's only a wee mouse,' he said. 'It'll not do ye any harm.'

'Aye it will,' she said. 'Ah'm warnin ye,' she said backing off. 'Don't bring it near me! Get rid of it.'

'Please yourself,' he said. He stood up and plunged his hand into the water in the sink. He heard his mother gasp behind him.

'Colin,' she whispered. 'Don't.'

'Too late,' he replied. 'And don't call me Colin… it's Colly, alright?' He could feel the mouse squirming in his hand and he looked into the sink, opening his hand slightly to see it struggling. Its tail whipped back and forth and he could see the little black beads of its eyes staring up at him through the water. It was looking at him. Its tongue poked out between the tiny fangs of its teeth and a string of bubbles escaped from its mouth, floating up to break on the surface of the water. Its little hands grasped his thumb and its rear legs pushed frantically against his fingers. He watched the mouse watching him and wondered what it was thinking. Wondered what he looked like to it – safe, in control. Alive. Not dying, powerless, in terror and despair.

He giggled.

The mouse struggled less and less. It gave a final, feeble

kick and went limp in his hand, but he didn't release his grip. He continued to stare into its dead eyes, searching with something approaching awe for a sign, some indication of the point where it crossed over from life to nothingness. What did it look like?

His head was snapped back by a hard blow across the face.

His mother stood there, nursing her hand and her eyes bulging with fury. 'Ya bastard!' she shouted. 'What did ye do that for?'

He wheeled round and threw the mouse at her. She leapt out of the way and its body skited into the corner, hitting the wall with a wet slap. He felt his face reddening where she had struck him.

'Ya cruel wee shite,' she said. 'Honest to God, what have Ah reared? Ah only asked ye to get rid of it, not to murder the poor wee thing!'

He rubbed his face and glared at her. 'Ah did what needed to be done,' he said. 'It was vermin, needed put down.'

'No,' she said. 'Ye could just as easy have taken it out the back green and let it go. Ye were enjoyin yourself, weren't ye?'

He bared his teeth at her. 'Go to hell, ya auld bag,' he said, and stormed through to the next room, slamming the door behind him.

The stupid bitch, she'd spoiled the whole thing, cutting off his thoughts about the mouse. He tried to focus, to bring back the feeling, to grasp the state of mind he'd just had. The feeling that had made his heart race and his pupils dilate. He had almost seen it... something at the edge of his comprehension... something unknowable, yet he had *almost* known it. Christ, what he would give to bring the feeling back. He swallowed the lump in his throat and flopped onto the sofa.

The idea about connectedness didn't hit him until later that same week. He'd avoided his mother for most of the time, but he overheard her on the phone speaking to his Uncle Jimmy. He was coming round at the weekend and there was going to be a party. *Weehoo!* Leggett loved parties, and he loved it even better when his Uncle Jimmy was coming. For one thing, his cousin Michelle sometimes came along, and though he knew there was something not quite right about it, he would sometimes get a snog from her in the back bedroom. She was sixteen now, and the last time he had seen her she looked pretty fit.

The other good thing about his Uncle Jimmy was that he always brought his guitar to parties. It was a battered old acoustic, with scratches and scrapes on the woodwork and a burn mark where he had left it too close to the fire one night, but Jimmy could play it good and he knew some great songs.

When Saturday arrived, Uncle Jimmy and his new girlfriend – a woman with a bad perm and a fag constantly hanging from her mouth – came round with a carry-out of super lager and vodka. There was no Michelle. Uncle Jimmy said she was out with some guy or other, 'Gettin her arse shagged off, no doubt!' But Uncle Jimmy had brought the guitar. That was a consolation at least.

They sent out for fish suppers and pizza, and the lagers were cracked open. Leggett sat in the corner chair, smoking a cigarette, watching and listening. He eyed up Sandra, Jimmy's girlfriend. Leggett thought she was pretty hacket, though her body wasn't so bad. Nice tits. Still, he'd have to be well drunk to even think about giving her a jump.

The talk was mostly about relatives and folk they knew, holidays and work. Occasionally, his mother would let out a long, braying laugh at some remark from Jimmy, and Leggett would smile, pretending he'd been following the story.

The time wore on, and Leggett became bored. It had turned out to be a crap party, a waste of a Saturday night. The room was too hot and everyone had a sweaty glow, shirt collars loosened and sleeves rolled up. Leggett felt clammy and seedy. The telly in the corner was blaring out some piss-poor variety special, nobody-you've-ever-heard-of acts strutting about like they were headlining the bloody Albert Hall. The fish supper wrappers were lying beside the fireplace along with the empty pizza box, cold chips and some crust spilling onto the carpet.

He was considering going down to the street corner, see if any mates were hanging around, when Jimmy reached round behind his chair and brought the guitar out of its plastic case. 'Anybody fancy a wee singalong?' he asked. The two women nodded enthusiastically, and Leggett sat up in his chair. Jimmy glanced at each of them in turn, one eyebrow raised quizzically. 'Oh, I don't know,' he said in a ropy American accent. 'I think we could drum up a little bit more excitement at this here party! Some good ol' country music is just what we need. Yeehaw!'

He set the guitar on his knee and began picking out a jangly rhythm on the upper strings. The women clapped their hands in time. Jimmy laughed, and Leggett found himself tapping his feet and smiling too. This was more like it. The tune twanged away, and Jimmy started to sing in a smoky drawl. An old Johnny Cash song, something about trains a-comin and a-rollin.

Jimmy was warming up, moving into the next verse. He turned a little in his chair, leaning towards Leggett. Now he was singing about his mama telling him not to play with guns. Leggett sat up straighter. Jimmy crinkled his face into a leathery smile and winked at him. And then came a line that stopped Leggett's heart in his chest. How the guy in the song was in some place called Reno and shot a man, just so he could watch him die.

There was something else about a train whistle, but Leggett didn't hear the rest of the words. His throat constricted and he could hardly catch his breath. *I shot a man… just to watch him die…* Fucking weehoo and holy mama; that was it! Oh man, oh man! It was as if an earthquake had ripped through his head, heaving his brain to one side and slamming it back down inside his skull. It was suddenly clear to him… *just to watch him die…* That was what he had wanted with the mouse, but with a man... that would *really* be it! He felt the connection ricochet around his head, screaming like the train in the song, barrelling towards him, out of control and trailing a blaze of white fire. If he could do that... if he could look into the eyes... then he would know, then he would see. He felt sick, his stomach churning and grinding. Jimmy's voice and the brittle, spiky sound of the guitar clanged in his ears. It didn't sound like music anymore. He jumped up and ran out of the room.

'Hey, wee man, what's the matter?' Uncle Jimmy called after him.

Two weeks later, and he saw the picture of Nguyen Ngoc Loan in the paper. It all fell into place for him then – the mouse, Uncle Jimmy and the picture.

Connected.

It became an obsession, gnawed at him, burrowed deep into his soul. He felt he would go insane – every waking minute was spent thinking about that fucking song and the way his hand felt wrapped around the mouse as it twisted and writhed in his grasp. He couldn't get it out of his head. He had to know, had to feel what it was like. That transition from existence to absolute zero.

He decided to do something about it.

He bought the airgun.

Things settled down a bit after that. He found plenty of use for the gun, oh yes. In the back courts, down by the canal, on the hills that ran down to the edge of the scheme. Cats, rats, even a dog or two. Though it made him feel better, it still wasn't enough. There was still that hot coal burning deep inside, glowing steadily, unquenchable, waiting to flare and flash into flame. But he knew he only had to bide his time. It would come. Soon, maybe later, but it would come. The time when Boddice would give him his chance. The opportunity to be like Kyle and Prentice.

Then he would know what it was *really* like.

***

His mobile phone buzzed and vibrated in his pocket and he jerked forward, feeling light-headed; mouth dry and sticky. He frowned at the drugs sitting on the table in front of him, as if seeing them for the first time. Outside, the snow had stopped, and a patch of blue hung like a high flag behind the heavy folds of the clouds. He pulled the phone from his jeans and keyed up the message.

Tears came to his eyes as he read it.

A message from Boddice.

It was the final connection.

Kyle:
Every December Sky

It was one of those days when the light in the sky gave Kyle the strange feeling that he had lived before. An intangible, light-headed sense in the back of his mind. Nothing he could grasp with any certainty, just a feeling... almost, but not quite, a memory that he'd had a previous life.

It was not an unusual feeling for Kyle – a smell or a song could trigger it, or a sound or a taste, but most often it was the dimming of the light on a day like this: getting towards dusk, low, dark clouds the colour of a winter sea, heavy with the threat of snow and, far on the horizon, a weak, watery sun filtering through the bleak greyness to cast a dim yellow glow on the Glasgow streets. Whatever caused it, it was as if the universe tilted on its axis for a moment and he felt himself struggling to grasp at memories he wasn't entirely sure were there at all.

Of course, he never mentioned any of this to anyone. They wouldn't understand, would think him an A-number-one candidate for the loony bin. But Kyle wondered if there were times when they shared the same thoughts and feelings. That maybe everyone had a trigger, a sequence of events, a coincidence of circumstances, that awoke a deep, latent memory, but, like him, they kept quiet about it.

Perhaps he attached too much importance to it. After all, it was just a feeling and, if he was honest, he didn't believe all this Buddhist-style shite meant anything.

Kyle parked his car in a side street and started to walk the couple of blocks down to the Palace. To park outside would just make it obvious to any nosy bastard who cared to look that there was something going on in the derelict bingo hall. Christ only knew why Boddice had picked this spot for the meet. The hall was due for demolition in a couple of weeks.

Safe enough for whatever Boddice had in mind. He always liked to have some sort of security for these things, especially if he was arranging a hit.

The sun finally disappeared behind the tower blocks in the distance and a squally wind threw sleet and rain in his face. Kyle pulled his jacket closer around him and ran his hand through his hair. It needed cut – he'd have to get Mary to go over it with the clippers. Number three all over. Boddice wouldn't allow them to have it any shorter, said it attracted unwanted attention. From wee neds wanting to have a go to see if you were as hard as you looked, to the polis cruising for someone who looked as if they needed to be flung in the back of the car. True, the shorter it was, the more aggressive and intimidating you looked – usually; Kyle thought it made some guys look like overgrown babies – but Boddice didn't want overt aggression. People knew what to expect if they saw that. Much better to go in with the softer look and then surprise them when things didn't turn out quite as they anticipated.

Whatever... he would get Mary to see to it later tonight. He was in danger of turning into a hippy. He smiled. Maybe that was what was behind all this previous-life crap.

He arrived at the Palace. Loose plaster hung down from the awning over the front doors and the black plastic letters *B N G* clung to their little attachment rails on the overhead marquee like the final notes in a musical score. A faded dayglo poster announced the appearance of Les Dennis on the fifth of March. What the fuck year must *that* have been?

The front entrance was boarded and shuttered, and cast -iron sliding gates were drawn across the stairs leading to the doors. Mounds of rubbish piled up behind the rails in scummy drifts. Kyle moved round to the side of the building, clambering through the overgrown weeds and mud-sludged puddles, and found the fire exit. The door was banging back and forth in the wind. He grabbed it and pulled it open, wedging it in place with a cement-crusted wooden board. Standing in the doorway, he looked up the stairwell that led to a dim flickering glow in the darkness above. He scrambled over a tarpaulin blocking the passageway and started up the stairs towards the light. At the top, he pushed open the swing doors, revealing the ruined carcass of the auditorium, and made his way towards the centre of the hall.

The Palace had once been a cinema, and the seats that had stood in rows of red-veloured splendour now lay scattered and broken amongst the rubble on the floor. Graffiti was sprayed on the walls, and someone had taken the trouble to draw a fairly impressive pornographic scene on the side of the staircase leading to the broken stage. Flurries of snowflakes drifted down from a hole in the roof and the matted carpet squelched under his feet as he walked across to the small fire that one of the guys had started in the middle of the floor.

It looked as if he was the last one to arrive. The Wilson twins stood off to one side, smoking; coats buttoned and collars turned up against the cold. Prentice sat on the edge of the stage, staring glumly at the dark recesses of the balcony, the light from the fire flickering in his eyes. Boag sat on his hunkers, warming his hands at the flames, his face drawn and pale. As Kyle approached, Boag glanced up and looked away quickly. Kyle hadn't seen him for a while and he wondered if he was sleeping rough. The thought crossed his mind to maybe lend him a wee bung when they were through with this. He gave Boag a nod and half a smile as he walked up to join him at the fire.

No-one spoke – except for the boy Leggett. He just wouldn't shut the fuck up.

'Wee-hoo!' he yipped to no-one in particular, kicking up a pile of yellowed bingo cards and clapping his hands excitedly. 'Oh man, oh man! Ah think this might be it. Ah think big Boddice is gonnae pick me this time! What do youse think guys?'

No-one paid him any attention. None of the others really liked him that much. Too much of a liability on whatever jobs he'd been trusted to take part in. Too much of a loose cannon. Too much of a fuckwit. Kyle put his hands in his pockets and stared into the fire.

'Oh aye,' Leggett went on. 'Youse've all done this kind of thing before, Ah know. Ah think it's gonnae be my turn now, but. Ah've been practising too…' Kyle lifted his head and looked over at him, '…using dugs and cats and that, and Ah know my wee air pistol isn't quite the same thing, but it does the business, ye know?' Leggett picked up a piece of plastic tubing from the floor and hurled it to the back of the hall where it clattered behind a balustrade decorated with little silver and gold crowns. 'The wee fuckers sometimes get away, but most times Ah get them clean. *Pow!* Right in the eye or the balls!' He spun round, cocking his thumb back and making a pistol of his hand. 'Wee-hoo! Ye should see them. They just fold up, all yelpin and whinin. Fuckin magic! And then Ah'll go over and step on their necks or their ribs till they stop.' He sniggered and shook his head. 'Aye. Ah think he's gonnae give me my chance, big Boddice.' He clasped his hands and straightened both arms in front of him, screwing up his eyes and taking aim along the length of his arm towards his thumb. '*Pow!*'

Kyle stared at him and spat on the floor.

Leggett turned his head. 'What's your problem, Kyle?' Leggett said, lifting his chin, curling his lip at him.

The twins turned to look at him. The others didn't move, couldn't be arsed.

Leggett folded his arms, took up a defiant stance. 'You not think Ah've got it in me? Eh, Kyle? You got a problem?'

You're fucking right I've got a problem.

Kyle was about to say something, walk over and wipe that stupid sneer off Leggett's face, when there was a sudden rushing of wind in the hall and the snowflakes falling from the roof swirled and danced above the flames of the fire. The door at the back of the hall opened and there was McLean, Boddice's right-hand man, his minder, his trusted lieutenant, striding down the aisle towards them.

McLean was a big man, tall and hefty, with his hair oiled and swept back and his greying beard neatly trimmed. He wore a long, dark overcoat with a yellow cashmere scarf tucked neatly around his neck. Black leather gloves covered his hands and the scent of expensive aftershave drifted towards the men as he approached. Leggett was looking at him expectantly, his hands fidgeting with the buttons on his jacket.

'Alright, boys?' said McLean. 'Glad you could make it.'

'Ah'm just fine, Mr McLean,' said Leggett, not realising the question didn't require an answer. 'Just fine.'

McLean didn't even look at him. 'Mr Boddice apologises – he has been unavoidably detained,' he said. 'But he will be glad to learn you all received his message and took the trouble to come out on this foul night to attend to business.' He reached into his coat and took out a bundle wrapped in a dark blue towel. McLean unfolded the package slowly to reveal a snub-nosed revolver, chrome-plated. It lay gleaming on the towel, reflecting the flames from the fire. He placed it carefully on the floor.

'Holy mother of all things holy,' said Leggett in a hushed voice. 'Fuck me, but that's a beauty! Can Ah touch it?'

McLean turned his head slightly and raised an eyebrow. 'Don't be so stupid!' he snapped. 'Mr Boddice paid over eight hundred for this weapon. Imported from Holland. Never fired.' He looked at each of them in turn. 'There's one bullet and then it goes back tomorrow. It'll be untraceable.' He turned to Leggett. 'So Ah don't want your grubby wee mitts on it alright?'

Leggett looked dejected.

'Not yet anyway,' McLean finished.

Leggett's eyes widened, and a grin spread across his face.

He hopped from foot to foot. 'Oh man, oh man,' he muttered under his breath.

'Okay boys,' said McLean. 'Sorry this has been a wee hike for most of youse. Mr Boddice hopes you will forgive him. But it's a single shot job. Ah don't need youse all for this one.'

They had heard all this before. Boddice always liked to have his full team at his disposal and usually didn't make up his mind who he would use on a particular job until the last minute. A wee text message on the mobile, giving the time and place for the meet, and he'd expect them all to be there. Failure to show and they'd never be used again. Simple as that. He'd make sure each of them got a wee something for their trouble, but it was never that much. Nevertheless, if any of them was picked for one of the 'special' jobs, the rewards were handsome; and that's what kept them coming back.

McLean stood for a moment in silence, contemplating. He took a deep breath. 'Leggett, it's you,' he said.

Leggett let out a wee gasp. 'Oh fuckin mama… yes!' he said.

McLean went on. 'And Kyle, Ah'll need you as well.'

Kyle's heart skipped a beat. He glanced over at Leggett who was still too excited to notice what McLean had said. *Oh fuck*, thought Kyle. *I think I know what's coming.*

McLean ushered the rest of them from the hall. 'Right lads. See the rest of youse soon. Let yourselves out the back.'

All the time Leggett eyed the gun as it lay glistening on the towel. It shone in the darkness like a bead of mercury. He licked his lips and looked up at Kyle, seeming to notice for the first time that he was still there, that they were a twosome. A small frown creased his forehead.

McLean came back down the aisle towards the fire, bent down and picked up the gun, holding it carefully in the towel, despite his gloved hands. Leggett shifted back and forth restlessly, barely able to contain himself, his eyes darting between McLean and the gun.

'Kyle,' McLean said, turning towards him. 'You've done this for Mr Boddice before, haven't ye?'

Kyle nodded.

He felt the universe tilt on its axis.

McLean came over and handed the gun to Kyle. 'Okay, do him,' he said, and walked quickly to the doors at the back of the hall.

Kyle turned to Leggett who was looking at him with innocent, uncomprehending eyes. Eyes that were growing wider by the second as it slowly dawned on him what was about to happen. Leggett started gibbering. 'No, it's alright, Ah don't need to know… Ah don't need to know.'

Kyle became aware of the banging of the fire exit door down in the depths of the building. It must have worked its way free of the board propping it open.

The sound reminded him of something. He couldn't quite place it.

He levelled the gun and squeezed the trigger.

Pow! he thought.

PART 2: THE BEST-LAID PLANS…

Boddice:
Nobody's Child

The Merc was becoming too hot. McLean had kept the heater running when he left, and Boddice felt stifled. He'd already reached over from the passenger seat and set the climate control to a cooler setting, but the combination of his overcoat, scarf and gloves meant he was still sweltered, the air in the car suffocatingly dry. Despite being a Mercedes, the people carrier wasn't his favourite among his cars, not by a long way, but it was necessary for tonight's wee job.

A trickle of sweat threaded through the stubble on his face. He couldn't stand it any longer. Sighing, he opened the door and clambered out into the thin sleet. Immediately, the chill sliced through him and he shivered violently. *Fuck's sake,* he thought, *from one extreme to the other.* He scowled and pulled up his collar.

The awning above the entrance to the Palace clattered and boomed in the wind, and Boddice thought of McLean taking care of business; in there; in the dark. Not that Boddice was concerned about Leggett – the spotty wee scrag meant less to him than the dogshit on the pavement. No, the thing that gave him pause was what was going to happen next.

The Announcement.

The Plan.

Whether it was going to work. And, more to the point, whether they were all up for it, ready for the change of direction. Without them on board, it would all go to hell. He needed the boys to carry it off, and he needed them to be fully behind him.

Later, when he was ready, he would reveal the wee twist in the story. Much later. Once they were committed.

He leaned against the bonnet of the car, fished inside his pocket and brought out a silver hip flask. He unscrewed the top, sniffed the contents. Laphroaig. The good old Leapfrog.

That would do the trick. He knew it was supposed to taste better if it was watered slightly, but Boddice preferred it raw and unadulterated. None of your namby-pamby tasting-notes shite. Just the whisky and nothing else. And this was the good stuff. Twenty-five-year-old. Four hundred quid a bottle. He put the flask to his lips and tipped it back. The whisky ran into his mouth, the pungent, peat-smoke flavour both warming and anaesthetising his tongue at the same time. He held it for a moment, savouring its fierceness, before letting the whisky slip down his throat.

The Plan. The change of direction. So much was riding on this. Of course, the money was one thing, and there was his standing in the drug world. But Boddice knew *that* had been declining for years. He wasn't self-obsessed enough to believe he was now not much more than a bit player in the great scheme of things. His star was no longer in the ascendancy. Sure, he was feared, he was loathed, he commanded respect, and rightly too – a guy would have to be one crazy fucker to even think about crossing him (as Leggett was just about to discover) – but now there were much bigger fish in the pond.

Boddice knew he was tolerated, allowed to run his little empire more by lack of interest than anything else on the part of those guys who had become the real movers and shakers; the guys with the book deals for a ghost-written autobiography, the television documentaries on their 'shady criminal underworld' shenanigans, and the publicists who made sure they were front-page regulars. He still moved in their circles of course, attended the same swanky dinners, the charity dos, the boxing bouts, schmoozed the room with the minor celebrities and the hangers-on, pressed the flesh, shared the dirty jokes. But he knew, and, more importantly, *they* knew, he wasn't the man he was. He didn't kid himself that if they ever were to express even the slightest curiosity in his business affairs, think about moving in, he wouldn't be removed from the scene without so much as a polite *good-night and thank-you*.

But this Plan... this could be different. This was something those newbies wouldn't dream of touching – not their scene in the first place – but, even so, something that could establish Boddice in an altogether different league. One where they would press their noses to the window and look on in awe at what he had done. He would show the fuckers.

Boddice shivered again. He was about to take another swig from the hip flask when the door of the Palace opened, juddering and scraping against the fake marble floor of the vestibule. He screwed the top back on the flask, smoothed his coat and stretched his neck over his shirt collar. *About time*, he thought, slipping the flask back into his pocket.

Boag was first. He shuffled through the rubbish in the doorway and made his way down the stairs towards Boddice without even lifting his head to notice him standing there. Prentice came out next, followed by the twins and then McLean, buttoning his jacket. Prentice nodded and gave a low grunt by way of a greeting, and Boag finally looked up, startled to see Boddice standing beside the Mercedes.

Time to turn on the charm.

Boddice smiled. 'Good to see you boys,' he said. 'Glad you saw fit to come along.' He turned to McLean. 'Everything alright with the boy and Kyle?'

McLean stuffed his hands into the pockets of his coat, glanced up the empty street. 'I don't see there being any problems Mr Boddice.' There was a dry, crisp bang from the bingo hall behind him, a sudden crack like the slap of a wooden plank on a stone floor. Boag and the twins gave a startled jump. McLean grinned. 'No problems at all.'

'You hear that?' Boddice scanned their faces. 'That, boys,' Boddice said, 'is the sound of justice, the sweet, reassuring noise that tells me I have someone I can trust to do what they are told. Not go fucking around behind my back or hope to pull the wool over my eyes.'

The door opened and Kyle came out shaking his head,

his lips pressed tightly together, forcing his mouth into a thin slash. He held the gun in trembling hands. He sat heavily on the stairs, his eyes fixed on the ground.

Boddice ignored him and carried on with his speech. 'The sound that, should any one of you even *begin* to think to try to scam me, to defy me,' he threw a sidelong glance at Prentice, 'to turn your back on me, will be the last fucking thing you hear.'

The door opened again and Leggett staggered into the street, his face as pale as the moon and with a piss stain darkening the inside of his trouser leg. Boddice waved Leggett over. 'It's the sound which our... come on son, over here, soon as you can... which our young cub, our wee baby spice, our thinks-he-knows-it-all fledgling entrepreneur, should have had echoing in his shell-likes as he breathed his last, lying on the sticky carpet of the illustrious Palace Bingo Hall.' Boddice put his arm around Leggett who stood blinking back tears. 'Which, you can clearly see, he has not. He has in fact...' Boddice wrinkled his nose. 'Have you shat yourself son? Had a wee wet fart and followed through? Understandable, I suppose.' He curled his upper lip. 'Anyway... as I was saying... Leggett here has in fact become a member of a very rare and elite band of people. We should get you a T-shirt made up... That's a good idea, I like it.' He winked at McLean. 'Andy, remind me about that tomorrow morning.' Boddice took Leggett's arm, began twisting it up behind his back, forcing the boy to his knees in front of the car. 'Yes, young Leggett is one of those unique people that have had the privilege of me, yes *me*, paying back a favour I owe *them*. More than that, he is one of the even more uncommon species of creatures that are alive and kicking when they should, more properly, be queuing up at the pearly gates.'

He kicked Leggett in the small of the back. Leggett fell to the ground, his shadow thrown far along the road by the car headlamps. Boddice knelt down beside him. 'You hear me son?' he hissed. 'You understand what I'm fucking saying to you? You've had a second chance here boy, and second chances are not usually my thing.' Boddice got to his feet. 'Consider us squared up.'

Boddice left Leggett lying on the road and turned to the others. 'I know what you're all thinking. What the fuck is going on? Why did I almost dispatch this wee toaly to meet his maker; and more to the point, you're probably wondering why I haven't, in fact, done so. Why is he still sucking air into his lungs, and not lying up in that hall waiting to be discovered by some scabby wee jakey three weeks from now?'

Boddice watched them shuffle uncomfortably. One of the twins, he couldn't tell which one, lit up a cigarette.

Kyle, still sitting on the stairs, looked over to Boddice. 'You're fucking right that's what we're wondering,' Kyle said, his voice shaking with anger. 'Ah've just psyched myself up to get rid of this wee prick once and for all, and what do Ah get? Nuthin more than a bloody ringing in my ear from a fucking blank.' He shook his head again. 'A blank!'

'I fully understand how you must feel,' said Boddice, smiling. 'You're a good man... *loyal*... and I took advantage. No doubt about that. But, rest assured, I'll see to it that you'll not go empty-handed for this. You're on a bonus Kyle.'

Leggett, still on his hands and knees, started to throw up on the road. Boddice laughed again. 'That's right son, get it all up. Better out than in, eh?' He was relishing his performance. 'You see lads, I brought you out here to observe this because I want you to know two things.' He kicked Leggett's arm away from him, sent him sprawling back to the ground. 'One, if you fuck with me, try to turn me over, this is going to happen for real, make no mistake.' Leggett had started to get back up. Boddice kicked him down again. 'Secondly, and I won't bore you with the details of what this wee shite got up to, but let's say I owed him a favour and now that's not only settled, but he owes me a few thousand pounds in lost revenue.' He grinned at Leggett. 'Let's just hope for both our sakes you've been squirreling it away under your clatty wee bed. A favour returned is one thing. Letting you get away with it is something altogether different.' He nodded to Kyle and Prentice. 'You two will go round tomorrow and do a bit of collecting. If he's not got it, break his fucking legs, tell him you'll be back the next day. And if… well, you know the drill.'

Boddice clapped his hands together, and rubbed them to get some blood flowing back in. 'But, anyway,' he said. 'There's also the real reason you're out here in this god-awful weather.' They all glanced up, except Kyle who fidgeted with the stock of the gun. Boddice swept his arms wide, shepherding them towards the Merc. 'I've got an announcement to make,' he said, opening the door and ushering them inside. 'In private.'

Boddice went back over to Leggett, who had finally scrambled to his feet. Boddice grabbed Leggett's shirt and pulled him close. 'As for you, ya wee prick, you're out. As of now, if I ever see you on this patch again, ever catch you with so much as a baw-hair on these streets, I *will* fucking kill you.' His breath condensed in the cold air causing each word to be punctuated by a small cloud of vapour. 'Don't for a second doubt me. I'll rip your plooky wee face off.' Boddice pushed him away. 'And that's not just a fancy figure of speech, believe me. You've been lucky tonight son. Luckier than you can ever know. Understand?'

Leggett stared at the ground and nodded his head.

'Say it,' said Boddice. 'Tell me you understand.'

Leggett blinked back his tears. 'Ah understand.'

'Good. Then we both know the lie of the land.'

Boddice turned his back on him and returned to the Merc.

He climbed into the front seat beside McLean who spun the car into the road and sped off, leaving Leggett, orphaned, under the Palace awning.

On the beach

McLean took the Merc onto the motorway, heading for the coast. Boddice turned in his seat and looked at the men sitting in the back. The twins and Boag seemed to shrink into their seats, unsure of what was going on. Kyle and Prentice stared out the windows on either side, watching the housing schemes slip past in the falling snow.

They drove in silence for forty-five minutes, the men knowing not to ask any questions or strike up any banal attempts at small talk with each other. Things would be made clear in due course.

When they reached Ayr, McLean drove through the town centre and down to the promenade, the car park deserted, not even a shaggin-wagon parked in a far corner away from the street lights.

Boddice touched McLean on the shoulder. 'Just pull up here Andy, this'll do fine.'

McLean turned into a space facing the beach and killed the headlights. They could just make out the waves breaking in long lines of white surf which surged onto the sand. The wind buffeted the car, rocking and bouncing it on the suspension. Prentice shook his head and muttered under his breath, 'Surely not here…'

Boddice opened his door. 'Afraid so, Davie. Thought we'd try somewhere different.'

'Ah'll say it's different,' said Prentice. 'It's fucking freezing out there. Ah'm not dressed for this.'

Boddice climbed out. 'Okay lads, follow me.'

They got out of the car and stood huddled beside it. Boddice leaned inside, spoke to McLean. 'Sorry Andy, it's just the boys for this one. Need-to-know basis and all that. What *you* don't know can't hurt you.'

'No problem, Mr Boddice. I'll be waiting here.'

'Good man. We'll not be too long.' Boddice made to close the door, but stopped. 'Oh, and Andy,' he said. 'Don't leave the heater running too high. Let's keep it down to sauna levels eh?'

McLean smiled. 'Will do.' He leaned across the front seat and pulled the door closed.

Boddice turned and headed down a small flight of steps leading to the beach. 'This way lads,' he called back to the rest of them. They followed him onto the sand, gritting their teeth against the icy wind whipping up from the sea. 'Keep up,' Boddice said. 'Keep moving, get the old blood circulating and all that. It's not too bad once you get used to it.'

'Aye, right,' Prentice mumbled. 'Not too bad if you've got on a stinkin great overcoat like that, instead of this crappy, paper-thin shite Ah've got.'

Boddice marched down the shore towards the waves which thundered onto the beach. He stopped at the edge, where the water swept and foamed towards his feet. The others came up behind him, stumbling on the ridges and hollows of the frozen sand.

Boddice turned to them, barely able to pick out their faces in the darkness. 'Right,' he said. 'I know this is cold and uncomfortable, but it's one of the few places we can discuss this matter with absolute certainty no-one will be listening in. It's important there is complete security on this.'

'What about the car?' John asked. 'Surely that's pretty secure? And warmer.'

Boddice stared him down. 'This,' he said, 'is where I want to have our discussion. Here and nowhere else.' He paused, taking the time to make sure he had their full attention. 'Understood?' They nodded, hugging themselves for warmth. 'Okay,' he said. 'This is the deal. I have a proposal... a plan, if you want.' There. He had said it: *The Plan*. 'I must warn you it's not without risk. I know you're not unfamiliar with violence and mayhem, the strong-arm stuff when dealing with the more unsavoury members of our society.' He looked at Kyle and Prentice. 'Well, some of you anyway.' The twins and Boag shuffled and stamped their feet against the cold. Boddice went on. 'This thing is different. There should be no need for any of that unpleasantness. But, if matters don't pan out as intended, one or more of us could wind up in the pokey. For a very long time.'

Kyle raised an eyebrow. 'So why don't you just tell us what's on your mind?' he asked. 'What's so risky about this plan?'

Boddice smiled. 'All in good time, Gordon. I need to know if you're all in first. If it all comes off, if we're successful, there will be handsome rewards for everyone. Very handsome. In fact,' he glanced at Prentice who was looking out to the churning sea, seemingly not paying attention, 'the rewards may be so great that we can all retire, go and do other things with our lives.' He brought a handkerchief from his pocket, dabbed a wind-blown tear from his eye. 'But I'm giving you the chance to refuse. Now, at the start, before things get too… involved. Before you know any of the details. You can walk away from it right now, and nothing will—'

'Ah'll do it.' Boddice turned. It was Prentice. He was still staring at the waves, face screwed up against the wind. 'Put my name down.'

Boddice grinned and tapped his nose. 'Ha! I knew you'd be first on board Davie. I can always count on you!'

Prentice drew back from the edge of the water, started kicking some seaweed. Boddice studied the others. Kyle shook his head wearily, raised his hand and walked over to join Prentice.

John cleared his throat. 'Ah don't mean to be awkward Mr Boddice, but Ah'm not so sure that…'

Campbell clutched John's elbow, began leading him away. 'Mr Boddice,' he said. 'Do you mind if I have a quick word with my brother before we commit to anything?'

Boddice blew on his hands. 'Be my guest,' he said. 'But be quick.'

Campbell pulled John a few yards back up the beach towards the promenade. 'What?' said John, seeing Campbell glaring at him. 'Ah only wanted to…'

'Shut up!' said Campbell. 'Do ye not see what's happening here?'

'Eh? What do ye mean?'

'Why do ye think we're down here, standing on this fucking beach? Do ye think we're here to build sandcastles?'

'Boddice said he wanted privacy, no eavesdroppers. You heard him yourself.'

Campbell snorted. 'Aye, he did say that, and it's probably true to a certain extent.' He put his arm around John's shoulder. 'But think on this. He said he's giving us a chance to get out if we want. True. But if we say anything, give any indication that we're not gonnae take part, ye can stake anything ye want, but we'll not be leaving this beach alive.'

'Aw wait a minute, ye can't—'

'Take a look about ye, John,' Campbell interrupted. 'Apart from us five, do ye see any witnesses?'

'No, but—'

'And did ye not notice that they two bastards Prentice and Kyle didn't even think about it? They didn't even wait to let Boddice finish. They're not stupid John. They know the score. If we turn this down, Boddice won't hesitate to slit our throats. There's too much—'

'Slit our throats? Ah don't think so somehow. Why would he do that?'

'Why? *Why?* Do ye even need to ask? For Christ's sake, think for once.' Campbell grabbed John by the shoulders. 'He's just told us something big is coming up. He wants us to be part of it. Now, we can turn him down, there's no problem with that, he's just offered us the chance hasn't he?'

John nodded.

'Sure, we can say no,' Campbell went on. 'But just work it out. Do ye suppose Boddice will just let us walk away from here, with us knowing that a really big job is just about to happen? He'll just let us go back to *Two's Tattoos* and forget everything? That it'll never cross our minds again, that we'll never let it slip to somebody that Boddice has some grand plan?'

John looked unsure. 'Well… it's a possibility that we…'

Campbell let go of John's shoulders. 'Forget possibilities John, it's a certainty. And you know what Ah'm talking about. Boddice is a psycho. More than that, he's a bloody *paranoid* psycho.' Campbell wondered if he'd said that a bit too loudly, and nervously glanced in Boddice's direction. He didn't seem to have heard – Boddice was deep in conversation with Boag. Campbell turned back to John. 'Even McLean isn't involved in this. You heard what Boddice said to him – what you don't know can't hurt you. Well John, *we* fucking well know don't we?'

'Aye, but not the details. He hasn't told us anything yet.'

'That's beside the point. We still know he's gonnae be up to something. Whatever it is, details or not.'

'Ah suppose.'

'Too right ye suppose.' The wind was making Campbell's nose run. He sniffed back a watery snotter. 'So, if Boddice has let us know he's got something planned, and let's not forget he wants us to be involved in this, then Ah think it would be madness to turn him down. Not just because of the rewards, whatever the fuck *they* might be, but because Ah honestly think he'll bump us off if we don't go along with it.' He gestured to Kyle and Prentice who were standing off to one side smoking. 'They two would do it right here and now without hesitation, believe me. All it would take would be a wee nod from Boddice. Who's to know, who's to see out here in the dark? Ye saw what happened with Leggett back there at the bingo hall.'

John shrugged and blew out a long sigh. 'Alright, alright, if ye really think that might happen then we'll go for it. But Ah think ye're imagining half of this.'

Campbell smiled. 'Thank Christ for that. Ye had me

worried there, brother. And ye never know, we might come out of this pretty well if what he says is true.'

'Aye, well, Ah'm not so sure, but Ah'll go with your gut feeling this time.'

'Good man,' said Campbell, guiding John back to where Boddice was talking to Boag. 'If nothing else, it'll get us out of this bloody freezing wind quicker.'

'Well?' Boddice asked as they came up. 'Made up your mind?'

'Aye,' Campbell said. 'Count us in.'

'Excellent news!' said Boddice. 'Young Boag here has also said 'yes'. Not much persuasion required there, eh son?' He gave Boag a hearty slap on the back, sending him staggering forward a few paces. Boddice looked at each of them in turn. 'Good stuff,' he said. 'Strange as it might sound, I need all three of you. If even one had called off, the ball would be on the slates, and your teas would be out, as they say.'

Campbell elbowed John in the ribs, muttering through gritted teeth, 'Told ye.' John kicked him on the shin.

'Davie, Gordon!' Boddice beckoned to Prentice and Kyle who made their way back to join the group. 'We have a team, gentlemen. We appear to be in business.'

'Maybe,' Prentice mumbled, scowling. 'But you haven't said anything about what sort of business we're supposed to be in. We're freezing our nuts off out here, volunteering for stuff, and we don't know what for. Some night this is turning out to be.'

Boddice's grin faded.

Prentice faltered. 'It's just, Ah mean, what kind of job needs the five of us? What's with all the extra secrecy?'

Boddice said nothing, simply held Prentice's gaze. The waves crashed in the background, plunging relentlessly onto the shore.

Prentice blinked and dropped his gaze.

He knew what was required. 'Sorry,' he said.

Boddice beamed. 'Apology accepted Davie, I appreciate how uncertainty can make you forget yourself. No harm done.' Boddice hugged himself, bounced on his toes. 'But you're right of course, it *is* bloody cold out here. Not sure my balls are gonnae drop off, but it's chilly sure enough.' He spread his arms. 'Come on lads, let's walk, warm ourselves up a bit. And while we walk, I'll explain.'

He set off along the beach, the others huddled in behind him, walking carefully to avoid unseen seaweed, tree branches, jellyfish that might be lurking on the beach in the dark.

'What do you know about the Dark Side of the Moon?' asked Boddice.

No-one said anything, unsure of what he was getting at. Prentice squinted out to sea, ignoring the question. 'Come on,' said Boddice. 'The Dark Side of the Moon, what does it mean to you?'

'A Pink Floyd album?' suggested Campbell.

'Who's Pink Floyd?' whispered John. Campbell increased his pace, pulling away from him.

'Aye,' said Boddice, 'it *is* a record by them. Never heard it myself. Meant to be not bad from what I understand. But that's not what I'm getting at.' He stopped and turned to them. 'It's something else.' He scanned their faces. 'Nobody?'

Boag cleared his throat. Boddice nodded to him. 'On you go son, spit it out.'

'It's a diamond, isn't it?' Boag said.

'How'd you know that?' Kyle asked.

Boag shrugged. 'Dunno. Seen it on some posters in the town centre maybe.'

Boddice laughed. 'It's not just any diamond. The Dark Side of the Moon is one of the rarest and most expensive in the world. It's a purple diamond. Deep, deep purple, and expensive not only because of its size, but because it's perfect. Absolutely flawless.'

John nudged Campbell, mumbled under his breath.

'Purple? Ah thought diamonds were white, see-through… ye know… clear.' Campbell took no notice of him.

Boddice carried on. 'It's a beautiful object, discovered in South Africa on the first day of the millennium. No-one could believe such a fantastic stone would—'

'Ye want to steal it don't ye?' It was Prentice.

'*Steal* it?' said Kyle. 'What the hell are you talking about?'

Prentice looked up. 'That's what he wants. Steal it. And he wants us to do it for him. That's his big plan.' He stared at Boddice. 'Isn't it?'

Boddice ran his tongue over his teeth and blinked a few times before breaking into a smile. 'Correct Davie! Absolutely spot on. You've hit the nail on the—'

'Wait a minute,' said Kyle. 'This fancy diamond, the Dark Side of the Moon, how are we gonnae steal that? Is it not kept in a big vault in New York or something?' The twins nodded. This didn't seem quite right.

'Geneva, actually,' said Boddice.

'But not next year,' Prentice interrupted. 'Next year, it's coming to Glasgow. For a whole month.'

'That's it!' said Boag, snapping his fingers. '*That's* what the posters were about. Ah knew Ah'd seen it somewhere. Glasgow – City of Jewellery, that big exhibition.'

Boddice grinned. 'Once again, you're right. I knew I had picked the right boys for this job. You're all so quick on the uptake.'

'Ah'm not so sure about that,' Campbell muttered, casting John a hurried sideways glance.

Boddice heard him. 'Don't be so down on yourself, you two are key to the whole thing.'

'We are?' said John.

'Oh yes,' said Boddice. 'But more of that later. It's true, the Dark Side of the Moon will indeed be in Glasgow next summer. The prize exhibit for the coveted City of Jewellery festival. It'll be on display for five weeks in Trusdale and

Needham. It's a major coup for the store.'

'A coo?' John whispered, covering his mouth with his hand. 'What the hell is he going on about?'

'Shhh!' hissed Campbell.

'While it's there,' said Boddice, 'we're going to take it.'

'Just like that?' asked Kyle.

'Of course, we're not going to waltz in on a busy Saturday and swipe it from under the noses of the security guards. But there *is* a way. I have a plan worked out. You all have your parts to play.'

'Maybe so,' said Prentice. 'But what's the point? This isn't exactly our usual stuff, is it? We've never done anything like this before, have we? It's always been drugs and extortion. Is this not a wee bit out of our league?'

'Call it diversification,' Boddice replied. 'A one-off move into something new and untried. It's perfect, because no-one is going to suspect us are they? Why should they? As you say, we're strictly drugs. We're not going to attract any attention from the law, cos, let's face it, big-time stuff like this isn't our game.'

'But Mr Boddice,' said Boag. 'How are we gonnae pull something like this off? We've not got any expertise in this kinda thing.'

'Ah, but you have,' said Boddice. 'You just haven't realised it yet.' He held his arm out, ushering them back to the car. 'Look, I'm not saying this is going to be easy. There'll have to be training and preparation. Lots of it. And, as I said, you'll all have your own specific function to perform. This job requires all of you.'

'So, for example,' said Kyle. 'What would ye be wanting me to do?'

'Not now,' said Boddice. 'I'll meet each of you in turn. In private. Spell out what I need from you.' He turned to the twins. 'Starting with you two. Your role is pivotal. I want to make sure that you're up to it before we commit to anything else.'

Campbell and John looked at each other. 'Us?' said Campbell. 'Pivotal?'

'Oh yes. You're right at the heart of this. I'll be wanting to see both of you tomorrow morning.'

'Hang on,' Prentice said. 'Listen, don't take this the wrong way. Ah'm not trying to be cheeky or anything.' He swallowed. 'Honestly. Ah've just got a question about all this robbery shite.'

'Shite?' said Boddice. 'Don't misunderstand me Davie. This isn't shite. I'm deadly serious about this.'

'Sorry,' said Prentice, holding up a hand. 'Figure of speech, that's all.'

'Fair enough,' said Boddice. 'What's your question then?'

'This diamond, the Dark Side of the Moon. It's really famous, it's worth millions…'

'Thirty at least,' said Boddice.

They all stopped walking.

'Thirty?' said Kyle, his voice breaking into a higher octave in astonishment.

'Holy fuck,' said John. 'That's… that's…'

'A lot of fucking dosh,' Campbell finished for him.

'My point exactly,' said Prentice. 'What are we gonnae do with it once we've got it? Assuming we do get it, that is.'

'What are *we* going to do?' said Boddice. 'I think I can take that particular burden from you, Davie. It'll be me who sorts that one out.'

'Well, whatever,' said Prentice. 'Ma point is, a famous diamond, worth thirty…' he shook his head, amazed, '…thirty million pounds, how do we get rid of it? We can't sell it – who could afford that kind of money? We can't cut it into wee bits – who would handle it, knowing where it came from? We'd never get anything for it. How would we—'

'Ransom it,' said Boddice.

'What?' Prentice looked incredulous.

'We'll ransom it back to the owners, or to Trusdale and Needham, whoever comes up with the best offer.'

Prentice burst out laughing. 'Ransom it? Oh for fuck's sake, that's just great. A ransom. Ransoms never fucking work. The crims always get caught. *Always*. There's never a—'

Boddice spun round and punched him in the face. The others backed away. Prentice dropped to one knee, holding his jaw. He glared up at Boddice.

'What the fuck is wrong with you tonight Davie?' said Boddice. 'You've been a growly bastard since the fucking Palace. Who spilled your pint?'

Prentice got back to his feet. He glowered at the others. 'It's nothing,' he said. 'It's just a mood, that's all.'

'I don't need moods, Davie,' said Boddice. 'I need you on board with this two hundred percent, no half measures.' He rubbed his knuckles. 'Now, I don't care what's bothering you… I need to know, are you in or out?'

Prentice could feel his rage rising, but was powerless to vent it. Not with Boddice. He slowed his breathing, closed his eyes. He felt all of this was a big fucking mistake. Boddice had been watching too many movies. Ransoms. Secret meetings. *'Are you in or out?'* Fuck's sake. Prentice bent and scooped up sea water from a puddle in the sand, massaged the coolness onto his jaw. He looked at Boddice, vaguely aware of the others gathered in the background. He flicked his gaze to Kyle, saw him mouth a silent, exaggerated, wide-eyed *Yes* as he fumbled a cigarette from a crumpled packet. Prentice looked up at the sky, feeling the soft flutter of the snowflakes landing on his face. 'Of course Ah'm in,' he said at last. 'You know fine well Ah wouldn't let you down.'

Boddice walked over and ruffled Prentice's hair. He drew him aside out of earshot of the others. Prentice stared at the ground. 'Of course I know that. You're my best man, Davie. The one I trust the most. But you're fucking worrying me with your behaviour tonight. I can't have you questioning me at every turn. Christ, we haven't even got into any of the nitty-gritty yet. There's something bugging you, I can tell. Has been for the last couple of weeks.' He dropped his voice to a whisper. 'This is serious stuff we're about to get into Davie. Make no mistake, it'll make us. Make us all.' He crouched down, brought his face up close to Prentice, studied his eyes. 'We will be able to retire after this.' Prentice jerked his head up at that. Boddice gave a wry smile. 'Yes,' he said. 'Think about it. We can get out of all this crap once and for all.'

'Will we?' Prentice asked in a low voice. 'Will we really? Somehow Ah doubt it.'

'Oh, if we do this right, you can count on it. If that's what you want, I'll make sure it happens.'

Boddice put his arm around Prentice's shoulder, a gesture of sly companionship, a cold excuse for friendship. 'Consider it Davie,' Boddice said. 'This isn't that much different from other jobs we've done.' He drew Prentice closer, squeezed him tighter. 'Maybe just a bit bigger in scale, but that's all.'

'Ah'd say it was considerably more than just a *bit bigger*,' said Prentice. 'This is off the scale, what you're suggesting.'

'Ah, but is it?' Boddice said, turning Prentice to face the others huddled against the wind a short distance up the beach. 'Think of the time we got that load of Italian suits from the warehouse at the airport, or the whisky job, remember that one? Ran like clockwork didn't they? Complete successes. This is just the same. Everyone has their part to play. We go in, we get out, job done and no sweat.' He released Prentice from the best-of-pals hug, let him walk a few steps. 'I don't know what you're worried about.'

Prentice stared at the wet sand. Aye, he thought, the whisky job; that was *exactly* the kind of thing he was worried about. Prentice remembered it very well. Sure, they'd got thirty grand's worth of finest malts, but they'd also got themselves a dead body to dispose of after Boddice slashed – no that was too mild a word for it – after he *pummelled* the delivery driver's face with a broken whisky bottle. Relentlessly. Mercilessly. And all because Leggett had forgotten to fucking blindfold the guy.

Meaning, of course, that the poor bastard had seen each and every one of their faces. Including Boddice's. And for that, he'd paid the price, Boddice standing over his body with the red-dripping shards of the bottle, gore-covered and grinning with a mad glee in his eyes.

And now here was Boddice, smiling, genial, mister everything's-fine-and-dandy, telling Prentice not to worry about this job – it'll just be like the whisky job. Aye, right.

The horror of the scenes from that night wrestled with the smiling, good-buddy persona of the Boddice who now stood before him. Prentice was in no doubt which was the reality and the dull throb in his chin from Boddice's punch only reinforced it, confirmed the charade.

There was nothing else for it.

Prentice sighed. 'Okay, okay,' he said. 'Ah've said Ah'll do it an Ah'm not going back on my word. Ah guess Ah'm just a bit nervous about it. New direction and all that. Too many uncertainties.' He gave a small laugh. 'But Ah have faith in ye. Ah just hope ye know what ye're getting us into.'

Boddice stroked his beard. 'Of course I do,' he said. 'Never been more confident.'

Prentice watched him walk back to the others. Sure, never more confident, he thought.

But he had caught the hesitation in Boddice's voice.

Darker With the Day

By the time Prentice woke up, the flat was freezing. One of his arms was outside the bedcovers. The deep, numbing chill on his skin was what had forced him awake.

It was still dark. He checked the radio alarm – quarter to eight. Was that morning or night? Morning, surely. He couldn't have slept right through the day, could he? He stretched out and flipped the switch for the radio to come on. It was a morning news programme. Thank fuck for that then, he thought. It had been a long time since he'd been on such a bender that he had missed out the entire next day. Though he felt he might have come close to it last night. A bottle of Grouse and some superlager to wash it down.

McLean had offered to drop him at the pub, maybe even come in for one himself after he'd let the others off at their various destinations and taken Boddice home. Prentice had said thanks, but no thanks. Felt like an early night, he lied. He suspected Boddice had put McLean up to it; get a few pints down him, see if he would open up about what was on his mind. Fuck that for a game of soldiers.

He found his tobacco pouch and Rizlas on the bedside table and rolled a thinny, spilling some of the tobacco onto the bedcovers. He sparked the lighter a few times, but no flame came. Cursing, he edged himself out of bed to go through to the kitchen, get a light from the gas ring. The living room was cold too. He felt a pang of envy for those people who had central heating, timers set to come on early, warm the place up before venturing into the morning. Maybe one day he'd be able to live in a house like that. Maybe Boddice's super-duper plan might actually succeed, and Prentice would be able to afford somewhere decent instead of this fucking toilet.

He went through to the kitchen and winced as his bare foot came in contact with a cold, gluey softness. He flicked on the light and looked down. It was the lid of a take-away carton, and he saw the best of the *Punjab Fountain* oozing between his toes. The smell of chicken jalfrezi hit his nostrils and his stomach heaved. Christ, he didn't even remember ordering a take-away, never mind eating one.

It's time to tidy this fucking flat, he thought. Since Elaine had left, he'd been living like a pig in shit. It was too easy to make do with curries and ready meals. The discarded boxes and foil cartons littered the kitchen worktops, and now the fucking floor. The living room was cluttered with old newspapers, overflowing ashtrays and porn DVDs.

He poured himself a glass of water and looked at the empties lying in the sink. Eight cans polished off, and the whisky was two thirds gone. He'd drunk more in the past, but it was still a fair whack.

No headache though. That was something at least. He'd Elaine to thank for that. She'd always had this ritual of drinking a pint of water before going to bed after a heavy session. She made a big thing of it, self-righteously sipping the water in bed, proclaiming it to be the best hangover cure bar none. Prentice had resisted at first, insisting it was all a load of crap, the best thing for a hangover was the hair of the dog that bit you. But eventually he had simply fallen into the habit as well. And it worked. No matter how out of it he was, he always managed to stagger to the sink and down some water. Made him have to get up in the middle of the night though, pishing like a horse.

He wiped his foot with the cloth from the sink, flossing the spaces between his toes to remove the last of the mess. He surveyed the kitchen. Later, he thought, later I'll get round to giving the place a wee redd up. He lit the roll-up from the cooker and went back through to the bedroom, stopping off in the living room to switch on the electric fire, get the place warmed up a bit before he came through to get dressed.

He slipped under the covers, grateful for the remnants of his body heat. He lay in the dark, smoking, thinking about the night before.

Why had Boddice decided to change tack all of a sudden? He had his fingers in all sorts of pies – some minor dabbling with minicabs, tanning salons – but, first and foremost, his business was drugs. He'd steered clear of the other obvious money-spinning opportunities – the construction and security stuff, minicabs, the nightclubs; said it was a CBA thing: *Couldn't Be Arsed*. Which was fair enough, Prentice supposed. The drugs had made Boddice money. Lots of it. He had a big house somewhere in a posh village out of town, he had the cars, the share in a racehorse and the motor launch on Loch Lomond. But that CBA attitude had also left him behind. There were other, bigger players in the city now; the guys who wanted their grubby little digits in *every* pie, no matter how big or small, leaving the likes of Boddice with much slimmer pickings. But Boddice seemed happy with that, though Prentice couldn't see it as a reason why he would unexpectedly turn to robbery. And not just robbery, but a fucking heist, ripping off some trendy new department store. And, since Boddice had mentioned they could go away for a long time if it all went tits up, probably involving guns.

To top it all, as far as he could gather from what Boddice had said last night, Prentice wasn't even going to be the main man. Those dopey twins and, he could hardly bring himself to think it, that glaikit wee jakey, Gerry Boag's son, were receiving most of the attention from Boddice last night. Vital cogs in the machinery, Boddice had called them on the way back from Ayr. Prentice couldn't see what was so fucking useful and indispensable about that unlikely trio. Kyle had felt it too. Prentice had seen him sulking at the back of the people carrier, avoiding eye contact with them. Was Boddice trying to teach them a lesson? Had they fucked up somewhere? Unlikely, with regard to Kyle. Boddice had still seen fit to trust him with Leggett's little fright. And what the hell had *that* been all about?

Prentice sighed. It was beyond him at the moment. Maybe

he was just imagining it. Sure, Boddice had been snippy with him last night, but then he was always a baw-hair away from exploding at the best of times. Maybe the best thing to do was just take a chill-pill, let things flow over him for a while. See how things panned out over the next week or two; it was more than likely the three amigos would fuck up somehow before things got too far advanced. Then life would settle back into more comfortable familiarity. A few more weeks of that and he could maybe bring up the subject of having a break from it all, quitting even. If Boddice would let him.

He took another draw on his roll-up, hating the bitterness of the cheap tobacco. The news on the radio was babbling on about some third-world shit-hole that desperately needed foreign aid. A drought had ravaged their crops or something. Tough titty for them, he thought. Get yourself a decent country in the first place. Take responsibility for your own fate.

He put his arms behind his head and lay against the pillow, the roll-up gripped between his lips.

Take responsibility for your own fate.

Aye, it was time for that.

He reached out to switch the radio off, but his hand froze above the power button. The announcer was concluding the headline story; the police were treating it as suspicious; they were asking for anyone with information to come forward, for persons with any knowledge concerning the discovery of the body of a baby on the upper deck of the number 39 early this morning.

'Oh fuck,' Prentice said. 'What have Ah done?'

Park Life

A metal park bench, one of those jobs designed to make it more difficult for the neds to vandalise: no wood or plastic to burn or melt. Nevertheless, the bench had its fair share of dayglo graffiti announcing such mundanities as *Fergie shagged Louanne here 15.11.08* or *Michelle is a fat cow* or the more prosaic *Billy ya Bass*.

John checked to make sure it was the correct one. McLean's instructions had been third bench from the entrance, just past the overflowing dog-shit bin. He looked at the pile of little plastic bags surrounding the foot of the metal pole supporting the bin. Some of them had burst, leaving keech all over the pavement. He sighed. This was it alright.

He took a paper tissue from his pocket, wiped the droplets of rainwater from the bench and sat down. The metal slats were freezing against his arse, numbing his legs. He tried to pull his jacket lower over his bum, but it was useless. He puffed his cheeks and blew out a long exhalation, watching his breath condense in an almost solid cloud. There was nothing for it but to sit it out, wait till his backside warmed the bench to a temperature that would at least let his balls drop back into their sac.

He thought about Fergie and Louanne. The fifteenth of November for fuck's sake. John doubted young Fergie would have been up to it – that time of year his knob would be more likely to be doing the incredible-shrinking-man routine than showing Louanne a good time. And 2008 – man, they probably had two sprogs by now. Louanne was maybe even a granny.

John checked his watch. Ten to two. Just in time. Never a good idea to be tardy for a thing like this. Err on the side of caution – that was the ticket. But Christ knew where Campbell had got to. He was nowhere to be seen. So much for being Mr Bright Spark, Mr Reliable. If he didn't hurry up, there was going to be some fun and games. And quite possibly broken teeth.

John scanned the park, looking for some sign of his brother. The place was almost deserted – hardly surprising given it was the middle of the week and cold enough to freeze piss. A dog took itself for a walk amongst the overgrown bushes lining the path. There was no sign of an owner. Ducks and swans cruised the edges of the pond, hoping for some ancient grizzled pensioner with a bag of crusts. Eventually he spied Campbell coming through the gate on the far side of the park. John waved to him, signalling for him to get a move on. Campbell continued his leisurely stroll.

'You're late,' said John, when Campbell finally arrived at the bench.

Campbell squinted at him. 'Late? What are you talking about?'

John pointed to his watch. 'Boddice told us to be here at the back of two, and it's seven minutes past now. You're late.'

'Ah'm no bloody well late, Ah'm on time. Seven minutes past two *is* the back of two.'

'No it isnae. Five *to* two is the back of two. What planet were you brought up on?'

'The same planet as… look, Ah'm no gonnae start that crap again. The back of two is *after* the hour, not before.'

'Ye're wrong. It's before.'

'After!'

'Befoooore,' said John in a sing-song voice, grinning.

Campbell threw his hands up. 'Okay, okay. Let's say for argument's sake that when Boddice said he'd meet us at the back of two he meant about five *to*.'

John nodded. 'Uh-huh, go on.'

Campbell spun around, arms outstretched, looking up at the sky then down at the ground with wide-eyed exaggeration. He moved over to where John sat, inspected under the bench, behind it. 'Well?' he said. 'Where the fuck is he then? It's nearly ten past and he's no here yet. Does that not tell ye something?'

'He's late too,' said John.

Campbell smirked. 'Oh, well you'd just better tell him that then, cos here he comes.'

John twisted round to follow Campbell's gaze. Boddice's car – the Lexus this time – glided through the park gates and drew up at the edge of the path with a spray of gravel and muddy puddle water. John made to stand up. Campbell laid his hand on John's shoulder. 'No, wait here,' he said. 'He asked us to specifically meet him here… right here at this bench. You know what he's like. Unless you want the full hair-dryer bawling out, let him come to us.'

John sat back down. 'Aye, ye're right.'

They watched McLean get out of the car, open the door for Boddice, who picked his way through the puddles and sodden leaves towards them. Campbell moved to stand beside John at the bench, arms folded across his chest.

Boddice was smiling – that was a bonus at least. He pointed to John. 'Okay guys, you know the routine. Denim jacket?'

'John,' said John.

'And so you, Mr Leather-Jacket, are Campbell.'

'Right,' Campbell replied.

'I hope I can remember,' Boddice laughed. 'Sleep well boys?' he asked.

'Alright,' said John.

'Fine,' said Campbell. 'Why?'

'Nothing really,' said Boddice. 'Just wondered if the excitement of last night had got to you. Kept you awake wondering what was going on.'

'Well, to be perfectly honest,' said John – Campbell sucked in his breath, wondering what was coming next – 'No, it didn't. Ah hadn't really a clue what was going on last night, but Ah didn't let it bother me.'

'But you're still interested, right?' asked Boddice.

'Sure we are Mr Boddice,' Campbell interrupted. 'What John's tryin to say is that we're still not sure what exactly is involved in this job. Especially with us having a pivotal role as you mentioned last night.'

'Which is exactly why we're here this morning, boys,' said Boddice. 'I'll admit I'm still going to be a bit vague about things… at least until I'm sure it's all feasible.'

He motioned for John and Campbell to come closer. 'Before we do anything else though, I need to check something. Jackets off and roll up your sleeves.' John and Campbell exchanged uncertain looks, but did as they were told. 'Let me see your arms,' Boddice said.

The twins held out their arms to show their black-and-grey sleeve tattoos which extended all the way from their cuffs to just below their shoulders. They each had similar patterns – a fantastical conglomeration of delicately-shaded clouds and sunbeams, overlaid with flower petals and storm-tossed waves, the occasional bird and fish. They were intricate, complex designs; closer inspection revealed further details and images emerging from the background – a skull here, a tiger there, a butterfly, a dragon. They represented months of work. Boddice examined them thoroughly. 'Okay,' he said eventually. 'I can't tell.'

'Can't tell what?' Campbell asked.

'They're different aren't they? The tattoos you both have?'

'Well, they both use grey-wash techniques with soft blends and they—'

'Cut the technical guff,' Boddice said. 'I mean the patterns, the pictures; they're different, right?'

'Yes, they're different. I've got a set of—'

'But it's hard to tell if they are, right? They pretty much look the same to me.'

'Not to us,' said John. 'A casual observer couldn't tell them apart maybe, but…'

'That's good enough for me,' said Boddice. 'And you've not got any others? On your back? Your chest? The crack of your arse?'

Campbell and John looked at each other. 'No, sleeves only. This is it,' Campbell said. He frowned. 'Why are you asking this?'

'I just needed to be certain.' Boddice checked the pathways, made sure there was no-one else who could hear him. 'For this to work, I need you to become one person.'

The twins frowned. 'One person?' Campbell said. 'What do you mean?'

Boddice chuckled. 'I want each of you to be able to pass yourself off as the other,' he said.

'Well, that's easy,' said John. 'We're bloody identical twins, aren't we? Christ, even our maw had a tough time tellin us apart.' Was the man mad?

'Ah don't think he means just that, John,' said Campbell. 'It's not just the looking like each other is it?'

'No indeed,' said Boddice. 'It's much more than that, much harder in fact. I want you to be able to become each other, act like each other, talk like each other. Transform yourselves into a new, single person. One individual. No-one must be able to tell you are two people. That's why I needed to check your arms.'

John furrowed his brows, shook his head. 'Look Mr Boddice,' he said. 'Ah know Ah'm not exactly Brainiac here, but Ah'm confused to fuck. What the hell do ye mean? Of course folk'll be able to tell we're two people. They'll see us!'

'Ahhh, but that's where you're wrong!' said Boddice. 'They'll only ever see one of you at a time.'

'Why?' asked Campbell.

Boddice sighed. He looked at John and raised an eyebrow. 'This is getting too difficult to explain easily, so I'll cut to the chase. As part of the plan you're going to get a job at Trusdale and Needham, a security job.'

'A job?' Campbell cut in. 'What about *Two's Tattoos*?'

'History,' Boddice replied. 'Wind it up, clear out the shop.'

'*What?*' said John. 'We've worked years to get that—'

'Forget it,' said Boddice. 'It's in the past. When this is finished, you'll never need to work again.'

John continued to protest. 'Aye, but—'

'I said forget it!' Boddice looked round, making sure no-one had noticed his outburst. He dropped his voice. 'Don't fucking argue with me. That's the way it's going to be. Deal with it.'

Campbell squeezed John's elbow. 'Don't worry about him, Mr Boddice,' he said. 'He doesn't mean anything by it.'

Boddice grabbed John's lapels, pulled him up close. 'Understand me son,' he said. 'Don't even think about jeopardising this fucking job with stupid ideas about your daft wee tattoo parlour, cos if you do I'll pluck your fucking eyeballs out and replace them with your nadgers. Got it?'

Campbell could see tears start in John's eyes. He pulled him back from Boddice's grip. 'It's okay Mr Boddice,' he said. 'He's got it. Don't bother about him.'

Boddice glowered at the both of them. 'Listen up the two of you, this is how it's going to be, and I don't want any fucking arguments, right?'

John brought out a tissue and wiped his eyes. Campbell held tight to his arm. 'Agreed,' Campbell said. 'Just tell us what you want us to do.'

Boddice smoothed down his coat, composed himself. 'As I said, you will get a security job at Trusdale and Needham, working all shifts. You will integrate yourself into the store, become one of the lads, a hard worker, dependable, nothing too much trouble for you. People will like you, respect you. And then, when the time comes, you will be our key to the door. It'll be you who gets us inside to take the diamond.'

'What one of us is gonnae do all that?' John asked cautiously.

'Both of you.'

'Both?'

'Exactly. You will both do the same job, day and day about.

Twin one goes in on the first day, twin two on the next, and so on. Every night you'll feed back to the other what happened during the course of the day's events. Over the months, you'll both become familiar with the job: the protocols and procedures, the people and the places, what happens where and when. And as far as everyone else is concerned, it's just one person they're working beside.'

'So why the both of us?' asked Campbell. 'I don't see the point of that.'

Boddice gave a resigned shake of the head, a schoolteacher dealing with the class dunderhead. Campbell felt his teeth grit. 'Because,' Boddice said, 'when we take the diamond, you will be someplace else. Making sure you're seen. Being very prominent indeed. And at the same time, you'll be in the store, helping us steal the diamond. You will, in essence, be your own alibi.'

Campbell went to say something, but couldn't think of the exact words to use. It was John who spoke. 'That's brilliant,' he said. 'We'll be in two places at the one time. Nobody'll suspect it was me… eh, him… Ah mean, us!'

'You see,' said Boddice. 'There now, the boy's a brainiac right enough!' John beamed with pleasure, glad to be back in Boddice's good books.

'How long will it take, all this set-up?' asked Campbell. 'Ah mean, this sort of thing doesn't happen overnight. We'd need to—'

'The diamond goes on display at the beginning of April,' Boddice said. 'For five weeks. That gives you at least three months.'

'Only if we start in January that is,' said Campbell.

'Which you'll do,' Boddice replied.

The twins shot each other a look. 'Eh?' said John. 'What, next month?'

'That's what I implied by my last remark, yes.'

'But… but what about landing the job, you know,

interviews and stuff?' asked Campbell. 'We can't just ponce our way into that kinda thing. We would—'

'It's all arranged,' said Boddice. 'The job's set up. It's yours already. Everything's taken care of. That's how pivotal you are to the plan. You're expected on January the fifth. Right in at the deep end in fact. All those crazy fuckers out to get a so-called bargain in the sales, taking no prisoners. You'll love it.'

'But how…?'

'Never mind that. Connections, that's all. You'll see soon enough what I've been up to.'

'But what do we do, just turn up on the day?' asked John.

'Exactly that, son. Uniform and everything will be ready and waiting.' Boddice paused, ran his hand over the back of the bench. 'That's assuming you pass the test, of course,' he added.

'Test? What test?' said Campbell.

'Oh bugger,' said John. 'Ah'm shite at tests.'

Boddice began cracking his knuckles absentmindedly. 'As I said earlier, I need you both to be able to pass yourself off as the other in order for this whole thing to work. If there's a single smidgen of doubt in the mind of anyone you'll be working alongside, the entire project is immediately in trouble. All it would need is some guy to see through what you're up to and we'd be fucked.'

'And *we'd* be more than fucked,' added Campbell.

'Indeed,' said Boddice. 'Which is why, before we enter into this, before we commit ourselves to all this hard work, I've decided to set you a test to see if it'll work.'

'What sort of test?' said Campbell.

'One that will replicate the situation at Trusdale and Needham. It's very simple. We've got a couple of weeks before you're due to start at the store. By the end of this week I want you both to set each other a task, some scam or scenario you instigate yourself, with no involvement of the other, only you. And it's important you don't let each other know what it is beforehand. It's then going to be up to each of you to carry on with that task in the guise of your brother, entirely left up to your own devices, no help, clues or advice from the other one, interacting and dealing with whatever third parties are involved. We'll see then if you can manage to pull it off successfully.'

The twins looked at each other. What the hell was all this about? Boddice had cracked. Tests? Tasks? This was the sort of stuff you got in some third-rate reality television show. It wasn't something drug dealers in Glasgow usually entertained. Campbell began to wonder if maybe they *would* have been better to have politely declined the opportunity to take part in the robbery. Perhaps John had been right to be apprehensive all along – his instincts were certainly basic, but usually sound.

No, that was stupid.

Stupid, stupid.

They both knew what Boddice was like. They were trapped. Whether Boddice was mad or not, he knew now they had no option but to go along for the ride.

Boddice went on, 'In fact, it could be a wee bit of fun, eh boys? Bit of a laugh?' He held up a finger. 'Wait, I've just thought of something. I want… I want you to write down your scam on a piece of paper and put it in an envelope. We'll have a wee handover ceremony later in the week, just the three of us, unveil the secret. And, I tell you what,' Boddice rubbed his hands, grinning, 'I don't want to know what it is you have to do till after the event. You can let me know how it all went after it's done.'

That confirmed it for Campbell; Boddice had lost the plot. Unless… unless it was all a joke. Maybe that was it. Boddice was just yanking their chain, seeing how far he could go with them.

'I can tell you think I'm off my head,' Boddice said, making Campbell flinch. Had Boddice read his mind? 'I'll admit it's all a bit theatrical, melodramatic even, but there's a serious side to it too. This is the very thing that might just save you from a long stay in the Big House, bed and board for a few years.' His face hardened. 'Just indulge me in this, alright?'

'Whatever you say Mr Boddice,' said John. Campbell nodded.

'Fine, that's that sorted then,' said Boddice. 'Now, if you boys have got nothing else to add, I'm off to see Boag. He's another one who's got an important part to play.' He hitched his coat, beckoned for McLean to bring the Lexus over. 'You know, it's funny… Usually, it's Kyle and Prentice who do the difficult stuff for me, all that hard-man grief we need to dish out, but this time it's you wee guys who are going to be in the driving seat. Who'd have thought it?'

McLean drew up and jumped out to open the door for Boddice. He slid into the passenger seat, closed the door and wound down the window. 'Remember, boys,' he said as he fastened his seatbelt. 'Later this week. McLean will let you know where. Have your tasks ready for each other. Sealed envelopes and all that.' The twins nodded their agreement as the car reversed to the main gate and slipped out into the traffic.

Campbell watched the car as it sped into the distance. 'Fuck's sake,' he said when it had disappeared. 'That's us, eh?'

'What do ye mean?'

'You heard him. *'You wee guys.'* That's me and you. That's where we stand in the great scheme of things. Wee guys. How's that supposed to make you feel? Does that not put your gas at a peep?'

'Ah never paid too much attention, Ah was too busy thinking about the tasks thing.'

'Aye, and what a load of shite that is. Can you believe it? Secret tasks. Ah ask ye.'

'Ah don't know,' said John. 'Sounds kinda good fun right enough. Should be easy.'

'Good fun? Easy? Listen, John. You'd better do this properly. If we just give this lip-service, Boddice'll know. He'll go nuts.'

'Ah know, Ah know,' John protested. 'Don't pish yer pants, Ah'll give ye something hard, don't worry.'

'Hang on,' said Campbell. 'Not so hard that it's gonnae be impossible to do. Do it properly, but do it fair.'

'Aye, aye, whatever. Anyway, Ah think Ah know already what Ah'll get ye to do.'

'Already?'

'Yup.'

Campbell pouted. 'Very good. Well, keep it to yourself till we meet up with Boddice.'

John stood with his hands in his pockets, scuffing his feet on the gravel path. 'Campbell?' he asked.

Campbell heard the catch in John's voice. 'What?'

'What about the shop? Ah like the parlour. Ah don't want to give it up. Seven months is a long time.'

'Ah know, but it doesn't look as if we've any option does it?'

'Ah suppose not.'

'Wait and see. Ah'll think of somethin. Maybe we could just say it's temporarily shut for refurbishment.'

'But what about the rent? How will we pay that?'

Campbell clipped John's ear. 'Ya muppet. Boddice is the fucking landlord. Ah don't think he's gonnae mind us going into arrears for a bit.'

John rubbed his ear. 'Ye never know,' he said. 'Ah was just thinking, that's all.'

Campbell started walking towards the gate. 'Are you coming? Ye've put it into my mind now. We should go back to the shop right away, start getting things in order. Tidy up after yesterday.'

John hurried after him. 'Campbell?'

'What now?'

'Ah could eat a scabby-heided wean.'

'Eh?'

'Or a horse between two mattresses.'

'What the hell are ye talking about?'

'Ah'm *starving*.'

'Well, ye should've had some breakfast then, shouldn't ye?'

'But Ah did. Beans and microchips... and some Lidl Crusti Crocs.

Campbell rolled his eyes. 'For fuck's sake.'

'And another thing,' said John.

'What?'

'We didn't ask Boddice about the time.'

'The time?'

'Aye,' said John. 'What he meant by the back of two.'

He just had time to dodge Campbell's kick.

Army Dreamers

Boag sat on the steps outside the old Cardenhall library, fidgeting with a little notebook Boddice had given him earlier that morning.

He hated being alone with Boddice. It didn't happen often: once when his old man was banged up and Boddice came over to 'see him right', and again when he'd fucked up a delivery, taken it to the wrong address at the wrong time. He'd had the full force of Boddice's wrath then.

Usually, it was McLean who relayed instructions. But this time was different. Boddice wanted to deal with him personally, had actually been pleasant, giving Boag a couple of hundred pounds to buy new clothes, get himself fixed up a bit. This on top of being put up in one of Boddice's Southside rental flats, with arrangements in place for him to stay there for the foreseeable future, all expenses paid. It was the first time in months Boag had a warm, comfortable bed to sleep in. Not that Boag regarded these luxuries as a gift. Somehow or other, he knew he'd be paying it back.

But the thing that was really making Boag anxious was Boddice's attitude. He'd been... the only word Boag could think of to describe it was, *ingratiating*. Falling over himself to be nice, praising Boag, and expressing his admiration at the way Boag had kept body and soul together in such difficult circumstances. Boddice even apologised for not being in touch recently, and for letting Boag slip through the net when it came to dishing out the work.

Boag wasn't fooled for a minute. Boddice wasn't a very good actor – charm and warmth had never been his thing, and Boag knew the mister-nice-guy performance was meant to soften him up. It had the opposite effect – Boag became more and more apprehensive, sensing that something he wasn't going to like was coming up. Sitting on the library steps, his stomach tightened and his jaws ached from constant clenching. He could feel a fluttering ripple of nausea rising in anticipation.

He thought of the old woman's lighter nestling in his back pocket. He had high hopes last night that she was right all along, that the damned thing *was* lucky, that his life might be about to change – this morning's events were not the sort of luck he had in mind, however.

It was the Army.

That was what had stirred Boddice's interest. Boag hadn't wanted to talk about it; it was years ago, but Boddice knew anyway – the dishonourable discharge, the court martial.

The accident.

Or, to be more accurate, the prank.

And that's what it had been: a joke that went wrong. Nothing more, nothing less. As far as Boag was concerned, it was all in the past. Christ, he'd been punished enough – the DD on his record made it virtually impossible to get any sort of job. But for Boddice, it was what made him ideal for the Plan. Boag had wondered why he was of such sudden interest. Now he knew.

Boag wasn't even an explosives expert – he was an electronics technician; for the first time in his life he'd found something he was good at, which he enjoyed. It was the other two – Christ, he couldn't even remember their names – who were the munitions guys, who had the access to the detonators, the concussion charges. Just a couple of other grunts who shared the same dorm, like himself a few months into basic training, not yet seen any combat action. They just needed him to provide the electronics to set the charges off. Why the Christ he'd allowed himself to be persuaded to take part, he couldn't answer; why he hadn't stopped to think that sabotaging a cannon demonstration at a passing out ceremony would be a pretty dumb stunt hadn't crossed his mind either. He had simply thought it would be a good laugh. A good story to tell the lads down the pub. The intention had been to produce a bigger bang, make the bigwigs jump. That was all. The outcome had been rather different – there had been the bigger bang alright, but perhaps just a bit bigger than they had anticipated. The dignitaries and officials shat a brick, and Colonel Morrice had the ignominious distinction of swearing rather inventively in front of some government bigwigs. What the hell had he been thinking? It was an idiotic practical joke in the wrong place and at the wrong time.

Boag cringed to think about it.

The army top brass didn't cringe though – Boag and his fellow conspirators' feet didn't touch the ground. Three months in military prison and the dishonourable discharge.

Boag had no idea how Boddice had found out about the incident, but he knew every detail. He may have heard it from the old man, though Boag could never remember discussing it.

And Boddice was delighted with the prospect. He seemed to think Boag had just the skills necessary to see his Plan through. Boag was less sure, but what Boddice proposed didn't seem beyond his capabilities.

At least at first.

Now, sitting on the steps, he faltered. Boddice had given him the notebook to jot down the kind of materials he would require in order to set up the diversions and distractions the robbery was going to require. Boddice would make sure the supplies were obtained in good time. Boag hadn't written a thing. His pen remained in his pocket. It wasn't that he didn't know what to do. That part was easy.

But the others. The others were not going to like this.

Not one bit.

The Wilson Twins:
Sartorial Eloquence

Boddice sprawled on the sofa in the back room of The Herdsman watching Campbell and John. They were perched on the stools in front of him blinking self-consciously and feeling conspicuous, vulnerable. Boddice was enjoying their discomfort. He sparked a match against the sole of his shoe and lit up a cigarillo, sent blue clouds of smoke rolling towards the ceiling. Boddice didn't offer them a drink. Through the glass of the swing doors Campbell could see McLean waiting on the other side, in the main space of the pub, making sure no-one disturbed them.

John attempted to break the ice. 'Nice jacket, Mr Boddice,' he said.

Boddice held out his arms, inspected the sleeves. 'I'm tempted to say "this old thing?"' he laughed. 'But that would hardly be truthful, seeing as I only got it yesterday. What do you think? Colour not too bright?'

Campbell had the urge to blurt out something about how puke-yellow really suited him, went with his eyes. Instead he said, 'Well, it's different. Not your usual style, if ye don't mind me saying.'

'I'm not sure of it myself,' said Boddice. 'It's a designer original, very classy, very expensive of course. But I'm not sure this shade is the right sort of thing for a dreich winter's day in Glasgow.' He stretched, leaned back, put his hands behind his head. 'Still, it brightens my mood a wee bit. That can only be a good thing can't it?'

'A good thing, aye,' said John.

Boddice sucked in another drag from the cigarillo and took a sip from his whisky. 'So,' he said. 'Are we ready? I see you have your envelopes prepared.'

Campbell tapped his envelope against his knee. He

had a bad feeling about this. He felt he'd picked something John could manage without too much of a problem, but still enough to make it a bit of a challenge. He just hoped he hadn't overestimated John's abilities.

'Who wants to go first?' said Boddice, rubbing his hands. He was relishing the situation, looking forward to the outcome. 'Remember,' he said. 'This has a serious purpose. If it doesn't come off, the whole plan will have to be changed.'

John pre-empted any discussion by reaching out to Campbell and taking the envelope from his hand. 'Ah'll go,' he said.

He ripped open the envelope, took out the piece of paper and studied it. He frowned and pointed to the sheet. 'Ah can hardly read your writing Campbell, what the hell's that word supposed to say?'

Campbell stood behind him, spotted the offending word. 'Enrolled,' he said.

'Enrolled?' said John. 'Looks like 'Brillo' to me.'

Campbell was losing patience. 'Well, it's 'enrolled'. Just get on with reading it.'

Campbell watched John scanning the paper, his lips moving as he read the words. He gave a little smirk and raised an eyebrow at Campbell. 'Alright,' he said. 'That seems doable.'

Boddice nodded, tapping ash onto the floor. 'Good, good,' he said. 'I like your confidence. That's just what we need.'

Confidence can be misplaced, thought Campbell. John's task seemed straightforward enough at first glance – Campbell had put his name down for lessons for a Heavy Goods Vehicle licence, in fact had undergone the first two sessions himself, was quite enjoying it. It would be up to John to complete the ten-day course. The difficult bit came with the fact that Campbell hadn't paid for the lessons yet. He'd persuaded the training school to let him pay in instalments and he'd so far failed to make a single payment. It would be up to John to sort out the melee that was surely about to follow.

John gave a self-satisfied grin, and handed his envelope to Campbell. 'Hope you're up for this one, brother!' he said, a malicious glint in his eye.

Campbell took the envelope and sucked in a deep breath. He stole a look at Boddice, who was watching the two of them with barely-contained glee. He loves this, thought Campbell. He's getting a real kick out of taking a rise out of us. They were used to being teased as twins of course, enduring the childhood taunts, the name-calling, the embarrassment of being dressed identically on a Sunday morning for church and the attendant oohs and aahs and cheek-pinching of ancient aunties and make-up-caked women in the street. It was all par for the course, it went with the territory. But as they grew older and began to develop their individual personalities, they became less tolerant of the jibes of the other kids, retaliated more often, got into more fights. Worked hard to make sure they won them too. Soon, the others realised it wasn't worth it any more; not unless they wanted a sore face. Things settled down. But to Campbell, this scheme of Boddice's didn't seem much more than a return to the bad old days. It was clear Boddice just wanted to have a bit of fun at their expense. He couldn't see how this plan depended so much on their pretending to be one person. He looked at John. He seemed to be enjoying himself as well. His face was split by a broad smile, and his eyes twinkled with amusement. Campbell ran his fingers over the envelope. Maybe he was being too sensitive. Maybe there wasn't any harm in it. Better to just enter into the spirit of things, get it over and done with.

He slipped his finger under the sealed flap and ripped open the envelope. He took out the piece of paper. He almost laughed when he saw that John had used a page from an old school jotter. He shook his head. Why on earth did John hang on to things like that, relics from their schooldays?

'Go on,' said John. 'Read it.'

Campbell unfolded the paper and read John's block capital scrawl. This couldn't be right. This had to be a joke, surely.

He turned to Boddice, almost showed him what this idiot brother of his had written. Boddice held up his hand, shook his head. Campbell blinked furiously, willing the words to change, to transform into something realistic, anything, just not what was written here. He looked at John, his mouth beginning to twitch. 'You cannot be serious,' he said.

John blinked, sensing Campbell's rising fury. 'Aye, Ah am,' he said. 'Totally serious.'

'This isn't one of your daft fucking ideas of a sick joke?' asked Campbell.

'Naw,' said John, flicking his eyes to the paper. 'That's your task. That's what ye have—'

He didn't get the chance to finish. Campbell launched himself at John. He toppled his brother from the stool, which smashed, the pieces clattering towards the fireplace. Campbell pinned John on the floor, pulled back his fist ready to pile into John's face, feed him his fucking teeth. His arm was jerked back by McLean who, at the sound of the commotion, had burst into the back room. Campbell screamed at him, kicking and twisting in McLean's grip. 'Let me go ya bastard, let me fucking at him.' McLean held him tight in a bearhug, lifted him off his feet and dragged him to the corner of the room. John picked himself up, backing away towards the sofa where Boddice sat with a face dark as a thunderhead.

'Ease up, pal,' said McLean, still wrestling with Campbell, who showed no sign of giving up the struggle. McLean pulled Campbell's arms behind his back, hoisted them above his shoulders and forced him to his knees. 'Ease up Ah said! Ah mean it!'

'Okay, okay,' Campbell said. 'Ye're hurting me. Let go!'

'Not till ye promise to settle down,' said McLean.

'Ah will, Ah promise,' said Campbell.

McLean began to relax his grip, but sensed Campbell about to lunge again and reapplied the pressure.

'Oyah!' Campbell shouted. 'That's sore. Cut it out!'

'Ah will,' said McLean 'As soon as ye calm down and stop yer carry on.' Campbell relaxed and McLean released his hold. 'What the fuck's got into you?' said McLean.

'I was just about to ask the self-same question,' said Boddice, rising from the sofa and moving into the centre of the room. He pulled the piece of paper from Campbell's hand. 'What the hell has your brother asked you to do that's so bloody difficult?' He started to unfold the paper.

'No!' shouted Campbell and John together.

John ran over, his face white. 'No, don't Mr Boddice,' he said. 'Don't... don't read it!'

'Why?' asked Boddice. 'What's so terrible? What's written here?'

'It's... it's just that... it's just that it would spoil the surprise. You know, when you ask us later how we got on,' said John, his voice small and constricted, edged with panic.

Boddice hesitated, the piece of paper flapping in his hand. 'I'm not so sure,' he said. 'I don't think I've ever seen one of you two lose the plot like that before. Quite impressive actually.'

'No, he's right,' Campbell blurted. 'Don't read it yet. Wait till we've tried it. See if Ah can make it work.' He bit his knuckles and scowled at John. 'See if it's, what was it you said, John, 'do-able'?'

Boddice looked from one twin to the other. 'There's something not quite right here,' he said. He tapped the paper against his teeth, continuing to eye each of them. 'But, okay,' he said eventually. 'Let's see how you get on with it.'

Campbell moved to take the piece of paper back, but Boddice drew it away, clenched it in his fist. 'Oh no you don't,' he said. 'I don't want you taking this home and changing it into something easy.' He went over to John and took his note too. He folded them both together and put them into the inside pocket of his jacket. 'No,' he said, patting them in place. 'They'll stay right here till next week, when we find out how successful you've been.'

John winced. This wasn't good. This wasn't what he had counted on happening. Maybe he shouldn't have picked something so difficult, so risky. But it was Campbell's own fault. He'd told him to make sure it wasn't too easy, to play the game properly. Obviously, Campbell didn't share John's interpretations of 'easy'.

It was too late to do anything about it, now. Boddice had the fucking note; John's set of instructions to Campbell.

The instructions that told Campbell about how John was having an affair with Boddice's wife, how he had to turn up next weekend when Boddice was away on business, give his wife a seeing to.

John thought about it. Yes, he could see why Campbell might get a bit upset about that. Maybe it wasn't such a great idea after all. He flicked a glance at him. Campbell had his head down, rubbing his arms and glowering at the floor.

Boddice stood up from the table, smoothing his yellow jacket and stubbing his smoke in the ashtray. He eyed the twins suspiciously. 'I don't know what's going on between you two,' he said. 'But calm your jets, alright? I don't want any monkeying about after I've left. Understood?' They nodded. 'You've drawn enough attention to me today as it is.' He opened the swing doors to the main bar. A few heads looked in their direction, before quickly returning to an intense study of half-finished pints. McLean went out first, clearing a path through the men crowding the bar. Boddice held the door open with his foot, turned back to the twins. 'And I don't want a mark on either of your faces. No bruises, no cuts. No fighting. Period.' He let the doors swing shut, leaving Campbell simmering, hands balled into fists, while John stood sheepishly examining his fingernails.

As Boddice reached the exit, he heard Campbell's roar from the back room, turning heads and raising a few eyebrows among the customers and the bar staff. A high, animal scream of rage, beyond mere words.

The Lexicon of Love

John was an idiot, a numpty, a bawheid, a stumor, an A-number-one moron, a cretin, a retard, an imbecile, a half-wit (no, make that a quarter-wit), a whole thesaurus-worth of stupidity, insanity, lunacy.

To Campbell, the very idea of even looking at Boddice's wife the wrong way gave him the jitters. If he ever *did* find himself in the presence of Mrs Boddice he would keep his eyes fixed firmly on the floor. No leering, no sizing up, no… appreciating. Who knew how Boddice might react? Campbell didn't want to think about it.

Which was, obviously, John's problem – he hadn't bothered to think about it. Or else he would never have got himself into the situation in the first place of not just looking at the boss's wife, but fucking fucking her.

'But she *made* me do it,' John whined, when Campbell forced him to explain.

Campbell was unconvinced. But he listened to his brother's story: *Boddice's wife comes in, says the big man sent her; she's taken a notion, wants a tattoo on her arse, big man says this is the place to come, the Wilson boys are the best in town… blah, blah-de-blah. As luck, or fate, would have it, Campbell's off somewhere else, stocking up on supplies, down the bookies, or having a swift one in the Swan, leaving only John to attend to her.*

And attend to her he did. As soon as she was bent over that chair, her black thong riding up the crack of her arse, John got to work on the tattoo.

But when he was finished he got to work on her too. 'It wasn't my fault. She started coming on to me man,' he whinged. 'Wriggling her bum at me, moaning, all that stuff. Ah couldn't help myself. Before Ah knew it, one thing had led to another…'

Aye, right, Campbell had thought. You couldn't help yourself. Prick.

***

So now Campbell found himself on Boddice's front doorstep, hoping for two things. Part of him (A pretty large fucking part, he had to admit) wanted the place to be deserted, everyone gone away for the weekend. He could turn around and get the hell away from here. But a tiny, trembling sliver of rationality hiding at the back of his mind knew if there was to be any way of saving the situation, he had to make sure his plan worked.

His plan – Christ, he'd had to think hard on that one: what could he possibly do that would salvage the situation? He'd tossed and turned at night, unable to find the oblivion of sleep, Boddice in his garish yellow jacket appearing every time he closed his eyes. He couldn't shake the image.

And then it came to him. A solution. A way out.

A plan.

And the only way this plan would work was to go through with John's task.

Campbell took a deep breath and rang the doorbell.

He waited.

There was no sound from inside the house; no movement that he could see through the frosted glass panels to the side of the door. He stepped back from the vestibule and scanned the building; no signs of life at the upstairs windows. A crust of snow clung to the roof tiles in patches, looking like a map of some newly discovered planet. Only the cloud of condensation billowing from the boiler vent at the far corner of the house gave any indication the place was occupied.

He waited a few minutes. Still nothing. Campbell breathed a sigh of relief; there was no-one home. He turned and started to head down the driveway when he heard the door opening.

'Sorry to keep you waiting.'

He spun round. The woman standing in the doorway was about fifty, maybe older, hair dyed jet black and pulled back into a pony tail. She was dressed to the nines in a classy cream suit and lots of jewellery. But the fake tan and heavy make-up gave her a severe, brittle edge.

'I could see you on the intercom,' she said, nodding towards the camera lens mounted above the door. 'But the bloody thing's broken; I couldn't activate the buzzer to let you in.'

'That's okay,' Campbell said, a strange fluttering catch in his voice.

'And I was on the phone to Norman, so I couldn't come down right away. He'd forgotten his shaver, was driving back to get it.'

Campbell frowned. Norman? Who was Norman? Was he the... Oh, my God. Dear Jesus in heaven. Norman. She was talking about Boddice.

'Mr Boddice!' he yelped. 'Is he...'

'Don't worry,' she said. 'I persuaded him just to buy another one when he got there. He can just throw the old one away.' She laughed. 'He's not coming back. My, the look on your face!' She took him by the hand, led him into the house.

'Ah'm sorry,' he said. 'It's just that...'

'Don't apologise,' she said softly. 'I'm just glad you decided to come back.' She slid her hand behind his neck, drew him towards her. She kissed him. Her tongue, slipping between his teeth, had the dry, metallic taste of cigarettes and coffee.

She pulled back. 'Why don't you go on upstairs? I'll join you in a minute. I just have a couple of things to attend to and then we can have a right good session.'

Campbell hesitated. 'Eh, what room is it again? Ah wasn't paying too much attention the last time.'

'The last time?' she said. 'What are you talking about? Last time was in the living room. On the sofa. How could you forget?'

Bastard. Campbell was going to throttle John when he got a hold of him. 'Oh aye, Ah know *that*, it's just that Ah thought, ye know...'

'Look, settle down,' she said. 'I appreciate you're a bit nervous.' She smiled. 'Relax. Norman won't be back until tomorrow. We'll be just fine.' She took him by the shoulders, steered him towards the stairs. 'We'll use one of the spare bedrooms this time. I've got it all sorted out. Up to the top landing, second door on the left. I'll not be long.' She sent him on his way with a squeeze of his buttocks.

Campbell climbed the stairs to the upper floor. He had never been in Boddice's house before. Christ, he hadn't even passed the front gate. This territory was strictly out-of-bounds. Not for the likes of him. Or his daft brother. Or any of Boddice's team, for that matter.

What the hell was John thinking? Not only had he come into Boddice's house, his inner sanctum, but the stupid prick had been shagging Boddice's wife. His bloody wife! This was just about the riskiest thing imaginable. And the glaikit bastard had now involved Campbell as well. If Boddice ever found out, they would both be dead men. And not just dead, but tortured, beaten, hot boiled eggs shoved up their arseholes, dipped in baths of acid and made to beg for sweet mercy beforehand. Campbell had a brief vision of Prentice and Kyle showing up at his door in the wee small hours one night, baseball bats in hand. Death would be the least of their worries.

Campbell reached the top landing, took his bearings. Christ, but this house was big. The corridor stretched into the distance, all polished floorboards, expensive rugs and fancy wall hangings. Tasteful stuff. Campbell thought he recognised a Vettriano hanging on one of the walls – the real deal, not a print – just a wee one, but it must have cost a small fortune.

He found the bedroom and went in, the door closing behind him with a tiny snick, like someone tutting. The curtains were drawn, shutting out the daylight, and tea-light candles burned in coloured glass holders on the bedside cabinets. An incense burner sent little coils of patchouli-scented smoke towards the ceiling. The bed was massive – Campbell thought you could probably get a decent five-a-side game on there. Red and black pillows were scattered against the wrought-iron headboard and the black silk sheets were turned down. A regular boudoir. If this was one of the spare bedrooms, what must the master be like?

Campbell sat on the bed and rubbed his palms on his trousers. There was still time to do a runner. Wherever Boddice's wife had gone, he could just bolt down the stairs, out the door and down the driveway. Let John deal with the fallout. But if he did that, the whole set-up with himself and John would be exposed. Boddice would find out.

He had no option but to go through with it.

Campbell kicked off his shoes and peeled off his socks, cursing John under his breath. What a bloody mess. He stood and stripped down to his underwear, placing his clothes on a wicker chair in the corner. He settled on the edge of the bed, drumming his fingers on his knee. There was something else worrying him. Boddice's wife was not exactly his type. If he was being honest, she looked as if she'd seen better days. Was John really that desperate? Then again, John had always been an opportunist – given the chance he would shag the buttonhole in a fur coat. Campbell considered himself to be a bit more discerning. And that was the problem. He was afraid he wouldn't be able to perform, wouldn't get it up.

He went through to the en-suite and ran the cold tap. He splashed some water on his face, inspected his pasty reflection in the mirror. His pupils were dilated. Less to do with the gloom of the bedroom than the fear of standing in nothing more than his scraggy grey boxers in Boddice's spare bedroom, waiting for the man's wife to show up.

Christ, what if Boddice had forgotten more than his shaver? What if he'd decided to cancel the whole fucking trip, come home and spend a nice relaxing weekend with the missus in front of the plasma screen? A few glasses of wine and an early night? A wee bit of reading before nodding off?

What if the bastard was pulling into the driveway right now? Climbing the stairs, wondering what *was* that smell of hippy-shit perfume coming from the spare bedroom? Has someone been sleeping in *my* bed?

He heard the bedroom door open and close. Campbell's heart leapt in his chest. Jesus, Mary and Joseph and all the saints with their shiny fucking halos, this was it. He was a dead man.

Campbell peered out from the en-suite. Boddice's wife leant against the bedroom door – she had changed out of her suit, slipped into something more comfortable as it were. She let her white satin dressing gown slide to the floor as she locked the door behind her.

'Like what you see?' she asked.

Campbell stared. Her hair was let down from its pony tail and she was wearing what appeared to be the contents of page one of the Ann Summers lingerie catalogue – black stockings and suspenders, black push-up bra and crotchless panties. The low-level lighting helped of course, but Campbell had to concede she looked sexy. She stood with her hands on her hips. 'Well?' she said. 'Does this turn you on, lover?'

Campbell cleared his throat. 'Yes,' he replied. 'It does.' He began to harden. His cock pushed and throbbed against his boxers.

She sashayed over to him, dragged her fingernails across his chest and looked down between his legs. 'So…' She smiled, licked her lips. 'Are we going to set him free then? He seems to be knocking at the door down there.' She reached towards him and tugged his boxers down. His cock sprung free. She gasped and jumped back. 'Oh my God!'

'What?' he asked. He'd never had *that* reaction before. 'What is it?'

'You're… you're…'

'What?!'

'You're… hairy!'

'Hairy? What are you talking about?'

'Last week,' she said. 'Last week, you were bald, shaved down there. You said it was a porno trick, made your cock look bigger.'

Campbell put his hand to his head. John – the bastard – he was setting him up. He must have believed that yarn the guy at the tattoo shop had told them, shaved his pubes, the idiot. But he had conveniently neglected to let Campbell know that little secret before he sent him off to shag the boss's wife. The arsehole. It was deliberate. Campbell would cut off more than the wee turd's pubes the next time he saw him. Time to think fast.

'Oh aye, that!' he said. 'Ah wondered what ye were talkin about.' He shrugged and gave a short laugh. 'It's no big deal. We're all hairy guys in our family, have to shave two, sometimes three, times a day. Just grows back like wildfire, can't contain it.' He pointed to his groin. 'Same down there, one day, out with the shaving foam and a plastic Bic, coupla days later – whoosh! It's back!' She was frowning. Campbell could see the doubt on her face. He tried a different tack. 'It's a virility thing. All that testosterone.'

She raised an eyebrow. 'Really?'

'Most definitely. Full to the brim with it.'

She placed her hand on his cock, sliding it down the shaft, and flashed her eyes at him. 'Why don't we put that to the test then?' She took his hand and led him to the bed, pulled his head towards her and kissed him hard, her tongue flicking and probing between his lips. She pushed him and he fell backwards onto the bed.

'Let's get started, shall we?' she said, sliding onto the silk sheets to lie beside him. She leaned over him and retrieved a dark blue bottle from under the pillows. She opened it and poured a thin oil onto her hands. 'Need to get you all lubed up baby,' she said, slipping her hand around his cock and slowly working it up and down. 'I want it slippery wet. I want you *gliding* into me, so slick, so quick... so *hard*.'

Campbell gulped, his Adam's apple like a billiard ball in his throat. She kissed him again, softly this time, while she slid her hand; up and down, up and down.

'Ready?' she whispered into his mouth.

'Mmm hmm,' Campbell muttered, not really wanting her to stop.

'I think you are,' she laughed. 'But let's try it this way this time.' She knelt on the bed, tucking pillows under her chest and settling herself onto them. 'Okay,' she said. 'I'm waiting for you lover. Roger me rigid.'

Campbell shook his head. This was it – the point of no return. He knelt behind her, looked down. He saw the tattoo John had done for her – a red devil on her left buttock, complete with evil grin and a wee trident. Not bad, but Campbell knew he would have done it better, made the grin a bit more wicked, put a little twinkle in the devil's eyes. Maybe used a deeper shade of red.

'What are you waiting for?' she asked. 'C'mon baby, do me.'

'Sorry,' he muttered. He took a deep breath and guided himself into her. His cock slipped in easily and she wriggled slightly, making herself more comfortable.

'Ooh, that's nice,' she said.

He began to move steadily, setting up a rhythm that would keep him going for a while without losing it too soon.

He was about to reach round, find her clit, when she lifted her head from the pillows. 'Make the noises again. They really turned me on the last time.'

'Noises?' said Campbell. What the fuck was she talking about?

'Yes,' she said. 'Like you did before. C'mon lover, pump me hard and do the noises.'

Campbell began to falter, lose his rhythm. What noises? He could feel himself becoming soft.

She pushed back onto him, moving her hips against him.

His cock perked up again.

Noises? Noises? What the hell had John been up to?

'Come on babes,' she said. 'The noises.'

He made a stab at it. 'Eeeee, eeeee…'

She turned her head, looked at him over her shoulder. 'What the hell are you doing?' she asked.

'Making noises?' he suggested.

'That's not the ones you did the last time, the ones that got my juices going.' She began thrusting, increasing her speed, making him follow suit. He'd need to be careful – if it got too fast too soon, he'd end up shooting early. She gripped the spars of the headboard, throwing her head back and sending her hair falling along her shoulders. 'The noises – c'mon sweetcheeks, same as before. Do it!'

He was at a total loss. He never even knew John made *any* sounds when he was shagging, let alone what the fuck they might actually be. Maybe he should just own up, tell her the truth, face the consequences. After all, she couldn't very well complain to Boddice, could she? *Could she?* That might be the best solution. He would… he would…

He had a brainwave.

'You first,' he said.

'What?' She buried her head in the pillow.

'You make them first this time,' he said. 'And I'll join in.'

She laughed. 'You dirty bastard,' she said. 'You really do know how to make me hot!' She slowed down, stretched luxuriously. 'Alright, you're on.' She slipped off his cock, turned round and pushed Campbell onto his back. 'But if I'm gonna do it, I want *you* underneath *me!*'

She pinned him on the bed and straddled him, guiding him back inside. She stretched behind her, undoing her bra. Her breasts fell out, massive and pendulous. She ran her hands through her hair, rocking back and forth, sliding along his shaft. Moving slowly at first, with each stroke out she moaned 'hoo!' and 'haa!' with each stroke back. 'Hoo-haa! Hoo-haa!'

Hoo-haa? In the name of the wee man – what had John been thinking? *Hoo-haa?* Did he do that every single time? What a prat. Campbell fought back the urge to laugh.

She settled down on top of him, letting her tits brush against his chest. 'Hoo-haa, hoo-haa, c'mon baby, join in. Hoo-haa!' She was increasing the pace, pushing him deeper inside her.

'Hoo-haa,' he said weakly.

'No, lover, same as you did before. I want you to shout it! HOOOOO-HAAAA!' she screamed.

Christ almighty, this was fucking ridiculous. Was she serious? 'Hooo-haaa!' he yelled.

'That's it! God, I love this so much – do me baby, do me hard! Hoo-haa, hoo-haa!' She was moving faster still. Campbell could almost imagine a guy at the foot of the bed beating a big kettledrum, oil glistening on his bare chest. Hoooo – left hand, Haaaa – right hand. Hooo! Haaa! Ramming speed!

He could feel himself getting close; it wouldn't be long now. He decided to join in, full gusto. They rocked together, thrusting faster and faster, Campbell pumping his hips up into her. 'Hoo-haa, hoo-haa!' they shouted in unison. 'Hoo-haa, hoo-haa!' faster and faster. 'Hoohaahoohaahoohaahoohaahoohaahoohaa…' Campbell was beginning to hyperventilate – he thought he might faint. He felt himself on the edge, tried to hold back for a few more seconds. He gave a final thrust – 'Hoooooo-HAAAAAAA!!' He exploded and arched his back, held her above him, his cock twitching and pulsing inside her.

He collapsed, exhausted, onto the bed. She was laughing. 'That was even better than last time,' she said. Campbell suppressed a smirk – that was one he could store up for a bit of ammunition later. *Better than last time eh, John? What do you think of that?* 'Only one thing…' she went on.

'Oh, what's that then?' he asked.

'Well, last time I got myself off too, you know? My little cherry bomb. And it was just delicious for me, remember?'

'Eh, aye,' Campbell said.

She rolled off him onto her back. 'So, what are you gonna do about it lover? Tongues or fingers? It's up to you.' She took his hand, steered him between her legs. 'And you can forget all the hoo-haa this time,' she said. 'Just get down to business.'

'Noises?' asked John. '*Noises?* What the hell are ye talking about?'

The twins were in the front shop of *Two's Tattoos,* making a half-hearted attempt to tidy the place. Putting everything in some semblance of order in preparation for their enforced shutdown, however long *that* might last. John was still trying to argue that they didn't need to close up, that business could carry on while they were working for Boddice.

Boddice had put them straight on that, however. There was no fucking way he would risk some punter coming in and recognising them from Trusdale and Needham's.

But the real reason they were mooching around the shop today was to meet Boddice, to give him the feedback on how their tasks had gone, how well they had done. Neither of them was looking forward to it. There could be trouble.

The *Closed* sign hung in the front door and Campbell had pulled down the blinds, making it clear to any potential customer they'd have to seek their body art elsewhere. He was just as put out by this as John was. *Two's Tattoos* was their business, their livelihood. It had taken them years to build up their clientele, their good name, and now Boddice wanted them to put everything on hold for some daft idea that sounded as if it had as much chance of success as John had of winning the Nobel Prize for Physics and Astronomy.

And now this. It was the first time they had met since Campbell's near disastrous encounter with Boddice's wife. Campbell had blasted John for not telling him about her requirement for audio accompaniment while they had been fucking, how that little secret had almost blown the whole thing. John had frowned, shaking his head in bewilderment. 'Noises?' he asked. '*Noises?* What the hell are ye talkin about?'

'You know damn well what Ah mean,' Campbell replied. 'Don't act the goat with me.'

John laughed. 'Sorry, Campbell, but Ah haven't a scooby what ye're on about. Ah don't know anything about making any noises, especially when Ah'm supposed to be on the job.'

'Hoo-haa?' Campbell prompted. 'Doesnae mean anything to ye? Doesnae ring any bells?'

John shrugged, shook his head, his mouth turned down in a *beats-me* expression.

It was Campbell's turn to frown. 'Ye mean, she never asked ye to do anything like that at all? No noises? Nuthin?'

John looked at the floor, bent down to pick up a fragment of paper towel, took it over to the bin, keeping his back turned to Campbell. 'John?' Campbell said. 'She did, didn't she? Didn't she? Ya wee shite, ye knew she would ask me and ye kept it from me.'

John shook his head and turned to look at him. Campbell recognised the expression on his face. After all, did he not have the same one himself from time to time? It was embarrassment.

'Wait a minute,' said Campbell, waving his forefinger. 'Hang on, there's something else isn't there? No noises, eh?'

John shook his head again.

Campbell narrowed his eyes, set his mouth in a firm line. He sensed John's evasiveness. His discomfort. 'Alright,' Campbell said. 'What was it she asked *you* to do then?'

John looked away, began studying the contents of the open drawer under one of the counters. 'Ah thought she'd get you to do the same thing,' he said. 'Ah thought it would be a laugh to think of you in that situation.'

'What situation?'

'Dancin.'

'*Dancin?*' Campbell raised an eyebrow. 'Ye mean ye had to dance with her first?'

'Well, not exactly. She didn't want me to dance *with* her. More on my own, like.'

'What do ye mean?'

'Exotic dancin, she called it. Just me.'

Campbell smirked. 'Ah don't get ye. Ye'd better explain.'

'She said it turned her on.'

'What did?'

'Me!' John shouted, exasperated by Campbell's pretence of failing to understand him. 'Me, dancin in the middle of the livin room. She made me wear this thing. A posing pouch. Leopard-skin pattern.'

Campbell couldn't hold it in any longer. He let out a long bray of laughter.

'She lay back on the sofa,' John went on, ignoring him, 'fingering herself while she watched me doing this stupid fucking dance on the rug in the middle of the floor, waving my arms about and swivelling my hips and stuff.'

Campbell could hardly picture it. 'Was there music?' he asked through his tears of laughter.

'Of course there was bloody music,' John said. 'It was… it was…'

'What?'

'It was… it was… the theme from Star Trek, if ye must know!'

Campbell completely lost it then. He doubled up, clutching his side. 'Oh man,' he said. 'That's fucking classic. Star Trek! Lieutenant Yahoorye, that's you that is.'

'Get to fuck, ya prick,' John said. 'At least when we finally got down to it, it was just normal stuff. Ah didn't have to *hoo* this and *haa* that like a fucking monkey.'

'Aye, well,' said Campbell, wiping the tears from his eyes, 'she seemed to make a monkey out of the both of us. In fact, she…' He stopped, his smile fading quickly. 'Hang on though,' he said. 'If that's the case, then that means that…oh, shit.'

'What?'

'It means that—'

He didn't get to finish. At that moment, the door opened, the bell on its little spring chiming cheerily, and Boddice walked in. Campbell flashed a look at John, warning him not to ask any further. John, more aware than usual, gave the smallest of nods.

'Bit dingy in here is it not?' Boddice asked, looking around the almost empty room.

'We've been tidying away,' Campbell explained. 'Getting ready for the shutdown. Ah've even made up a wee sign.' He moved behind Boddice and picked up a large cardboard square.

Closed until further notice for refurbishment.
***Two's Tattoos* will be back soon!!**

The sign was scrawled in black magic marker.

Boddice probed a nostril with his index finger, absently inspected what he'd found up there. 'Right,' he said. 'Pushed for time today, boys, I'm afraid. No luxury of fannying about.' He flicked something small and grey from the end of his finger. 'Let's find out how you boys got on, eh? I've been looking forward to this.'

John and Campbell exchanged glances as Boddice went into his inside jacket pocket and retrieved the two sheets of paper containing their tasks. John had gone white, swayed slightly, struggling to catch his breath.

'You okay, son?' Boddice asked.

John nodded, wiped a bead of sweat from his brow.

'You don't look so good,' Boddice said. 'Too many pints last night?'

'Something like that,' John replied.

Boddice opened the first sheet. 'Well, let's see who's first then.' He took the piece of paper, held it at arm's length as he read, his mouth pursing as he tried to decipher the writing. He looked up. 'HGV driving, eh? Who had to do that?'

John raised his hand, and Campbell noticed the tips of his fingers were trembling.

'Ye know,' said Boddice. 'That might actually be a pretty useful thing.' He looked at Campbell. 'Good choice, son.'

Campbell gave a thin smile in reply.

'So, how did it go?' Boddice asked. 'Did you get the licence?'

'Well, aye and no,' John said, staring at the floor. 'Ah picked it up easy from where Campbell left off. They couldn't tell it was me.' He kept his head down, but stole a look at Boddice, watching for his reaction. 'Ah passed all their tests and that, but they'll not submit my forms until Ah pay the fee. Ah kept putting them off, telling them the cheque was in the post, and for some reason they believed me, but they'll not let me sit the official test till Ah give them the money.' He looked up at Boddice, his chest puffing with pride. 'But Ah know Ah'll pass. It's a doddle.' He had a natural aversion to tests or exams of any kind, but he had excelled at these, actually found them enjoyable.

'Very good, son,' said Boddice. 'Ye did well. Good job. Ah'll make sure they get their money, and you'll have your licence.'

Ordinarily John would have beamed with pleasure, grateful for approval from the big man, happy that he'd done something right in Boddice's eyes, something to raise his profile. But not this time, not now that Boddice was unfolding the second piece of paper. John felt as if his legs were made of powder, and there was a piledriver hammering relentlessly in his chest. Why the fuck had he been so stupid – no, make that insane – as to pick such a ridiculously dangerous task? And to write it down on a bit of paper? One that Boddice had in his hand at this very instant.

The room became clammy and grew dimmer by the second. A sour juice trickled down the inside of John's cheeks, and a pulsating, buzzing sound in his head waxed and waned with a steadily increasing frequency. The floor took on a life of its own, pitching and yawing like a ship in a storm.

Boddice used his stubby fingers to smooth out the sheet of paper.

The last thing John saw before he hit the floor was Boddice

turning the sheet of paper the right way up, scanning the words, a frown beginning to crease his brow. John screamed, '*Noooo!*', but even as he fell he knew the sound which came out of his mouth was nothing more than a weak, watery moan.

***

He couldn't have been out for more than thirty seconds. Campbell was kneeling beside him with an arm around his shoulder, gently shaking him awake. John looked up at Boddice who stared back, his face set in a dark scowl.

Boddice held up the sheet of paper. 'No wonder you were reluctant to let me see this,' he said. 'And this explains why your brother threw a flaky when he read it.' He took a few paces forward, towering over the twins on the floor.

John noticed a small white thread clinging to the leg of Boddice's trousers in the shape of the letter 's'. He couldn't look away, and he wondered why, at this critical turning point in his life, he should become absorbed in something so trivial.

Boddice folded his arms, crumpling the sheet of paper against his chest. 'You been dipping your wick somewhere you shouldn't, eh son? Tasting forbidden fruit?'

John started to stutter an answer, but Campbell halted him with a firm squeeze of his arm.

Boddice turned to Campbell, his voice matching the glowering, thunderous look in his eyes. 'This must have been very tricky for you, being placed in such a delicate situation, having to sneak in and out, make sure you weren't spotted. Being compromised like that, all because of your brother's fondness for a bit of rumpy-pumpy.' He turned his back on them, directed his next question to the wall: 'And were you successful, son? Did you manage to convince when you got your tadger out? Were you… good enough?'

John looked from Boddice to Campbell and back again. Campbell was taking his time in answering and John felt as if he was going to throw up. 'Ah was fine, Mr Boddice,' Campbell said eventually. 'No problems in that department.'

Boddice swung round, and John had to cling on to Campbell to prevent himself falling over again. 'Superb!' Boddice said, clapping his hands and breaking into a wide grin. 'I knew you boys had the right stuff, that my trust in you wasn't misplaced.' He balled the sheet of paper and threw it onto one of the counters.

John allowed Campbell to help him to his feet, guide him to one of the stools in the corner. Campbell sat him down, giving him a knowing wink as he did so. John flinched, bafflement and surprise playing across his face.

Boddice glanced at his watch. 'That's all I needed to know boys, all the information I require. I need to be making tracks, but before I go, a few final instructions. You can start work on Monday. Everything's in place, just present yourself at Trusdale and Needham, the security office at eight in the morning, there'll be someone there to take care of you.'

'Who?' Campbell asked. 'The insider?'

'Of course not,' snapped Boddice. 'They're not going to reveal themselves to the likes of you. No, as far as everyone's concerned you'll be the new start. Just make sure you don't fuck up. Turn and turn about, remember? One day you, the next day, him.'

Campbell nodded. 'We get the picture, don't worry.'

'Oh, I'm not worried, son. If things go tits up, it'll be you who needs to worry, not me.' Boddice adjusted the collar on his coat, straightened his sleeves, pulling them over his wrists. 'But time's pressing, boys. I'll just leave you to…' He looked around the shop. '… to whatever it is you're up to.' He turned to John, grabbed the front of his jacket, almost lifting him off the stool. 'And you, son, you just watch yourself the next time you feel like competing for a medal in the humptathlon, okay?' He let him go and opened the door, stepping into the street. 'Eight o'clock on Monday. Don't be late,' he called over his shoulder.

The door blew shut, rattling the *Closed* sign and sending a shudder through the shop.

John got up from the stool. Disoriented, unsure of what he'd just witnessed. His legs felt funny, like he had stepped onto an escalator that wasn't working, standing for a second, swaying while his body expected to be carried up. It wasn't just that he'd fainted, but more that Boddice had let them off scot-free. No questions asked, no recriminations. How in the name of jumping Jesus had that happened?

Campbell picked up the notepaper Boddice had thrown on the counter and gave it to John. 'Check it out,' he said.

John unfolded the sheet and scanned the message scrawled in uneven block capitals:

> I'VE GOT APPOINTMENTS AT THE
> VD CLINIC AT THE SANDYFORD. YOU
> HAVE TO GO AND GET YOUR KNOB
> EXAMINED NEXT TUESDAY.

'What…? How…?' John spluttered.

Campbell grinned. 'It's as well one of us has a functioning brain cell isn't it?'

'*You* did this?' asked John. 'But how did ye manage to get…?'

'It was easy really,' Campbell interrupted. 'You remember that hellish yellow jacket Boddice was wearing when we met him in the back room of the pub?'

'Aye, it was hideous, what about it?'

'Well, thank fuck it was hideous, or else Ah wouldn't have found it in his wardrobe.'

'His wardrobe? What do ye mean? When were you in his…?'

'After Ah'd played hide the sausage with his wife, complete with vocal performance and everythin, she fell asleep. She snores like a rusty chainsaw, by the way. Anyway, Ah sneaked out, all tippy-toes and quiet as a mouse with slippers on. Ah found the main bedroom and there was the yellow jacket hanging in the big mirrored wardrobe. Into the inside pocket, and there were the bits of paper. Ah hate to think what we'd have done if they weren't there.'

'So, what did ye do?'

'Ah replaced it.'

'What, my note?'

Campbell nodded.

'And she never heard ye?'

'Ah don't think so. When Ah got back, she was still sleepin. She woke up later on and Ah had to go through the whole hoo-haa thing again. In the armchair this time.'

John started to laugh, sheer relief flooding through him. 'Man, that's really funny. Ah can just see the two of youse, shagging away, creating all that racket.'

'But John, it isn't funny.'

'Aye it is, at least Ah only had to do a daft wee dance.'

'That's my point exactly,' Campbell said. 'Ye know what this means, don't ye?'

'We're both arseholes?'

'No, much worse than that. It means she saw right through us. She *knew* we weren't the same person. We were rumbled.'

'And that means…'

'That we failed the test.'

They were silent for a few minutes. John picked up a bottle of red ink, placed it in one of the overhead cupboards. Campbell lifted the blind and stared out into the street. 'Well, at least Boddice didn't find out about what we were up to,' John said eventually.

'What *you* were up to, ye mean. Ye can keep me out of it.'

'Aye, well it's all finished now.'

'How do ye mean?'

'She's called it off, doesn't want to see me any more, says she's got somebody else.'

'Oh aye? And Ah wonder what that poor bugger's gonnae have to do to give her the jollies. Dress up as Batman?'

'Or Robin.'

They looked at each other and laughed. 'Holy Johnny Bag, Batman,' Campbell said. 'Missus Boddice is sending out the shag signal again!'

'Man, we got out of jail there though, didn't we?' said John, puffing his cheeks and blowing off a stream of air.

'No thanks to you, ya tosser,' Campbell said. 'You know somethin?'

'What?'

'You're lucky to have me.'

John tilted his head. 'Ah know that,' he said, smiling. 'Ah know that.'

PART 3: HOPE AND ARGYLE

Going Underground

The subway station was packed. An electrical fault somewhere on the Inner Circle had delayed the trains and the platform was crowded with commuters and shoppers jostling for position.

Kyle stood in the queue which backed up onto the steps, and looked over the heads of the crowd to the far end. There was no space. Just a sea of angry, frustrated travellers.

When the problem was finally resolved and things started running again, it was fifteen minutes and two trains before the throng thinned out.

The third train into the station was busy, but Kyle managed to get onboard and actually found a seat. The other passengers looked weary and frazzled already, and they hadn't even made it into the city yet. The guy beside Kyle slumped in his seat listening to his iPod on a pair of sling-back headphones, drumming his fingers on his knee in time to the music. Kyle could faintly make out the sounds of Led Zeppelin – *When The Levee Breaks*. A bit of class at least, he thought.

The doors closed and the train juddered into the tunnel. From the corner of his eye, Kyle studied the guy with the iPod. He had the dreamy, distracted expression so many people wore while listening to music on headphones, playing games on their phones; turned in on themselves, not quite present in the real world. It reminded Kyle of his previous-life feelings; it had the same quality of dislocation, of existing in two places at the one time. The tilting of reality.

He had felt it again that night at the Palace, levelling the gun at Leggett's chest as the boy backed away, scrabbling blindly for the exit, and pulling the trigger, standing slightly outside himself, adrift in consciousness. He considered it a defence mechanism, something which protected the fragile marrow of his soul, shielded it from the horrors of what he sometimes had to do. Of course, the incident with Leggett had jolted him back to the harsh physicality of the world. The gun had fired, and Leggett had collapsed to the floor, but in fright and terror, not as a result of a gaping, gushing wound in his belly. Kyle had stood over him, blinking in amazement, while Leggett burst into tears, sobbing uncontrollably. Kyle had examined the gun, checked the loader, searched for something that could have gone wrong. The gun was fine, no problems there. It had been the bullet. A fucking blank. A dud. A useless piece of junk.

He'd been tricked.

Boddice had used him. Boddice had his methods, and there was often madness in them, but this time Kyle felt betrayed and exploited. He had killed many times in the past, but it was never an easy thing, not a task to undertake lightly. Boddice could command him to carry out a hit, but Kyle was certain Boddice hadn't the slightest inkling how much emotional effort it actually took. To fool him into thinking he was about to do it again, to force him into that gut-wrenching decision for a bit of fun, just to put the frighteners on a wee scumbag like Leggett, was cruel and heartless.

It might even have been different – in fact Kyle *knew* it would have been different – if Boddice had let him into his little secret in the first place, kept him in the loop. No doubt Boddice had his reasons, deeper machinations were presumably at work. Gradually, Kyle's rage had subsided. He'd never had cause to question Boddice's decisions before; perhaps it was better just to let the big man do whatever he was going to do. Go with the flow.

There was a commotion near the door. The train had arrived at the next station and more passengers had come on. It was standing room only now. A guy had shuffled in on crutches and he stood leaning against the glass partition next to the door. The straggly beard, pale blue shell suit and holey trainers gave him away – Kyle had seen it too many times to mistake it for anything else – the standard-issue uniform of the druggie: the beanie pulled tight and low over his forehead, the sagging jaw and the slow, hooded eyes, perpetually focused on a point somewhere in the middle distance *(no-one living in this house)*, reinforced the image. All it needed was the whiney, slurred voice, the elongated, sliding vowels, and the picture would be complete. Kyle didn't have to wait long.

The train pulled away with a jerk, sending the standing passengers lurching into each other. The guy with the crutch almost lost his balance, but was held up by the press of bodies around him. In the middle of the tunnel, he let out a yell. 'Can youse smell it, man?'

People in the centre of the carriage turned to see who had shouted, craning their necks for a better view, while those nearest to the door and crutch-guy shot each other a quick *Oh-no* look and stared at the floor. The guy looked around, wild-eyed now, struggling to focus. 'Can youse smell it ya bastards?' he shouted. There was a shuffling of feet and people tried to back away a few inches, get some clear space between themselves and the nutter. He shouted again, 'Can youse smell my fuckin leg, man?'

An Asian girl, long hair so black it seemed to suck light from the air, put her hand to her mouth to stifle a laugh. She offered crutch-guy her seat, but he ignored her.

'Can ye smell my leg?' he asked again. 'Eh?' Passengers turned away, looked out the window at the walls of the tunnel rushing past, found something interesting on their jacket to fidget with, decided now was a good time to check the keys in their pockets.

The poor buggers who were stuck right beside the guy flashed nervous, jealous looks at the smug bastards standing in relative safety in the middle of the carriage. The smug bastards in the middle of the carriage looked on sympathetically, but grateful they weren't in any immediate jeopardy. Kyle folded his arms and sighed. What a fucking day this was turning out to be.

The guy started on a new topic. 'Brillo pads, man.' Kyle raised an eyebrow. What was coming now? 'That's what Ah'm gettin now. My shites are comin out like brillo pads.' Kyle heard someone mutter, 'For fuck's sake,' and the guy took this as a signal to warm to his theme.

'It's no what Ah'm eatin,' he said. 'That's just chips an stuff, but my arse is red-raw with these jaggy shites Ah'm doing.' He gave a wheezy laugh. 'Anyway,' he went on, 'this fuckin leg of mine is pure bowfin, man. Been like this for days. Can youse no smell it? An Ah tell ye whit, there's—' He stopped dead. His attention had been caught by something at his side. He stuck his chin down onto his chest and hobbled a few inches to his left on his crutches. He nudged a man in a business suit, nodded to the case the man was carrying.

'Is that a computer, pal? In there? A computer, eh?'

The businessman transferred the case to his other hand and turned his back on the crutch-guy. 'Your job is it?' he went on, undeterred. 'What is it ye do?' The man ignored him. The crutch-guy raised his voice. 'How ye no talkin to me, eh? You too good to talk to the likes of me?' Kyle could feel the mood of the other passengers slide a little further up the tension scale, a short, sharp glissando of anxiety. This was a turning point. They all sensed it. The guy had asked the question they all knew had the potential to tip the whole situation over the edge. They were poised on the crest of a wave, balanced between the plunge down the other side or a safe glide back into calmer waters. The businessman kept his back to the crutch-guy, ignored him.

Despite the roaring of the train as it sped through the tunnel, a silence descended in the carriage. The guy lifted one of his crutches, used it to tap the businessman on the leg. 'Heh, you,' he said. 'Ah'm talkin to you.' The businessman still refused to acknowledge him. He turned to the other passengers. 'Youse are all the same, ya pricks. Youse all think Ah'm scum, don't youse? Well, ye can just fuck off.' He was about to launch into another rant when the train pulled into St Enoch. The people nearest the door streamed onto the platform, many of them glad to just get the fuck off the train and away from the guy with the crutch; they could walk the rest, or wait for the next train – anything but spend another second beside this arsehole.

The people waiting for the train began to board, innocent and oblivious of what they were about to encounter. 'Stop bumpin me, ya bastards,' the guy shouted at the oncoming crowd. Some of them glanced at him warily, others scrambled on regardless. 'Heh! Ye're duntin my leg! Can youse smell it?'

Kyle got up and went over to the guy, took him by the arm and guided him to the seat he'd vacated. 'Here pal,' he said. 'Settle down. Just sit here till it's time to get off.'

The guy flopped into the seat and propped his crutches between his knees. The people beside him shifted uneasily. He frowned and looked around him, still struggling to concentrate on his surroundings, a thin thread of saliva running down his chin.

Kyle made his way through the standing passengers to the door and hopped off. Just as the doors slid together, Kyle heard the guy shout in a muffled voice: 'Ho! This is my stop! Hold on, this is me!'

The train pulled away and Kyle had a last view of the guy falling backwards in the carriage, taking out two or three other passengers in the process, his face contorted in a furious, wild-eyed yell, crutches and limbs flailing in a tangled confusion.

***

At the top of the escalator, Kyle saw Prentice waiting beside the station exit. Like Kyle, he was dressed for the job: good suit, black polo shirt for that air of careful casualness, clean-shaven.

He didn't look pleased though. 'What kept you?' he asked.

Kyle explained about the delayed trains, but didn't say anything about the crutch-guy. He couldn't be bothered getting into it all with Prentice. It had been weeks since the meeting at the beach and Kyle had hardly had any contact with him. That was unusual in itself – they normally worked together on everything – but what little time they'd spent together since then had been punctuated by scowls and bad moods. Whatever had been bothering him, Prentice had kept his own counsel.

Now, he was barely listening to what Kyle had to say. He just turned and headed off to Argyle Street, leaving Kyle shaking his head in frustration and hurrying to catch up. Today was an important part of the plan, a crucial scouting expedition, and there was no point in carrying an attitude onto the job. It would make them too conspicuous. Kyle remembered a slogan he'd seen printed on a T-shirt somewhere – *I don't have an attitude problem, you have a perception problem.* Prentice might as well have it printed on his forehead.

They crossed the road and walked through the Heilanman's Umbrella, the dank, dismal part of Argyle Street which ran under Central Station. At the far end Kyle could see their destination suspended in the air.

Trusdale and Needham's was only eighteen months old, but already it had become a Glasgow icon. The flagship of the Trusdale and Needham consortium (they would never call it a 'chain'), it was hailed as the most stylish department store in Europe, not just by the glitterati, the fashion gurus and the self-appointed 'beautiful people', but equally by the ordinary punters, the Joe Soaps and the merely curious. Architecturally, it was considered a masterpiece – a fusion of old and new, symbolic of Glasgow's dynamic thrusting leap into the future, springboarded from the solid foundations of heritage and history. Or so the publicity blurb said. To most people it was simply a stunning building.

Trusdale and Needham had chosen their site well, on the corner of Hope and Argyle. The design had involved demolishing the jaded office block at one end, taking the old Edwardian buildings running up Hope Street and fusing them to a gleaming burnished copper spike which soared and curved over the intersection with Argyle Street, seeming to strain against the tendons of black-coated steel beams which both supported the spire and anchored it to the main building. Below this, a glass bubble, two storeys high, was suspended from the spike, like a giant bead of water caught in a spider's web of cantilevered cables and struts. The bubble was joined to the main building by a slender walkway, also encased in glass, where customers paraded high above the street below, giving them the illusion of walking on air. The whole structure was an unlikely balancing act, held in place by the subtle interactions of gravity and the biomechanical grace of the suspending cables and stanchions which sprung from the copper spike. After dark, the bubble was illuminated by spotlights and lasers mounted on adjacent buildings and it glittered and sparkled in the night like a mirrorball.

This was where the Dark Side of the Moon would be put on display. A diamond within a diamond.

Kyle and Prentice emerged from the gloom of the Umbrella and stood looking up at the giant bauble hanging above them. Despite its glass construction, they noticed it was actually difficult to make out anything inside in any detail. The curvature of the walls had a curious lensing effect which distorted the view from the ground.

'Impressive, eh?' said Kyle.

Prentice shrugged. 'Ah suppose so, if ye like that kinda thing.'

Kyle looked at him. 'C'mon, shake yourself. Ye've got to admit, there's nothin like it.'

Prentice sucked his teeth and stared at the ground, refusing to meet Kyle's gaze. Kyle grabbed his arm and steered him to the nearest doorway. 'What the fuck's eatin you, man?' he asked. Prentice shrugged him off, turned his back on him. Kyle seized

Prentice by the shoulders and spun him round, pinning him against the wall. 'Don't ignore me, ya prick. There's somethin botherin ye. Tell me what it is.'

Passers-by turned to look at them, curious to see if anything was going to kick off, but cautious of getting too close. Prentice pushed Kyle away. 'Back off,' he said quietly. 'Don't fuckin get me started. You know what Ah'm like and you don't want to aggravate me, right?'

Kyle caught the menace in Prentice's voice, knew it was safer to hold back a bit. But this behaviour wasn't good. They needed to co-operate, to get their act together. 'Look,' he said. 'Let's just get this over and done with, eh? It'll not take long. In, out… and that'll be it. We can go get a pint or two later, you can tell me what's up. Christ, ye've got a face like a bulldog chewing a wasp.'

Prentice glowered at him, his eyes hooded and emotionless. 'Let me ask you something,' he said.

Kyle nodded for him to carry on.

'Why do you do it?'

'Do what?' Kyle asked.

'All this stuff for Boddice, all the shite we have to put up with, all the shite we have to dole out, what do ye do it for?'

Kyle frowned. 'Ah don't know what ye mean.'

'Exactly,' said Prentice. 'Ye don't, do ye? Ye never stop to give it any thought. Ye just get on with it. Whatever Boddice asks ye, ye just get the job done, no questions asked, no consideration of the ins and outs of things.' He shook his head. 'It never crosses yer mind, does it? To ask what it's all for. What we, personally, get out of it.'

'Boddice sees us right,' said Kyle.

'Does he?' Prentice asked. 'Does he, really?'

'Of course he does. We get our money every time.'

'Aye, and sometimes it's not much more than pocket money.'

'We do alright. What more do ye want?'

Prentice laughed. 'Aye, we do alright don't we? That's how you and me are stayin in shitty wee one-bedroomed flats in Maryhill, and not in some big mansion in Blantyre with fitba players and bank managers for neighbours. We're doing great aren't we?'

Kyle found himself getting angry. 'Ye don't know where we'd be without Boddice. Mary and me are fine in that flat. Christ knows what our situation might be like if it wasn't for the cash we get from Boddice. How else would we survive? We've got zero skills, you and me, what else can we do?'

Prentice ignored him. 'All Ah see recently is that Boddice gets all the profits, and the most we can expect is scraps from the table.'

Kyle jerked a thumb at the Trusdale and Needham building opposite. 'In there,' he said. 'Is that gonnae be scraps?' He dropped his voice, made sure no-one was listening. 'The fuckin diamond man, that's not exactly leftovers from the mince and totties is it?'

'Maybe not,' said Prentice. 'But don't think for a minute that we'll be gettin the lion's share. We'll be doing all the dirty work, riskin all the danger, maybe even gettin caught, and Boddice'll be safely out of harm's way, controllin things from the sidelines, the general commanding from the rear. Make no mistake, we're the ones that'll be feelin the heat if things go wrong.'

'Ah don't understand why ye're being like this,' said Kyle. 'Ye never used to question anythin the big man wanted. Why are ye startin now? Now that we've got a chance to do somethin big. Somethin that could set us up, get us to fuck out of they flats in Maryhill. Why do ye not trust him?'

'Kyle, that's always been your problem,' said Prentice. 'Ye've never questioned anythin, have ye? Ye just do whitever ye're told. Ye're like a fuckin robot, man. When Boddice says jump, you ask how high.'

'Have you ever been any different?' Kyle asked. 'You've

always been the fuckin tough man, Boddice's Doberman. Ah've never seen *you* soundin off to his face.'

Prentice looked up at the glass structure hanging above their heads, the blue sky reflecting from its gleaming walls. 'Aye, well it's about time we did some thinking, Kyle. Some serious analysis. Stop following blindly.' He looked Kyle in the eye. 'You and me, we deserve better. And the funny thing is, Ah think you know it.' He walked to the edge of the pavement, waiting for a break in the traffic. 'C'mon,' he called over his shoulder as he crossed the road.

Kyle hurried after him, wondering just what in Christ's name was happening to everyone. Prentice was wrong; Kyle was quite happy in his flat. So was Mary. They had a lot to thank Boddice for and shouldn't be complaining. Life could be much worse. But there was a strange niggle at the back of his mind, a little seed of doubt, that maybe, just maybe, things were about to get worse anyway. Perhaps the incident with the guy on the subway had unsettled him more than he thought, had queered his pitch for the rest of the day. Bad karma and all that.

More hippy shite.

He caught up with Prentice at the entrance to the store. The main door was in one of the older buildings on Hope Street. Neither of them had been in the shop before. They stood outside, staring at the ornate wood and brass doors, the T&N symbol carved in blonde ash inlay on the arch overhead and an array of high-powered micro-spotlights blazing a criss-cross pattern on the walls of the vestibule. Even in daylight, the effect was dazzling.

They pulled on handles shaped like strange musical instruments and went inside. The store opened before them – a huge, cavernous white space criss-crossed by wooden staircases and walkways which spanned the higher levels, ramps and bridges leading to galleries of clothes, high-end furniture, jewellery, furs. A glass ceiling vaulted over the central sales area where perfumes and cosmetics were displayed on islands of polished black stone, beautiful girls in an assortment of scanty uniforms hovering in anticipation of pouncing on any customer who paused long enough to fall into their trap. Here and there were mannequins set on plinths, dressed in expensive big-name designer clothes and posed in various attitudes of exciting-young-thing-ness. A steady thrum of voices circulated in the air, a buzzing undercurrent of exhilaration at the sheer pleasure of being in such a brazenly opulent environment.

Dominating the space was an enormous golden arrow, the shaft perhaps six feet in diameter, which looked as if it had pierced the building high on the left-hand wall and plunged into the floor in the middle of the concourse in front of them, the glittering arrowhead burying itself in the polished floorboards. Where the shaft came out of the wall, perhaps seventy feet above them, the brickwork had been constructed in such a way as to make it appear as if the bricks and plaster had been damaged beyond repair, hanging precariously, ready to crash to the floor. The shaft of the arrow housed the supporting cables which ran through the copper spike outside. The cables suspended the Bubble and they travelled down the main body of the arrow to anchor points secured to the underground ballast deep beneath the store. It was a stroke of genius to disguise the structural engineering in such an outrageous and audacious manner, to transform it into a work of art.

Even Prentice was moved to comment. 'Now *that* looks fuckin good,' he said. 'Ah like that.' He rubbed his chin and shook his head in amazement. 'Could ye imagine if it broke? Some sweep-up operation outside if that happened.'

Kyle felt a surge of relief as he saw Prentice break into a smile. Whatever had been bugging him earlier hadn't passed, but at least his mood had mellowed. Kyle considered saying something to break the ice that had formed between them, but thought better of it. It was as well to let Prentice come round in his own time.

On their right, a sweeping wooden staircase led to the first floor. Slender illuminated cones sprouted from the handrails every few feet to light the way. Kyle and Prentice climbed slowly, taking in the view of the ground floor, checking the layout of the various stalls and sales islands, mentally noting the floorplan. A giant banner slung between two of the overhead galleries announced the arrival of the Dark Side of the Moon in just over two weeks, a photograph of the diamond glittering on a white velvet pillow as its centrepiece.

As they arrived onto the first-floor landing Prentice nudged Kyle. 'Look,' he said.

Kyle followed his gaze and saw one of the Wilson twins standing in a little alcove set into the wall. He was wearing a smart green uniform, with yellow stripes running down his trouser legs, a green shirt and bow tie completing the outfit. A walkie-talkie poked from a pouch attached to his belt. He stood legs apart and with arms folded, surveying the shoppers from beneath the skip cap pulled down tight on his forehead. 'Looks the part, eh?' said Kyle.

Prentice continued to stare at the twin, Campbell or John, whichever one it was – he could never tell the fuckers apart. 'Ah'm gonnae test him,' he said. 'Let's see if *this* bit of the plan works at least.'

Kyle was about to tell him to hold back, not to risk any exposure, but perhaps there was some sense in this after all. Worth seeing how it goes, he thought.

'Excuse me pal,' Prentice said as they came up to the twin. 'Can you tell us where we can have a look at some expensive jewellery? Something rare and unusual? A gift for a friend?'

The twin didn't even blink. He turned to them with a studied indifference; unsmiling and cold. 'Certainly sir,' he said. 'You'll want the second level in the Bubble.' He pointed to a gantry, two or three floors above them, which led to a mirrored and spotlit doorway. 'You can gain access from the Stewart Gallery which will take you onto the Sky Walkway. Just follow that, and you're there.' He refolded his arms and looked off to the right. 'There's an elevator further along here which will take you up.'

'Thanks pal,' said Prentice. 'Ah think Ah know where to go now.' He led Kyle away. 'Very smart, by the way,' he said to the twin as they left.

'Sir?' said the twin.

'Your uniform,' Prentice said. 'It suits you.'

The twin stared after them as they walked to the lift.

When it arrived, the lift was empty. They got in and pushed the button for the Stewart Gallery. 'Not bad,' said Kyle as the lift ascended. 'Didn't faze him at all, whatever one it was.'

Prentice grunted.

'*Stewart Gallery*,' announced a cool, sexy voice from the speaker as the lift came to a halt and the doors slid open. Ahead of them was an array of hats. Nothing but hats. All colours, all sizes, all styles. Kyle and Prentice stepped out and looked about them. Prentice examined the nearest hat. It was a green and red monstrosity, shaped vaguely like an upturned boat, with yellow feathers spraying out at the back. Or was that the front?

'Who the fuck buys these kinda things?' Prentice asked. 'More to the point, who wears them?' He picked it up. 'Ah mean, look at the state of this. It's a joke.'

'Ah don't know,' said Kyle. 'It might go with that yellow jacket Boddice has been wearin recently. Might just set it off.'

Prentice stared at him, one eyebrow raised, and then burst out laughing. 'Man ye're right,' he said. 'What the hell is he thinkin? He looks like a bloody banana.'

'Oh aye, and are you gonnae tell him that?' asked Kyle, laughing now too.

'*Nobody'll* tell him. That's why he's still wearin it man, thinking he's the business.'

They both laughed again. Prentice put the hat back on its

stand, noticing the six hundred pound price tag. They walked round the gallery, following the signs for the Sky Walkway.

'Listen,' said Prentice. 'Ah'm sorry about before, ye know, outside. Having a go at ye. Ah was out of order.'

'Consider it forgot,' said Kyle.

'No, Ah mean it,' said Prentice. 'Ah shouldn't have taken it out on you.'

Kyle let him walk ahead for a few paces, considered what to say next. 'Want to talk about it?' he asked.

Prentice turned back. 'Not really,' he said. 'Just wondered what Ah was makin of my life, ye know, where Ah was gonnae be in five, ten years' time. Still doing all this shite.' He stopped and leaned over the balcony, examining the shoppers on the ground floor. He turned to Kyle. 'Do ye ever think what life would be like if ye *weren't* doing this?'

'What, ye mean workin for Boddice?'

'Aye, that, for sure. But just in general. Ah mean, let's face it…' Prentice glanced along the balcony, made sure no-one was in earshot. '…we're *criminals*.' He smiled at the absurdity of the statement. 'But it's not even that. We're just bit players in the whole thing. If we were bumped off, say by big Drurie's lot or somethin, nobody would actually notice. Maybe a report in the paper or the news, but nobody would care.'

'Boddice would,' said Kyle.

Prentice laughed, but there was no humour in it. 'Would he hell. He'd soon get somebody else to step in. Christ, look at the way he took to that wee shite Leggett.'

'Don't talk to me about him,' said Kyle.

'Aye, sorry, but my point is that you and me… we're auld.'

'Speak for yourself,' Kyle said.

'No,' said Prentice. 'We are. In terms of *this* game.'

'What about Boddice then?' asked Kyle. 'He's aulder than us.'

'Aye, but he's a mover and shaker isn't he? We're just minions.'

'So what are ye gettin at?'

Prentice shrugged. 'Ach, nothin really, but have ye never thought about gettin out?'

Kyle's eyes widened. 'Cutting ties with Boddice?'

'Exactly.'

Kyle took a step backwards. 'No, never.'

'Never?' Prentice wasn't convinced.

'Ah owe him too much,' said Kyle. 'Ah told ye earlier, he's always been good to me.'

'So ye said, and Ah don't suppose ye'll change yer mind on that one.'

Kyle spread his hands. 'Look, it's a loyalty thing. Ah just don't see myself chuckin it.'

Prentice sighed and turned back to look at the crowds below. 'Ah don't know,' he said. Kyle felt Prentice was talking to himself as much as anything else. 'Ah think Ah'm ready for it. Ready to give it a rest.'

Kyle tried to catch his eye, but Prentice refused to meet his gaze. 'Look,' said Kyle. 'Don't kid yourself. It's not the kinda thing ye can just walk away from. Boddice will always have some sort of hold over ye. He'll never let ye go.'

'Ah could try,' Prentice said.

'Aye, ye could, but don't expect to have much success.'

Prentice finally turned to look at him. 'Ah think he knows already.'

Kyle narrowed his eyes. 'Boddice knows? Knows what?'

'He senses Ah'm restless, Ah can tell.'

Kyle leaned beside Prentice on the brass handrail of the balcony and stared across the void to the other side where Australian wall hangings and Mexican prints lined the walls. 'If he suspected somethin, Ah don't think he would let you in on this job. He'd keep you on the streets, collecting money, noising folk up. You'd be sidelined. Boddice would—'

'Do ye not think we're sidelined right now?' Prentice interrupted.

'Sidelined how?' asked Kyle.

Prentice shook his head. 'You don't see it at all, do ye?' He spread his hands, indicating the store spread out below them. 'This whole idea, robbing…' he dropped his voice to a whisper, '…*robbing* this fucking shop of not just some stupid wee bits of jewellery, but some bastard diamond that's the most famous in the world or something, and where do we fit in? We haven't even been invited to the party yet. No, it's goons like Boag and they twins that Boddice wants. Not us.'

'That's just the now,' said Kyle. 'Boddice has his plans for us, he…'

'Plans?' said Prentice. 'Ah don't see any evidence of plans. Boddice seems to be makin this up as he goes along.'

'Trust him,' said Kyle. 'He'll let us know when the time comes. For God's sake, we're here aren't we? Scouting the place, getting the lie of the land.'

'Lie of the land? All we've been told is get into the glass bubble, see what's what. We don't even know what we're supposed to be looking for.'

'Which is why we should just get on with it,' said Kyle, moving off along the gallery, following the signs for the Sky Walkway. 'C'mon.'

Prentice waited a few seconds before following, muttering under his breath.

The Stewart Gallery led to a ramp which climbed to the mirrored doorway they had seen from below. As they passed through into a short corridor, the same sophisticated voice from the lift relayed a recorded message, this time accompanied by a synthesised heartbeat: '*In two weeks' time… an event to take your breath away… to widen your eyes… a unique opportunity… for the wonderful people of Glasgow… exclusive to Trusdale and Needham… we present the jewel in the crown…*' The heartbeats became louder and the surging music began to crescendo. '*… the stone of destiny… the Dark Side of the Moon!*' The music finished in a blazing chord with accompanying timpani and cymbal crashes just as they emerged from the corridor onto the glass covered Sky Walkway which led to the Bubble.

'Aye, very good,' said Prentice. 'Ah nearly came in my pants there.'

Kyle laughed. Ahead of them they could see the Bubble, improbably suspended from the great spike which arched high over their heads, customers and staff milling about inside. They could feel the Walkway bounce and swing slightly as they walked towards it. Behind them the message started up again as another customer entered the corridor.

'How are they gonnae control the crowds comin to see this thing?' Prentice asked. 'This walkway doesn't seem that safe to me, never mind what it'd be like with hundreds of folk tryin to get in.'

'Rota system,' said Kyle. 'It's ticketed, apparently. Gives ye the date and time to turn up, so no queuing. Or so they say.'

They came to the end of the Walkway and entered the Bubble. Soft synthesised music washed over them and a smell like freshly cut grass drifted out from the air -conditioning units. Sales assistants in white trouser suits smiled toothpaste-advert smiles as they approached customers with brochures and samples. Through the walls Kyle and Prentice could see the sandstone and glass of Central Station, trains snaking along the platforms, while below them the traffic and pedestrians on Argyle Street scuttled soundlessly in all directions. The effect of the whole place was strangely soothing and reassuring, despite being dangled forty or so feet above the busy intersection by nothing more than a few steel wires.

But the warm, safe glow that had settled around them was shattered as they rounded a corner and saw what was in front of them.

Kyle felt the blood drain from his face. 'Oh fuck,' he said.

Altogether Now

'We saw it, and it doesn't look good,' said Prentice. 'Or, rather, it looks too fuckin good. We don't stand a chance.'

It was after nine at night. They were gathered in the storeroom of *Two's Tattoos*, waiting for Boddice. Boag sat in the corner beside a mop and pail. The twins were at a small table, smoking. Prentice paced back and forwards in front of the sink, making scuffing sounds on the linoleum.

Kyle glared at the twins. 'Right,' he said. 'What Ah want to know is why neither of you two thought to tell us about the fact that the security system for this diamond is like somethin out of James fuckin Bond.'

When Kyle and Prentice had entered the viewing room in the Bubble they'd seen the full extent of the protection that would surround the diamond when it finally went on display. A golden plinth, sweeping up from the floor in a graceful curve – it reminded Kyle of the Eiffel Tower – to a tiny platform set on a spike at shoulder-height where the diamond would sit in all its glory. But surrounding this was a whole array of lasers and sensors banked to either side of the plinth, and with a further ring of lasers suspended just above the apex sending beams down to even more detectors at floor level.

'We thought you knew already,' said John. 'Did Boddice not say anythin to ye about it?'

Prentice snorted. 'No, he didn't,' he said. 'Not a peep.'

'Me and him,' Prentice nodded at Kyle, 'were sent to case the place, get the lie of the land. But nobody said anythin about fuckin laser beams and grilles and electric fields and who knows what else. But you two knew about it all the time.'

'Too right,' added Kyle. 'You've been workin in there for the last however many weeks. Did you not think a wee hint might have been useful? Give us a wee bit of warning, what to expect?'

John started to say something, but Campbell laid his hand on his arm, stopping him. 'Wait a minute,' said Campbell. 'The security system was only brought in last week, and, even then, we weren't sure what all the bits and pieces were for. It wasn't till the day you showed up that they actually fired it up. We weren't allowed near it. And, anyway, what did ye think was gonnae happen? Did ye think they would display somethin like this in the middle of the shop floor? Maybe put up a wee sign saying *Please Help Yourself?*'

'Don't get lippy with me,' Prentice growled. 'Ah'll break your fucking nose. Maybe then we could tell you two pricks apart.'

'Calm down,' said Kyle, stepping between Prentice and the twins. 'This is getting us nowhere.' Prentice continued eyeballing Campbell. Kyle pulled him away. 'Leave it,' he said. 'We're in this together. Let's start acting like a team, eh?'

Prentice looked at him. 'A team is it?' he said. 'A team's supposed to have a bloody goal to aim for. So far we've got more in common with decapitated poultry than any semblance of a team. Maybe we're the Z-team, eh?' He scowled at Campbell who dropped his gaze to the floor. 'We don't even know what each other is supposed to be doing,' Prentice said. 'Boddice has told us fuck all. You two are supposed to be some sort of insiders, playing at being each other. That's as much as Ah can fathom.' The twins shifted uneasily, shot each other a quick glance. Prentice turned at last to Boag. 'And you,' he said. 'Ah haven't got a scooby where you fit into all this.'

Boag had been dreading this. Boddice had kept him apart from the others, feeding him nonsense about how he was an essential element of the whole scheme, how he was going to secure the getaway, make sure everyone got out intact and with the diamond safely ensconced in the old swag bag. But he'd had no contact with the rest of them since the meeting on the beach, and he now knew Boddice hadn't told them anything about what he was expected to do on the night of the robbery.

For whatever reason, Boddice had kept them out of the loop. Actually, perhaps Boddice had been right to stay quiet about it. He couldn't imagine they would be particularly pleased with what Boddice had in mind.

***

Boddice had taken him to see the Rastahman. They had driven out into the countryside, north of the city, to an old cottage in the centre of a Forestry Commission plantation, miles from anywhere, Sitka spruce as far as the eye could see. There was no McLean, it was just the two of them.

The Rastahman turned out to be an old guy called Jim Aiken (Boag had groaned when Boddice told him), early seventies at the youngest, by Boddice's estimation. Despite the rain, he was waiting for them in the driveway to the cottage as the four-wheel drive turned in at the entrance, bouncing over the rutted road. Aiken was a wiry figure, unshaven and with a shock of untamed hair flying in thin strands from below his baseball cap. His eyes seemed too wide apart for the size of his head, giving him a strange, fish-like appearance. Three lean and mean Dobermans barked at his side. 'Lennox! Larsson!' he shouted. 'To yer beds!' Two of the dogs slunk back to the house, while the third moved round to stand in front of the old man, its docked tail standing erect like an aerial. As Boddice and Boag got down from the car, the dog moved forward a few paces, wrinkled, quivering lips drawn back, baring its teeth in a silent snarl. The old man said nothing. Boddice walked straight up to the dog, hand out, palm upwards. The dog, still showing its teeth, hesitantly advanced a couple of steps to sniff Boddice's hand. Once it had his scent it gave a single bark and trotted back to the old man's side.

Boddice smiled. 'Ah yes,' he said. 'Faithful old Dalglish. Still going strong I see.'

The old man hacked a phlegmy cough from some dark

recess of his lungs. 'Aye,' he said. 'And would have your throat at my word, never fear it.'

'I don't doubt it,' said Boddice. He motioned for the old man to join them. 'How you doing, Jim? Long time, no see, eh?'

The Rastahman sent Dalglish back to the house and walked over to shake Boddice's hand. 'Not bad,' he said. 'Been better, been worse. You know how it is.' He jerked his head back towards the cottage. 'Roof's been leaking these last few weeks, and nobody comes to see me much. You're the first person Ah've seen in a fortnight.' He looked at Boag, seemingly noticing him for the first time. 'You and the boy here, that is,' he said. 'Is this the one you were telling me about?'

Boag shuffled nervously. Boddice and this guy obviously went back a bit, but whether they were old friends or adversaries wasn't exactly clear. Boag struggled to identify the tension between them, and he didn't trust the old man's dismissive attitude towards him.

Aiken stood silently for a moment, his rheumy, red-rimmed eyes narrowing to crusted slits as he scanned Boag's face. Whatever internal debate was going on in his head came to a conclusion. 'Right,' he said. 'The stuff you're looking for will cost you, but I have it. Come with me.' He turned and went round the side of the cottage to a large barn, the roof a patchwork of corrugated iron panels and wooden slats. Aiken ushered them in. The barn was full of old garden and farm implements, rusting and decaying in a forest of weeds which sprang from the muddy floor. At the far end, Aiken opened a door which, to Boag's surprise, led to a set of stairs descending to a small cellar. Aiken pulled an overhead cord, switching on a dim lightbulb. 'Down here,' he said.

Boddice and Boag followed him down the stairs. The walls of the room were lined with metal shelving units stacked with an assortment of boxes and containers. The old man bent down to one of the lower shelves and pulled out a grey

Samsonite box. He undid a padlock on the lid and snapped open the fasteners. He placed the box on the seat of a broken chair and opened the lid. 'This is what you're after, I take it?'

Boddice had grinned and rubbed his hands together. 'Oh yes,' he said. 'Absolutely.'

Boag had looked into the box and needed no explanation of what the long metal cylinders were. They were very familiar indeed.

***

Now, sitting in Kyle's kitchen with everyone staring at him, he knew the answer to Prentice's query would set the cat among the pigeons. Prentice nudged him with his foot. 'Out with it dopey-boy. What's your task in all of this?'

Boag grimaced and looked around the rest of the men. 'Explosives,' he said in a small voice.

'Eh?' said John. 'Did you say…?'

'Explosives,' Boag repeated.

The others exchanged puzzled looks. Prentice went over to the window, muttering under his breath. He leaned his forehead against the pane and spoke, as much to himself as to the men in the room Boag thought. 'That's just brilliant isn't it? We're blindly waltzing into this plot… this heist… Whatever ye want to call it, and Boddice has set this arsehole up to blow the bloody place to Kingdom Come. Christ on crutches, this is a bloody shambles. You realise what will happen to us if we're caught with a… a *bomb?*'

'No, you've got it wrong,' said Boag. 'We're no gonnae blow the place up, it's—'

'Don't tell me, it's to blow the security system, or a safe, or some stupid *Mission Impossible* pile of crap.' Prentice's voice was breaking. 'This is us we're talking about here. *Us!* We don't do this kinda stuff. We're well out our depth here. It's all just…'

'It's not a bomb,' said Boag. 'They aren't big explosives,

just detonators. Low energy, they just—'

'*Detonators?*' said Prentice. 'Well, thank Christ for that. Ah thought it was somethin dangerous, no somethin innocuous like a wee toaty detonator.' Boag didn't miss the sarcasm in Prentice's voice. 'To detonate what?' Prentice asked.

'Nothing,' said Boag. 'We're gonnae use them to start fires.' Before the others could burst in with their protests, he carried on. 'But… only if we have to. It's our safety net. We only use them if things go wrong and we have to get out quick.'

'Get out quick?' said Kyle. 'And how exactly are fires supposed to help us do that?'

'By providing a distraction,' said Boag. 'If things go wrong, if… and it's only if… if we mess up, the alarms will go off, the polis will be there in a couple of minutes at the most. Mob-handed. Boddice has asked me to set up fires here and there throughout the whole shop.' The rest of them stared at each other, incredulous. 'Just wee fires. At strategic points. Ah'll control them remotely by an electronic rig Ah'll set up. *If* the alarms go off, the polis will think it's just a fire. At first anyway. If they suspect anything else, they'll be too busy dealing with the fires to be bothered looking for us.'

'Wait a minute,' said Campbell. 'If the alarms go off, would the best thing to do not be to run like fuck? Ah know that's what Ah'll be doing.'

'Too far,' said Boag. 'Boddice said that where you'll be will be too far to get out before the polis get there. You'll… *we'll*… get caught.'

'No it isn't too far,' said Kyle. 'We've been there. We could make it.' He glanced at Prentice, who nodded. 'With time to spare.'

Boag shrugged. 'Maybe you could. But Boddice doesn't think so, he doesn't want to take that chance. The fires will buy time. Don't bla—'

'—Well said, young Alistair.'

They all turned to see Boddice standing in the doorway.

'You really should spend more time listening out for a chap on the front door,' said Boddice. 'And also make sure that the bloody thing is locked.'

Boag took a deep breath and shrank back into his chair. His heart was thumping in his chest, a small animal trying to punch its way out. He had no idea how long Boddice had been standing there listening, but, if he hadn't interrupted, Boag might just have got his last sentence out – the one where he asked the rest of the team not to blame him if the whole scheme was as fucked up as a whore's fanny on a two-for-one sale offer. Good God, what if…

'So,' said Boddice, cutting off his thoughts. 'I gather from what you've been saying that you've got round to discussing what exactly is going to take place on the big night.' He pulled up a chair and sat at the table. 'And I'm also guessing you've seen the security system for the diamond, am I right?'

Kyle and Prentice exchanged glances.

'Don't worry about it too much,' Boddice went on. 'I have a little something up my sleeve with respect to that particular problem. A wee surprise. In the meantime, I'm sure you'll figure out some way to tackle it on your own.'

'Ah don't like surprises,' said John.

Boddice gave him a cold stare. 'I don't care what you like or don't like,' he said. 'Just you do your bit and you'll be fine, and so will everybody else.'

Prentice spoke up. 'Just exactly what *are* our bits that we're supposed to do? Nobody knows what anybody else is doing. For God's sake, we've just discovered that this wee plook,' he jerked a thumb at Boag, 'is gonnae be walking in with some sort of hi-tech Molotov cocktails in his bag. What other revelations are in the pipeline?'

Boddice nodded gravely. 'You're quite right, Davie,' he said. He walked to the door and opened it a crack, peered out into the shop. 'Okay,' he said, satisfied there was no-one lurking outside. 'The plan. Let's get it sorted.' He laced his fingers together and stretched his hands outwards, cracking his knuckles. Boag winced at the sound. 'Rather than having me spell it all out,' said Boddice, 'you lot can do it. You've heard part of what Boag's going to be doing already, and there'll be more from him later, but let's start with the twins.' He flicked his gaze to Campbell. 'Let's start with the party, shall we?'

Campbell cleared his throat. 'Two parties, actually,' he said. 'The first one is on the night the diamond is unveiled…'

The Model

They were grudging, but they gave Boag credit anyway. He'd spent hours at it, measuring, sawing, gluing, nailing.

Knitting.

Well, not knitting exactly, but certainly indulging in wool-related activities.

They'd gathered round Boag's life-sized model of the Dark Side of the Moon display plinth which he'd set up in the living room of his flat – inspecting, judging, questioning. Boag was handy; not in the good-man-to-have-in-a-street-fight sense of handy, but in the good-at-building-things-from-scraps-of-wood sense. He'd done a very decent job on this, if he said so himself.

'And you're sure this is the right size, the proportions are all correct?' Kyle had asked.

'Ah told you before,' Boag replied, exasperated. 'Ah took everything from the picture you took on your mobile. Scaled it all to Campbell's height.'

***

After the session in the tattoo parlour, when Boddice had set out the details of their tasks, Kyle had gone back to the store on his own. Posing as an excited rubber-necking tourist, an eager beaver desperate to see where the mighty Dark Side of the Moon would be displayed. The perfect excuse to grab a photo of the display plinth on his mobile, made easier, of course, by Campbell being on security in the Bubble that day. A few days later, and it would be the big boys, the Securarama heavies, watching the place, even though the diamond was still a thousand miles and a fortnight away. Anyone whipping out a camera or a mobile phone *then* would have politely, but firmly, been told to shove it the fuck up their arse.

Once they had the picture, Boddice had pulled Boag aside and told him he was 'tasking' him to build a life size model, something to practice on. *Tasking.* Fucking management speak; where had that come from for Christ's sake?

Still, by having Campbell standing to attention beside the plinth in the picture, and by measuring his exact height, Boag could easily work out the relative proportions of the structure – the height, the diameter, the angle of taper as it swept up to the apex holding the single spike on which the diamond would rest. But most importantly, he could calculate the dimensions of the array of lasers surrounding the whole construction.

Boag painstakingly reproduced the whole set-up, using fishing line to suspend the mock-up of the laser grid from the ceiling so that it floated above the plinth at just the right height, and arranging the positions of the 'sensors' on the floor surrounding the base of the plinth. The really tricky bit was replicating the path of the beams; Campbell had told him that each of the lasers was angled such that the beam fell not on the sensor immediately underneath, but on the one four along to the left, clockwise. This gave a slanted pattern of forty-eight beams that Boag reproduced using strands of red wool. There were a further two banks of lasers and sensors running down either side, sending horizontal beams criss-crossing those coming down from above.

More measurements, more foutering about with red wool.

Finally he'd got it completed, brought the others in to see it. All in all, it looked good. It looked impressive. It looked the business.

It looked impenetrable.

***

They stood back, arms folded, chewing bottom lips, stroking chins, biting nails. 'How in the name of fuckdom are we going to get through all that?' asked Kyle. 'Ah mean, it's like a chain-link fence or something. One of they things wee lassies make with bits of string between their fingers…'

'A cat's cradle,' offered John.

'Aye that's the thing,' said Kyle, eyeing John suspiciously. 'There's no way we can grab a pea through that, never mind a diamond the size of whatever.'

'But we can try,' said Prentice, moving to the window and looking out at the street below. 'It's what the big man wants, so we've got to give it a go.'

He crouched in front of the model, his knees popping, and pushed his hand up between the strands of wool, reaching for the apex where the diamond would sit. It was no use. Whatever way he inserted his arm he always pushed the wool away; if this had been the real thing the beams would have been broken, the alarms ringing all hell in their ears.

'Do you want any of us to try?' asked Campbell. 'We might have skinnier arms.'

Prentice shook his head. 'No, it's too tight for even a wean's arms.'

The others crowded round, pushing, jostling, exploring the model from every angle, looking for a way in. John stumbled and caught his sleeve on one of the strands of wool, pulling the laser mock-up out of alignment. The suspended array swung like a drunken puppet.

'Jesus Christ! You're all a bunch of fuds! Get back the lot of you.'

They turned to look at Boag, who pushed past them and moved quickly to stabilise the structure, grabbing the swaying wooden frame and smoothing the oscillations in the strands of wool. 'This isn't some sort of toy, you know,' he said. 'This took me bloody ages, and you lot are acting as if it's just a Lego model.' He caught the look on Prentice's face, but ignored it. 'This is delicate, it's precision-made.'

'Aye we get it,' said Kyle. '*Vorsprung durch Technik* and all that shite.'

Boag's face reddened. 'Aye, you can mock, but you're forgetting Ah built this. Days and days Ah've been at this.' He straightened a cord at the top of the plinth, made an adjustment to the angle of one of the top boards. 'And because of that Ah know it inside and out. Ah know every nook and cranny.' He went into his pocket and brought out a golf ball. He parted the strands of wool and stretched his hand into the centre of the plinth, leaving the golf ball balanced on the little platform on top of the central spike. 'And the thing is…' he gave a weak smile, '… Ah know a way through. Ah know how to get in.'

Prentice cocked an eyebrow. '*You?*' he said. '*You* know how to get in?' He laughed. 'Aye, that'll be right. Ah don't believe you.'

'Wait a minute,' said Kyle, laying a hand on Prentice's shoulder. 'Let's see what he means.' He extended his arm, bowing and motioning towards the model in an exaggerated sweeping gesture. 'Be our guest. Show us.'

Boag went to the corner of the room and picked up a plastic bag. 'A wee trip to B&Q, that's all you need to beat this thing,' he said. From the bag he pulled a long metal contraption with a handle grip at one end and what looked like a pair of crab's claws at the other.

'What the hell's that?' asked John. 'It looks like—'

'A bloody litter-picker,' Prentice finished, laughing. 'You know, the parkies use them, saves them getting their hands dirty when they have to pick up crisp pokes and Buckie bottles and the like.' He shook his head. 'You mean to tell us that you're gonnae crack this hi-tech mega-security system with a five quid piece of shite from a DIY shop?'

Boag chewed his lip. 'Aye,' he said. 'It's all low-tech, DIY crap, but you better believe me… it works.' He held up the litter-picker. 'Ah've modified this a wee bit to make things easier.'

Prentice laughed. 'Easier than what?'

Boag shook his head. 'Did you ever play that game

Operation when you were wee? Remember the game where you have to take out a patient's bones and organs and stuff using a wee pair of tweezers, and if you got it wrong, if you touched the sides of the wee slots then a buzzer went off and you'd killed the patient, lost the game?'

'Was that not a lassie's game?' asked John.

'Or a game for fucking nancy-boy cissies,' growled Prentice.

Boag stared at him. 'Naw, it wasn't, and anyway it doesn't matter who played it, the point is that this is just a bigger version of that game. It's the same principle.' He pushed the others aside and positioned himself in front of the model. 'Watch carefully,' he said.

Boag took the litter-picker and lowered himself onto his haunches. He squinted up through the maze of red fibres and gradually threaded the litter-picker through a tiny gap, a channel through the intersecting strands. He advanced the contraption, slowly moving up and into the depths of the model, all the while avoiding contact with any of the strings. After a few minutes the head of the picker was in front of the golf ball. Boag gently pulled the trigger on the picker's handle and the claws at the end opened. He edged the picker forward the final two centimetres and released the trigger. The claws closed over the golf ball, gripping it between their serrated edges. Boag lifted the ball from the apex of the plinth and began to withdraw the picker, smoothly backing out through the same channel.

'Here, give me a go at that!' Prentice elbowed him out of the way and grabbed the litter-picker from Boag's hands. The golf ball fell from the picker's claws and bounced out from the base of the model, rolling under the settee. Boag fell back on his arse on the floor.

'What did you do that for?' said Boag. 'I nearly had it out there.'

'Aye, we could see that,' Prentice replied. 'But it's best

to leave a job like this to one of the big boys, somebody who knows what they're doing.'

'Ah want a shot as well,' said Kyle. 'We need to see who's going to be the best at this, who's got the steadiest hands.'

Boag looked from Kyle to Prentice, toothy grins of enthusiasm breaking out on their faces. Now that they could see that it was possible they were suddenly such fucking big shot heroes, desperately determined to show that they were the only bastards who would be capable of pulling it off. The pricks. They didn't give a runny shit about the time, the effort, the planning and measuring that he'd put into this. Or the hours he'd spent working out a possible route through the pattern of beams. Oh no, that mattered less than a flea on a dog's arse.

Boag got to his knees and crawled over to retrieve the golf ball from under the sofa. He stood and placed it back on its spot on the plinth. 'On you go, have yourselves a fucking ball.' He turned and left them to it.

***

In the end it turned out Prentice had the steadiest hands; it would have to be him wouldn't it? But there was no doubt, he was the best. He managed to pick the ball out on his first go, and repeated it on every other attempt. No mistakes. No touching the wool. Perfect, in fact. The others (though the twins were never going to be allowed to be involved, that much was clear) were too clumsy, never quite getting the hang of the litter-picker or coming to grips with the technique required; obviously none of them were masters of the good old Operation game. None of them were cissie enough.

Except Prentice, that was.

All Tomorrow's Parties

The Trusdale and Needham bash was in full swing. The entire ground floor of the store had been transformed into one giant party room. It was just after eleven thirty, everyone who was anyone had already arrived, and no-one had been so uncool as to leave early.

The store was mobbed. The invitation list had run to over six hundred bodies, and no-one had passed on the opportunity. Movers and shakers, politicians, celebrities major and minor (a combination of film stars, models, writers, fashion designers, hairdressers and STV sports presenters) and general hangers-on glided and floated around the ground floor sales area, keeping a weather eye open for a networking opportunity, a potential tryst, a chance to score some coke. Designer suits and dresses (little black numbers were the flavour of the night, with maximum exposure of cleavages and butt-cheeks *de rigueur*) competed with each other for attention in the general throng. At the far end of the room a small kitchen had been set up, dispensing Chinese food in little cartons. Sounds of flash-frying were accompanied by clouds of steam and the flaring of yellow and blue flames above the gas stoves as the chefs threw noodles and diced chicken, peppers and onions around the woks. People struggled with chopsticks, attempting to manipulate the hot, succulent food to their mouths.

In another corner a bunch of revellers danced to the house band's easy-sleazy version of Minnie the Moocher, the tuxedoed, Brylcreemed frontman almost fellating the microphone. Searchlights high in the roof vault swept their beams across the crowd below, reflecting off the champagne glasses, earrings and gold necklaces of the women, creating a swirling, glittering galaxy of dazzling lights.

The press had been and gone – an allotted half-hour at the start to snap the arrivals of the great and the good, including

Maggie Trusdale and Jaclyn Needham themselves, who had flown in from New York especially for the event. They posed with studied elegance on one of the upper balconies, all big hair, high heels and scarlet lipstick, their trophy husbands relegated to adorning the wall behind them, as the cameras flashed and journalists jostled.

Of course, there had been other events in various galleries and museums throughout Glasgow as part of the City of Jewellery festival, but they were all small fry; this was the big one, the exhibit everyone had been waiting for. It wasn't just the Scottish press which had turned out, but the London dailies and Sunday supplements, the international style magazines, the glossy, glitzy gossip garbage and the lager-lads' soft-porn comic books were all in attendance, all forced cynicism and trying too hard to be unimpressed.

It was now time to get down to some serious partying. The noise levels ramped up, fuelled by the free bar and the kind of hedonistic atmosphere which only the delusionally self-centred can generate. The dancers in the corner were giving it *hi-di-hi-di-hi-di-hi* and *ho-di-ho-di-ho-di-ho*, arms raised above their heads, punching the air in time to the music. Groups of people congregated around the candle-lit tables, laughing and eating, drinking and flirting.

Campbell stood beside the door to one of the lifts, a spot that offered a good vantage point to scope the comings and goings of the people on the walkway above, queuing to enter the Bubble for the chance to be one of the first to see the famous Dark Side of the Moon. The diamond itself had arrived the day before, the store closed to the public as the specialist Securarama guys took over, all sharp suits, shades and earpieces. The rest of the staff were made to stand to one side as they brought in the small steel box containing the diamond and transported it to the Bubble where they unpacked it with a slow, devotional grace.

Now, with the party shifting up into top gear, an excited

babble erupted as those in the queue stood on tiptoe, or leaned over the handrail of the walkway, trying for a better vantage point to catch even the slightest glimpse of the stone before they were ushered along the connecting glass passageway into the Bubble itself.

A man in a white tuxedo and red bow tie reeled up to Campbell, his eyes focused on a point somewhere over Campbell's left shoulder, a cocktail glass sloshing a blue liquid onto his sleeve.

'Okay, pal?' the man said, his words slurring. Campbell said nothing, staring straight ahead. 'Lisssen…' said the man. 'I rrreally want to have a wee shot at seeing this diamond, eh? Eh?' Campbell remained mute. 'Annnyway…,' the man went on, 'I don't really see why I have to queue up with the rest of the plebs to do that. I was therefore wondering,' he brought out a tenner and stuck it in Campbell's breast pocket, 'if you could see your way to fast-tracking me, so to speak, perhaps let me ride up in a secret lift or something,' the man spread his arms wide, spilling yet more of his drink, '… you must have something like that eh? Eh?'

Campbell turned his attention to the man, gave him a full-toothed smile, turned on his most polished voice. 'I'm so sorry sir,' he said. 'We don't have the facility to cater for your request.'

'Awww, come on,' said the man. 'I know…, I know…, I know there must be special passes and suchlike, Vee-Eye-Pee treatment, eh?' The man brightened, seemingly struck by a brilliant thought. A change of tack. He pulled himself into a full upright posture, straightened his shoulders, stuck out his chest. 'Do you know who I am?' he asked.

Campbell resisted the urge to ask him if he'd lost his memory. 'Of course I do sir,' he said, though, in truth, he didn't have a fucking clue who the hell he was.

'Excellent!' said the man. 'So we understand each other then?'

Campbell failed to see what there was to understand, but

knew that this guy wasn't going to go away until he got what he so obviously thought he deserved. Any attempt to dissuade him could lead to trouble. There was only one thing for it. Campbell flashed his smile again and winked at the man. 'Understand completely sir,' he said, raising his forefinger. 'Please wait one moment and I'll sort this out.' Campbell scanned the room. A short distance away he spied Murray and Malloy, two of the other security officers. He waved them over.

Murray and Malloy were typical security material – heftily built, military moustaches, small, piggy eyes. Campbell and the drunk watched as they marched over to join them. 'My colleagues here will see to your request sir,' Campbell said.

He gave Murray and Malloy a sharp, business-like nod as they came up.

'Hello Orr,' said Malloy.

'Mr Murray, Mr Malloy, this gentleman has asked for some preferential treatment with respect to the Dark Side of the Moon. I think we should be able to accommodate him.' Murray and Malloy turned to the man and each gave a curt bow of the head. 'I wonder,' Campbell went on, 'if you could make sure to be discreet and take the gentleman to the level zero concourse?' Campbell held out his arm, gesturing for the man to follow his two escorts.

The man beamed at Campbell and swayed slightly as he stepped between the two security guards. 'Well, thank you,' he said. 'Thank you very much.'

'Oh, and sir,' Campbell said fishing the tenner from his breast pocket. 'There's absolutely no need for this. We're happy to be of assistance.' He handed the money back to the man who looked up at Malloy towering above him on his right and then Murray on his left. 'Onwards men,' he said. 'And thank you again,' he called over his shoulder to Campbell.

Campbell gave a small smile in return. You won't be thanking me when you find out the level zero concourse is the fucking pavement, he thought.

★★★

Campbell had taken some time to get used to his and John's alter ego – Johnny Orr. They'd decided on sticking with John's first name, mainly because Campbell didn't feel John could be trusted to answer to anything else. If the whole double-act thing was going to work, they had to be secure in the knowledge they wouldn't blow it by getting their name wrong. Campbell remembered the scene in *The Great Escape*, where poor old Gordon Jackson is tricked into answering the German guy in English just as he's about to get on the bus to Switzerland. He could envisage John falling for some idiotic mistake like that. Better to leave nothing to chance and avoid any risk of John forgetting who he was supposed to be. But Campbell had almost flunked the test himself in those first couple of days. He'd find himself being addressed as 'Johnny' and returning a blank stare to whoever was talking to him before cottoning on he should be saying or doing something in response.

It all settled down after a week. He and John would turn up to work on alternate days, just as planned, clocking in, sharing a joke or two with the other guys in the security office, patrolling the store, noting the routines and patterns of the different shifts. They would feed back to the other at night, filling in the details of what had happened that day, who had been late, any incidents on the shop floor and, more importantly, all the trivial chit-chat that had passed between the security guys that day. Conversations ranged from the usual football stuff, to politics, to the most recent example of hot tottie spotted in the store. All inconsequential drivel, but important for Campbell and John to maintain a sense of continuity when they took their alternate turns on the job. For the most part it worked, and any slip-ups were forgotten or dismissed as the effects of a shitey memory. John and Campbell quickly built up a familiarity with the ins and outs of the job and none of their workmates suspected anything.

The only problem was Miss McKinnon. She was the head of store security services – a manager rather than a hands-on supervisor – all power-dressed super efficiency. She had a reputation as a ball-breaker; no sufferer of fools or slackers. 'Johnny' had already had a few run-ins with her – stupid, petty instances: ties not done up properly, missing scheduled stops on the 'tour of duty' around the store, taking too long on a lunch break.

Campbell wasn't entirely sure if she suspected anything, but she had initially questioned how 'Johnny' got the job in the first place. She didn't recall any unfilled position coming up for interview. Campbell had fobbed her off with the stock answer Boddice had fed him: that he was employed by the agency, that they'd had a request for an extra body in the run-up to the exhibition, and he was it. Campbell felt uneasy giving this answer. He had no idea who Boddice's insider was, the one who'd arranged for 'Johnny' to get the job. Christ, McKinnon was supposed to be the head of security, surely she would have been kept informed of something like that? She seemed satisfied with his answer though, which was a relief. He thanked God the question hadn't arisen when John had been on duty. She might not have been so willing to believe such a story if it had come out as a rambling, stuttering string of unrelated facts and figures, finally getting round to the point of the question five minutes later.

Campbell could see her now, walking towards him, skilfully manoeuvring across the crowded floor, avoiding contact with any of the jostling, heaving mass of people. She looked different out of her normal business suit. She had avoided the ubiquitous black and was wearing a long, red dress, a little badge identifying her as one of the store staff and a walkie-talkie clipped to the opening of her handbag. Campbell guessed she was between thirty and thirty-five, neat short hair, just the right amount of make-up. She had certainly made an effort tonight, appearing as glamorous and chic as any of the so-called celebrities on the invitation list. It was all part of the store image of course – look, even our on-duty staff are as hip and trendy as our customers, *that's* the kind of shop we are.

She walked over and stood at his side surveying the crowd, biting her bottom lip in concentration as she scanned the room and upper galleries for any sign of anything untoward. She kept her eyes on the assorted glitterati as she spoke to him. 'I saw how you handled that guy, Orr,' she said.

'Oh aye?' he replied. He wondered what was coming.

'Yes,' she said. 'It was well done. Very judicious.' She turned to look at him. 'You're not as daft as you appear are you? Or as you act sometimes.'

Campbell stiffened. 'What do you mean?'

She brought out a pocket mirror, checked her lipstick. 'Oh, nothing really,' she said. 'Just that occasionally you can seem… what's the word…? Distracted. Not quite connected to planet Earth.'

'Well, I…'

'And at other times, like just now, you're absolutely on top of the situation.' She dabbed the corner of her mouth and put the mirror back in her handbag. 'That little incident had the potential to become just a tad unpleasant. Of course, you probably wouldn't know, but he's Jim Burns – writes Juicy Jim's column in the Evening Echo. A man who must have had major cosmetic surgery to disguise the rather large penis that usually grows out of his forehead.'

Campbell laughed. 'He was just a wee bit drunk that's all. But a dickhead nevertheless, Ah suppose.'

'Yes, a wee bit drunk now, but nasty drunk later on. Nevertheless, you sorted it out without it becoming messy. Well done.'

'No problem,' said Campbell.

'Okay,' she said. 'Just try to keep up that standard instead of dicking around as you sometimes do. I could be forgiven for thinking you've got some sort of split personality.'

Campbell felt his stomach muscles tighten. He said nothing.

'Anyway,' she said. 'Must get going, see what's happening upstairs. Don't want it getting too crowded up there.'

McKinnon checked her watch, adjusted her earrings and headed back out into the crowd, smiling and nodding to various punters.

Campbell watched her thread her way through the masses. Halfway across the floor, she was stopped by Mr Tennant, the store's Director of Operations, who exchanged some words with her and motioned her to a group of four or five men in full evening suits clutching glasses of no-doubt-expensive malt whisky. Campbell didn't recognise any of them, but they looked like the real thing; *Vee-Eye-Pees*, as the dear departed Jim Burns might have said. She did some gladhanding, smiling politely as she listened to what the men were saying. After a few moments, she guided the group over to a lift in the corner. She inserted a key in the lock beside the lift and the doors slid open. She shepherded the group inside and Campbell caught a last glimpse of her over a trail of streamers from a party-popper just as the doors closed.

Now, that's unusual, he thought. Where was that little tour party heading? There had been nothing about this in any of the security briefings. Campbell knew that particular lift was the private transport direct to the manager's office. Only those and such as those were allowed up there. What was going on?

The thought was dislodged from his mind by the sound of breaking glass to his left. Some stupid old cow had stumbled over a display case and had been sent sprawling onto a table full of empties. He hurried over to help her.

When he returned to his station and looked over the heads of the crowd to the lift, he played back the scene in his head. Just as the doors had closed, he could have sworn that McKinnon turned her head and stared directly at him, fixing him in her mind, holding his image till the closing doors cut him off. The more he reviewed it, the more certain he became.

She was clocking him.

He felt a shiver ripple through his belly. Could she possibly know? Did she suspect anything?

It wasn't till she walked in on the whole team in the Bubble exactly a week later that he got his answer.

Leggett:
Unfinished Sympathy

They thought they were all so fucking smart. Thought they had everything tied up. Leggett sniggered.

They knew bugger all. Oh yes, they were all a bunch of arseholes. So full of themselves, the smug, cocky bastards. He had seen the looks they gave him as Boddice humbled him on the street outside the Palace: the hard, cold stares, the surprised confusion, the pity.

No, not the pity. There had been none of that. They had all been glad. Leggett could sense it. They had been dancing inside, whooping it up at his demise, his exit from their cosy little team.

Wankers. They didn't know who they were dealing with.

As they drove away into the night he had felt a cool, calculated serenity descend on him, despite the hot tears that ran down his face. When Kyle and Prentice came round the next day to collect the money *(his fucking hard-won earnings!)* Leggett had been calmness personified. He didn't flinch when Prentice laughed in his face, when Kyle shook his head at him, called him 'sonny'. No, he sucked it up, quietly handed over the money and closed the door in their faces.

They suspected nothing.

They thought they had won. The idiots. They still thought they had the upper hand. But Leggett knew they had dismissed him altogether. Which was their big mistake. Oh yes, they had underestimated him.

Big time.

And Boddice, with his carefully stage-managed humiliation, his big speech, setting an example to the rest: who the fuck did he think he was? Making out he was paying back a favour by being so kind as not to shoot Leggett dead. *Shoot him dead!* The prick; Boddice should be paying him to *stay* in the fucking team, not looking to bump him off. As far as Leggett was concerned, Boddice's debt to him was far from repaid. The big bastard had a short memory.

Leggett's entry to Boddice's little group had been a classic case of right-time-right-place, back in the days when Hutchison had been Boddice's man on the street; a grey, almost skeletal figure who lurked outside the pubs and bookies, endlessly shifty, one eye on the lookout for the polis, the other scanning the street for the next likely customer.

Leggett had been vaguely aware of the drug dealing that had been taking place in the toilets of the local pub, but had steered clear of actually approaching Hutchison himself, knowing him to be one of Boddice's goons and so to be avoided unless you were intending buying something.

That was until one Friday night, waiting for the last bus home from the pub.

It was late summer and there was still the last shimmering of light in the sky, aqua green on the horizon fading to deeper purple overhead, one bright star winking in the heat rising from the city. Further up the street, a gang of five or six neds was fooling around with a plastic picnic table nicked from someone's back garden. Leggett prayed for the bus to hurry up before they got to the bus stop. He was roughly the same age as them and he could probably get away without any confrontation, but if they were sufficiently fuelled up on Buckfast or MD 20/20 then there was always the risk they would give him a kicking. Just for laughs.

A scuffing sound across the street caused him to turn his head. He recognised Hutchison lurching unsteadily from lamppost to lamppost, outstretched arms waving in mid-air, seeking purchase on some imaginary support. Too much to drink, Leggett supposed. He watched Hutchison fall to his knees and attempt to get back up. When he finally got moving again, Hutchison stumbled into the gutter, skinning the heels of his hands and letting a small groan escape from his mouth.

He got to his feet slowly and stood with his hands on his knees, swaying. He pitched forward again, his legs buckling under him, and he fell heavily onto the pavement, his head hanging off the edge of the kerb. He didn't get up.

Leggett looked up the street. The neds had disappeared up some close or other and there was no-one else about. He crossed the road to where Hutchison was lying and crouched beside him.

Hutchison's eyes were closed and a thin layer of grit from the pavement crusted the side of his face. Leggett stood and prodded him with his foot. There was no reaction. He tried again, a bit harder. Still nothing.

He knelt and turned Hutchison onto his back, his head making a hollow clonking sound as it bumped against the kerb. There was no reaction.

Leggett saw an opportunity. He checked no-one was coming and unbuttoned Hutchison's coat. A deep red stain leached out from a small nick on Hutchison's polo shirt, a poppy blooming on the white fabric. Leggett examined the coat and saw a ragged gash at the same spot on the front.

Leggett's heart was racing. 'Weehoo...' he whispered. Man, oh man, some bastard had knifed him. Who had the balls to do that to one of Boddice's men? Leggett lifted Hutchison's limp form by the lapels of his coat and let him drop back to the pavement. The head whacked hard onto the ground, but Hutchison didn't so much as flutter an eyelid.

He was gone.

Leggett scanned the street again. A light blinked off in one of the tenement windows and a warm wind ruffled the pages of an old newspaper in the bin by the bus stop, but there was no other sign of activity. He knew he had to act quickly now. If he were spotted crouching over Hutchison's body he would have a hard job explaining that the body had fuck-all to do with him.

He fumbled in the inside pocket of Hutchison's coat, the

smooth satin of the lining soft and cool against his fingers. He found what he was looking for – a package wrapped in a Kingsmill bread bag. He'd seen Hutchison pull this very bag from the depths of his coat many times in the pub, knew what it contained.

He stuffed the packet under his shirt and stood, ready to sprint down the street, get himself to hell away from here. But something held him back, pulled him with an irresistible magnetism to the lifeless figure lying on the pavement. Leggett knew he was taking a risk, that he might be seen at any second.

He knelt again beside Hutchison, bent close and let his gaze wander over Hutchison's face, taking in the tiny details – the day's growth of stubble, the little pits and pockmarks around his nose, the wayward eyebrow hairs, the creases on his forehead. He leaned closer, brought his mouth to within a centimetre of Hutchison's, and breathed in. He got a faint taste of cigarette smoke, and a sweeter whiff of alcohol underlying that. Nothing more. There was no sudden revelation, no secret whisper of the nature of death, only the stale halitotic remnants of Hutchison's last breath.

A dog barked in one of the close mouths across the street, and Leggett sprang to his feet. For a moment he felt dizzy, the street lights seeming to flicker and flare, and a low buzz thrummed in his ears. Stood up too quickly, he thought, although some part of him thrilled at the possibility that maybe he really had the essence of the dead coursing through his arteries, that he had absorbed some part of Hutchison's departing spirit.

A small titter began to bubble to the back of his throat and he quickly stifled it. Wiping his mouth on the back of his hand, he walked quickly across the street, slinking through one of the close mouths to the back green, where he navigated through flapping, fluttering sheets to a wall that led to an alleyway behind the tenements. He climbed the wall, jumped into the deserted lane and disappeared into the night.

Back home, he checked the contents of Hutchison's Kingsmill bag and smiled. There must have been a couple of grand's worth of coke wrapped in little cling-film packets in the bag. They were his for the taking, for the selling on. But an insistent voice in his head told him to wait. Bide his time.

He gave it three weeks.

There had been a brief flurry of police activity investigating Hutchison's stabbing, but this soon faded away as the cops lost interest and life returned to normal. It was then that Boddice's goons began to reappear on the scene. Leggett clocked one of them – Kyle as it turned out – a sullen figure, hanging around the pub and outside the bookies, taking money from local neds and junkies and passing on the usual wee packets, re-establishing Boddice's control.

Leggett waited till there was a lull in the number of folk indulging in their own form of retail-therapy and sidled up to Kyle, let him know he had something which might be of interest to Mr Boddice. Kyle had stared at him with practised do-I-give-a-shit impassiveness. When he dropped his little bombshell of where and how he had found it, Leggett was gratified to see Kyle's composure falter, his attitude changing to one of cautious interest.

After that, it all moved quickly. Leggett explained that he'd taken the gear from Hutchison's coat to prevent it being found by the rozzers and that he was simply handing it back to its rightful owner. Kyle eyed him suspiciously, but called Boddice on the mobile anyway. Within the hour Boddice came round personally to collect the goods, oozing charm and goodwill, giving it all sorts of crap about liking the cut of Leggett's jib and doling out plenty of backslaps. Of course, Leggett fell for it all, and had practically pissed himself when Boddice suggested coming on board, explaining how he could use someone with Leggett's obvious talents, how Leggett would make an ideal replacement for the late, lamented and sorely missed Mr Hutchison.

One of Boddice's famous impulses, Leggett later learned. A whim to be indulged and humoured. None of the others were consulted on his joining the team, which put their noses well out of joint.

Tough on them, Leggett thought; dry your eyes and deal with it.

Months passed before Leggett discovered the true value of what he'd handed back to Boddice – not one or two grand, but *seventeen* big boys. And what had he got in return? A shitty dead-end job dealing smack in deepest Cardenhall, the arse-crack of Glasgow.

That was no return for what he'd done for Boddice. Boddice owed him. Owed him big.

True, he'd had a chance at a couple of the bigger plans Boddice hatched from time to time and, true, some things hadn't always gone as predicted, but that wasn't his fault. If the others had just trusted him a bit more, shown him more respect, everything would have been okay. But no, they just didn't give a fuck about him, couldn't see what he was *really* capable of, how far he was willing to go.

Oh, but they would know now alrighty. He'd been sneaking. He'd been watching.

Watching closely.

And now they were going to pay.

All of them.

The fuckers.

PART 4: ON THE DARK SIDE

Party Fears Two

For all that it belonged to such an upmarket, style-conscious store, the rear loading bay of Trusdale and Needham was just as messy as that of any other shop in Glasgow. There seemed to be an unwritten rule that such places had to be littered with cardboard boxes in various stages of rain-soaked decomposition. Crates and pallets piled in untidy towers. A plastic tarpaulin caught on a splinter or a nail, flapping in the dark like a trapped pterodactyl. As an additional requirement, the driveways and ramps must be covered in oil stains, with the smell of diesel hanging in the air in an almost tangible smirr. Tonight, it was no different.

Campbell led Prentice, Kyle and Boag down the short lane that ran from Wellington Street to the loading bays. Each wore a small rucksack, carrying the tools and accoutrements they would need for the night's work.

The yellow glare from the sodium lamps threw shapeless shadows along the walls and into the corners of the bay, and the stark fluorescents from the security office window shone a bleak light into the alley. Campbell and the others moved around a container trailer and slunk behind a hopper bin, careful to keep out of sight of the security office. The stench of rotting food filled their nostrils.

'Okay, wait here,' whispered Campbell.

'Here?' said Prentice. 'It bloody stinks, man.'

Campbell gritted his teeth. It felt odd to be in charge. Fuck, more than that, it was all the way past odd, round the corner and down the street to bizarro. This was Prentice he was dealing with here, ordering around. Good Christ. 'Look,' he said. 'Just for a couple of minutes, okay? This is the best spot, believe me. And Prentice, keep your... keep your voice down, alright?'

Prentice gave him a long, cool stare. Kyle reached out

and touched him on the arm, shook him by the sleeve. Boag shuffled his feet in the background, eyes like clocks. Campbell, his heart racing, stood his ground, forced himself to stare back. Prentice blinked a few times and sighed. 'Just hurry the fuck up then,' he said.

Campbell licked his lips. 'Right,' he said. 'Wait here while Ah go in and see who's on duty in the office. Give me a couple of minutes and Ah'll send him out to you. Just make sure you're ready for him and, remember, don't rough him up. This one at least has got to be unharmed.' He scanned their faces. 'Got it?'

Kyle and Boag nodded, while Prentice looked away. 'Aye, we'll just lurk here in the dark till ye're ready,' he said. 'We're good at that. Lurking.'

Campbell took three big breaths and walked out into the loading bay.

This was it.

The point of no return.

***

Got to give them credit, John thought. Trusdale and Needham really did buy into the whole we're-all-equals-here thing. Treat the staff as partners, not employees; make sure everyone worked together in harmony; keep everyone happy and content in their job. At least that was the theory; the image that let the corporate suits sleep a little easier at night. We're all equal in the great Trusdale and Needham empire; we're all just working towards the same retail goal of excellence and quality. Yes, except that not everyone was on a hundred grand a year or more for their valued and committed contribution to the company. Not by a long way.

Still, their generosity did extend to this party. It couldn't have been cheap to hire the Hilton grand ballroom for the night, provide a free meal and, more importantly, a free bar, for the whole staff. Plus, a chance for a wee dance and a spot of karaoke later on. Not many companies would stretch that far for a celebration of some one-off event that was only going to last a month. True, there was no invite to the big celebrity bash the week before but, credit where credit's due, Trusdale and Needham were pushing the boat out for the staff, no doubt about that.

Everyone was having a good time. John had found a seat at a table with a bunch of whooping, hollering sales staff from the womenswear floor and a few of the guys from the sports department. The normally demure, genteel girls from Womenswear – Marie, Gayle, Eileen and Christine – usually the epitome of sweet, deferential efficiency, turned out to be a gang of foul-mouthed, filthy-joke-telling wild things, tanked up on cava and Red Bull, Southern Comfort and Breezers, making a play for any guy who happened to walk past the table. The guys from Sports looked uncomfortable in their suits, more accustomed to the tight white T-shirts and trackies that was their usual uniform. Bottles of Stella and Beck's were lined up on the table in front of them, like a small army awaiting inspection.

One of the girls was telling a story about a customer who thought a push-up bra was a sports accessory that kept her boobs out of the way when she was doing her press-up gym exercises. 'Aye, and she needed it too,' she was saying. 'She was *huge*. Tits like a dead heat in a Zeppelin race!'

John laughed along with the rest of them, but scanned the room out the corner of his eye, checking that everyone seemed calm and relaxed, no-one rushing off to answer an urgent call from the store. He caught sight of the top table, the senior management and their various partners grinning and bearing the horror of mixing with the plebs and their ideas of what constituted having a good time. Just a bit different from the glitz and glamour of the previous week. Still, it had to be endured. All for the sake of corporate equality. The thought made John laugh all the harder. He loosened his tie and took another sip from his coke. This had the possibility of turning into not too bad a night.

Not too bad at all.

★★★

Campbell opened the door and walked into the security office. It was Pat Murray who was on duty. He looked up in surprise as Campbell came in.

'What the hell are you doing here?' he asked, pushing his cap back from his head. 'Should you not be up at that party? Having a high auld time to yourself?'

Campbell shook his head. 'Naw,' he said. 'Couldn't be arsed. Ah don't like they kinda things. Too busy, too many drunks for my liking.'

Murray looked at him in disbelief. 'What? You mean to say you could've been sat here instead of me?' he said. 'Ah was desperate to get a ticket for that do. Just my luck Ah missed out on the ballot and ended up having to work tonight.'

'Aye, but ye get the vouchers for a night away at a hotel for you and the wife as compensation, do ye not?' said Campbell.

Murray raised an eyebrow. 'Ah'd much rather be partying the night away at the Hilton, chatting up they nice perfume-counter lassies, than sitting with the wife all through a meal at some hotel in the back of beyond.' He shook his head. 'Christ, if only ye'd told me, we coulda done a swap.'

Campbell nodded. 'Ah know,' he said. 'Sorry, mate.'

Murray looked him up and down. 'You still haven't answered my question yet,' he said.

'What's that?' said Campbell.

'What brings you here at this time of night when you're not supposed to be working?'

'Oh that,' said Campbell. 'Nothing really, was just passing, thought Ah'd pop my head round the door.'

Murray looked unconvinced. Campbell had to get him

outside. This little exchange had gone on too long.

'Listen,' said Campbell. 'You've got to get a look at this. You'll never guess what Ah saw on the way in, just out there in the loading bay.'

'What was it?' asked Murray.

'You'll never believe it,' said Campbell. 'There's an auld jakey trying to get some meat off a dead dug.'

'You're joking,' said Murray. He keyed up the CCTV cameras for the rear entrance, brought the images onto the main monitors on the security desk. 'Ah can't see anything,' he said.

Campbell moved closer to look over Murray's shoulder. There were three cameras trained on the loading bay. He could see the hopper bin where the others were hiding, but thankfully they remained out of view. 'No,' he said. 'Ye can't see it from here. Ye'll need to go out to have a look.' He put his hand on Murray's shoulder, guided him to the door. 'You've gotta see this for yourself, man. The depths some folk'll sink to.'

Murray looked at him, still a bit unsure.

'On ye go,' said Campbell. 'Ah'll look after the station while ye check it out. In fact, ye'd be as well to hunt the auld bastard, tell him to get lost.'

'Eating a dead dog, eh? For fuck's sake.' Murray indicated the security station. 'You'll look after this while Ah'm out there?'

'No problem,' said Campbell, ushering him towards the door. He returned to the security station and watched on the monitors as the dark figure of Murray opened the outer rear door and crossed to one of the loading bay ramps where the second camera picked him up, his image walking down towards the hopper bin. Campbell turned his attention to the view from the third camera and watched the silent scuffle as the three figures emerged from the shadows behind the bin and jumped Murray, bundling him to the ground and pulling a dark sack over his head. The struggle was short and intense –

Murray put up a good fight, but, in the end, the three of them were too much for him.

So far, so good, thought Campbell. Murray had seen no-one but him. And who was going to believe him when he later told the story it had been Campbell – or rather Orr – who had set him up?

And how could that be the case when Orr was having such a good time at the party?

***

A certain degree of leglessness was now the common state of most of the Trusdale and Needham workforce. There was a lot of shouting, a few glasses had been knocked over, and some food spilled on the floor. The Hilton staff, for the moment at least, were turning a blind eye. There had been no major damage, and John presumed T&N had come to some arrangement with the hotel to cover any substantial losses as a result of overexuberance on the part of the revellers.

Earlier, one of the high-heid-yins at the top table had got up on his hind legs to make a speech about the true spirit of Trusdale and Needham, the soaring, magisterial ethos which informed and encompassed the company mission statement and how this was trickled down to even the lowliest operative (the idiot had actually used those words). The crowd at the janitors' and cleaners' tables lifted their glasses in a mock toast at this, and one voice, raised a little too high for discretion, urged the speaker to 'Get away, and lie in yer ain pish!'

The management suit appeared to take heed of this exhortation, since he quickly mumbled something about having an enjoyable time for the rest of the evening and sat down in a red-faced fluster to a polite ripple of applause, which turned into a raucous cheer as the band burst into Kool and the Gang's *Celebrate*. The crowd rushed the dance floor, clapping in time to the music and responding to the band's request to celebrate good times with the obligatory *WooWoo!* John tapped his finger against his glass in time to the music. In the space of a few seconds, the party had gone from Dullsville, Arizona to fucking New York, New York.

John had taken up a position at the bar. He was ordering vodkas with a bottle of coke, but tipped the vodka onto the carpet when no-one was looking, topping up his glass with the coke instead. He made sure he kept up the same drunken behaviour as the rest of the crowd, but it was all an act. He couldn't afford to get steaming on a night like this. He was going to need all his wits about him, later, when things would kick off in earnest.

He spied McKinnon talking and laughing with some of the admin staff at one of the tables near the front of the room. That was a good sign. She was entering into the spirit of things, though not so much that she would get up and dance when someone tried to drag her onto the floor. At least she was busy, distracted, not thinking for a minute there might be four guys prowling the store, inching their way to the most expensive diamond in the world.

John checked his watch. Ten forty-two. It wouldn't be long now till he performed his little party piece.

★★★

Kyle and Prentice dragged the hooded Murray into the security office. Murray struggled a bit, kicking out and squirming as they pinned him to the floor.

'Stay at fucking peace,' said Kyle. 'Or you're gonnae regret it.' He brought out an iron bar from his rucksack, tapped it against the side of Murray's head. 'Feel that?' Kyle asked. A muffled acknowledgement came from inside the sack. 'Good,' said Kyle. 'Cos if you create anything here pal, this is coming down on yer skull big time.' To reinforce his point he rested the bar against Murray's forehead. Murray relaxed, went limp on the floor. Kyle knelt beside him. 'Now, you see that's the sort of co-operation that will have you going home to the wife and weans in one piece, with a good story to tell the lads in the pub, instead of waking up in the Royal Infirmary not able to feel yer legs.'

Kyle signalled to Prentice, who came over with a plastic cable tie which he used to bind Murray's hands and legs. He took a cord from his pocket and gagged Murray through the folds of the sack.

'Can you breathe in there?' asked Kyle.

'Fuck him if he can't,' said Prentice.

Kyle ignored him. 'Just nod your head if you're okay,' he said.

Murray gave a muffled grunt, but nodded anyway.

Prentice grabbed Murray by the wrists and dragged him into the corner of the room, throwing him against a set of filing cabinets. He turned to Campbell. 'Right,' he said. 'What next?'

Campbell rummaged in his rucksack and brought out a large horseshoe magnet which he placed on the desk in front of the security monitors. 'We'll need this in a minute,' he said. 'But first, there are three other security boys on duty, patrolling the store. We need to take care of them.' He flicked a couple of switches on the security console on the desk and spoke into the store intercom, deepening his voice to make it sound more like Murray. 'Security base room to Patrol. This is Pat here.' Prentice went over and placed a foot on Murray's chest, preventing him from making a sound. 'Hey guys,' said Campbell into the mic. 'Got a wee bit of a situation down here. Couple of neds fannying about in the loading bay. Wonder if you could come down, give us a wee hand?' There were a few seconds of static and then three replies clicked through in quick succession. They were on their way.

As they were arriving at different times from various parts of the store it was an easy task to pick them off one by one as they came through the door of the security office. Prentice and Kyle worked quickly – lunging from behind the door, a sharp thump with the iron bar to the base of the skull, and they dropped as if their plug had been pulled. Boag hauled them into the corner beside Murray and tied and gagged them, covered their heads with a sack. Campbell roped the four men together and secured them to a pillar beside the filing cabinets. With the exception of Murray they were going to be out of it for a long time. Campbell hoped they would suffer no lasting injuries; he'd worked with these guys, shared a joke or two, discussed the football, had a laugh. They were ordinary, honest blokes trying to scrape a living.

'What's the magnet for?' asked Boag.

Campbell took the magnet from the desk and opened a cabinet at the rear of the office. Inside was a bank of computer monitors with an array of black boxes with blinking red and green lights set below. Campbell slowly passed the magnet over each of the black boxes. He turned to see the others looking at him quizzically. 'CCTV,' he said. 'All the images are stored and recorded on hard drives inside these gizmos. Magnet erases the whole shebang, fucks them up goodstyle. There's no way they'll be able to extract anythin from these now.'

'Are ye sure?' asked Prentice. 'Ah don't want some tiny wee flickering image of me to be left in there somewhere, just because your magnet didn't work right.'

'Don't worry,' said Campbell. 'Watch.' He drew the magnet over one of the computer monitors. The image distorted and fragmented, the pixels drawn towards the powerful field generated by the magnet, finally freezing in a jumbled, multi-coloured mosaic, a soft fizzing sound coming from the screen. 'See?' said Campbell. 'That's just the effect on the screen. The hard drives themselves are completely fried by this sort of thing.'

Prentice grunted, and took the magnet from Campbell. He swung it down onto the disc drives, smashing the front panels and shattering the electronics inside. 'There,' he said. 'Now Ah believe ye.'

★★★

The gate had been left open. Again. Boddice wondered why the hell he'd spent five grand on a security system if Shirley wasn't going to bother her stupid arse to close the bloody gate to the driveway.

He swung the Lexus through the entrance, sweeping up the monobloc drive towards the house. The living room lights were on and a solitary candle burned in the window of one of the bedrooms. Shirley was probably up there, doing whatever it was she did when she locked him out of the bedroom.

For almost a year now, he hadn't been able to satisfy her. Shirley had always been insatiable (*Shag-me-Shirley* they called her at school), but now the problem was he couldn't even *begin* to satisfy her. His dick, for whatever reason – physiological, mental, anatomical – refused to do the business. It wasn't tiredness, or lack of desire, or even lack of lust if it came to that. Christ, he still wanted it, was desperate for it – no problems there. It was just the mechanics of the thing or, more accurately, the hydraulics.

It just wouldn't stand up.

Of course, it drove Shirley mad. She had tried everything to get him going – the sex games, the kinky stuff, the role play, the sensual massage. Ordinarily he'd have been front of the queue for stuff like that, enthusiastic as a spaniel. But it simply wasn't happening. Shirley had even left some Viagra for him on the breakfast table one morning, a mocking note – *Try these lover* – sitting beside them. The bitch.

He did try them anyway. Nothing.

Eventually, Shirley had taken matters into her own hands, so to speak. Locking herself in the bedroom, turning to artificial means to get her jollies, and Boddice would sometimes stand in the hallway outside listening to the quiet buzz and soft moans coming from her room. He even suspected she might have been seeing someone else – God help her (and lover-boy!) if that ever turned out to be true.

In the end, Boddice decided it must be psychological – a vicious circle kind of thing. Perhaps the more he thought about it the worse it became. The simple fact of dwelling on the issue was what was causing it to occur in the first place. Yes, that was it. The more he considered this, the more he became convinced it was true. Amateur psychology to the rescue.

He needed a distraction, some diversion that would take his mind of the Shirley Problem. And what more of a distraction could there be than his Plan, which, by his reckoning, should now be in full swing at Trusdale and Needham.

He unlocked the front door, kicked off his shoes and went through to the living room to pour himself a large malt. He settled onto the sofa and thought of what was going on, right now, at the store.

He allowed himself a smile. If – no, when – it all came off, his life was going to change for ever. He would get his mojo back.

And Shirley could go fuck herself.

Literally.

***

John made his way to the stage, taking care to stumble on the last few steps, almost sprawling his full length but recovering at the last instant. A roar of laughter went up from the dance floor. Someone shouted, 'Too many fingers of the old fire-water there, pal!' John smiled inwardly as he stood at the microphone and gave an exaggerated salute to the crowd. He turned to the band, swaying slightly and blinking slowly.

'You sure you're up for this?' asked the band leader. 'This isn't the easiest song to sing you know.'

John wondered why that was now a consideration. Since the karaoke section of the party had started there had been a string of screechers and wailers murdering everything from *Like a Prayer*, through *Angels*, to *A Hard Day's Night*.

The idea was simple. The band leader had passed a sheet of song titles around the tables during the meal, and if you felt like making an arse of yourself in front of everyone all you had to do was print your name beside the song you wanted to sing. Each volunteer was then called to the stage to do their turn. John saw it as a perfect opportunity. If ever there was a way to start drawing attention to himself, this was it. He had scanned the list of songs and this one had jumped out at him.

His party piece.

They were going to love this.

John rubbed his hands and smiled at the band leader. 'No problem,' he said. 'Ah'll be just fine.'

He turned back to the crowd and started clapping his hands above his head, urging everyone to join in. Soon, there was a forest of waving, clapping hands raised above the bobbing heads and smiling faces. John started moving across the stage, dancing and strutting in time to the rhythm of the handclaps. It was bloody brilliant! He was glad he was sober, could take it all in. He shuffled back to the microphone stand and turned to the band. This was something he'd always wanted to do. 'Hit it boys!' he shouted.

The brass section came crashing in, stabbing out high, pulsing bursts while the drums followed with a sledgehammered double beat. Whoops and yells went up from the crowd.

John grabbed the mic from the stand and dropped to one knee. He brought the mic up to his mouth and began to sing.

Jailhouse Rock.

Man, he'd waited years to do this.

***

Campbell was leading the way from the security office through to the main shop floor. They passed through dim, grey corridors, a far cry from the classy white surfaces, the mirrors and the glass of the public side of the store. This was the utilitarian, behind-the-scenes innards of the building, bland and gloomy, unpainted walls and bare concrete floors.

At last they came to a chrome double door. 'Right,' said Campbell. 'This is us, the ground floor area is through there.' He looked at the others. Again he had that feeling of unreality, of plain weirdness, that he was ostensibly in charge at this point. Kyle and Prentice were waiting for *his* instructions. Boag still kept to the back, unwilling to make any fuss.

But this was where Boag's role started.

Campbell signalled for him to come forward. 'This door,' he said. 'If we run into problems through there, if things start to go tits up and the alarms go off, this is where the polis will come through. So, here is where the first fire will have to be. They'll have to turn back. It'll give us more time to get out.'

Boag nodded. 'Ah know,' he said. 'Ye don't need to explain it to me.'

Campbell raised an eyebrow. 'Okay,' he said. 'And you're sure where to set the rest?'

Boag tutted. 'Aye,' he said. 'The main entrance, the two side entrances and the three main fire exits.'

'Just make sure ye leave us a clear path to the second-floor fire escape at the back,' said Kyle. 'If you get us trapped in here Ah'll fuckin kill ye, understand?'

Boag took two steps back. 'Don't worry,' he said. 'Ah know what Ah'm doing.' He took off his rucksack, laid it on the floor. 'Ah just hope the rest of youse can say the same.'

'Hey, ya wee shite-licker,' said Prentice moving towards him. 'Ah don't like the tone of yer—'

'Leave it!' said Campbell. He tapped a finger to the side of his head. 'Job in hand, remember? Let's concentrate.'

Prentice glowered at him, his jaw muscles working. He looked from Campbell to Boag and back again. 'Ah can hardly believe this,' he said, shaking his head. 'Okay, let's bloody well do it.' He walked to the door and held out his hand to push it open.

'Wait!' shouted Campbell.

Prentice turned. 'What now? Have ye not given the order yet, or somethin?'

'No,' said Campbell. 'Gloves.'

'Eh?' said Prentice.

Campbell pointed to the door. 'See that?' he said. 'Nice shiny door isn't it? Just right for leaving lovely sets of fingerprints is it not?'

Prentice glared at him. 'Give me them,' he said.

Campbell fished in his pocket and brought out several pairs of latex gloves which he threw to the others.

Prentice snapped his on, and, without waiting for the others, pushed open the door and went into the shop. Kyle hesitated for a second then followed him.

Boag began unpacking materials from his rucksack.

'You be alright?' Campbell asked.

'Ah'll be fine,' said Boag. 'Ah've got the plans ye gave me. Just let me get on with it. Ah know where ye'll be.'

'Okay,' said Campbell. 'But don't hang about. We don't know how long all this is going to take, but hopefully it'll not be too long.' He looked at the explosives laid out on the floor. 'And hopefully we'll not be needing to use any of that stuff.' He gave one last glance up the corridor, checked that everything was clear and pushed through the door to the store.

***

John had more than just a few drinks laid out for him on his table when he returned, the applause still ringing in his ears. His shoulders were aching from all the slaps he'd received on the way back, his hair tousled and his hands pumped by well-wishers. *Man, that was brilliant!... I didn't know you had such a great voice... It was just like Elvis was in the room... Hey, Johnny-boy, that was magic!* Even the band were clapping, glancing at each other with big grins on their faces. John was loving it. A few shouts of *More!* went up around the room, but John held up his hands, shook his head, mouthing *sorry folks* to the crowd. All those years of practice: standing in front of the mirror with a hairbrush, singing along to the '68 Comeback Special, getting the poses and the moves just right – had paid off in spades. He never thought he'd get the chance to do it with a live band – Christ, he'd never even tried it at a karaoke night – but he knew he'd be good at it, knew he had the talent. Campbell would be mortified if he was here. John laughed at the thought of his brother cringing somewhere in the background as he endured John's star turn.

He took a vodka and coke from the table and scanned the room. People were still staring and smiling at him, lifting drinks, gesturing cheers in his direction. He smiled back, remembered the act he was supposed to be putting on. He made to sit down but deliberately missed the chair, ending up on his arse on the floor, the drink conveniently spilling over his shirt. There was laughter, and a couple of guys helped him to his feet, got him seated. John thanked them, throwing an inane, glazed smile in their direction.

But something wasn't right. Something was missing. He slumped in his seat, made a show of loosening his tie and wiping the sweat from his brow with a napkin, but all the while he was searching the room, trying to identify the source of his unease. His heart beat heavily in his chest. Someone else had taken to the stage – one of the girls from the stockroom – and was not so much singing *Nothing Compares 2 U* as yelling it at the top of her voice in the mistaken assumption that volume equated to tunefulness. The crowd were focused on her now, egging her on, her mates drunkenly yelling encouragement and derision in equal measure. John's gaze wandered to the tables at the front of the room, nearest the stage. The girls from admin were shouting at each other across their table, trying in vain to hold some sort of conversation above the din from the stage.

It was then John realised what was out of place.

McKinnon wasn't there. He was sure he'd seen her sitting with the others as he weaved through the tables to get to the stage, convinced he had spotted her nodding along as he belted out the chorus. But now her chair was empty, her jacket no longer draped over the back, handbag gone. She might be paying a visit to the loo, powdering her nose, but the vacant space at the table had a permanent air about it.

John felt his chest tighten. Where the fuck had she gone?

***

The store looked different at night. An eerie silence settled around Campbell and the others as they picked their way through the gloom, the feeble yellow light from the security lamps throwing lurching shadows ahead of them. The only sound came from their footfalls, which echoed faintly from the overhead galleries and walkways. Display mannequins loomed threateningly from behind pillars, their featureless faces and the flat blank space where their eyes should have been made them look strangely malevolent.

'Kinda spooky, eh?' said Kyle.

Prentice and Campbell turned to look at him. 'Want one of us to hold yer hand?' asked Prentice.

Kyle laughed. 'Aye, and kiss my arse as well!'

'Over there,' said Campbell, pointing to the opposite end of the room. 'The stairs lead up to the Sky Walkway.'

'What's wrong with the lifts?' asked Prentice.

'No use,' Campbell replied. 'They're immobilised at night. Fire safety.'

Prentice shook his head and sighed. 'C'mon then.'

They crossed the shop floor and climbed the polished beech stairs to the third floor, the edge of each step inlaid with an array of tiny bulbs which illuminated their legs as they pushed upwards. They followed the signs for the Stewart

Gallery, Kyle noticing the display of expensive hats had been replaced by a series of identical white handbags. Prentice and Campbell hurried ahead towards the ramp which led to the Walkway door.

Kyle hung back. He leaned over the gallery rail. Below, Boag slinked amongst the counters and sales points, carrying his rucksack in one hand, and a torch in the other. He bent low to the floor, zigzagging between the mannequins and podiums. He stopped and glanced up, gave Kyle a small wave. Kyle lifted a hand in response, turned it into a thumbs-up. Boag returned it and carried on towards one of the side entrances.

'Hey!' Prentice hissed from up ahead. 'Stop admiring the view and get your arse in gear!'

Kyle jogged along the gallery to join the others. 'Sorry,' he said. 'Just wanted to check something.'

'Check what?' Prentice asked. 'We're no exactly on a guided tour here.' He tapped his watch. 'Let's get this thing over and done with. The sooner we're out of here the better.'

Kyle held his hand up. 'Okay, okay,' he said. 'Ah understand. Let's go.'

The mirrored door to the Sky Walkway was ahead of them, the vestibule duller than the last time they'd seen it now that the surrounding spotlights were switched off. They crept along the ramp towards the entrance. Prentice made to pull on the door handle. 'Wait,' said Campbell grabbing his wrist. 'It's locked. We need a code to get in. The door's alarmed – any vibration will set it off.'

'Christ almighty,' said Prentice. 'How could ye no have told us that before?'

Campbell shrugged. 'Ah just didn't, sorry.'

Kyle pushed him in the back. 'Open it,' he said. 'And sorry isn't good enough. Next time there's anything we should know about, ye'll give us plenty of warning or ye'll get ripped, okay? The whole thing could've went off the rails right there, and we'd be spending the next few years twiddlin our thumbs in the jail.'

Campbell nodded. 'Sure,' he said. 'Ah didn't mean anything by it. Just slipped my mind.' Campbell went over to the keypad set in the wall. 'Alright,' he said. 'Wait until Ah tell ye before ye open the door. The code might not work first time.'

'What?' said Kyle.

'It changes every night,' replied Campbell. 'There's a cycle of seven different codes.'

'And you know them all, right?' asked Prentice.

'Of course Ah do,' said Campbell. 'But…'

'But, what?' said Kyle.

'But… we only get three chances. If we don't get it right in three goes, the alarm will go off.'

'The alarm will *what*?' said Prentice. 'Ah don't believe this. Boddice! Where the hell is he? Eh? Every step of this stupid thing is fucked to buggery. Nobody's tellin anybody the straight truth about anythin. We're stuck in here and he's swanning about somewhere, well out the way, and we're the ones that are risking everything—'

'Calm down,' said Kyle.

'No, Ah'll not calm down,' said Prentice. 'Ah've had it up to here with calming down, and going along for the ride, and just doing as Ah'm told, and kowtowing to every wanker that thinks they know better than me.'

'It's open,' said Campbell.

'And another thing,' Prentice went on. 'How come we…'

'It's open,' Campbell repeated.

'Eh?' said Prentice.

'While you've been ranting, I punched in a code and it's open. Look.' He grabbed the handle of the door and pulled it towards him. 'We're in.'

Prentice stared at him. 'How many times?' he asked.

'How many times what?' he asked.

'How many times did you enter the code?'

'Got it first time,' Campbell lied, forcing himself not to blink. 'Ah'm not that daft that Ah would risk going all the way to the third time if Ah wasn't sure.'

'What does it matter?' said Kyle. 'It's open now. Let's get cracking.'

Prentice didn't move. 'You better not be fuckin us about,' he said to Campbell. 'You can do what ye like when it's just you and your dipstick brother, Ah couldn't care less, but when Ah'm involved don't ever consider making a decision that puts me on the line.' He opened his jacket, revealing a hunting knife jammed into his waistband. 'Do we understand each other?'

Campbell nodded.

Kyle pulled Prentice away. 'Stop fannying about,' he said. 'Let's go.'

Prentice shrugged him off, shot a final scowl at Campbell and followed Kyle through the door.

They stopped in the short connecting corridor. The Sky Walkway stretched ahead of them, the streetlights from the intersection below shining up through the glass floor panels, and the spotlights on either side of the building scanning back and forth along its length. At the far end the entrance to the Bubble was a dark square against the background glow of Central Station. It was perhaps thirty yards away.

'We're exposed here,' said Kyle, looking at the street below. 'We could be spotted.'

'No,' said Campbell. 'We're okay. The walls are a kind of mirror thing. We can see out, but nobody can see in. Stops perverts standing on the street below, looking up the women's skirts when they're walking across.'

'Are you sure?' asked Prentice.

'Trust me,' said Campbell. 'Ah've tried it.'

Prentice laughed. 'Alright,' he said. 'Ah trust ye. Let's go.'

They stepped onto the Walkway and started to cross to the Bubble.

'Gentlemen!' a voice boomed out from behind them. Campbell threw himself to the floor, a reflex more than anything else, while the other two spun on their heels, Prentice

grabbing for his knife. *'And Ladies!'* the voice continued. *'You are moments away from the experience of the year, the pinnacle of…'*

'It's a fuckin recording!' said Kyle.

Prentice laughed at Campbell. 'Check you!' Campbell was sprawled on the floor, arms outstretched, face pressed against the glass panels, watching a guy and his girlfriend cross the street arm in arm forty feet below him.

The pre-recorded welcome message continued to prattle on for a few more seconds, culminating in a blazing fanfare. Prentice and Kyle grasped Campbell under his arms and lifted him to his feet. 'Ya plonker,' sneered Prentice. 'Shitin yourself like that. Show a bit of backbone, will ye?'

Campbell clenched his jaw. He should have known better. He should have remembered about the motion sensors which triggered the message for the visitors to the exhibition. Should have stayed on his feet instead of collapsing like a frightened poodle. He tried to think of something to say. Something to show he was still in control of the situation, that it was a daft mistake anyone could have made. Nothing came to mind. 'We're wasting time,' he said, turning away from them and marching down the Walkway towards the Bubble, head high, back straight, in an attempt to restore his dignity.

Kyle and Prentice let him get halfway across before they started to follow. Campbell could hear them speaking to each other in low voices, their words just below the threshold of hearing. He stepped into the Bubble and turned right towards the exhibition room.

The room itself was enclosed within a smaller space, shut off from the main body of the Bubble. Two mock golden gates stood at the entrance, gleaming dimly in the light coming through from the Walkway. To open them, Campbell quickly keyed the security code into the box on the wall, his heart hammering as the fear he felt at the Walkway door returned. He hadn't told Prentice that his first two attempts had failed.

How the little red light on the keypad had winked mockingly as his fingers trembled above the numbered squares of the keypad. He couldn't explain why he'd decided to stab in a third attempt, why he'd risked the whole operation on a statistical probability, a twenty percent chance he'd hit the right code, but, for better or worse, it had worked. Perhaps he wanted the plan to fail, get himself the hell out of this stupid situation. Just run away.

The gates clicked open with the insect buzzing of a solenoid and swung inwards. Prentice and Kyle came up behind, and the three of them stood at the entrance peering into the darkness towards the plinth in the centre of the room. A brass banister ran in a circle around the perimeter of the display area, limiting how close the punters were allowed near the diamond. No way were the riff-raff going to be allowed to get up close and personal with something like this. The Bubble shuddered slightly as a bus rumbled across the junction below them. Ahead, the lasers which surrounded the plinth formed a small galaxy of red pinpoints extending from the floor to the ceiling, and cast faint, blood-tinged shadows on the walls.

On the top of the plinth, at the apex of a single golden spike, sat the Dark Side of the Moon itself, glowing like a solitary deep red eye, illuminated from below by its own cluster of lasers which were set into a circular array like the rings of Saturn.

'Holy shit,' said Kyle. None of them had actually seen the diamond in the flesh before. On their previous visit, Kyle and Prentice had only come across the plinth and the security system; the display itself had been empty. Campbell had been strictly on Ground Floor duty since the diamond had arrived; only the Securarama boys were allowed up here during the day – 'Special Forces' the other security guys called them. He hadn't been able to get near the Bubble with them prowling around all the time.

'It's bigger that I thought,' said Prentice. 'How much did Boddice say this thing was worth?'

'Lots,' said Campbell. 'Lots and lots, and then add a whole tower of more fucking lots on top of that.'

They looked at each other, unsure of who was going to take the first step. Campbell took the bull by the horns. 'Okay,' he said, walking towards the plinth. 'Ultra-fucking-cautious from here on. Got it?'

The others nodded and followed him into the exhibition room.

***

John did his best impression of a sailor in a force ten storm as he wandered over to the admin staff table. He made sure to nudge a few backs, bump a few tables on the way.

'Awwright gurrrls,' he said as he arrived, spilling his drink on the table. 'Enjoyin yourselves? Having a gooood time?' He gave them a leering wink.

The admin girls looked up at him, their conversation halted by his sudden appearance, glasses half-raised towards lips, heads turning, eyes wide in recognition of the fact they had a seriously drunk half-wit leaning over them. A few of them were well-puggled themselves, but not so far gone their innate sense of self-preservation at the prospect of ridicule and humiliation didn't kick in. They laughed nervously.

John blinked slowly, cleared his throat. 'Izzhis no a great party?' he said. 'Ah mean 'sfuckin brilliant, eh?'

'Eh… aye, it is,' said one of the girls, her smile flickering uncertainly.

'Brilliant, aye,' said John. 'Free bar, cannae whack it.'

'So we see,' said another of the girls. 'You seem to have been making a fair attempt to get as much out of it as you can.'

'Of course!' he shouted, drawing some looks from the adjoining table. 'It would be the baddest manners no to accept the hoshptality of our employers. Verry graishusz of em.'

The admin girls squirmed in their seats, tried to avoid eye

contact with him. Good, he thought, they're still falling for it: hook, line, sinker and annual subscription to the Angling Times. But the niggling worry at the back of his mind remained. Time to find out.

'Ananurrthing,' he said, rocking back on his heels.

'Eh?' said one of the girls, the one wearing a bright red dress with a neckline that plummeted all the way to her pierced belly button.

'Nannurrer thhing,' he replied. They still looked at him blankly. He tried again. 'And. Another. Thing.'

'Oh,' said red dress. 'What?'

'The great thing about zhiss parrty iszh that evrybiddy joins in. Abslootly evrbiddy.' He waved his hand around, haphazardly indicating the crowded room. 'Furrzample,' he went on. 'Errz all ra bosses at the top table there, having a good time, laughin an jokin like the rest of us.' He pulled up a chair and sat down. 'And… and… even that stuck-up bitch, whasirname? McKinnon. Aye, *Miss* McKinnon. Even her, she's here, livin it up, gettin it on.' He made a big show of looking around, frowning in slow exaggeration. 'Where is she anyway? Was she no here earlier?'

'Thank God she's away,' said one of the girls. 'She's a right bloody madam that one. And, no, she wasn't living it up or getting it on. She was just the same as she is in the shop, a bossy bastard, thinking she's better than us, all hoity-toity and up her own arse.' She turned to the others. 'I don't know about you lot, but I sure as hell didn't believe her when she said she had a sore head. I think she just couldn't wait to get away from the likes of us.'

'You mean she's left?' spluttered John. 'She's not at the party?'

'Away home to a couple of paracetamol and a stiff whisky, she told us,' said another of the girls.

'A stiff dildo more like,' said someone else, and the girls burst out laughing.

'Aye, that's the only thing she'll ever get between her legs!' said red-dress to more laughter.

A bowling ball deposited itself in John's gut, settling in a weighty knot that almost buckled his legs. Christ almighty, why had she left? Surely she couldn't know what was happening at the shop. Could she? Did she have some secret link to the store's security systems? Something linked to her mobile, an alert or text message perhaps? It was possible. That was her job after all. It wasn't beyond the realms of possibility she had such a set-up. Or maybe he was just being paranoid, freaked out by the pressure of the situation, the stress. Maybe the girls were right and McKinnon was just a snobby bitch who'd had enough of mixing with the commoners, jealous of their shop-floor friendships and cliques, their cosy banter and in-jokes. Better to hit the road before she outstayed her welcome. On reflection, listening to the girls' opinion of her, that seemed the most likely scenario. He was being stupid, oversensitive, that was all. He forced himself to relax, bring his heart rate back down to normal.

'Heh, you've went awful white,' said one of the girls, a blonde with badly plucked eyebrows and way too much make-up plastered on her face. She was one to talk about skin colour. 'Are ye okay?' she asked.

He broke into a wide smile and stood up. 'Abslootly fine, never better,' he slurred. 'In fact,' he said as he manoeuvred away from the table, 'Ah might just strut my stuff on the dance floor. Embdy fancy joinin me?'

'Nah, ye're alright John Travolta,' said red-dress. 'You away and get on down. It's the getting back up again that might give ye problems.'

The girls started laughing again, and John careened across the room towards the top table where the bigwigs and head-bummers were sitting, looking as uncomfortable as ever, sickly smiles pasted to their faces, fingers lamely tapping the table in time to the music. The band had just kicked off a new set with a rollicking version of *Brown Sugar*, big, bold and brassy and a sure-fire floor-filler. John hitched his trousers. This was it. Time for the big finale.

If people hadn't noticed him before, they sure as fuck weren't about to forget him now.

***

Now that they'd actually made the decision to cross the threshold into the exhibition room, they each found a curious desire to be the first to approach the diamond. The three of them formed an almost reverential procession which gradually gathered pace as they drew nearer, footsteps quickening and breaths held in anticipation.

Campbell, feeling Prentice and Kyle jostling him from behind, held up his hand, drew them to a halt before they got too close. The diamond glittered in the light from the lasers, sitting in the dark like a drop of blood on a dagger-point. It seemed to possess a black weight, a gravitational field, sucking them towards it. The very air seemed thicker here as if it was drawn to condense around the diamond.

To his surprise, Campbell's eyes were watering. He pretended to rub them in tiredness to clear his vision. Up close, he could see the detailed elegance of the cutting pattern, the subtle angles and contours of the facets. The diamond was the size and shape of an egg, slightly flattened, and its dark, unnatural colour gave it a brooding malice which unnerved him. It seemed to exist in a world other than their own, a different plane of reality which had somehow manifested itself in the shadowy gloom of this room in the centre of Glasgow. The others felt it too. Campbell could hear their slow, heavy breathing.

They looked at each other and nodded. There was no going back. Without speaking, they each unhitched their rucksacks and set about their business. Campbell brought out a can of deodorant, while Prentice retrieved Boag's modified litter-picker from his bag. Kyle circled the diamond's plinth, inspecting the array of lasers and sensors.

'Oxter-spray?' asked Prentice. 'Ah know ye're a smelly bastard, but this is hardly the time or place, is it?'

Campbell gave him a sarcastic smile, and sprayed the deodorant in wide circles in front of the Dark Side of the Moon. Immediately, a criss-crossing lattice of red beams flared up around the diamond, reflecting from the microscopic droplets of perfumed mist. The beams ran in impossibly thin lines from the laser source to the little mirrored sensors opposite, just as Boag had reproduced in his model. They formed the same complex three-dimensional grid of horizontal and vertical shafts cut across by diagonal beams from further lasers set into the floor and ceiling. The whole array stood out like red-hot spars of an impenetrable cage surrounding the diamond and its plinth, before fading as the deodorant dissipated.

Kyle came around from the other side of the plinth. 'It's the same back there,' he said. 'Exactly as we thought.'

'Okay then,' said Prentice, interlacing his fingers and making a show of cracking his knuckles. 'No time for fannying about. Here goes.' He positioned himself in front of the plinth, stood with his legs apart, bracing and steadying himself. He kept the litter-picker at his side and motioned Campbell to join him. 'Right,' said Prentice. 'Spray the stuff again, and keep it going for a bit longer this time.'

Campbell moved behind Prentice and pressed the nozzle on the can, sending a fine jet of perfume into the air. He moved his arm back and forwards in a wide arc until all the beams were illuminated.

Prentice coughed. 'Fuck's sake,' he said. 'What *is* that stuff? It's honking.'

'*Minotaur*,' said Campbell. 'Ah think that was some sort of mythological bull or somethin. Ye must have seen the adverts on the telly. Guy chasin a big cow through a cave.'

'It smells like a bloody cow right enough,' said Prentice. 'Anyway, keep spraying.' He got down onto his haunches and squinted through the gaps between the bars of light, seeking out the pathway he'd used in his practice sessions. It was almost impossible, every potential avenue had a final red barrier punching across the path from below or from the side. But Prentice knew where the weakness was; he'd spent long days lying on Boag's floor, inching the litter-picker up the steep narrow channel through the strands of wool that ran from just above floor level to the golf ball sitting on its mount at the top of the model.

But something wasn't right.

Now that he was in front of the real thing, somehow it didn't look the same as the mock-up.

Not the same at all.

The angle of the beams was steeper than in Boag's model; the whole plinth looked taller as it loomed above him. Prentice frowned. How could this be? He gingerly edged the litter-picker into the gap, his precious opening, the one he'd used so often on the model he felt he could do it with his eyes closed.

It was too tight. The gap was too narrow.

He got back to his feet, rubbed the stubble on his face. The height. There was something wrong with the height of the top section where the lasers were housed.

'What?' said Kyle. 'Is there a problem?'

'Fucking right there's a problem,' said Prentice. 'The model's wrong. This is different. Boag, that stupid wee wank, has screwed the whole thing up.'

'But the photo, the measurements he took,' said Kyle, 'He told us he'd been meticulous, that he'd—'

'*Meticulous?*' Prentice rasped. 'How in God's name could he have been meticulous when something as simple as how high this thing's supposed to be is completely fucked?' He grabbed Campbell and dragged him to stand beside the plinth.

'Look! This is above shoulder height. In the model it's lower than this. The angles of the beams are all buggered because the height is all to cock.'

Kyle looked at Campbell standing beside the plinth. Prentice was right; it *was* different. Campbell said nothing, just stared at his feet.

Kyle walked round the plinth again, frowning. 'Wait a minute,' he said. 'Wait a bloody minute…'

'What is it?' Prentice asked.

Kyle gestured to Campbell. 'You,' he said. 'Give me your phone.'

Campbell continued to stare at his feet, distracted.

'Hey! Dozy boy! Give me your fucking phone.'

Campbell looked up quickly, wide-eyed. He took his phone from his pocket and handed it to Kyle. 'I think I know what—' he began.

'Let's just check something first,' said Kyle.

Prentice shook his head. 'Will somebody tell me what in the name of crippled Christ is going on?'

Kyle skipped through a few keystrokes on Campbell's mobile, brought up his pictures album. He looked at Campbell, looked at the plinth, Campbell again and then back at the phone. 'I fucking knew it. They've changed the bloody plinth, the bastards have switched it.'

'No, they haven—' Campbell tried to say.

'Show me!' said Prentice, snatching the phone away from Kyle. He looked at the screen. The picture of Campbell standing beside the plinth glowed in the half-light of the Bubble. It was true. The top section was lower in the picture. Not by much – an inch maybe, not much more.

But enough to make a difference.

'Bastards!' said Prentice. 'The fucking basta—'

'They didn't switch it,' said Campbell.

'Eh? What do you mean?' Prentice said. 'Look at the bloody picture. It's fucking lower.'

'No it isn't,' said Campbell.

'Are you fucking blind as well as stupid?' said Kyle. 'Of course it's—'

'It's not lower in the picture,' said Campbell. 'It's me that was taller.'

Prentice and Kyle gaped at him, mouths working like newly-landed fish.

Prentice screwed his eyes shut. 'You were fucking *taller? Taller?* Holy shite, what did you do between then and now, chop a bit off your legs?'

Campbell shook his head. 'No. Shoes.'

Kyle raised an eyebrow. '*Shoes?*'

'Platforms,' said Campbell. 'The store makes all the security guys wear them. To make them look taller. More intimidating.' He looked at Kyle and Prentice, the uncomprehending looks on their faces. 'You know... for the customers.'

'Christ almighty,' said Kyle. 'You mean that...'

'Ah forgot,' said Campbell. 'When Boag took his measurements, my height, Ah forgot Ah'd been wearing the shoes in the picture. It's my fault, not his. My mistake.'

Prentice shook his head. 'Your *mistake!* Well, that's a fucking understatement.' He paced the floor behind the plinth, 'Your mistake has just screwed the whole bloody deal, hasn't it? Ah mean, what the fuck are we supposed to do now?' Prentice took the litter-picker and hurled it into the corner where it smashed against the wall.

Campbell flinched. 'Ah'm sorry, it wasn't intentional it just slipped my mind.'

Kyle sucked air in through his gritted teeth. 'Look,' he said. 'There's fuck all we can do about it now, is there? Is there no way we can just try it, give it a go? You know, now we're here?'

Prentice laughed at him. 'No way, José. You can try it if you like, but the angles are all wrong. It's too narrow now. The pincers won't fit through. And, short of just grabbing the bastard and running like fuck, Ah don't see any other possibilities. Mind you, if we do that, there's that wee matter of the security grills and the alarms and the two dozen polis that'll be here in three minutes flat. Oh aye, and the twenty fucking years in prison, there's always that too.'

'Hang on, hang on,' said Kyle. He picked up the litter -picker from where it lay in the corner. He held it up before Prentice's face. The plastic grips which covered the pincers had broken when Prentice had flung it against the wall and had fallen away, leaving only the exposed metal of the pincers themselves. Prentice saw what Kyle had noticed.

They were thinner than before.

Thinner.

Campbell looked from Prentice to Kyle and back again. 'Do you think…?'

Prentice took the picker from Kyle and squatted down on the floor before the plinth. 'We'll need to see won't we?' He squatted before the plinth. 'Get spraying and let's have a look.'

Campbell moved to the right of the plinth and started spraying. Once again the diamond was enveloped by the bright red threads of light. Prentice cocked his head and settled lower onto the floor. He held his breath, squinting up through the beams and then at the picker in his hand. Five, six times he did this, each time puffing his cheeks and blowing air slowly from his lungs. 'You know,' he said finally. 'Ah think it'll go through… Ah think the fucker will actually make it.'

Kyle and Campbell broke into wide grins.

'Okay,' Prentice said, getting to his feet. 'Ah need to practice this. It's an awkward position, Ah need to make sure Ah can get the right angle.' He moved away from the plinth and lay down on his back.

Kyle and Campbell stepped aside to give him room. Prentice took the picker and advanced it slowly in a rough approximation of the path he would have to take, bracing his arms against his chest. He tried it three times more, shifting position slightly each time to give him a more comfortable approach. At last he stood up. 'Right,' he said. 'Ah think Ah'm ready.' He walked back to the plinth and settled himself on the floor at its base, squirming to adjust his shoulders to the right angle.

Campbell fished in his rucksack and brought out another can of deodorant for Kyle. 'Better with the two of us,' he said. 'Make sure we don't lose the beams while he's in there.'

Kyle nodded. 'Good idea.'

They knelt either side of Prentice. 'Ready?' Kyle asked.

'Ah suppose,' he said. 'We're well past the point of no return, so let's get this over and done with.'

Kyle and Campbell began spraying, the beams flaring into view again, while Prentice moved the litter pole into the space between them. The clearance on either side was no more than half a centimetre. His progress was painfully slow; Prentice was acutely aware that the slightest tremble in his arms would be magnified by the length of the pole, causing the far end to dance dangerously close to the path of the beams.

The pincers edged towards the diamond. The gap, narrow enough to begin with, seemed to close in, the perspective of the passageway tricking Prentice's eyes as he struggled to maintain a steady hand.

The smell from the deodorant was overpowering, with both Kyle and Campbell spraying inches from his nose. Christ, if he should start to sneeze now! Prentice put the thought out of his head, tried to concentrate on the job. He was almost there, perhaps two or three inches from the end of the golden spike. A few more seconds and he would have it, a minute or two more and it would be in his hand. They could get out of this fucking place. They would be rich.

He slowly stretched his arm till the pincers were a centimetre in front of the diamond. He squeezed the trigger on the handle and they opened. Campbell and Kyle continued to keep the beams lit, but he could sense their anticipation, knew they were staring bug-eyed at how close he was, willing him to clasp the diamond, finally make contact.

He released the pressure on the trigger and the jaws of the pincers closed on the Dark Side of the Moon. There was a tiny crystalline *clink* and the diamond rocked slightly on its mounting at the top of the spike. Prentice smiled – a thin slice of satisfaction – and prepared to lift it clear and withdraw back down through the gap in the beams.

'*Gentlemen!*' a voice sounded from way behind them.

They froze, Prentice straining with the effort of keeping the diamond in place.

'*And Ladies! You are moments away from the experience of the year…*'

Someone had entered the Walkway. They stared at each other.

'It's Boag,' said Campbell. 'It must be!'

'He was under instructions to stay put!' said Kyle. 'Why would he come up here?'

They heard the *tok-tok-tok* of high heels coming down the Walkway towards the Bubble.

'Well, unless he's been raiding the women's shoe department, Ah don't think that's Boag, do you?' hissed Kyle.

'Fuck!' said Prentice. 'Fuck, fuck, fuck!' He let go of the diamond which dropped back into its holder, and began backing out of the space between the lasers. 'Help me! Quick!'

They abandoned the deodorant and began pulling on the pole, keeping it as steady as they could and as far away from where they supposed the paths of the beams would be.

They made it. The pincers came clear. They breathed a collective sigh of relief.

But the footsteps were coming closer.

'Quick,' Campbell hissed. 'Over here.'

They scrambled across the floor and into the space behind a counter holding a selection of souvenir catalogues and guides.

A figure emerged from between the two golden gates at the

entrance to the exhibition area, dark and indistinct in the light seeping through from the street below. It stepped into the room, a firm, confident stride, business-like and efficient. They could now see it was a woman; neat tailored jacket over short blue skirt, high heels and dark, cropped hair. She walked forward to the plinth and stood sniffing the air. Campbell winced. The deodorant. Christ, what a giveaway.

From the corner of his eye he saw Prentice about to stand up, his knife in his hand. Kyle was crouched ready to move too. Campbell stretched out, grabbed Prentice by the arm, widened his eyes, signalled for him to wait. She hadn't seen them; there was still a chance.

The woman placed her hands on her hips and scanned the room. As she turned towards them, Campbell ducked behind the counter, but just had time to see it was Miss McKinnon. Fucking hell, what was she doing here? She was supposed to be at the…

His thoughts were interrupted by McKinnon's laughter, a deep belly laugh which rolled around the confined space of the exhibition room. She put a hand to her forehead and shook her head. 'You boys,' she said trying to compose herself. 'You really crack me up. This place smells like a fucking bomb went off in a Rightguard factory.'

Campbell, Prentice and Kyle were rooted to the spot. *You boys?* What the hell did she know? More to the point, *how* the hell did she know? They shot each other quick glances, unsure what to do next.

'You truly are amateurs,' she said. 'I warned Boddice, but he wouldn't listen, wanted to plan things his way. And this is what you get.' She shook her head. 'I tried to make things as easy as possible for you… smooth the way. A bit of research wouldn't have gone amiss, boys.'

She stepped forward and reached towards the Dark Side of the Moon, stretched her arm across the beams and lifted it from the plinth.

'No!' shouted Kyle, getting to his feet. 'Wait!'

At the same instant, Prentice rose up and vaulted the counter, lunging at McKinnon in a swift sweeping movement, his knife raised high above his head.

He never made contact.

Seemingly without thinking, McKinnon spun away from him and in the same movement landed a spiked heel directly on his balls. Prentice crumpled to the floor, clutching his wounded testicles and folding into a foetal position. Kyle and Campbell sprang round the counter and sprinted towards her. 'Stop!' she shouted, holding up her hand.

It wasn't the way she had dealt with Prentice (*Prentice* for fuck's sake!), or their surprise at the commanding tone of her voice that caused them to halt in their tracks. It was the diamond.

There it was.

In her hand.

And nothing had happened. There were no alarms, flashing lights or security grilles crashing down around them. No police sirens in the distance. Zilch. Nada. Rien.

She had just walked up, stuck her hand in and took it.

She laughed. 'Look at you,' she said. 'Could you be any more slack-jawed?'

Prentice got to his knees, still clutching his balls. 'Who the fuck *are* you?' he snarled through clenched teeth. Campbell and Kyle stepped forward and helped him to his feet. He shrugged them off. 'Answer me!' Prentice shouted. He made to rush her again, but Kyle and Campbell held him back.

'Good move boys,' McKinnon said. 'You don't want to be messing with me, Davie, unless you want more of the same.'

'Answer him,' said Kyle. 'Who are you? How the fuck do you know his name?'

'She's Miss McKinnon,' Campbell said.

'Miss Who?'

'McKinnon. The head of security for the store,' Campbell replied.

'Correct,' said McKinnon. 'And wrong too.' She motioned for them to move back behind the counter. They stood their ground, a chest-puffing act of defiance. Did she have any idea who the fuck she was dealing with here? 'Fair enough,' she said, smiling. 'Makes no difference to me.' She stretched her hand towards them, the Dark Side of the Moon lying in her open palm. 'Here. Take it.'

They looked at each other, frowning. 'Look,' said Kyle. 'Gonnae chuck the mystery shite and just tell us what's going on here?'

'Okay,' she said, tossing the diamond towards them. Campbell caught it and closed his fist around it, feeling its weight and coolness. 'Miss McKinnon,' she said. 'Head of Security at Trusdale and Needham. Or not, as the case may be. Not everything is as it seems sometimes, Campbell.' She walked over to the plinth, stood directly in the path of the beams. Her face, her arms, her dress were studded with little red pinpoints which glowed fiercely in the dark like undiscovered constellations.

'Take this, for example. Pretty crap security system is it not, when you can just walk up and snatch the world's most expensive diamond and there's not so much as a doorbell ringing. You'd expect something approaching the third world war to be kicking off right now, wouldn't you?'

'Get to the fucking point,' Prentice said.

'This *is* the fucking point, as you so eloquently put it,' she said. 'Did you really think something as important as this would be left sitting here overnight, unprotected, except by a bunch of low-paid drones who don't know how to wipe their own arse without being given instructions?'

'Hey!' Campbell said.

'Present company excepted, of course,' McKinnon said. She walked around the plinth, stroked the gold spike with a long, red-varnished fingernail. 'All this is just an elaborate hoax. None of it is real. That stone you're holding isn't the real deal.

It's just a bauble, a fake, a trinket put on display for the proles to gape at after their hour and a half of queueing.'

Campbell lowered his head and examined the gem in his hand, its improbably dark interior leaching the light from the room.

'Don't get me wrong,' said McKinnon. 'As a fake, that one's worth a considerable amount of money. It's an accurate replica, right down to the tiny variations in colour of the real thing, same weight, same dimensions. But it's a fake nonetheless.' She looked at each of them in turn. 'If you'd bothered to do any homework before your daring little raid tonight, you'd have discovered these laser beams are old hat, passé. No security system worth its salt uses something like this these days. You're only likely to see these in some crappy Hollywood spy movie, that's all.' She smiled at Prentice. 'Something with wee Tom Cruise or Matt Damon. If anything, the beams would be infra-red, if they were used at all. Invisible to the naked eye.' She swept her arm in a wide arc, taking in the room. 'All this is just showmanship. A crowd-pleaser. Let the public think they're getting involved with something slightly dangerous, something exotic. They can say they've been part of it. Tell their friends about it. Brighten their dismal little lives.'

'Fuck all that,' said Prentice. 'If it's a phony, then where is the real diamond?'

'Ah,' she said. 'The real Dark Side of the Moon is, in fact, in an altogether different room within the store. A room only those and such as those are invited to, well away from the prying eyes of the great unwashed. Private viewings only, I'm afraid.'

'We've wasted our fuckin time,' Prentice said. 'Boddice knew all along this was never gonnae work. He's hung us out to dry.'

'Wait,' said Kyle. 'Why is she telling us all this?' He glared at McKinnon. 'You still haven't answered his question. Who are you?'

'You don't need to know who I am.' She turned to Campbell. 'But my name's not McKinnon.'

'And you're not the security chief for the store are you?' Campbell asked.

'Oh, but I am,' she said. 'You work for me, remember?'

'Aye, but…'

'There's always a 'but'.' She shook her head in exasperation. 'In fact I—'

'In fact she works for Boddice,' said Kyle. 'She's a plant. He's had her hidden away in here for… how long? Months? Years?'

She smiled. 'Let's just say a while, shall we? You're almost right, Gordon. Well done. But I don't work for Boddice. I work for myself. Boddice has just hired my services, that's all.'

'Hired? What do you mean?' asked Prentice.

'What part of that word don't you understand, Davie? What would you prefer? Rented? Engaged? Employed?'

'Don't get smart with me,' Prentice said. 'Ah'll come over there and—'

'And what?' she said. 'You're the one nursing balls that are going to be the size of melons before long. And I didn't even need to try hard.'

'Aye, but there's three of us now.'

'And?' she said. 'There were three of you before. Believe me it wouldn't have made much difference.'

'Ah've had enough of this crap. Ah'm out of here.'

'Wait, Davie,' said Kyle. Prentice turned to him. 'Think about this a minute. How does she know our names? Why is she here, right at this particular time? The very night, the very minute we're about to lift the diamond. Maybe there's somethin in this after all. And she says she works for Boddice.'

'Aye,' Prentice replied. 'And why did Boddice leave that wee detail out of the plan he discussed with us? Do either of you mugs seriously believe this shite? How do we even know she's tellin us the truth about the bloody diamond?' He went over to Campbell and took the stone from him, turned it over in his hands. 'For all we know, she's just spinnin us some yarn to stall for time. This doesn't look like a fake to me.'

'Feel free to take it then,' McKinnon said. 'You can pass it on to Boddice and take a ringside seat to watch his face when he tries to raise some money from it. That should be good fun.'

'Okay,' Kyle said. 'Suppose this is all straight up. Will ye just tell us what in the name of Christ is going on?'

McKinnon grinned. 'Follow me.'

***

John caught disjointed snatches of conversation as he approached the top table. A couple of guys on the end, bow ties slightly skewiff, glasses of red wine poised halfway between table and lips, were discussing lawnmowers. *Lawnmowers*, for fuck's sake! Something about the advantage of petrol-driven models for the larger garden. Further on, an older couple – man and wife? Boss and secretary? It was hard to tell – were in the middle of an argument. 'If you loved me, you'd want to take me with you!' the man whined.

John ignored them. His goal was further along the table. There, isolated from the rest of the group, seemingly by choice, sat Sir James Corrigan, the Chief Executive and Managing Director of Trusdale and Needham, UK, and his wife. Sir James looked as if he'd rather be eating a runny shit sandwich than slumming it with the minions in Scotland. John almost felt sorry for him. Everyone else had a fucking PhD is having a good time, while Sir James wore the downturned mouth of the terminally crabbit. And now his evening was about to get a whole lot worse.

John staggered to a halt in front of Sir James and his wife, planted a crooked smile on his face. Sir James looked up, glowering under his wild eyebrows.

'Zzhorry,' said John. 'But Ah... Ah just had to ask... is this...'

'Go away,' Sir James said.

'No, no, wait… hear me out. Ah only wanted to know if—'

'Look, you're being unpleasant. We're not your sort. Go away.'

'Ah'll go away in a minute, but Ah just wanted to ask a wee question, just a wee one.'

'And you promise you'll depart after that? Leave us in peace?'

'Ye have my word,' John said. He could see Sir James looking past his shoulder, seeking some sort of help from the room behind, trying to catch the eye of a waiter, anyone who could come and remove this lout.

'Very well,' said Sir James. 'What do you wish to know?'

John clapped his hands. 'Magic!' He arranged his face into serious mode, made a show of composing himself. He cleared his throat. 'Am Ah right in assumin this is your good wife? Lady Anne, Ah believe?'

Sir James's wife eyed John with suspicion. Sir James sighed. 'Yes, you're correct. This is Lady Anne. You have your answer. Now will you go away?'

'No, no, that wasn't my question. That was just a premlin… a pre… a prelminary question. That wasn't the real thing Ah wanted to ask.'

Sir James banged his hand on the table. 'For God's sake man! Will you just get on with it then?'

John blinked in mock hurt. 'Awright… it's no big deal. Ah just wanted to make sure that Ah was askin the right person.'

'What are you blithering about? Just ask your question and go!'

'Okay,' said John. 'Ah was just wonderin if Lady Anne would like to have the next dance with me.'

'Are you out of your tiny excuse for a brain?' Sir James said, his face reddening. 'Of course she doesn't want to dance with you!'

'Aw, listen,' said John, looking over his shoulder to the band on the stage. 'They're playing *Money For Nuthin,* that should be right up your street, should it not?'

'What?' spluttered Sir James.

'Never mind,' John said. He was aware a few other faces at the end of the table were now turned towards them, curious to see what the commotion was about. The guy on the stage was singing about playing *geeetars on the emmteevee.* 'One last question then. For Lady Anne.' Sir James was getting to his feet now, ready to put an end to this once and for all, but his wife was smiling at John, either humouring him, or enjoying the floorshow playing out in front of her. 'Do ye like wine gums?' John asked.

Lady Anne spoke for the first time. 'Wine gums?'

'Aye,' said John. 'Wine gums. Do ye like them.'

She frowned, unsure of the point he was making. Sir James was on his tiptoes, signalling for someone to come over, get rid of this lunatic.

'Why, yes,' said Lady Anne. 'I do believe I enjoy wine gums from time to time.'

John undid his trousers and dropped them to the floor, followed by his boxers. His dick dangled between his legs. Lady Anne gasped in surprise. John jumped onto the table, grabbed his cock and flapped it in front of her face. 'Well,' he said. 'Wine yer gums round this!'

That was when all hell broke loose.

***

Davie Prentice rarely experienced the emotion of panic, but he was feeling it now. Panic, or something close to it. Events were slipping away from him. Christ, he'd felt edgy enough before tonight – so many things in the lead-up were balanced between incompetence and ineptitude; this whole plan of Boddice's wasn't just flawed, it was a downright insane, fucked-up, half-arsed attempt at some big-shot criminal mastermind shite that had as much chance of success as a ten-man Scotland beating Brazil six-nil in the World Cup Final. All this crap about setting explosives throughout the shop, using a litter-picker – *for fuck's sake!* – to steal the world's most famous diamond, and, despite Boddice's suggestion to the contrary, no bloody plan to speak of.

Chaos. That was what it was. And the thing pushing him to the brink of an uncontrollable bout of the heebie geebies was the fact that none of the others seemed to be bothering about it. The stupid arseholes. They couldn't see what he saw: the potential for disaster. The whole operation was one loose nut away from coming off the rails.

And underneath it all, feeding the fire of his disquiet, bringing his rage up to the boil, was the death of the baby. Wee Jackie. Prentice had tried to muffle the tormenting guilt, submerge it with the distraction of the preparations for the robbery, but it kept bubbling back to the surface, nagging away, a constant reminder of the consequences of his selfishness, his self-absorption.

He'd tried to rationalise the guilt; perhaps the news stories were about another baby, some other unknown infant found dead on a bus – that was wishful thinking more than anything else. Maybe she was sick to begin with, after all, she'd been in that room for how long? Days? Possibly. Rosco was certainly stinking the place up by the time Prentice had found him. How long did it take for a body to get into that state? If the baby had been there for days, no food, no water, it was entirely possible she was at death's door and he hadn't noticed.

But in the end, he had failed her. Abandoned her, alone and unwanted in the bleak fluorescence of the rear of the bus, her short life ebbing towards its final breath. Prentice had left her to die. He could have done something about it then, but no, Boddice and his fucking hare-brained scheme were more important.

This stupid plan that was now falling apart big time.

And now this McKinnon woman. Boddice's *insider*. But Prentice hadn't imagined it would be someone like her. It hadn't even crossed his mind it would even *be* a her. Christ, his balls were aching; her kick had been aimed just right, hitting him bang in the sweet spot, the one place where, no matter how fired up you were, how ready to have a right old go, you were guaranteed to fold to your knees, avoiding any sort of movement. She knew what she was doing alright.

Now she was leading them back down to the ground floor, Campbell and Kyle following like meek sheep, eager to go along with this as if it was all perfectly normal. Prentice watched her lean close to Kyle, mutter something in his ear. Prentice bit his lip, hung back a pace or two. He didn't trust this woman. This could all be an elaborate ruse; she was the head of store-fucking-security after all – there could be a whole posse of polis lying in wait for them at the bottom of the stairs: *thanks very much Miss McKinnon, we've been after these boys for years.*

Prentice still had the diamond in his pocket. Was it the real thing or not? Would she have let him keep it if it wasn't a fake? There was no way of telling. Not yet anyway.

They reached the foot of the stairs. McKinnon led them to the centre of the shop floor, where the shaft of the giant arrow dived into the floorboards. They stopped at the spot where the arrow seemingly disappeared into the floor. McKinnon turned to Kyle, gave a single nod. 'Call him,' she said.

Kyle looked around him, scanning the sales floor. 'Boag!' he shouted. 'Are you here? You can come out, everything's fine.'

Prentice fought back the urge to shout out that everything was very fucking far from fine.

'Boag!' Kyle shouted again. 'Where are you?'

A small voice came from behind them, in a distant corner of the room: 'What the hell's happening? Are you finished?'

'No, we're not finished,' Kyle shouted back. 'Just come out and we'll explain everything.'

There was a clatter as a mannequin fell over, and Boag

emerged from behind a partition displaying a poster of a bronzed couple cavorting on a beach.

'Hurry up!' McKinnon called to him. 'We don't have all night.'

Boag broke into a trot, and Prentice shook his head in dismay as he saw yet another of the team capitulate to her, this time without so much as even speaking to her.

Boag came up to them, his rucksack bouncing on his back, out of breath with the short jog. He eyed the group quizzically, scrutinising McKinnon. 'Who… what…?' he began. 'Ah didn't get them all done, Ah've still got—'

'Change of plan,' Kyle said. 'And don't worry, we're as much in the dark as you.' He took McKinnon by the arm. 'But we're just about to get an explanation, aren't we?'

At fucking last, thought Prentice. Kyle wasn't completely won over by her.

McKinnon slapped Kyle's hand away. 'Don't start any funny business,' she said. 'It'll be you who comes off worst, I guarantee it.'

Prentice stepped up to join Kyle. This was more like it. Now they were getting somewhere.

Instead of retreating, McKinnon moved forward to meet him. 'Goolies not sore enough for you, Prentice? Want some more of the same? Because I'll be only too happy to oblige.'

Prentice was ready for her this time. He started to bring his fist up, eager to pummel it into her sneering face, when his arm was grabbed from behind. He stumbled, caught unawares.

It was Campbell. The freak-brother. Mister I'm-in-charge. Who did he think he was, manhandling Prentice like this? 'You can't start a sentence with because,' Campbell said to McKinnon.

Prentice struggled to get free, twisting and wriggling to release Campbell's hold. 'What the fuck are you talkin about, ya prick? Let me go.'

Campbell's grip tightened and Prentice turned towards him, powering up to head-butt the fucker into oblivion. But

Kyle stepped in and grabbed Prentice's other arm. The two men wrestled Prentice to the floor, pinned him down.

'Listen, Davie,' said Kyle, breathing hard. 'Ah'll say this only once. Calm. Down. We need an explanation here. We need to hear what she's got to say. This isn't the time for blood and guts stuff.' Kyle got to his feet, allowed Prentice to do the same, signalling to Campbell to let him go. 'She's working for Boddice, Davie. We need her to tell us what the hell this is all about.'

'She's working for Boddice is she? How come we've never heard of her? How come she's not been part of this big plan, this fucked-up excuse for a robbery? Eh? Tell me that, ya tosser.'

'If you're quite finished,' McKinnon said. 'I was just coming to that. You are, of course, entitled to an explanation, and I forgive your outburst Davie. I know this must be an unexpected turn of events.'

Prentice glowered at her, but said nothing. It was Campbell who spoke up. 'That would be a good idea, Miss McKinnon,' he said. 'We're not exactly—'

'What's with this *Miss* McKinnon shite?' said Prentice. 'Tell us yer real name ya bitch.'

'That's impossible,' she replied. 'But if it makes you feel any better you can call me... Debbie.'

'Okay, *Debbie*,' said Prentice. 'Freak-show here has got it right. For once. It *would* be a good fucking idea to tell us. Right now.'

McKinnon rubbed the back of her neck. 'Okay, but this is going to have to be quick. A potted summary. And then you're going to have to do exactly as I say.'

'We don't have to do anything,' Kyle said. 'But on ye go.'

'Alright,' McKinnon said. 'Consider me a freelancer, a hired hand. A job here, a job there, whatever takes my fancy.' She smiled. 'And I'm not talking your usual legitimate lines of employment. That sort of stuff doesn't meet my financial requirements. Although getting the Head of Security gig in this place was easier than you might think. It's surprising the number of employers who don't actually check the details on CVs or references once they've interviewed you.' She ran her tongue over her top lip and blinked once, slowly. 'And, of course, I do have a very good interview technique.'

'Aye, good for you,' Prentice said. 'Get on with it.'

McKinnon made a small bow. 'A new store like this provides interesting opportunities – expensive merchandise, rich, no, make that *very* rich, customers, politicians, celebrities, royalty. I decided to get in right at the start, see what came up. Of course, when the advance announcement was made that the Dark Side of the Moon was coming, it was too good an opportunity to miss. Your Mr Boddice has employed my services in the past. He pays very handsomely, which is to our mutual advantage. I get in, get out, he receives whatever it is he's after. On time, no fuss, no trail leading back to him.'

'What kind of things are ye talkin about?' Kyle asked.

'That's the other aspect of our agreements,' she said. 'He pays me, I keep schtum. You can ask *him* if you like, but I doubt he'll give you an answer either.'

'Which is very convenient for you,' Prentice said. 'We still have no way of knowin if ye're tellin us the truth.'

'Then you'll just have to accept it, won't you? It's the way I work.' She glanced at her watch. 'Anyway, I saw a chance, for me and for your boss. Don't misunderstand, I'm not getting a cut of any money Boddice makes from this. I get paid up front. In fact, I've already *been* paid. I won't be asking for a penny more. As soon as tonight is over and done with, I'm gone. Until the next time.'

'But surely you'll be linked with the robbery then?' asked Campbell. 'If you disappear after this it'll be an obvious connection to make. The shop, the polis, they'll know.'

'Makes no difference to me,' she said. 'They won't be able to track me down. I have ways of disappearing.'

'And what about me and John, then? How will our story stand up, when we're expected to return to work?'

'You're forgetting,' she replied, looking at her watch again. 'Around about now your brother should be getting you both sacked. Your services, as of tonight, will no longer be required. And, conveniently, when whoever it is you've bundled into those sacks in the security office tries to identify you as the perpetrator of tonight's business, then it's going to look more than likely he's lying. Especially if your brother has something special planned.' She raised an eyebrow, her eyes twinkling. 'You couldn't tell me what it is could you?'

'Haven't a clue,' Campbell replied. 'Ah just hope he gets it right, that's all.'

Prentice held up the stone they had taken from the Bubble. 'You've still to explain this wee bit of the story.'

Boag gasped. 'Is that…?'

'No,' Kyle said. 'At least, we don't know if it is or not.'

Boag's brow furrowed as he scanned the faces of the others. 'Well if it isn't, then where is the real thing?' he asked.

'The question I'm sure the rest of you want answered as well,' McKinnon said. 'And if we could just learn to trust each other a bit more, we might have got to this stage a bit sooner.'

Prentice spat on the floor.

McKinnon ignored him. 'Okay, as I've already pointed out, the stone in your hand is a fake, a very good one, but a fake nonetheless. The real Dark Side of the Moon is within a steel box inside a safe in the manager's private entertainment suite.'

'And where would that be?' Kyle asked.

'It's a side room accessed from the manager's office, on floor nine,' she replied.

'That's the room you can only get to by the special lift,' Campbell said. The penny dropped. 'That's it,' he said, clicking his fingers. 'That's where you were taking the bigwigs on the night of the big party.'

'Correct,' she said. 'Restricted viewings for the *very* privileged few. Invitation only. Everyone else has been duped.'

'So what are we standing here for?' Boag interrupted. 'Where's this lift? Let's get the bloody thing and get out of here.'

'Wait a fucking minute,' Prentice said. 'This doesn't add up.' The others turned to look at him. 'Would somebody tell me why we've just spent the best part of an hour trying to steal a fake diamond? Why in the name of Holy Christ did Boddice send us on a wild goose chase for something that's...?'

'Because,' McKinnon butted in, 'I didn't think you were up to this job.' She raised her hand, stopping their objections. 'I wanted to use my *own* contacts. Guys I trusted. Capable, competent men. Not a bunch of sorry half-wits who couldn't find their arse with both hands.'

Prentice stepped forward. 'Oh, aye? And just what...?'

McKinnon cut him off. 'However, your Mr Boddice had complete faith in you, said you were just the boys. That you would... what was it he said? You would *rise to the occasion.*' The four men looked at her, stony-faced. 'I still didn't believe him. So, I demanded a demonstration of your abilities. A test to show you'd be able to pull something like this off.' She walked over to Prentice, laid a hand on his shoulder. 'I had to be convinced that you could organise yourselves enough to at least get to the point of taking the fake diamond.' Prentice shrugged her off and she spread her arms, beaming a large grin. 'And here you are... you did it. More or less. Boddice was right and I was wrong. You passed the test.' She turned to the others. 'You're here now. You're close. *Now* is the time to present you with the real plan to steal the diamond.' Her smile faded. 'But here's the thing. Do *you* think you're up to it? Was Boddice really right?'

'Wait a minute,' Kyle said. 'The *real* plan?'

'Ah don't like the sound of this,' Prentice said.

'Yes,' said McKinnon. 'The real plan.' She turned to Boag. 'Unfortunately, Alistair, it's not as simple as taking the lift to Nine and walking into the manager's office to swipe the diamond.

That particular room *is* very heavily secured. Extremely hi-tech stuff. You couldn't come within ten feet of the doors without setting off the alarms. Not that you'd hear them, of course. Everything, including the CCTV images, is relayed directly to both the local police station and the Securarama bases in Glasgow and London. Any breach and the whole ninth floor goes into lockdown. The outer reception area for the manager's office has been equipped with special reinforced doors with unique interwoven four-inch steel deadlock bolts which will be slammed into place by a combination of compressed air and hydraulic hammers. There are no windows. No skylights. No other doors. The whole room is practically a safe in itself. You'd be trapped inside without any way of escape.' She gave Boag a pat on the cheek. 'Incendiary devices, or not.'

'And we wouldn't even have gained access to the inner office, never mind this other room where the diamond is,' said Kyle.

'Exactly,' McKinnon replied. 'The whole area is as safe and secure as Fort Knox.' She grinned. 'Or so they think.'

'What do ye mean?' asked Prentice.

'The entire system was set up by the Securarama team months in advance. The operation was personally supervised by the chief security consultant from the store's insurance company as well as representatives of the diamond's owners. There was nothing left to chance, even down to creating the illusion the real diamond was displayed in the Bubble. They were – no, *are* – so sure the system is fail-safe that they don't even see the need to post guards on the room during the night.' She raised her index finger, flicked her gaze from Prentice to Kyle and back again. 'But they overlooked one small, but important thing. Their complacency led them to forget that this building is *old*. Sure, the Bubble and the spike and the interiors are all glossy, shiny and brand new. But the actual building, the shell, is over a hundred years old and,' she paused, looked at each of them in turn, 'this is the important bit. There are some features of the old building which had to remain intact.'

Prentice sucked his teeth. Where the hell was she going with all this architectural crap?

McKinnon seemed to read his thoughts. 'They forgot about the dry riser.'

'The dry what?' asked Boag.

'Riser,' McKinnon repeated 'It's the channel in the wall that carries the pipes for the building's sprinkler system and fire hydrants. There are several of them running in the walls throughout the building. They're leftovers from the original building, and one of them...' A sly smile crept across her face. 'One of them runs directly up to the manager's entertainment suite.' She paused to let her statement sink in. 'That's right, it leads straight to the room with the diamond. There's no need for you to go through the outer office, you can access the room through the very wall itself.'

'Eh, am Ah missing something here?' Prentice asked. 'Only, it kind of occurred to me that if what you say is true, how in the hell are we supposed to get in *behind* the fucking wall in the first place? How do we get into this dry riser system ye're talkin about?'

McKinnon walked over to the Arrow and patted the shaft above the point where it flared into the points of the arrowhead. A ring on one of her fingers made a dull *ting* against the metal. She looked up along the length of the shaft as it rose steeply to the place where it burst through the wall five floors above. 'There,' she said, pointing to the ceiling immediately above the shaft.

The four men looked at each other, then back to McKinnon. They said nothing, but their blank faces prompted her to explain further. 'The Arrow houses the cables which support the Bubble outside. Where it goes into the wall up there the cables continue for another couple of metres, over a pulley system built into the wall. Something like that.' She waved one hand dismissively. 'Whatever it is, the engineer guys have to check out the mechanism every few months, make sure everything's hunky-dory. Just above the Arrow, in the ceiling, is an inspection hatch which allows them to gain access to the gantry above the cables.'

Campbell, who had heard the other security guys talking about this before, now noticed the upper surface of the shaft had a series of subtly countersunk rungs running along its length. He found his saliva drying up, his tongue sticking to the roof of his mouth like a flake of burnt cardboard. He knew what was coming next.

'The space that houses the gantry,' McKinnon continued, 'connects to the old dry riser system for the original building. Get in there, and you're into the riser. Then it's a little bit of manoeuvring, and up four floors and you're at the room with the diamond.'

'And how exactly do we get into the inspection hatch?' asked Kyle. 'The only way Ah can see is to climb up this fucking arrow here.'

McKinnon bit her bottom lip and blinked at him, shifted her gaze to something over his right shoulder. Kyle frowned. 'Wait a fucking minute, you don't mean…'

Prentice burst out laughing. He slapped his thigh. The others turned to look at him, surprised by his outburst. 'Jesus, Mary and Joseph…' He stopped to wipe tears from his eyes. 'Oh, fuck me with the blunt end of a ragman's trumpet, but this is so good, so fucking typical…' He trailed off, trying to catch his breath.

'What do ye mean?' asked Boag.

'Ya bunch of fannies, ye don't see it do ye?' Prentice shook his head, still struggling to contain his laughter. 'Kyle's hit it right on the head. That…' he pointed to the Arrow, '… that *is* how you get to the hatch. She expects us to climb up this fucker and then squeeze through a door at the top.'

His laughter stopped as abruptly as it had started, his face wild-eyed and furious as he marched over to McKinnon.

She stood her ground, unflinching, and let him thrust his face up into hers. 'You!' he shouted, the tendons on his neck standing out. 'You're taking us for a fuckin ride, you… you and Boddice both, you think we're just a bunch of worthless scum, disposable as a piece of toilet paper after ye've wiped yer arse.' His lips drew back in a spittle-flecked snarl. 'Sure, it's fine for the likes of *us* to risk fuckin life and limb so that some other bastard can make a profit out of us, but don't expect to get yer own hands dirty or ye might break a nail. No, leave it up to us… us…' he searched for the word, '…us *minions* to carry out the risky business, the likes of Kyle that'll crawl through shite with an open mouth if Boddice asked him, or Boag, that doesn't know any better.' He spun round to direct his rage at the others. 'Ya spineless bastards, ye're all just the same. Ye're nothin but puppets, never stopping to find out what the big picture is, to see that we're no more than… than…'

He stopped his ranting, the beginnings of tears in his eyes. He looked around at them, a curl of contempt standing on his lips, and sniffed back a trickle of snot.

'Look at youse,' he said, calmer now. 'Look at *us*. We're a sorry bunch of pricks, are we not?' Prentice gave a short humourless laugh. 'You know something? She's right, what she said earlier. We *are* a bunch of amateurs. We're fuckin clueless. How in the name of Christ did we end up here, tryin to do this? This isn't us, this isn't what we do, is it?' His voice dropped to a whisper. 'Since when did this become our lives?'

Prentice dragged a finger across his lower eyelid, examined the moisture on its tip, before rubbing it away against his thumb. 'Ye know what?' he said, looking around the room, at the upper floors, the galleries and the stairways, at the golden Arrow sweeping down from above. 'Ye know what?' His voice tailed away, distracted. He looked at McKinnon, and then at each of the men in turn, and smiled. 'Ach, fuck it,' he said, and tossed the diamond to McKinnon. He turned on his heels and made for the door.

'Hey!' Kyle shouted, and started to run after him. McKinnon grabbed his sleeve, held him back.

'Leave him,' she said.

Kyle shucked her off and called after Prentice again. 'Hey, ya bastard! Where are you going?'

Prentice carried on walking in silence. When he got to the door leading to the staff-only area he gave a short wave without looking back and pushed through, letting the door swing shut with a soft *whump*.

Kyle set out after him, shouting for him to come back.

'Let him go,' McKinnon said. 'He's no use to us now.'

Kyle wheeled. 'What the fuck just happened here? Eh?' He jabbed a finger towards McKinnon's chest. She slapped it away.

'It seems Davie wasn't up to the job,' McKinnon said.

'What the hell do ye mean by that?' Kyle said. 'That man is up to anything. Anything!'

'But he's not here, is he?' She raised an eyebrow. 'Are *you* up to it Gordon? Are any of you? How much do you want this?'

'How much does Boddice want it?' It was Campbell. 'Prentice is right. We're the ones doing the hard work, and where the hell is Boddice tonight?'

'Who knows?' she said. 'But the fact remains, we're here, the diamond is upstairs, and, from what I understand, you boys will now see your share going up, what with Mr Prentice no longer part of the scene.'

Kyle inhaled sharply, held the breath in his lungs and turned his back on the group. He leaned on a glass display case, looked down on an assortment of watches laid out like so many exclamation marks.

What the fuck to do now?

He considered following Prentice. It would be easy, to just turn his back on all this crap, waltz out the door.

But there was Boddice.

And the money. Oh aye, there was that alright.

He sensed Boag and the twin waiting, watching him. Whatever he decided, he knew they would go with him. The bastards were too gormless to do anything for themselves. *Spineless*, Prentice had called them. *Puppets*. But he had included Kyle in those remarks. But it was Prentice who was spineless, not him. Prentice who'd walked out. Maybe McKinnon was right. Prentice couldn't hack it. No balls. No cajones. Not up to the job.

He dug the heels of his hands into his eyes, pushed until they throbbed and he saw little lights forming at the back of his retina, blue and green sparks which fizzed and splashed in the blackness. He drew his hands down his cheeks and looked up to the glass roof above. 'How long have we been in here?' he asked without turning to the others.

Campbell looked at his watch. 'Fifty-three minutes,' he said.

Kyle closed his eyes. 'Alright,' he said. 'What is it we have to do?'

***

Prentice walked to the security control room, his steps echoing in the bare corridor, unsteady and erratic. He had expected some sense of relief, of a burden lifted from his shoulders, the tightness in his chest and throat to have dissipated. He had made the decision. He was out of it. For better or worse, he had defied Boddice, had finally broken the bonds. Of course, there were sure to be consequences, retributions possibly. But he felt confident he could handle them, at least in the short term. And now that he'd done it, he felt there ought to be some change in his mood; if not elation then at least a lightening of his spirit. There was nothing. No easing of the pounding in his temples, no slowing of his heart. The darkness which gripped his mind remained – a heavy, oily dread sunk deep in his soul.

It was still the baby. It was still that. What he'd done *(hadn't done)*.

He kicked open the door to the security station, sending it crashing against the wall. The men hooded and shackled in the corner jumped at the sound. They scuffled and thrashed, struggling to free themselves. Muffled cries came from the sacks covering their heads; stifled swearing and pleading. Prentice moved in front of the men, careful to stay beyond the reach of their flailing legs and feet. 'Shut the fuck up and lie at peace,' he shouted, kicking one of the men in the stomach. They quieted. 'Good,' he said. 'Now just keep it like that.'

Prentice surveyed the room. The wreckage of the security computers lay on the floor, a half-full coffee mug – *I Need My Caffeine Jolt!* in quirky letters – sat beside the night's paperwork piled on the desk alongside the anglepoise lamp. He pulled off his latex gloves and stuffed them in the wastebin in the corner. Fuck the fingerprints.

He pulled open the security office door, and walked out into the night.

***

Prentice took the whole flight of stairs in a single leap as he jumped down from the doorway to the loading bay ramp and ran towards the street. He didn't notice the short dark figure sneaking along the wall behind him, a liquid shadow, just getting to the door in time to catch it before it snicked shut, and slipping inside with a smooth, almost balletic grace.

***

McKinnon went behind one of the display counters and fetched a carrier bag emblazoned with the gold flourish of the T&N logo. She looked from Campbell to Kyle. 'You'll need these,' she said, letting the bag fall to the floor with a clinking of metal and plastic.

Campbell picked up the bag and looked inside. 'What are these?' he asked, fishing out a red and blue nylon strap with two D-shaped steel rings attached at either end. There were seven or eight of them in the bag.

'Carabiners,' McKinnon replied.

'What the fuck are carabiners?' asked Kyle.

'Courtesy of our outdoor leisure department,' McKinnon said. 'Mountaineering section.'

Kyle flicked his gaze towards Campbell and back towards McKinnon. 'Ah don't get it,' he said.

McKinnon took the carabiners from Campbell and fished in the bag for a few seconds. She brought out a different, larger metal contraption. Campbell thought it looked like the handle of one of those extending dog leads. 'And this too,' she said. 'This is an ascender.'

'Okay,' Kyle said. 'Similar question: what the hell's an ascender?'

She moved to the bottom of the Arrow, shaking her head. 'You don't look the outdoor type, so I suppose it's not that much of a surprise.' She held up one of the D-rings. 'Look,' she said, pushing the straight side of the ring. It had a spring-loaded hinge at one end allowing it to open inwards like a clasp, forming a hook which she slipped through a hole in the handle of the ascender. She closed the carabiner and took the assembly to a brass-coloured cable which ran the length of the Arrow from floor to ceiling.

'Ah never noticed that before,' said Campbell, indicating the cable.

McKinnon manoeuvred the cable, sliding it into a groove on the inside of the ascender's handle grip. The device was now securely fastened onto the cable. 'This is how the maintenance guys do it,' she said. She went into the bag again and brought out a harness attachment and hooked the other end of the carabiner onto it. 'You wear this harness and you're safe and sound as you scramble up. If you slip, the ascender holds you onto the cable.'

Kyle took the harness from her, pulled against the straps connecting it to the ascender. It held fast to the cable.

'Now push it up,' McKinnon said.

'Eh?' said Kyle.

'The ascender. Push it, slide it up the cable.'

Kyle took the handle and pushed it up the cable. It went up smoothly.

'Now pull again,' she said.

Kyle tugged hard on the harness. The ascender again held tight to the cable.

'You see?' she said. 'All you have to do is climb up the shaft a bit at a time, moving the ascender as you go. It moves upwards freely, but the mechanism grips the cable if it goes backwards. If you fall, it will catch you.'

Kyle and Campbell looked less than convinced.

She sighed. 'Trust me. It works. You'll see once you get up there.'

'Aye, *if* we get up there,' Kyle said. 'Ah'm still not sure about this.'

'Damn right,' said Campbell. 'How come it's us that has to go up? Ah'm scared of heights. How can you not do it?'

McKinnon gave them a wry smile. 'In these shoes? I don't think so.'

'And then what?' Kyle asked. 'What do we do when we get up there, get into this special room?'

McKinnon held out the stone from the Bubble. 'You take this and swap it for the real diamond. It won't make much difference in the end, but for a wee while at least they'll think we were just a bunch of opportunist amateurs, that we only went for the display version. It'll take them a day or two to figure out the one in the vault upstairs isn't the real deal.'

'And by then, we'll be well away,' said Boag.

'Exactly.'

'Ye still haven't answered my question,' said Kyle. 'What do we do in the room? How do we get our hands on the real diamond?'

McKinnon drew Campbell and Kyle in close, put her arms round their shoulders. 'That's why we need the both of you.'

***

The cold seeped into John's arse as he sat on the steps outside the hotel. He'd pleaded with the bouncer to let him wait here for a minute or two, take the chance to sober up a bit. Not that he needed to; he was very far from drunk, and the rough handling he'd received on the part of the hotel security after the little incident with his dobber and Lady Anne had focused his mind somewhat. The bastards had been right up for it, as if they'd been waiting all night for something to kick off and John had given them the perfect excuse. If it hadn't been for a few of the guys from the stockroom stepping in, persuading the bouncers he was just wasted, he could have found himself on the receiving end of a right good kicking. As it was, John sensed the bouncer at the door behind him was biding his time, humouring him, waiting till the crowds thinned out a bit before he called up a few of his mates on the old walkie-talkie, dragged John round to the service entrance, out of sight.

For the moment, however, he was safe; there was a steady trickle of punters filing out from the hotel, flagging down taxis, singing at the tops of their voices (Christ knew what the residents in the rooms above were making of it all). One or two of the revellers spotted him on the steps, came over to offer congratulations, commiserations, express admiration, call him a bloody fool. There were shoulder punches, bearhugs, shaking of hands, shaking of heads.

John played up to it all, offering a crooked grin and a sheepish shrug, a slurred reply or two. Enough to make sure he was still visible, still someone who would stick in their memory later on.

He leaned forward, his hands dangling between his knees, and turned his head in the direction of the store. He couldn't see it, but a shifting glow in the sky behind the intervening buildings gave an indication of where the Bubble hung, illuminated by the floodlights and lasers. He looked at his watch. Right now, this very second, the guys were in there. Stealing the diamond. He hoped. The fact that he hadn't received any text on his mobile, from them or from Boddice, meant it wasn't over yet.

***

The carabiners and the harnesses were all very well, but Campbell was still anxious. He and Kyle were about two thirds of the way up the Arrow and the floor seemed thousands of feet below. The upturned faces of McKinnon and Boag now looked like small pennies at the bottom of a well. McKinnon had given them head torches to light the way once they got through the hatch and Campbell felt unbalanced by the weight and the tightness of the strap against his forehead.

Kyle moved ahead of him, inching upwards, hand over hand on the recessed rungs. The nylon straps of the carabiners connected them to the lifeline of the cable. McKinnon had been right of course; the ascender contraption gripped the cable without any problem. If they slipped, they would fall only a few feet before being halted by the carabiners attached to their harnesses. Still, Campbell wasn't entirely sure he trusted the whole set-up. The nylon straps, for one thing. They didn't look as though they were capable of holding his weight if he was to go over the side. Plus, he would be left swinging in mid-air. Getting back onto the shaft didn't look as if it would be too easy a task. He tightened his grip on the rung in front of him – *let's just make sure there's no going over the side involved.*

As they climbed, the cable thrummed and sang like a plucked guitar string, a deep low drone, the sound amplified by the hollow chamber of the shaft, such that Campbell felt he was playing the world's largest musical instrument. Concerto for shaky man and fucking enormous arrow.

Kyle was like bloody Spiderman. He'd hooked himself on at the bottom, gave McKinnon a brief smirk and started up the Arrow as if he'd been doing it all his life, pulling himself, metre by metre, along the length of the shaft. Within a matter of minutes, they'd climbed to the height of the second floor, and Campbell had to call for Kyle to ease up a bit, take a breather. Christ, his thigh muscles were burning like buggery, struggling to keep up with the pace Kyle had set. Kyle had looked at him over his shoulder, snorted his contempt, but waited till Campbell got the blood flowing back into his legs and signalled to go on.

Above them they could see more clearly the inspection hatch McKinnon had pointed out earlier. It was obvious now they knew what to look for. From the top of the Arrow, where it met the wall, to the ceiling looked a good five, maybe six, feet. It would be a bit of a stretch to reach the hatch and undo the bolts holding it in place. Awkward at the best of times, but a fucking liability when balancing on a smooth, shiny cylinder seventy feet above the floor. A smooth, shiny cylinder at a forty-five degree slope. With nothing to hold onto.

Which turned out to be not exactly true. When they finally got to the top they saw that the shaft had a small level platform, again recessed, perhaps eight or ten inches across. It made enough of a ledge to stand on. The wall above the shaft had two white rungs, blended into the paintwork so that they would never be visible from the ground. Campbell waited a few feet below and held tightly to the handle of the ascender as Kyle unclipped his carabiner and reattached it to the lower of the two white rungs. Campbell noticed Kyle's legs were trembling, whether from fatigue or sheer terror he couldn't tell. He felt vaguely reassured by this – at least he wasn't the only one who might have the skittering shits. Kyle turned his head slightly, directed his voice over his shoulder. 'If Ah slip here, you be bloody well ready, okay? Just in case, right?'

Campbell licked his lips. 'Don't worry,' he said. 'Ah'll be on my toes.' Like hell he would. If Kyle slipped, Campbell would be making damn sure he was out the way of any falling or flailing that might be going on. Kyle would just have to fend for himself.

Kyle let go of the rung and reached upwards to grasp the handles of the hatch above. Campbell was horrified to see him lean back, away from the wall *(away!)*, letting the harness take his weight and support him as he released the latches and swung the door down on its hinges. The opening gaped like a black, toothless mouth. Kyle switched on his head torch and looked up. The rungs continued upwards for a few feet on the other side, ending at a metal catwalk which stretched off to the right.

Kyle looked down at him. 'So far, so good,' he said, a grin spreading across his face. 'The next bit's gonnae be the hard bit.'

The hard bit? The climb up hadn't exactly been straight out of the really easy book of easy things to do on a Friday night. If that wasn't hard, then what…?

The last vestige of strength was sucked from Campbell's legs as the reality dawned on him. Kyle's next move only confirmed the awful truth. Dread and panic swept over Campbell as he watched Kyle unclip the carabiner from the rung, letting it dangle from the harness, and climb up into the hatch unfettered.

Kyle scrambled onto the edge of the hatch and sat down, his legs swinging in the void. 'Piece of piss,' he said. He held out his hand. 'Come on. You next.'

Campbell shook his head. 'Nup,' he said. 'Ah can't.'

'What do ye mean ye can't?' Kyle called down, his voice

small and echoless in the confined space of the hatchway. 'Get your arse in gear. We've not got all night.'

Campbell tried to slow his heartbeat, contain his panic. A voice in his head repeated: *Don't Look Down... Don't Look Down... Don't Look Down... Don't Look...*

He looked down.

The Arrow's shaft dropped away beneath him, tapering to a bright thread as it reached the floor. Boag and McKinnon were staring up at him, one of them – Christ, he couldn't even tell which one it was from this height – pointing and gesturing. His calf muscles started to tremble, a knotting pain building in them like little balls of hot lead.

'Hurry the fuck up!' Kyle yelled, making Campbell jump and white-knuckle his grip even further on the handle of the ascender. *You can do this*, he told himself. *A wee bit at a time.* He brought his other hand across and slowly unclipped the carabiner. As soon as it slipped free from the ascender, before he had time to think, he closed his eyes, let go and lunged forward, scrabbling for the rung in front of him like a first-time swimmer thrashing his way to the side of the pool. His hand made contact with the cool metal and his fingers locked around it.

Kyle gave a low whistle. 'Man, you nearly went over the edge there,' he said. 'That was pretty close.'

Campbell blinked up at him, catching his breath. 'Was it?' What a stupid bloody thing to do. He could have been a pile of red jelly on the floor. 'Was it really?'

'Nah, Ah'm only yanking your chain. You were fine. A bit undignified, maybe, but fine.'

'Don't fuck about with me,' said Campbell. 'Ah'm shitin myself as it is.'

'Aye, well just get on with it. Ah'm beginning to lose patience.'

Campbell drew a deep breath and exhaled sharply, a quivery, horsey sound. He made to let go of the rung, but it was as if his hands had taken on a life of their own, some primal hard-wired instinct shouting out it was plain crazy to release his grip. Wasn't it obvious this was what was keeping him from plunging to his doom? His hands refused to budge. He felt his gullet begin to heave and contract. Oh Christ, he was going to puke. He tried to hold it back, his eyes and nose watering, but to no avail. He felt the acidic onrushing liquid rise to the back of his throat and he could contain it no longer. He spewed a spluttered spray of bright yellow vomit, sending it tumbling, disintegrating, to spatter on the floor far below. A faint yell, Boag's voice – *Hey ya tosser!* – rose from the depths.

Campbell spat the remaining vomit from his mouth. This was ridiculous. Kyle was waiting above him, the expression on his face a mixture of contempt and twisted merriment. He was enjoying the sideshow. *Come on, just do it!* Campbell told himself. *He thinks you're no more than a fucking wank-stain. Show him different.*

He sucked air in through his clenched teeth and forced his fingers to open. The voice in his head started up its little chant again – *Don't Look Down… Don't…*

He made himself stare at the wall in front of him. He tried to convince himself it was no different from climbing a ladder to get into the loft at home. It's exactly the same, he thought, just higher. Aye, seventy feet higher.

He moved his hand up, grasped the next rung and pulled himself upwards. Gingerly, he lifted his right leg and placed his foot on the rung. He felt like some daring high wire act in the circus, the people below tense with the possibility, the anticipation, of seeing him fall. Left hand, left leg, up again. He breathed a sigh of relief, it was working. Right hand up, and he felt Kyle grab his wrist, haul him towards the lip of the hatch. Campbell slithered into the opening on his belly, his legs kicking in mid-air, seeking purchase on something, anything, that would propel him onto a solid surface. Kyle seized his belt, yanked him onto the hard metal frame of the catwalk.

Campbell got to his feet and grabbed a railing to steady

himself, careful not to step backwards towards the open hatch.

'Don't say thanks or anything,' said Kyle.

'Maybe if ye hadn't dragged my kegs up the crack of my arse Ah might be more grateful,' replied Campbell, adjusting his trousers.

'Right, head torch on, and let's get moving,' Kyle said. 'And watch you don't bang yer head on any of these stanchions.'

'Aye,' Campbell sighed. 'Onwards and upwards.'

***

Boag watched Campbell's flailing legs disappear into the space in the ceiling above, the glow from the head torches fading into the gloom as the two men moved deeper into the access corridor.

Beside him, McKinnon shook her head. 'Amateurs…'

Boag looked around the room, unexpectedly shy and nervous in the presence of this woman who had appeared from nowhere and now seemed to be in charge of the whole affair. He felt his old army indoctrination begin to kick in; the almost automatic deference to figures of authority. He couldn't decide whether he should tell her he hadn't finished planting his devices, that there was one more to go; that he should be getting back to work, get the job finished. He cleared his throat. 'Eh, Ah was just—'

She held up her hand, cutting him off. She glanced at her watch. 'Not just now,' she said. 'I need to go.'

'Go?' Boag said.

She took a silver oblong cylinder from her pocket. 'Yes,' she said, turning the object over in her hand. To Boag it looked like some kind of miniature torch. 'I need to do the security check.' She tapped the end of the cylinder. 'This is a portable electronic sensor. A data logger. The guards dock it with the security points around the store, at least once every ninety minutes. That sends a signal to the central computer, telling it that everything's fine, the guards are doing their rounds as they should be. You must have noticed these sorts of things before?'

Boag shook his head, mystified, embarrassed he didn't know about it.

'Whatever,' she said. 'But if the computer doesn't get a signal during each inspection period it sets off the alarms.' She put the cylinder back in her pocket. 'With our bunch of merry men tied up in the front office, if I don't make the rounds we'll be in trouble.' She moved off towards the grand staircase. 'So, if you don't mind, I'll just get on with it.' She cast a look over her shoulder. 'I'll see you soon.'

Boag watched her go, climbing the stairs to the darkness of the second floor and disappearing through the door to the electrical goods department.

He did mind actually. Why was he the one who was left behind? Everyone else had gone off to do something important and here he was, left alone to kick his heels. Johnny-no-mates.

He sighed. He might as well make himself useful. He could always do something about the last detonator, find somewhere to set it up.

If he could be arsed that was.

***

The cables which came up through the Arrow shaft passed over a series of massive pulleys and gears, greased and oiled with a foul-smelling yellow gunk which coated their spiralled cords like some alien secretion. They creaked and groaned, adjusting the weight and tension as the Bubble swung and bounced imperceptibly in the night air. Campbell briefly marvelled at the scale of it all, the forces and balances involved in keeping the whole structure in place.

'C'mon doughhead,' Kyle called from up ahead. 'No time to admire the scenery.'

'Aye, aye,' Campbell muttered. 'Don't pish yer pants.'

'What was that?'

'Ah'm comin.'

They eased slowly along the narrow catwalk, the beams from their head torches sending pale cones of light ahead of them. After a short distance the walls on either side changed from the smooth white panels of the hatchway to rougher brick with crumbling mortar. The air had a dry, dusty odour: the smell of spiders and dried paper.

'This must be the old part of the building,' Kyle said. 'It can't be long now.' They could see the passageway stretch twenty feet or so until it narrowed to a dark, thin slit where the metal gangway of the catwalk ended. 'What do you think?' asked Kyle. 'That looks like it, eh?'

They crept towards the black fissure, the walls and ceiling closing in on them until they were moving through little more than a tunnel. They halted where the catwalk ended abruptly at a small parapet in front of the narrow gap in the wall. Kyle leaned over, stuck his head into the space and looked up. Campbell gripped the rail of the catwalk and joined him, their torches showing a black iron pipe which rose up into the dark where it disappeared from sight in the shadows above. The cavity housing the pipe was perhaps three feet by four, and God knew how high or deep. Thankfully, whoever had built it all those years ago had seen fit to include a set of rungs running beside the pipe. At least they wouldn't have to shimmy up the pipe itself.

'You okay with this?' Kyle asked. 'You're no gonnae have another flakey are you?'

'No, Ah'm alright,' Campbell said. 'Ah feel better, this'll be fine. Ah can't see the drop. And if Ah don't think about it Ah'll be—'

'Good,' Kyle interrupted. 'But Ah'm going first anyway. If you fall off Ah don't want ye comin down on top of me.'

'Thanks for the vote of confidence,' Campbell said.

Kyle swung into the gap in the wall and grabbed one of

the rungs. 'No offence intended, by the way,' he said. Campbell grunted. 'We'll go slow,' Kyle went on, 'This'll be hard work Campbell.'

Campbell. That was the first time he'd ever heard Kyle use his name, that he'd ever addressed him directly, as a person. Wonders will never cease, he thought. He wasn't daft enough to think this constituted their being new best buddies, but it was a surprise nonetheless. He edged himself into the crack, reaching out to find the nearest rung. Rust stains bled from the iron hoops onto the bricks like the trails of some peculiar red slug. A draft of warm air rose from the depths below, ruffling his hair. He looked up to see the soles of Kyle's boots a few feet above and started climbing to catch up. 'Why did you not go with him?' he asked.

'What?' Kyle replied. 'Go with who?'

'Prentice,' Campbell said. 'When he left. Why did you not go as well? You two do everythin together. Why split up now?'

'Fuck's sake,' said Kyle. 'You've picked a funny time to strike up a conversation.'

'Sorry,' Campbell said. 'But, you know, it should be Prentice that's climbing up here with you, not me. That's the usual way of things. You two are partners, are ye not?'

'Don't read too much into that,' said Kyle. 'He does his thing and Ah do mine. We're not married or anything.'

'You still haven't answered my question though. Why did ye not go as well?'

'Why? Ah'll tell ye why. Because Boddice said so, that's why. Same reason as you're here, is it not?'

'Not really. Ah'm here out of fear. John too. But it's different for you. You don't have to worry about things like that.'

Kyle stopped and looked down, breathing hard from the exertion of the climb. Campbell blinked against the glare of the head torch. 'You believe that?' asked Kyle.

'What?'

'That it's any different for me?' Kyle wiped the dust

from his nose. 'Listen, pal, it's fear for me too, don't think otherwise. Ah do as Ah'm told, end of story. No arguments, no complaints. Prentice thinks there's a way out of this. But he's wrong. He made a mistake tonight. A big one.' He turned, resumed his climbing.

Campbell started after him. 'Maybe so,' he said. 'But it doesn't change the fact it's you that punishes the mistakes. You and Prentice.'

'Aye, well Prentice will see soon enough who's gonnae be on the receiving end.'

They climbed in silence for a while, and then a new thought came into Campbell's head. 'What's the worst thing you've done?'

'Eh?'

'The most grisly thing you've had to do for Boddice. Ye know, as punishment.'

Kyle laughed. 'Fuckin hell, you're in a talkative mood all of a sudden. What do ye want to know that for?'

'No reason really, just... ye know... curiosity. Ah'm interested.'

'Ah get ye,' Kyle said. 'Ye want to know what might lie in store for ye if ye step out of line?'

'No, not even that, though now that ye've mentioned it...'

'Alright, ' Kyle said. 'Ah'll tell ye. Ah've done plenty of horrible things, gruesome things, but the worst thing wasn't somethin Ah did for Boddice. It was for Prentice.'

'Prentice?'

'Aye. Years ago. Prentice used to have this auld Alsation dug. Thor it was called. Bad-tempered bastard it was. Take the hand off ye if ye looked at it the wrong way. Well, one day it was tied to a table in the pub and some eejit took a kick at it for no reason other than the guy didn't like the look of it. Nuthin much, but enough for the dog to let out a yelp.' Kyle stopped climbing for a second. Wiped sweat from his eyes. 'Ye might imagine how Prentice would have reacted, kicked the guy's head in there and then, put him in hospital for a month. But no. He waited. Bided his time.' Kyle grabbed the next rung and began climbing again. 'Me and Prentice got a hold of this guy when he came out his work one night, bundled him into the back of the motor and drove out to this remote car park at the Gleniffer Braes outside Paisley. High up, great view of the city. Not that we paid much attention that night. We gave the guy a right good pasting, and then Prentice went into the boot of the car and brought out this big bucket of paint.'

'What, emulsion? For doing up yer house?'

'Exactly, yellow paint. A big industrial-sized bucket of the stuff. Prentice opened it and picked the guy up off the ground.' Kyle was puffing now, breathless from the climb. 'The guy was still conscious. He looked from Prentice to me and then to the bucket of paint. Prentice was calm and cool. He knelt down and lifted the guy's chin. 'This is for Thor, pal.' The guy just looked at us. 'Remember my dug? The one ye kicked?' It was clear the guy didn't have a clue, but it didn't matter. Prentice signalled to me. Prentice held the guy's arms behind his back, while Ah took his head and plunged it into the bucket.' Kyle halted his ascent again, stared at the decaying bricks in front of him. Remembering. 'The guy struggled like fuck. You could tell he was tryin not to breathe in, not to get that paint into his lungs, but it made no difference. Ah just held him down until he could hold it back no longer and he sucked it in, through his nostrils, through his mouth, that yellow paint gurgling deep into his lungs.

'We let him go after that, watched him stand up, tryin to catch his breath, coughin, splutterin, blindly staggerin about, arms outstretched, seekin help. But it was no use. The paint was coating the inside of his lungs. He collapsed onto his knees, still hawking paint, makin this horrible noise, hopin to get his lungs inflated, get that precious air into his body. But no. His head hung forward and – Ah remember this more than anything – the paint oozing out of him like a burst egg yolk, long strands of yellow stuff stringing from his nose and mouth. He vomited up a plug of paint and blood. He tried opening his eyes, but the paint was in them too. He couldn't see a damned thing. Started pawing at the air, frantic and futile, gaspin for breath.'

Kyle climbed a few feet more, then paused and looked back at Campbell. 'It took him a good two or three minutes to die. To drown. And me, standing watching with my hands all yellow, and Prentice at my back, laughin.

'For days after it Ah would find wee splashes of paint on my fingernails or on my jacket, in the creases of my trousers. Wee reminders... That... That was the worst...' His voice tailed off.

Kyle's face was lost in the glare from his head torch and Campbell felt a tinge of regret at asking the question. Regret and fear.

Kyle cleared his throat. 'Right,' he said. 'Ah think we're nearly there.' He pointed to a valve in the pipe a few feet above his head. 'This is the one.' They had passed three of these valves on the way up, a rusting, knurled wheel protruding from the main body of the pipe. According to McKinnon these were the water outlets for the old fire appliances. She had told them to count four of these, one for each of the floors as they moved up through the dry riser. Opposite each valve was a panel in the wall, a red door with latches at each corner. Campbell hadn't quite followed the logic of what she'd told them, but supposedly if there was a fire, water was pumped up the pipe to the sprinkler system and to these valves where the firemen could open the panel and attach their hoses.

The fourth valve – the one just above them – was directly opposite the panel which led to the manager's office.

Kyle scrambled up the last few feet and hooked his arm through one of the rungs. Campbell joined him, his own hands gripping the rungs tightly, acutely conscious of the empty drop into the dusty blackness of the shaft below. They directed their torches onto the panel in the wall. The panel had four latches, each secured into little metal slots in the brickwork at one end and rotated about a hinged bracket on the panel at the other. Kyle reached out to the first latch and twisted it. Nothing happened. 'Bastard's stuck,' he grunted through gritted teeth, straining with the effort.

'Want me to try?' Campbell asked.

Kyle raised an eyebrow.

'Aye, well, okay… keep going,' said Campbell, giving him a thumbs-up, or at least the best approximation of one he could manage with his hand spot-welded to the ladder rung.

Kyle gave the latch a bang with the side of his fist and tried again. This time it screeched open, the metal bar grating against the rusting grit surface of the panel. Kyle grinned. 'One down, three to go.'

The other latches were less problematic, turning smoothly with little forcing. As the last one came free of its securing slot the panel slid forward into the room beyond, landing on the floor with a heavy dull clang.

A thin blue light oozed from the room, leaking an eerie spectral glow into the shaft and casting inky shadows on the wall behind them. A blast of air-conditioned coolness ruffled their hair, carrying with it the same cut-grass smell they had encountered in the Bubble what now seemed like a year before. Kyle and Campbell stuck their heads through the opening and surveyed the space before them.

They were in.

***

Boag kept hearing noises: little ticking sounds as the building settled in the cooling night, the muffled echoes of Kyle and Campbell as they clambered through the spaces in the ceiling and walls high above, the banging of doors in the depths of the store as McKinnon went about her business with the security checker.

But there was something else; something different. He couldn't be entirely sure he had heard anything at all, he thought perhaps it was just the intensity of the situation that had heightened his senses, made' him aware of the least thing; or it was his mind playing tricks on him – the empty store, the dark corners, the mannequins with their weird faces; they were all freaking him out. Nevertheless, there had been clicks and thuds, a faint scraping once or twice, sounds that didn't seem part of the normal night-time vocabulary of the building.

He put it to the back of his mind, tried to focus on the task in hand. He opened his rucksack and took out the last unused detonator rig, together with the remote trigger. He placed them on a glass display case containing an array of silk scarves, gold bracelets and necklaces. He felt he'd done a more than passable job with the remote; a set of eight toggle switches feeding through a digital relay to a model aeroplane radio transmitter. Each detonator rig had a small receiver which picked up the signal from the different switches, a separate frequency for each one.

It had been good to put his training to use once more. Transistor-transistor logic pulses, optical isolators, microchip controllers, it all came flooding back to him. He had actually enjoyed himself, sitting in his tiny kitchen with all the gear spread out on the table, assembling the rigs and the remote. Sixty quid's worth of cheap and cheerful goodies from Maplin's had got him everything he needed, Boddice footing the bill of course.

The only weak link was the detonators themselves; the stuff the Rastahman had provided was old, second-rate, one step removed from being junk. Fuck knows where Aiken had picked them up, but at the time Boag hadn't felt himself to be in a position to point out the somewhat shite quality of the goods, not with Boddice acting the big cheese, pretending he knew what he was talking about.

Which was why Boag had added his own little pièce-de-résistance.

All in all, Boag was pleased with what he'd managed to achieve with the shoddy materials provided, how he'd added his own little something extra to spice things up. In fact, he felt rather proud; he'd been useful again, had made a proper contribution to the work of the team for once. It was a pity, if everything went to plan, that no-one would get to see how good a job he'd done.

He gave a contented sigh; in a way, he might have turned a corner, begun to get some self-respect back, maybe even...

There it was again.

Close this time. Somewhere just behind his left shoulder. A shuffling scuff against the floor.

He spun around.

He just had time to register the crouching figure in front of him before the punch slammed into his nose and everything went dark. As he crumpled to the floor and consciousness seeped away, his fading mind struggled to comprehend the leering face behind the fist. The name seemed to glow like a red neon sign in the blackness that closed in on him. The last feeling he had before he went under was one of puzzlement.

Leggett?

***

The strongroom differed from the ostentation of the Bubble in so many ways: no glittering pedestals, no triumphant music, no crowd-control barriers, and, most of all, no lasers. The room was a study in understatement: a solitary white sofa sat on a dark blue carpet, facing a pale desk the colour of a full moon behind clouds. The surface of the desk was bare save for a small white cushion which sat in the centre. On the wall behind the desk, illuminated by a cool blue spotlight was a black metallic panel, the size of a hardback book, and with a red LED blazing from its centre. On either side of the panel, perhaps five or six feet away and also set into the wall, were two six-inch computer monitors with a digital keypad mounted underneath. The whole set-up reminded Campbell of the crazy computer in that space odyssey film; the one that lost its marbles and started killing the crew of the spaceship.

Kyle gripped the edge of the hatch and hoisted himself into the room, Campbell following somewhat less elegantly. The two men stood in the middle of the floor breathing heavily, glad of the clean air after the stale brickdust of the shaft. They looked at each other, wide-eyed, barely able to believe they had made it this far.

Kyle let out a low whistle. 'This looks the business alright,' he said. 'It's somehow scarier than all that hi-tech shite downstairs.'

'More evil,' suggested Campbell.

Kyle looked at him and nodded slowly. 'Aye, ye're right.' Kyle moved towards the panel with the red LED, squinted at the thin handle which ran horizontally across its otherwise featureless face. 'This'll be it then. The safe.'

'Ah guess,' Campbell said. He picked up the dry riser door from the floor and rested it against the wall. The inner fascia was identical to the woodgrain panels of the office wall. Campbell smiled; when the door was in place it would be practically invisible. Someone's head was going to roll for not paying enough attention. He could just imagine some poor schmuck trying to explain it to the corporate suits: *'What do you mean you didn't know there was a door in the wall? What the fuck were we paying you for?'*

Kyle snapped his fingers. 'You ready for this?' he asked.

Campbell straightened, walked towards him. 'As ready as Ah'll ever be.'

McKinnon's instructions were simple. Kyle delved into his pocket and brought out the piece of paper she had given them down on the shop floor. The safe opened by inputting two sets of numbers into the computers on either side of the safe. Easy-peasy. The catch, though – the element that required both of them to be here – was that the numbers had to be punched in simultaneously to both keypads. Any appreciable delay beyond a few hundred milliseconds and the alarms would be triggered. On top of that, the numbers were not just a straightforward sequence. No, they were much more than that; the computer screens showed a five-by-five grid of coloured squares. Each square corresponded to a number written on a similar pair of grids on the paper McKinnon had passed to them:

0	6	18	14	22
13	24	2	5	16
7	15	11	23	4
21	3	9	17	10
19	12	20	1	8

LEFT GRID

21	2	8	14	15
13	19	20	1	7
0	6	12	18	24
17	23	4	5	11
9	10	16	22	3

RIGHT GRID

When activated, the computer would flash a particular square on the screen, a different one in a different random position for each control panel, and the corresponding number found on their piece of paper had to be entered from the keypad as quickly as possible. When all the squares were completed, the resulting table formed what McKinnon said was called a *magic square* – all the numbers in any single column, row or diagonal added up to the same value: 60. The thousands of different combinations of possible squares meant that the code would be almost impossible to break.

Unless, of course, there was access to the kind of information McKinnon had left them on the sheet of paper.

Kyle studied the numbers. 'Ah hope to fuck this works,' he said. He folded the paper and carefully tore it down the middle, giving Campbell the left-hand grid.

They positioned themselves in front of the keypad. Below

the coloured grids on the computer screens a single stark message blinked: *Press 0 to initiate sequence.*

Kyle adjusted his latex gloves, laced his fingers and cracked his knuckles. Campbell winced at the sound. Kyle blew out a long exhalation and nodded to Campbell. 'Ready?'

Campbell swallowed and nodded back.

'Okay,' Kyle said. 'Here we go. On my count... Three... two—'

'Wait!' Campbell shouted.

Kyle wheeled on him. 'For fuck's sake!' he yelled. 'What the hell is it? Ah thought ye said ye were ready?'

'Ah did... Ah know... it's just, should we not... ye know, practice this before we start? Make sure we can do it right? Get in synch with each other.'

'Practice? *Practice?* Jesus Christ, we don't have time for any of that shite. We've spent long enough in this place. Any minute now the polis could walk through that door, and there would be me and you tryin to explain how we're just workies doing a night shift repair on that big fuckin hole in the wall. That's gonnae be convincin isn't it?'

Campbell stared at the floor.

'So, if it's all the same to you, we'll just forget the practicin bit and get straight on to the job in hand, eh?'

Campbell looked up. 'Sorry,' he said. 'Ah'm a wee bit twitchy, that's all.'

'Fuck twitchy, let's just do this and get the hell out of here.'

'Okay.'

Kyle sucked his teeth and poised his finger over his keypad. 'Right. Again. Let's go... three... two... one... now!'

They both jabbed the square with the zero on their respective pads. The computer gave a tiny beep and the relevant square of both grids on the screen turned black. Immediately, Campbell's grid flashed the centre bottom square, while Kyle's flashed two along and three down. They checked their sheets and keyed in the correct numbers as quickly as possible – *20* for Campbell, 6 for Kyle. The coloured squares went black and the next flashed up.

Thin pellets of sweat snaked through the stubble on Campbell's cheek as he keyed in the rest of the numbers, the tension in his muscles forcing his hand into a tight claw with only his index finger protruding to stab at the digits on the keypad. By the time the last square was left blinking on the now black-filled grid, his hand was shaking so violently he almost fumbled the very last number, his finger brushing against the adjacent 5 as he prodded the final 4.

His screen went completely blank.

Campbell glanced across to Kyle who appeared equally drained by the experience. Like Campbell's, his screen was also blank.

Nothing appeared to have happened; the room was silent, no message appeared on the screens, no beeps from the keypads, though, more importantly from Campbell's point of view, no alarms going off or sliding bolts sealing the doors to the room.

'What happens now?' he asked Kyle.

'Fuck knows.' Kyle licked his lips. 'Maybe there's—'

'Wait!' Campbell shouted. He pointed to the panel on the wall. 'Look!'

The LED had changed from red to green. It burned like a brilliant star, a vivid, electric spangle against the flat black of the metal plate.

'Do ye think…?'

'Only one way to find out,' said Kyle, placing his fingers on the handle below the green light. He pulled gently and the door slid open with a liquid heaviness to reveal the dark space within.

Campbell joined him and they both leaned forward to look inside. The light from their head torches flooded the interior of the safe. At the back, resting against the rear wall of the compartment, sat a plain black box, perhaps six inches to a side, unadorned except for a picture of a crescent moon etched onto its upper surface. The detail in the etching was such that individual craters and ridges could be seen, the line marking the boundary between the light and dark sides jagged and fractured by encroaching mountain ranges and crater rims. Kyle reached into the safe and ran his index finger along the top of the box, tracing the raised lines of the etching. He looked at Campbell and smiled. 'This is it,' he said and lifted the box from the safe.

At that instant a loud explosion rocked the floor beneath their feet. Campbell frowned. *What the fuck was that?* His mouth made the appropriate movements to accompany the words, but Kyle never heard them.

A second explosion, much closer this time, obliterated any sound Campbell might have made, and this time the alarms did go off.

Big time.

***

Boag had a cold. A deep, heavy, snotter-filled, nose-clogged stinker of a cold. He sat on the sofa in his gran's house trying to pinpoint when it had first started. He didn't remember having it yesterday. *Yesterday?* What had he been doing yesterday? He couldn't bring that to mind either. Was there something to do with arrows? Arrows and diamonds? He shifted in his seat; something was digging into his back, making him uncomfortable, something sharp and angular, pressed hard against the skin between his shoulder blades. Was it an arrow? He thought it might be. There was an idea there. Yes, an arrow. Or a diamond. Had he been shot by an arrow? His nose was streaming and he blinked back tears that were beginning to brim in his eyes. This fucking cold. This stupid fucking...

A huge bang, a dry, chest-thudding thump, brought him awake with a start. He sat up quickly, struggling to get his bearings. His surroundings tilted and swayed and he closed his eyes in an attempt to steady the lurching pitch of the floor.

He felt the warm, slick trickle of blood oozing from his nostrils, the sensation triggering an almighty sneeze. Immediately his head exploded in a white-hot flash of pain, his legs buckling beneath him. He brought his hands up to his face, cradling his smashed and splintered nose and fighting the promise of the sweet bliss of fainting.

'Wee-hoo mama!' came a high-pitched voice off to his right. 'Ah'm fuckin back ya bastards! Ah'm a weapon of mass destruction!' Boag opened his eyes to see Leggett standing with the detonator remote in his hands, his finger poised above the second switch on the control panel.

Boag stretched out a hand towards him, flapping feebly at the black plastic box. 'No, wait!' he shouted.

Leggett turned towards him, a gleeful malice sparkling in his eyes. 'Oh-ho!' he said. 'Managed to rouse yourself, Ah see.' He held up the remote. 'This is an interestin wee toy isn't it? See what happens when ye throw these wee switches? It's fucking great!' He flicked the next switch and a second shuddering boom, this time on one of the upper floors, shook the building. A fine white powder silted down from the ceiling far above. Boag shook his head, tried to clear the fug in is mind. The action sent another jolt of blinding pain through his forehead, but at least it forced him to get to his feet. He wiped the blood from his mouth, inspected the clotted slickness of it between his fingers. A howling blare sounded in his head, rising and falling in a deafening, grating discord. At first, he thought it was the pain from his broken nose crystallising in a yammering wail in his skull and he clutched at one of the display counters by his side to steady himself. Leggett swaggered towards him, his head tilted back as he echoed the sound in Boag's head: '*Eeee-oooo, eeee-oooo, eeee-oooo!* Look at me, Ah'm fuckin howlin at the moon, man. Ah'm a werewolf bastard, *eeee-oooo, eeee-oooo*. Holy mama and sweet Christ on the cross,' he punched the air to punctuate his words, 'Ah've fucked youse up good style! *Eeee-oooo!*'

The wailing noise went on and Boag realised the sound wasn't in his head but was coming from the klaxons mounted on the walls. 'Ha, ha, ya pricks,' Leggett shouted above the clamour. 'Let's see what youse are gonnae do now.'

He threw another switch and a new explosion burst from behind them. The door leading to the security office blew back on its hinges and flames jumped from the small pile of kindling Boag had left there earlier. The fire crackled and sparked for a few seconds before the overhead sprinkler system kicked in, showering freezing water onto their heads. Leggett looked up in surprise and Boag made a lunging grab for the control box.

'Aw no ye don't,' Leggett said, easily sidestepping the wheeling thrashings of Boag's arms. He brought his knee up and caught Boag in the groin, sending him crashing to the floor. Leggett gave a contemptuous laugh. 'Who the fuck do ye think ye are ya cunt?' He kicked at Boag's head and Boag felt his cheekbone yield under Leggett's boot. Boag struggled onto his trembling elbows, his eyes swirling blindly in their sockets, before collapsing, unconscious once more, to the floor.

***

'Tosser,' Leggett said, pushing wet hair back from his face. The sprinklers were continuing to flood the sales area, a relentless torrent from a gantry of pipework set into the ceiling far above. His clothes were soaking and the floor was beginning to puddle and pool. Despite this, he noticed the small fire at the door showed no sign of going out. On the contrary, it blazed merrily, sheltered from the downpour by the overhang of the lintel above. Already a secondary fire had sprung up in the corridor beyond, this one rather more substantial than the original.

Leggett smiled. This was great fun. He looked around the shop; man, but there must have been thousands of pounds worth of damage already. The place was drenched, and everything sparkled in the rain falling from the ceiling – the fancy coats and jackets, the dresses, the expensive watches; all ruined. He glanced up to where one of the overhead walkways joined the upper gallery. A thin plume of black smoke snaked from a set of glass doors, behind which a yellow-red glow flickered and danced. He allowed himself a giggle. Just a tiny one. Nobody was around to hear after all. He examined the control box in his hand. The asymmetry of the three thrown switches annoyed him. It just didn't look right. Or so he convinced himself.

Flick, flickety-flick he sang to himself, his fingernail brushing, teasing the remaining switches, clicking against the little metal toggles. He pulled his hand away and quickly stuck his thumb in his mouth, biting down hard to prevent a fit of uncontrolled sniggering. Oh, but this was just too good. Of all the revenge scenarios he had envisaged this surpassed even his wildest imaginings. Whatever the bastards were up to in this poncy shop – and he had seen enough to suggest it must be something pretty damned big – he now held in his hand the means to royally fuck them up. Oh aye. And not just destroy their careful little plans, but quite possibly destroy those tossers into the bargain. Wherever the rest of them had buggered off to, these wee bomb devices the Boagster was in charge of were the dog's bollocks, *weehoo*, the perfect thing to wreck their stupid plan.

He couldn't contain himself any longer – the five remaining switches on the control panel stood to attention beside their fallen comrades, goading him. He bit down onto his lower lip, his eyes flashing with greedy anticipation, and flicked over the rest of the switches one by one.

Explosions rocked the building, the sound of shattering glass echoing in distant upstairs corridors carrying over the incessant grainy sirens of the alarms. With each successive blast Leggett's grin grew wider. A grin which was instantly wiped off his face as he flipped the last switch and the final detonator rig exploded on the display counter where Boag had left it.

The blast was mild in relative terms, but it was enough to throw Leggett six feet backwards, send him crashing against a fluted marble column. The wind was knocked from him and he fell to his knees amongst the glass and metal remains of the display unit. He looked up to see silk scarves drifting lazily through the air like slow-motion birds. Some of the scarves were ablaze, and Leggett struggled to focus as he watched two of them land and drape across the shoulders of one of the mannequins, setting fire to the pink shirt it wore. Soon the whole figure was in flames, regardless of the water falling from the sprinklers, an inhuman torch standing in a curious pose of exaggerated elegance. *Mama, mama*, thought Leggett, this was better than the movies. He felt exhilarated despite the pain in his lower back where he had slammed into the pillar. Further fires had broken out on the upper levels and a dense rope of black smoke was coiling down one of the high stairways with an oily slowness.

Leggett got to his feet, energised by the thought the others were up there somewhere. Trapped, or panicked, running from room to room, blindly seeking the way out. Man, oh man, this was something he had to see. Especially that shit-eater Kyle. Leggett hoped that bastard was roasting like a fucking pig on a spit right now. He stepped over Boag's unconscious form, and ran towards the nearest stairway.

***

Conscience.

McKinnon had no place for it in her moral repertoire. It belonged with other woolly concepts such as *empathy* and *pity* in the mental garbage bin marked SENTIMENTALITY.

She had not time to deal with any of that crap right now. Something had clearly gone wrong. Whether it was an accident with the explosives or something else, she didn't know and didn't care, but when the first blast rumbled from the depths of the building her commitment and allegiance to Boddice and his half-arsed heist had evaporated instantly. It was all part of the deal, McKinnon's standard *modus operandum* – payment, in full, up front (and, as Boddice knew from past experience, she didn't come cheap), with the complete understanding that if things went arse over tit she was out of there. No questions asked. No retributions. No refunds. She would simply disappear. Boddice had been happy enough to accommodate her; the times she had worked for him before had been fruitful, and he'd seen no reason to refuse her conditions this time, even with the high price tag. He made a song and dance about the amount of money she was asking for, though she knew fine well it was, if not easily, then certainly tolerably, affordable for him. Besides, if this whole diamond thing came off, he would be beyond caring about money.

All that was academic now, however. McKinnon had already begun to make her way to the second-floor fire escape, the team's planned escape route, when the second explosion went off and the alarms and sprinklers came on. Part of her mind, still in security officer mode, made a note of the fact that nothing had happened after the first blast. That wasn't good. The T&N empire would not be pleased with that little lapse in the building's automatic emergency procedures. She smiled; that wasn't going to be her problem any more.

She reached the door to the fire escape and that word swam up into her mind again.

Conscience.

What she was about to do would cost the lives of the men still inside the store: Kyle and the twin somewhere in the walls of the building itself, and Boag... well, who knew what had become of Boag? Those explosives were his responsibility. It sounded as if he'd fucked up.

As if to confirm her feelings, a further set of explosions shook the building. She opened the door to the fire escape and a swirl of cool air blew into her face.

She dragged her hands through her soaking hair and flicked the water onto the floor. Ahead of her, a metal staircase ran down to the alley at the rear of the store. Above the door, a green illuminated sign with a picture of a running man bathed the stairway in a sickly light. This doorway was now the only way out of the building. The other exits were likely blocked by fires now that the other detonators had gone off. No point in feeling sorry for those left inside. They couldn't be allowed to get out alive. If the police nabbed them they would blab about her role in all of this. She would be compromised.

McKinnon closed the fire-escape door. The release bars slid into place on the other side. Preparation was all, exploring every possibility for things that could go wrong, contingencies devised. This particular one had been top of the list. Once she knew of Boddice's proposal to steal the diamond and how he planned to carry it out, she recognised the high probability it would fail. Trusting fuckwits to carry off such an involved scheme was madness. The fact they had actually got this far surprised her. Nevertheless, she had anticipated every eventuality and had made sure she was prepared. Attached to the metal railing of the stairway she had left two cycle cable locks – high-quality, expensive ones. She unlocked them and looped each through the handles of the fire-escape doors in a double figure of eight. She fastened the ends of each cable into their respective locks, making sure they were tight and secure. She tested the doors against them. They held fast.

McKinnon descended quickly to the alley and walked out into the street. She glanced behind her once, looking up at the fire-escape door – a blank square beneath the green exit sign.

She drew her wet coat around her.

Fuck conscience.

***

As soon as he got to the junction with Hope Street, John knew something was wrong.

A growing feeling of unease had crept up on him as he sat on the steps outside the hotel, a worry that he should have heard something by now – a text message at least – but there had been nothing. Unable to stand the tension any longer, he'd made the decision to go to the store for a look. John knew he'd done enough for the night back at the party. He even felt a slight pang of regret for what he'd done to Corrigan's missus; she was an innocent party in the whole affair after all, didn't deserve to have some idiot's walloper flapping in front of her face. Still, it was a necessary evil; no-one was going to forget him and what he'd done in a hurry. Mission accomplished.

He'd made a point of catching the eye of a crowd of guys from the audio and hi-fi department who were having a smoke outside and offered some slurred excuse about not feeling too good, needing to stretch his legs, get some exercise to clear his head. They sent him on his way with a couple of hearty slaps on the back from the ones who hadn't seen what he'd done and disapproving grunts from those who had.

Hope Street was almost deserted as John rounded the corner, a few late-night stragglers making their way to Central Station or looking for a kebab shop. He leaned against a traffic signal at the pedestrian crossing and squinted towards the glowing Bubble suspended above the intersection with Argyle Street. A distant but distinct bang sounded from the bottom end of the street. John frowned; what the fuck was that? A flurry of pigeons flew up from nearby window ledges and a couple kissing at a bus stop broke off and turned to look towards the sound for a few seconds before getting stuck back into each other.

John picked up his pace and jogged towards the store. That didn't sound right. Not right at all. His sense of foreboding ramped up a few notches. As he got closer, a second blast came from somewhere high above followed by the shrill crash of falling glass as a window blew out on the store's third floor. A girl on the opposite side of the street screamed and ran into the doorway of a shop. The wailing of alarm sirens rose and fell in the still night air and blue lights strobed from metal boxes beneath the first floor balcony. The passengers on a bus waiting at a stop crowded to the windows, looking up at the dark façade of the building to see what had happened. John broke into a run and sped down to the store entrance. He skidded to a halt at the main door, almost losing his footing on the slippery pavement. The spotlights in the window displays and those surrounding the main door flickered once and went out, and the street suddenly became darker.

John tried the doors, knowing they would be locked, but pulling hard nonetheless. He stood back, aware that a small crowd had grouped on the road behind him. He ignored them and began searching for another way in.

The explosions meant something had gone wrong with the robbery and the guys inside would be making their getaway via the second-floor fire escape; if that was the case, it was best for John not to get involved.

But he had a feeling deep in his gut that the plan had now gone to hell in a handbarrow, an intuition something much more serious had happened. He had to get into the store. No use going round to the back. He didn't have time for that now. No, a more direct approach was needed.

He wheeled round and the people behind him, a middle-aged couple, a railway worker and two or three drunks, backed off a few steps. John crossed the road to a rubbish bin sitting at the edge of the pavement. He opened the little door on the side of the bin and dragged out the metal inner container. He dumped the contents onto the street and crossed back to the store, carrying the metal box above his head.

'Heh, what're ye gonnae do with that?' asked an old guy in a check jacket with matching bunnet.

John ignored him and carried on walking, pushing through the small crowd. In the distance, beyond the crest of the hill at the top of Hope Street, a police siren could be heard. A girl in the crowd was filming the scene on her mobile phone, panning from the ground to the top floors of the store. John grabbed the phone from her hand and threw it onto the road.

'Hey!' the girl shouted. 'My phone!'

'What's your problem pal?' asked a burly guy with a shaved head, moving towards him. 'Where do you get off flingin that poor lassie's phone into the… *Whoa!*'

He was cut short by John launching the metal bin over his head and into the large plate glass window of the shopfront. The bin bounced back from the glass and clattered onto the pavement, leaving the window unharmed.

The guy with the shaved head glared at him. 'Are you off yer nut, pal?'

John paid him no attention. He picked up the bin from the pavement and made to swing it back onto the window when there was another set of explosions – five of them in rapid succession. John dropped to one knee and reflexively raised an arm to shield himself, though no debris fell. Several people in the crowd screamed. Everyone except John ran back across the street to safety, huddling behind a parked van.

The last explosion was close, and the concussion from the blast rocked the whole store front, sending the contents of the window displays flying against the glass and causing the window itself to bow outwards momentarily before it snapped back into position in its frame. Through the wailing of the alarms John heard a thin crackling sound. He looked up at the window. A hairline fracture had started at the bottom right-hand corner of the glass and was now inching slowly upwards, moving diagonally across the window, creaking and splintering as it went.

John wasted no time. He grabbed the bin and hurled it at the window. It struck midway along the fracture line which shot upwards with a loud crack. The glass hung in place for a fraction of a second before separating into two large triangular sections which slid from the window frame in slow motion, smashing to the ground as John dodged to the side. He jumped into the window display, vaulting over a collapsed plasma screen television and surround-sound speaker system.

The plasterboard wall at the rear of the display had been blown out by the blast. John kicked through the tatters of its remains and scrambled into the store. He was confronted by a confusion of smoke and flames, water and debris, noise and chaos. The familiar layout of the shop had been thrown into a jumbled, rain-soaked shambles. He was quickly becoming drenched by the overhead sprinklers yet, despite the volume of water being sprayed over the shop, he could see several fires blazing brightly throughout the ground floor and smoke belching from a number of doors and passageways on the upper floors.

John shot a glance upwards to the walkway leading to the entrance to the Bubble. It looked clear, no evidence of fire or damage. He waited for a few seconds to see if the others might emerge from the doorway, running to the escape point on the second floor.

John was about to cup his hands to his mouth to shout Campbell's name when a sudden bolt of searing, snapping pain shot up his right leg, causing him to buckle at the knees and crumple to the floor in agony. *What the fuck was that?* He folded into a foetal position on the wet carpet, clutching his leg and fighting the urge to scream at the top of his lungs.

Almost as abruptly as it had arrived the pain started to disappear, melting away like mist in a breeze. He got to his feet and gingerly put his weight on his right leg. It was fine.

John bent to rub his hand along his leg, feeling for any sign of injury, all the time staring wildly about the sales floor. There was nothing – his leg was perfectly okay, no indication that anything had happened to it.

He had only ever experienced something similar once before, many years ago, when he and Campbell were just boys, walking home from school on his own, his guts had erupted into sudden excruciating pain for no apparent reason. No reason except that Campbell, who was at home in bed, had developed acute appendicitis that very same day.

He knew now that things were far from alright. Very far indeed.

★★★

As soon as the alarms started, Campbell pulled the box from the safe and opened it. He had no time to register the purple darkness of the diamond lying in the white velvet folds of the container; he simply grabbed it and stuffed it into his pocket, quickly replacing it in the box with the fake one. A heavy clunking sound came from the adjacent room, causing the floor to shudder; the sound of huge bolts slamming into place, sealing the doors to the outer room and entombing Campbell and Kyle inside.

'Come on, come on!' Kyle shouted from behind him. 'Get a move on!'

Campbell placed the box back in the rear of the safe and closed the door. The LED on the door changed from green to red again. Campbell tugged on the handle. It was locked. He turned to Kyle. 'Okay, Ah've got it. Let's go.'

'Hurry up, get in,' Kyle yelled above the howling of the alarms.

'What? Me first?' said Campbell.

'Too right, you first. You and yer brother are the kinda guys who can't wipe their arse without getting shite on their thumb. So it's just gonnae be the same as on the way up, Ah'm no having you panicking and losing yer grip when ye're above me, come crashin down on top of me.' Kyle grabbed Campbell's sleeve, pulled him towards the opening. 'So shift yourself and get in.'

Campbell gripped the edge of the hatch and hoisted himself through, reaching across to grab the rungs of the ladder. Kyle followed with the hatch door held in his right hand. They struggled with the door, manipulating it onto its hinges and slotting the latches into position. More explosions shook the building, sending loose masonry and flakes of brickwork tinkling down through the riser shaft.

'What in the name of holy fuck is happening?' Kyle said.

Campbell shrugged. 'Whatever it is,' he said, 'we need to get out of here.'

'Ye're a master of the understatement,' Kyle said, fiddling with the last of the latches which was refusing to fit properly into its slot. 'Look, you make a start. Ah'll catch ye up when Ah get this done.'

'You sure?'

'Aye, just get going. Ah'll be quicker getting down than you anyway. If we go at the same time ye'll just be holdin me up.'

Campbell could see the logic in this. 'Okay,' he said, and started to descend the ladder, leaving Kyle grunting with the effort of trying to secure the final latch.

Going down on his own, in the dark, with nothing but the glow from his head torch casting a tiny cone of light, was unnerving. Campbell, trying not to think of the drop below, edged down, inch by inch, rung by rung, setting as fast a pace as he dared. A faint smell of smoke drifted up from the depths of the riser. Above him, he could make out the yellow circle of Kyle's torch bobbing and dancing in the darkness. He turned back to the wall in front of him, concentrating on placing his hands and feet in the right place.

As he worked his way down he thought at first he was losing his sight; the rungs and the bricks seemed to be fading, he had to make more of an effort to locate his hands in the correct position. He looked down and realised he could no longer see his feet.

Then it dawned on him.

It wasn't his vision. It was the head torch.

The batteries were running out.

'Fuck! Fuckfuckfuckfuck!' Campbell reached up and tapped the side of the torch. It was the worst thing he could have done. The torch flickered briefly and blinked out, leaving him in complete darkness.

Campbell froze. Christ, this was all he needed. He thought briefly of waiting for Kyle to make his way down to join him but knew that wasn't the best idea; Kyle already thought he was a dickhead without Campbell acting like a big wean; scared of the dark and frightened to move, waiting for someone to come and hold his hand. Plus there was the small matter of getting out of the store without being caught. In other words, getting out as quickly as possible. On top of that, the smell of smoke was stronger now; something, somewhere, was definitely burning.

He took a deep breath and tentatively lowered his foot to the next rung down, finally exhaling when his foot made contact. Okay, okay, he could do this. It wasn't so bad. He carried on for another few rungs and let out a sigh of relief. It was going to be fine, there couldn't be too far to go now. He looked up to see Kyle had also started to descend, the light from his headtorch getting closer, and this increased Campbell's confidence further. He began to go down a little quicker, finding a rhythm between hands and feet. He even managed a smile to himself, and was about to shout up to Kyle, kid him to get a move on, when his foot slid off the next rung, slipping through the narrow gap between the ladder and the wall.

He started to fall and scrabbled for purchase on the rungs in front of him. It was no use. His momentum carried him backwards and his outstretched hand missed the metal bars. His head collided with the wall behind him and he began to drop down the riser. His leg, trapped in the space behind the ladder, twisted impossibly as he fell.

Campbell felt something snap below his knee and a

white-hot shard of pain speared up through his body, exiting in a piercing scream of agony as he came to rest hanging upside down in the shaft, his leg still wedged in the ladder.

Kyle came scurrying down the ladder towards him. 'Jesus Christ!' he said. 'What the fuck happened?'

Campbell continued to scream, flailing wildly, trying to lift himself up to relieve the weight on his trapped leg. 'Help me!' he finally managed to get out, his voice cracking. 'Pull me up!'

Kyle hooked his arm through a rung and stretched down, making a grab for Campbell's hand. He couldn't reach, only managing to brush Campbell's fingertips with his own. 'Wait a minute,' he shouted and edged down a little further. He could see Campbell's leg, the raw edge of bone protruding from his ripped trousers like a splintered stick. 'Give me your hand,' he said. 'Reach up.'

Campbell tried to raise his body to stretch towards Kyle, but the movement only caused him to slip further down the shaft, his leg shifting and grating against the rung. Campbell screamed again, a long tortured howl which ended in a series of burbled choking gasps as he vomited.

Kyle looked for a way to get down to Campbell. It was hopeless. There was no way he could manoeuvre past Campbell's shattered leg.

That realisation brought him up short.

If he couldn't manage to get Campbell upright there was no way Kyle was going to be able to get out of the shaft. Kyle was stuck above him.

He was trapped.

Unless…

Campbell started howling again and Kyle had to shout to make himself heard. 'Hey! Listen! There's only one way Ah can help ye.' Campbell quieted to a series of low moans. 'Ah can't reach ye from here. Ah'll need to go back up, get out through one of the other hatches up above.' He could vaguely make out the pasty oval of Campbell's face staring up at him through the gloom. 'Ah'll find a way back down to the Arrow and climb back and get ye from below.'

'No!' Campbell screamed. 'No, ye won't! Ye're gonnae leave me here.'

'Ah'll come back for ye, Ah promise,' Kyle replied, knowing as he said it that it was a lie.

'Ye don't have time. Ye'll just save yourself and to hell with me. Ye'll let me die here.'

'Ye're not gonnae die, get a grip of yourself.'

'Ah will,' Campbell said. 'Can ye not smell that smoke?'

Kyle hadn't noticed, but now that Campbell mentioned it, there *was* a burning smell in the shaft. 'It's nothin,' he said. 'Boag said there'd be wee fires. That was the point of the explosives.'

'Aye, and wee fires can get out of control. Ah'm tellin ye, don't leave me here.'

Kyle had had enough. It was time to act. 'Look,' he said. 'This isn't going to work. Ah'll come back. Climb up and get you from below.'

'Ya prick,' Campbell yelled. 'Ye're gonnae do it, aren't ye? Ye're actually gonnae desert me.'

Kyle started to make his way back up the ladder. 'Ah'll be back,' he shouted down. 'Ah promise. Ah'm no gonnae let ye down.' The words rang hollow, even to his own ears, and he knew as soon as he was out of the riser he would be looking for the nearest exit.

Campbell began to struggle, pushing his back against the wall in an attempt to lever himself upwards. 'Come back ya scumbag,' he shouted. 'Come back!' His squirming contorted his leg further and another brilliant blaze of pain scorched through him.

This time he fainted.

***

John ran through the debris of the lower sales area, pulling aside toppled mannequins and climbing over broken display cabinets. Panic constricted his throat. A serious fire had taken hold in the far corner of the room, black smoke billowing thickly towards the ceiling far above. Other, smaller fires were crackling and flickering around the expanse of the shop floor.

Where the fuck were the others?

John negotiated a pile of lifesize golden dogs which had been thrown together by the blast and strewn across the floor. He vaguely recalled they were part of a 'pampered pooches' display, advertising jewelled collars and fur-lined coats. Now, they lay across each other in various attitudes and postures, like some weird canine orgy. To his right was an aisle relatively clear of rubble and wreckage. It led to the grand staircase. He could get up to the second floor that way. If, as he hoped, the others had made it to the fire escape he could catch up with them there. If not, he would carry on up to the Bubble, see if they were still there.

The water on the floor lay half an inch deep and it splashed about his feet as he sprinted towards the stairs. He began calling for Campbell as he ran, but it was useless – his voice was drowned in the clamour of the alarm sirens. As he got to the stairs, a small movement to his left caught his eye.

A bloodied figure crawled along the floor towards him, and as John skidded to a halt it lifted its head to look at him. John frowned. Was that Boag? Good God what on earth had happened to him? His face was mashed to a blood-spattered ruin, his nose flattened and crushed. Boag rolled onto his side and sat up, leaning against the base of a perfume counter.

John knelt beside him. 'Fuck's sake man, you been getting some plastic surgery? Cos Ah'll tell ye, it hasn't worked.'

Boag managed a smile. 'Bad as that is it?' He wiped a string of clotted blood from above his lip and examined it. 'It was Leggett,' he said through gritted teeth.

'*Leggett?*' John asked, wide-eyed. Boag waved away an answer.

'What about Campbell?' John asked. 'Where is he?'

Boag pointed up to the hatch at the top of the Arrow.

'You're pullin my plonker. What in the name of Christ is he doing up there? What about the Bubble?'

Boag shook his head. 'No time to explain. But that's where he is. Him and Kyle.'

'The two of them?'

'Up there,' Boag said. 'They climbed.' He pointed to the arrow, then to the ceiling.

John swallowed hard. 'Jesus Christ… okay, if you say so, but look, Ah can't explain it, but Ah've got a feeling something's wrong, something bad's happened.'

Boag made a show of looking at the chaos surrounding them. 'No shit, Sherlock.'

'Aye, very good,' John said. 'But there's something else, call it instinct if ye like. Ah think they're in trouble.'

He stood, walked over to the base of the Arrow and hoisted himself on top, grasping the recessed rungs. He sucked his teeth, inspecting the length of the Arrow. 'Okay,' he said to himself. 'Ah think Ah see how this is done.' He turned to Boag. 'You wait here,' he said. 'Ah'm gonnae see what the score is up there.'

'But you might slip,' said Boag. 'They had harnesses and stuff.'

John laughed. 'Harnesses are for wimps. Just watch this.' He gave Boag a thumbs-up and began to climb.

***

Kyle made his way up the ladder, leaving Campbell behind in the inky blackness of the riser shaft. He would make better progress now he didn't have that fool to nanny any more.

The twin had been right about one thing though – the smell of smoke *was* pretty strong. Too strong to be just the result of the small fires Boag had been intending.

When he finally got to the next access panel he reached out to undo the first of the latches, ready to get out of this pit. He drew his hand back in surprise. He'd burned himself. 'What the fu—?' he said aloud, his voice deadened in the confined space of the shaft.

He licked his forefinger and placed it on the flat surface of the hatch. Again, he had to pull back. It was hot. Very hot. He felt around the brickwork surrounding the panel – it too was warm. This wasn't good. There shouldn't be any fire this high up – Boag was only supposed to set them on the lower floors. If a fire had spread this far...

He began climbing again, picking up the tempo. Each footfall on the rungs clanged with a dull, metronomic regularity which pushed him harder. At the next floor he stretched out his hand to test the panel, breathing a sigh of relief as he encountered only cool metal.

He quickly undid the latches and pushed the hatch open, letting it fall to the floor on the other side. He climbed through into a storeroom filled with box files and stationery. A faint rumble from the fire on the level below came through the floor. Kyle opened the door and went out into the corridor beyond. He ran to a stairwell at the far end – a utility, staff-only, concrete-and-steel affair. Wisps of smoke curled up and around the spars of the handrail but he could see no flames or flickering below. He had no option but to risk it – down was the only choice.

He vaulted the stairs, taking a whole flight at a time. A sign on each level announced the relevant floor and he made it as far as Level 4 before he was stopped in his tracks. The smoke had been getting thicker and the temperature higher the further he descended and now he saw the source: a wall of flame flared from the door leading to the main corridor, cutting across his path on the stairs. The heat from the fire seared his face, and he could feel the tear film on his eyes evaporating. The smoke was overpowering and Kyle doubled over in a hacking convulsion of coughing, forcing him to retreat back up the stairs to the floor above. There had to be another way down; it couldn't just be this.

He slammed through a doorway marked Level 5, and ran down the corridor pushing open random doors as he passed, hoping for access to some other passageway which might lead out. They all led to offices and store cupboards, one even to a room which was empty but for a single champagne glass standing in the middle of the floor.

Kyle let out a yell of frustration. This was hopeless. He stopped, tried to think it through. Maybe the next floor up would provide a route. It was the wrong direction, he couldn't keep going up all the time, but he didn't see what else he could do. He ran back and opened the door to the stairwell. Immediately a sheet of flame burst into the corridor, throwing him to the floor. He forced the door closed with his feet and scrambled across the floor on his hands and knees. Kyle rolled onto his back and stared at the ceiling which now had little curls and licks of flame slinking along its underside.

'Aw man,' he said. 'Not this, please not this.' He got to his feet and stumbled to the end of the corridor, as far away as he could get from the flames. Looking back, he saw small drips of thick molten material dropping from the ceiling onto the carpet which now began to smoulder.

Kyle considered going back and trying to stamp it out, but the stuff from the ceiling, whatever it was, was now coming down so fast it would be impossible. He looked round and spotted the final door in the corridor. It was a proper fire door and, if nothing else, it would provide a temporary refuge from the blaze and from the smoke which was now advancing along the ceiling with a slow creeping menace. It didn't escape his consciousness that the room would also serve as a trap – once inside there would be nothing left for him to try. This was the last resort. His only chance was that the fire brigade would get to him in time. But even that was a forlorn hope – as far as the emergency services were concerned there was no-one in the building; why would they bother to search some obscure corridor on an upper floor?

Fuck it, there was no choice now. He took one last look at the flames which were steadily progressing towards him, tried to estimate how much time he had left, and pushed the door.

It opened into a large open plan office. The air inside was cool and clear, the only light coming from a small window set in a door at the opposite end.

He did a double-take.

Kyle started laughing hysterically. It was true. There *was* another door. Another fucking door, a way out. 'Ya beauty!' he shouted, punching the air. 'Oh, ya dancer!' Tears came to his eyes.

He ran to the door and squinted through the window. The passageway on the other side was clear – no smoke, no fire. He pulled on the handle. The door didn't budge. Kyle could hardly believe it. The bastard was locked. No, this was too much. Not now he was so close.

Kyle yanked on the door again, braced his feet against the jamb, strained with all his might.

It didn't move.

Frantically he searched the room for a key, throwing open desk drawers and filing cabinets, tossing paperwork and books aside. There was nothing.

Fuck.

He checked the window; that wasn't a possibility either – it was too small and, besides, it was wired security glass. He'd never manage to smash it.

He was about to sink to the floor in despair, resign himself to the fact that this was finally it, when he spotted movement in the passage beyond the door.

His heart leapt. Someone was there.

He began pummelling on the door, yelling for help.

The figure in the corridor halted and walked slowly back towards him through the gloom.

'Hey, pal!' Kyle shouted. 'In here! Ah'm in here! Get me out. Hurry!'

Kyle took a step back from the window, slackjawed, as the figure came closer and he saw Leggett's leering face materialise on the other side of the glass.

'Oh mama, mama,' breathed Leggett, shaking his head. 'Whoop-de-doo and shag me sideways, but this is just fuckin perfect.' He broke into a wide smile. 'Kyle, my man. Kyle, Kyle, Kyle. Don't ye just love it?'

***

Campbell came to in the pitch black of the shaft, the blood pounding in his head as he hung upside down. The pain from his leg was like a razor-edged corkscrew slicing and twisting into his spinal cord. He let out a weak moan.

He was going to die here. Stuck in this fucking shaft, hooked like a side of meat in a butcher's freezer. The stench of his own vomit filled his nostrils and he could feel the sticky wetness of it on his forehead and in his hair.

He fumbled to find one of the rungs behind him, seeking some sort of purchase by which he could lift himself and relieve the weight on his injured leg. It was too awkward – any movement he made seemed only to serve to redistribute his centre of gravity without releasing the tension on his leg. He slumped, exhausted by his efforts.

Prentice had been right after all. They'd risked everything for Boddice's stupid adventure, and what sacrifices had that fat bastard made? Not a single fucking thing. Campbell and John had even given up *Two's Tattoos*, a genuine legitimate business they'd spent years perfecting. And for what? Just so he could end his days trapped like a ferret in a stovepipe? Boddice could go fuck himself if he thought Campbell was as expendable as that. Prentice was the only one amongst them with guts enough to walk out on the whole thing. Even Kyle was a coward –

Campbell knew that now, only too well – too scared to think for himself. Did Campbell really want to bracket himself with the likes of that?

Did he, fuck.

That bastard, Boddice.

Anger boiled up inside him. He could do this, by Christ. He could get himself out of this mess. A few moments ago he'd been ready to give in, roll over, play dead. But now, with the image of Boddice lording it up in his big mansion swimming through his head, Campbell found an unexpected well of hatred in his heart and he took a grim satisfaction in sinking a borehole to extract every last drop of venom. He'd be damned if he was going to let the cunt get away with it.

He steadied himself as best he could and took in a huge breath. He let it out again in an immense shriek of defiance. As he did so, he barelled all his energy into his stomach muscles and forced himself to sit up, curling his body up towards his knees. The pain in his leg spiked and spiralled to new heights but he yelled all the harder and ignored it. He brought his hands up to grab the spars of the ladder above and in the same movement hauled his body upwards, releasing his leg at the same time. It scraped up and out of the tight space behind the rungs.

He'd done it. He was free.

He held onto the ladder and rested his weight on his good leg, breathless and spent. In the deep dark of the shaft, he wept.

After a while Campbell pulled himself together. He wiped the tears and vomit from his face and managed a smile. His shattered leg felt numb and weightless. In a way, he was glad of the darkness. He didn't feel ready to see for himself the damage that had been done. His priority was to get out of here.

Gently, Campbell eased himself down the ladder, taking his time, making sure he didn't jar his injured leg. He didn't enjoy total success, and a couple of times searing jolts of pain were sent whipping through his leg.

Sooner than he expected, he touched down on the access platform at the foot of the riser. My God, he'd made it. He was down. This time he broke out laughing.

His joy dissolved as it slowly dawned on him that he'd only negotiated the easy part. There was still the Arrow to contend with. How in Christ's name was he going to manage *that?*

He felt around his waist. He was still wearing the harness and carabiner. That was something at least. He searched for the railing at the side of the platform and used it to support himself as he hobbled along the walkway towards the hatch above the Arrow. In the distance Campbell could see a faint orange glow and black fingers of smoke drifting along the gantry. The sound of the alarms came up from below, sounding like the very voices of the damned. He hurried as best he could, hirpling and shuffling towards the opening, shielding his broken leg from any contact with the spars and struts of the walkway.

At last he reached the hatch and looked down from his high vantage point onto a vast space filled with roaring red flames and dense shrouds of smoke; a vision of Hell.

A vision of Hell, with his own face looming up at him.

***

On the whole, Leggett didn't believe in God. Life was life, and that was all there was to it. However shitty or fucked-up things were, that was the way of the world, and you just had to get on with it; no divine intervention was ever going to change things.

But there were times when even he thought he felt the presence of something greater than mere humanity. Something guiding their lives, placing obstacles in the way, providing unexpected opportunities. Now and again all of these things happened at more or less the same time and Leggett was almost convinced of the reality of a deity.

Times like tonight.

After he left the Boagster lying in a heap of splintered

cartilage on the floor (and how easy had that been, by the way?), Leggett had spent the best part of half an hour wandering amongst the deserted shop displays and counters, picking up the odd trinket and gadget (*knick-knacks-for-dickheads* he called them). He stopped once to grab a double handful of TAG Heuer watches and stuff them into his jacket pockets – he could make a tidy wee profit on those down the pub later.

But he couldn't find the others. No sign of them anywhere. Hurrying along one of the upper galleries, he could see the extent of the fires below – they had certainly taken hold and were spreading quickly. He would have to be quick if he was going to witness those bastards getting their comeuppance, catch the looks on their stupid faces when they saw it was him, Leggett, who had been instrumental in bringing about the downfall of their precious plan. *Weehoo*, Boddice or no Boddice, they would see he was his own man, he would show them just what he was made of.

Leggett gave up searching the main area of the shop and snuck into the back room area of the upper floors – the storage spaces, the offices and cleaners' cupboards. Even here the sprinklers sprayed cold water relentlessly, and the corridors were partly flooded. This part of the shop was just as extensive as the sales areas and Leggett soon found himself disoriented in the intricate passageways, repeatedly covering the same ground, passing the same rooms and doorways.

It was luck (or was it God?) that made him decide to try one of the anonymous-looking doors at the end of the corridor. *Yee-haa!* It opened onto another stairway which led up to a series of open-plan offices and a large area filled with tables and chairs and kitchen counters – what he guessed must have been the staff restaurant.

He exited into yet another identical featureless corridor. Jesus Christ, the wankers who worked here must need a bloody map to let them know where the fuck they were. Everywhere looked the bloody same.

He had just about given up hope of ever finding the others when God came knocking again. Leggett had passed an ordinary-looking door and was carrying on down the corridor when he heard a frantic thumping coming from behind him, accompanied by pleas for help.

His heart flipped over in his chest.

It was a voice he recognised. A voice that was going to pay. Oh yes indeed.

He stopped in his tracks and closed his eyes. A shudder ran through his body.

He turned and walked back to the door. He saw Kyle's eyes behind the little window in the door, dancing in fear and panic. He saw the flutter of recognition and puzzlement cross Kyle's face and Leggett smiled.

'Oh mama, mama,' he whispered.

He felt God standing at his right-hand side.

***

'What the hell are *you* doing here? More to the point, *how* did you get here?' asked Campbell.

'Nice to see you as well,' John replied. He looped one arm round a rung on the wall, pulled himself onto the platform under the hatch. 'You look terrible by the way.'

Campbell grimaced. 'It's my leg.'

'Show me,' John said.

Campbell couldn't bear to look at it himself, but hopped closer to the opening to let John have a look at his injured limb.

John winced and sucked a breath into his lungs. Campbell's shin bone had completely snapped; the bottom half had sliced through the skin and ripped through his trousers and was now freely sticking into the air in a crag of sharp white splinters. His lower leg dangled lifeless and loose.

'Man, no wonder ye look like shite. What the fuck happened?'

Campbell shook his head. 'No time.' He grabbed the handrail behind him and leaned over the edge of the hatch, surveying the scene below. 'We have to get down off here.'

John gave a wry smile and cleared his throat. 'Aye, well there's the thing.'

'What?'

'Well, Ah got up here no problem, but now that Ah'm here Ah'm no sure how Ah'm gonnae get down.' He threw a glance over his shoulder at the Arrow sweeping down to the floor. 'Ah've… em, Ah've just discovered Ah don't like heights.'

Campbell rolled his eyes and groaned. 'So, let me get this straight. You've come up here on some sort of rescue mission and ye've got no idea how to actually do the rescuing?'

'Oh, aye,' said John, bristling. 'There's a whole queue of idiots down there just waitin their turn to climb up here and give ye a hand. It's just your bad luck ye got me first isn't it?'

'Sorry, ye're right,' said Campbell, softening. 'It's just Ah'm no feeling too good. Ah'm cold, clammy and Ah keep feelin Ah'm gonnae puke.'

'Puke again ye mean. Have ye seen yer hair? What is it? Spew-dio Line? For that extra hold.'

Campbell managed a laugh. 'Anyway, sorry. Ah'm glad ye're here.'

'Fair do's,' John said, squinting up at Campbell. 'But first things first, let's get ye down from up there. Ah can hear bangin and stuff below. Fire brigade's here Ah think.' He steadied himself on the platform below the hatch. 'Ye think ye can do this with one leg?'

'Do Ah have an option?'

John raised an eyebrow. 'No,' he said.

'Okay, let's do it.' Campbell settled his backside onto the edge of the hatch and, still refusing to look at it, gingerly manoeuvred the wreckage of his right leg out over the abyss, shuddering with the pain.

He stopped, slapped his hand to his forehead. 'Christ,

Ah nearly forgot.'

'What?'

Campbell put his hand into his pocket and brought out the diamond. He held it up for John to see. 'This,' he said. 'This pathetic wee thing. This is what has brought us here. It's that important Ah plain forgot Ah had it.'

'*You've* got it?' John asked. 'How the fuck did you…?'

Campbell held up a hand. 'Later.' He turned the diamond over, rotating it and holding it up to the flickering half-light that shone up from below. It seemed blacker than ever, almost a sculpted lump of polished coal. 'Think on it. We wouldn't be here if it wasn't for this. We would be safe and happy doing tattoos for bikers and punks.'

'Ah liked the tattoos,' John said dreamily.

'Aye, so did Ah,' said Campbell. 'And if Boddice hadn't stuck his oar in, we'd still be there, doing our own thing.' He tossed the diamond in the air carelessly and caught it in his other hand. 'And just so he can get his grubby paws on this.' He inspected the stone in his palm. 'Ye know somethin? Ah don't actually give a fuck about this any more. As far as Ah'm concerned, Boddice can cover it in butter and shove it up his arse.' Campbell looked past John to the shop floor far below. 'Who's down there?' he asked. 'Is Boag still on patrol, or has he fucked off?'

John thought better of telling Campbell about Boag and Leggett and the rearrangement of Boag's features; things were complicated enough as they were. 'Aye,' he said. 'Ah think he might still be there. Though not for much longer, if they fires get much worse, or the firemen manage to get in.'

'Hey! Boag!' Campbell shouted down.

'He'll not be able to hear ye,' said John. 'The alarms—'

'Boag!' Campbell yelled again, his voice cracking. 'Are ye watchin? Do ye see this?'

'Ah told ye, he'll no… Campbell! No! What are ye doing?'

Campbell extended his hand over the drop and slowly turned his palm downwards, letting the Dark Side of the Moon fall like a black teardrop into the flames beneath.

John's mouth hung open, struggling to take in what Campbell had just done. 'What the fuck have ye... do ye realise...?'

'Of course Ah realise,' Campbell said. 'And do ye know? Ah feel a million times better.' His face broke into a bitter grin. 'It's a weight off my shoulders. Boddice'll never ask us to do anything for him again. Not after this.'

'Aye, but...'

'No 'buts'. What's done is done. Now, let's get ourselves to fuck out of here.'

The first of the two rungs in the wall which led to the platform was about three feet below. Campbell took a deep breath. 'Right,' he said. 'Ah'm gonnae lower myself slowly. You be ready to support me.'

John tightened his grip and nodded.

Campbell turned onto his stomach and shuffled to work his torso over the lip of the hatch, balancing his upper body on the edge. John held out his free arm, hesitating to make any sort of movement that might upset either his own or Campbell's balance.

Campbell's left foot blindly searched for contact with the first rung.

'You're too high,' John called. 'Ye need to lower yourself a bit more.'

Campbell cursed but wormed further down, cautiously adjusting his handhold on the spars of the walkway above. It wasn't the best of grips, but if he could just... He took a deep breath and released his right hand, taking his full weight with his left.

His foot came within an inch or two of the ladder.

'Here, let me help,' John said, reaching out to guide Campbell's foot to the rung.

Campbell shouted, 'No! Wait, Ah'm not...' He felt himself begin to overbalance. His left hand slipped from its grip and he desperately sought some purchase as his body slithered over the edge and into the void. Campbell screamed as he plunged towards the shaft of the Arrow, his body twisting and wheeling in the air.

'Campbell!' John lunged to grab Campbell's arm as he fell past him. He managed to catch his outstretched hand just as Campbell hit the Arrow, his shattered leg crashing against the metal cylinder with a sickening crunch. John felt the violent wrench as he suddenly took up Campbell's weight and he was jerked from the platform above, falling headlong onto the Arrow himself. He began sliding over the curve of the shaft, pulled by Campbell's swinging body. John threw out a hand, wildly clutching at the recessed handles on the Arrow. He missed, but his fingers closed around the cable running beside them.

His grip held.

Campbell dangled below him. 'Don't let me go!' Campbell shouted. 'Don't let me... just... just hang on to me!'

John grunted, straining against Campbell's weight and the razor sharpness of the cable which was slicing into his hand. 'Don't worry,' he said. 'Ah won't drop ye.' He tried to pull himself up, his arm muscles trembling with the effort. It was no use; he couldn't raise himself more than an inch. Blood trickled down his arm as his palm started to bleed, the flesh stripping away as the cable bit deeper. 'Stop wriggling will ye?' he shouted. The hand holding Campbell began to weaken, muscles cramping and trembling. He needed to take his mind off it, give himself a chance to gather his strength. A distraction was required. He looked down at Campbell suspended above the flames below, his brother's eyes wide with fear and pain. 'Ye know somethin?' he said.

'What?' Campbell said through his gritted teeth.

'Ah wouldn't shag one of they lassies if ye paid me.'

'*What?*' said Campbell, straining.

'They lassies in the posters, ye know the ones in the

lingerie department, advertising knickers and bras and stuff. They're no shaggable lassies like that.'

'What the fuck are ye talkin about?'

'Do ye not think if ye had the chance, ye know, to give them a jump, ye wouldn't bother?'

Campbell shifted his weight, taking some of the pressure off John's grip. 'Wouldn't bother? They're beautiful. They're supermodels.'

'No they're not. Ah mean, aye, they're good-looking lassies Ah suppose, but they've always got this kinda scowly look on their face. Ye know, greetin-faced.'

'Aye maybe, but it'd be different if ye were shaggin them.'

'How would it? They'd just be lyin there with their face like fizz, as per normal, all disinterested. It'd be shite. They're no worth shaggin, lassies like that.'

'Oh aye,' Campbell said, rolling his eyes. 'And like you have them queueing up at the door, burds like that? Aye... ye've always been lucky that way haven't ye?'

'Well Ah might be, what point are ye tryin to make?' John grunted, adjusting his position slightly.

Campbell smiled up at him. 'No point,' he said. 'But Ah know what you've been doing. You and yer stupid conversations.'

John smiled back, the smoke from the fires stinging his eyes, bringing tears which flowed down his cheeks. 'Campbell,' he said. 'Ah can't hold it any longer. Ah'm slippin.'

Campbell nodded. 'Ah know,' he said, blinking back his own tears. 'Ah know. Don't let me go.'

John looked at Campbell and gave him a crooked smile. 'Don't worry brother,' he said. 'Ah'll not let ye go. Just close your eyes.'

'What?'

'Close your eyes, it'll be okay.'

Campbell closed his eyes.

John sighed and let his fingers slip from the cable.

***

'Open the door. Let me out.'

Leggett laughed. 'You've got a fucking short memory ya bastard. Open the door? Why the fuck would Ah entertain that idea?'

Kyle banged his fists against the door. 'Open it!' he yelled. 'Open it ya wee shite or Ah'll—'

'Or ye'll what? Stare at me? Cos that's about all ye can do in your position.' Leggett held his hands out, showed his open palms. 'And anyway, how am Ah gonnae let you out, Ah don't have any keys do Ah?'

'Well, help me. Do somethin,' Kyle urged.

'Oh, don't worry, Ah'm gonnae do somethin. Weehoo, aye.' Leggett smirked and stood back from the door, folding his arms. 'What Ah'm gonnae do is... man, oh man Ah can hardly believe it... Ah'm just gonnae stand here and watch you.' He made a pistol of his fingers, pointed it at Kyle and cocked his thumb. 'Watch you burn, ya fucker.' He pulled his imaginary trigger. '*Pow!*'

Kyle screamed with rage. Already smoke was streaming into the room via the ceiling space and the crackling of flames could be heard up there.

'Holler all ye like,' said Leggett. 'It adds to the whole experience. Ah'm enjoyin it, Ah really am.' He held a finger to his chin, striking a thoughtful, considering pose. 'In fact, Ah've got an idea. Why don't ye tell me what ye're feeling? What's going through yer head right now? Now that ye know ye've not got long left. What does that feel like?'

Kyle punched the door in fury. 'Bastard! Ah'll ram my fist into yer plooky face so hard ye'll be shitin teeth for a month.'

Leggett gave a sardonic laugh and shook his head. 'No ye'll not, ya tosser. This is it for you.' He leaned close to the glass, cupped his hands to his eyes to get a better view. 'Is it gettin warm in there? Feelin toasty?' Leggett giggled.

It didn't matter who heard him. Not Kyle, not anyone. Not now that he was so close. Finally, he was going to see it, after all this time it was really going to happen; Kyle was the 'man in Reno' and now Leggett was going to watch him die. Holy mama! He felt like dancing. Dancing for joy and gratitude, giving thanks to a God who was so generous.

Kyle had to scramble against the wall as the suspended ceiling at the far end of the room collapsed with a crash, sending smoke and cinders rolling in a black wave along the floor towards him. He heard Leggett whoop on the other side of the door. Kyle could see roaring flames in the space between the ceiling and the concrete roof, licking through from the corridor beyond and hungrily probing into the office. He began coughing, choked by the dense smoke, but he stared through streaming tears at the flames, gripped by what he could see up there; there was something… something.

It was a last chance.

'*Woo-wee!*' yelped Leggett, clapping his hands. 'This is where the fun really starts. Oh mama, Ah love it!'

Fuck this, thought Kyle. He ran over to one of the desks and pulled a sheet of paper from a drawer. He tore a couple of pieces of Sellotape from a dispenser on top of the desk and ran back to the window.

'Get it up ye,' he shouted, and taped the paper to the window, cutting off Leggett's view.

Kyle was surprised to hear Leggett actually howl. 'Nyaaaa!' he cried. 'Naawww, ye can't do this! Not this time! Ah want to seeeee!' Kyle allowed himself a smile, pleased to hear the defeat in Leggett's voice.

But he had to move quickly. He could hardly breathe, and the heat from the flames was fierce. He dragged the nearest desk across the floor and jammed it against the door. He went back to gather a smouldering chair and placed it on top of the desk.

'What are ye doing in there?' Leggett shouted, a catch in his voice. 'Why are ye movin the furniture?'

Kyle said nothing, but climbed onto the desk and then onto the chair. Spluttering and gagging, he reached up through the smoke and pushed aside one of the ceiling panels. He shone his head torch into the space.

He was right.

It was what he'd seen through the flames at the other end of the room. The breeze blocks above the door didn't extend all the way to the roof. There was a small gap – two feet, no more – below the concrete of the floor above. Small, but large enough for a man to crawl over and into the space above the corridor outside.

Another crash close behind him signalled the disintegration of a stationery cupboard in a spray of sparks and embers. Kyle quickly hoisted himself up into the ceiling space. The metal rods and supports which were the loadbearers for the ceiling panels groaned and buckled under his weight, but held fast.

The fire was twice as ferocious up here in the enclosed space and flames shot in brilliant, flaring arcs towards him, sucked on the powerful air currents from the wind tunnel he'd created by the removal of the ceiling panel. Kyle felt the fire lick at his legs and he frantically pulled himself over the breeze blocks above the door. An awful, scorching pain enveloped his legs and he knew his trousers had caught fire. He kicked out desperately, an involuntary series of spasms, trying to get his legs away from the terrible heat and pain.

He cried out in agony, an anguished primeval yowl of terror and despair.

It was answered from below by a braying laugh from Leggett. 'Yeeeooww! Oh man, you go for it, give it laldy big man.'

Kyle hauled himself over the brim of the low partition above the door and launched himself onto the ceiling on the other side. He smashed through the panels and crashed to the floor below, sending Leggett springing away in horror.

But then Kyle made a mistake. Landing awkwardly, he stumbled to his feet, his instinct to get as far away from the fire as possible. As he rose, the flames from his legs leapt up greedily to engulf the rest of his body, setting his jacket ablaze. Leggett backed away screaming, horrified by what he was seeing. Kyle staggered towards him, wildly flailing his arms about his chest in a futile attempt to douse the flames.

In the depths of his mind, in the inner kernel of his soul which existed far beyond the pain and torment he was experiencing, Kyle knew his time had come. The universe remained steady on its axis and he felt the empty void of eternity, cold and vast and pitiless, yawn before him.

He swung around and his arm made contact with the retreating, terrified Leggett. In a last act of defiance (a last act of any kind, he knew now), he lunged forward blindly and caught Leggett in a bearhug. Leggett's screaming spiralled upwards in a wordless crescendo of panic, fear and, now, pain. He struggled frantically, kicking and thrashing against Kyle's relentless flaming grip. Kyle's hand sought out the carabiner which still dangled from the harness around his waist. He fumbled the mechanism open, hooked it into one of the belt loops on Leggett's jeans, and snapped it shut.

'Now,' he said through the flames which engulfed them both, 'Now you can see what it's like.'

***

Boag ran up the grand staircase to the second-floor gallery. Behind him he could hear the yells of the firefighters as they finally broke through into the blazing sales area. Minutes before, he had watched horror-struck as the twins slipped from the top of the Arrow, plummeting soundlessly, hand-in-hand, to crash to the ground five floors below.

It was all his fault. The explosions, the fires. If Boag hadn't been so keen to demonstrate his technical prowess and ingenuity by adding that wee bit extra 'spice', things wouldn't have got so out of hand. What had he been thinking? His own private recipe, a subtle mixture of nitrates and phosphates, a little bit of sugar, packed into cigar tubes and secured to his explosive rigs, had seemed just the ticket to offset the shitey obsolescence of the Rastahman's detonators. A bigger bang for your buck.

Aye, well they had got that hadn't they? A much bigger bang. And the fires that went with it.

If he was being rational about it, he knew it was Leggett's fault, not his. The explosives should never have been used; there was no need, everything had been going well until *he* showed up (and where the fuck did he come from anyway?). It was yet another Leggett fuck-up.

All that was academic now. It didn't change the fact that people had died; the twins certainly, and what the hell had happened to Kyle? Why hadn't he appeared at the top of the Arrow along with Campbell? What had happened up there?

Boag had no time to worry about these things now. He'd lingered long enough.

At the top of the staircase, he raced along the right-hand walkway of the gallery; to his left, the gallery was a confusion of blazing handrails and stanchions, melting wall-mounted displays cascading onto the floor like a Dalí painting. Boag was confident the firefighters hadn't seen him; they were too preoccupied with getting their hoses into place and establishing a plan of action to notice him sprinting along the balcony above their heads.

He burst through a set of double doors and ran towards the green fire exit sign at the far end, each pounding step jolting the crushed meringue of his nose. Twice he slipped in the water pooling on the polished floor, skidding and floundering to regain his balance.

He slammed into the fire-escape door, grateful to finally be free from the broiling hell of what remained of Trusdale and Needham.

He was thrown back onto the floor. Confused, he got to his feet and pushed the door again. It didn't budge.

'Aw fuck!' he shouted, kicking the door. 'What now?' He pushed and rattled the doorbars, heaved with all his might. Nothing.

He looked up at the ceiling, took three deep breaths and closed his eyes. There was one option. 'Right,' he said. 'For once in yer life, take control. You know what ye've got to do.'

He fished in his pocket and brought out the last of his cigar tubes, the one he'd kept back as a spare, packed with his patented nitrate-phosphate-sugar mixture. It would be enough to blow the door, and then some.

In the breast pocket of his denim jacket he had a couple of receipts for the clothes he had bought with Boddice's advance; he took one and rolled it into a thin cylinder. He unscrewed the lid of the cigar tube and inserted the paper cylinder into the powder inside. He was aware of the incredible risk he was taking – the mixture was extraordinarily unstable, so much so he was surprised it hadn't already gone off with all the falling and stumbling he'd been doing.

Gently, he rested the cigar tube against the base of the fire-escape door. He went back into his pocket and brought out the old woman's lighter and struck it. He smiled as it lit first time. He studied the grotesque face and the words – *La Guerre* – written below. Not for the first time, he thought the expression changed as he looked at it. Almost a conspiratorial wink, a knowing acknowledgement of complicity. What the hell *was* that?

Fuck it, he thought. He lit his makeshift taper and ran for cover.

He only managed a few steps before an almighty blast threw him head over heels into darkness and silence.

PART 5: SHINE ON YOU CRAZY DIAMOND

Nobody's Fault But Mine

Prentice sat alone, upstairs at the rear of the number 39, hot and slick in the heat of the late morning. He wondered if this was the same bus. Was this the exact spot where wee Jackie (or whatever her real name had been) died? He remembered her tight little face, screwed up against the world, the tick-mark scratch on her cheek. He gripped the back of the seat in front, hands in knuckled knots, jaw clenched. He couldn't allow himself to think about her. Not yet.

There was business to attend to first.

***

After he'd left Trusdale and Needham, he strode across the street to Central Station and found an empty bench in the main concourse. The station was quiet, just a few stragglers waiting for the late trains and the sleeper to London. A pair of ragged derelicts wandered as aimlessly as the stump-foot pigeons on the station floor, barely bending their knees as they shuffled from the closed newsagent to the centre of the concourse and back again. Prentice held onto the armrest of the metal seat and rocked back and forth, muttering and cursing under his breath. A middle-aged woman, bleached hair that didn't so much look styled as hacked into random clumps with a razor comb, stared at him, assessing him, her mouth working incessantly on her chewing gum. Prentice gave her a *back-off* scowl and she retreated towards the Costa shop.

Prentice forced himself to calm down, gulping deep breaths and directing his gaze to the floor. Now that he'd finally done it, defied Boddice so blatantly and completely, he knew things were going to change. He was on his own now, and, sooner or later, Boddice would be coming for him.

He had no idea how long he sat there, staring at the floor,

finding meaningless patterns and structures within the cracks and irregularities, the glazed flakes of stone, embedded in the tiles. When he finally looked up he saw a crowd of people gathered at the side exit from the station onto Hope Street. Necks were craning and bodies jostled for a better position. A railwayman in a fluorescent yellow jacket sprinted from the station office to join them. The rest of the concourse was deserted; everyone seemed to have gravitated to the exit passageway.

Prentice stood, and wandered over to see what the fuss was, gradually becoming aware of the distant sound of sirens and alarms as he approached. He frowned. What was going on here? He pushed his way through towards the front. Two cops were holding the crowd back to prevent them from spilling onto the street. Prentice pressed his back against the wall and snuck along the edge of the throng, ducking under the blue and white tape strung across the entrance.

'Hey, you,' called one of the cops. 'Get back here.'

Prentice pretended not to hear and walked steadily down the street towards the store.

Ahead of him, the sky was lit up in a brilliant orange glow and smoke billowed and boiled in rolling black clouds into the air. Flames leapt from broken windows high above, while fire-fighters ran in a confused rabble amid the blue strobing lights of the tenders. A great screaming roar came from the tortured ruin of the Trusdale and Needham building, almost as if the structure itself was crying out in pain.

Prentice stopped in his tracks, slack-jawed. Jesus Christ, he thought, what in the name of fuck has happened? Even from this distance he could feel the intensity of the fire. He stepped back into a recessed doorway, kept out of sight and watched as the fire continued to rage out of control.

They were in there. Kyle, Boag, the twin, the McKinnon woman. Somewhere in that inferno, they were... what? Trying to get out? Trapped? Dying? Already dead? Or had they already managed to escape? Prentice somehow thought that was unlikely. This looked much more than just the result of Boag's little diversionary explosions. He brought out his mobile and keyed Kyle, then Boag and the twin. Each time the same message – *The number you are calling is unavailable. Please try again later.*

He looked up. Something was happening. The fire-fighters were regrouping, retreating further up the street, pulling back. There was shouting and running. Prentice sensed an air of panic about their withdrawal.

One of the fire-fighters, a woman, ran past his hiding place in the doorway and, by chance, glanced in his direction. She skidded to a halt and grabbed him by his arm, pulling him away.

'What are you doing there?' she yelled. 'Come with me. Hurry. It's coming down.' She yanked him forwards, almost sending him stumbling to the ground. He regained his balance and looked over his shoulder as he ran back to the crowd at the station.

The copper spike that supported the Bubble began to bend in the middle, buckled by the heat from the fire. The Bubble itself swayed precariously above the intersection below. The cables and struts strained and groaned against the shifting weight. Prentice jumped as one of them sprang free from its mooring on the wall with a colossal whipcrack. The cable snapped up into the air and lashed against the sides of the neighbouring buildings, bringing down masonry and glass onto the road below. The Bubble tipped to one side, shuddering and bouncing on the remaining cables which struggled to accommodate the weight. The spike warped further, flexing and twisting, the whole structure complaining with a grinding metallic screech. An awed hush settled on the crowd as they watched further cables snap and tear away from their anchor points.

The Bubble lurched downwards and recoiled as it reached

the limit of the final few cables which still held. It swung in a wide circle for a few breathless seconds before the cables finally gave out, their severing signalled by three loud cracks which rang out over the thunder of the flames. The Bubble collapsed to the street below, a slow-motion descent through the last twenty feet, landing in a tangle of girders, glass and smoke. The ground shook beneath their feet.

The crowd gasped and someone near the back broke into applause. 'Quality, man,' cried a high-pitched voice. 'Pure quality.'

A fireman ran up the street towards them, waving his arms. 'Get back, get back!' The gable wall of the building, weakened by the collapse of the Bubble, started to bulge along the edge adjoining the corner, accompanied by a deep, almost subsonic, rumble. Huge sandstone blocks came free from the wall, crashing down to the street, crushing and flattening the cars below, and sending clouds of dust into the air to join the smoke and flames. A series of loud booms ricocheted along the street as vertical fissures opened up in the wall, red flames licking through the gaping wounds in the stonework. The façade of the store fell away with a long, ear-splitting roar which echoed through the dark canyons of the city centre. As the wall came down, the floors of the building caved in, tumbling like a spilled deck of cards. Beams and trusses, walkways and gantries, thrust up and out in crooked shards, backlit by the raging inferno beyond.

Prentice blinked, unable to take it all in. No that wasn't quite right – *unwilling* to take it all in. *This is fucked*, he thought. *So fucking fucked.*

He turned and barged back through the crowd and continued up Hope Street, fighting against the rising tide of rubberneckers emerging from the pubs and clubs, eager to see the free-to-view spectacular at the store. He kept walking, robotically marching through the streets, step after step, eyes fixed ahead, not stopping till he arrived at his flat, finally slumping onto the sofa to sit in the dark in a glazed stupor.

How had it come to this?

He sensed his life crumbling around him, a collapse as catastrophic as that of the Trusdale and Needham building. Everything had changed. Nothing was going to be the same again. It was his own stupid fault for listening to Boddice. And now the price was paid. Kyle, the others, all gone – he knew in his heart they hadn't made it – and for what? To satisfy Boddice's greed and lust for money and power?

Fuck him. The words spat in his mind. Fuck. Him. Prentice began banging his head against the back of the sofa, emphasising each word.

Fuck him.

Fuck him fuck him fuck him fuck him fuck him fuck him fuck him fuck him...

He fell asleep, the words swirling around his brain, losing their meaning by repetition, becoming nothing more than an abstract electrical buzzing as he slipped into unconsciousness.

***

And now Prentice sat on the bus. With business to attend to.

He'd made the call first thing, forcing McLean out of his bed, and requesting – no *demanding* – a meeting with Boddice. Prentice could picture McLean's raised eyebrow at the other end of the phone, his smug amusement at Prentice's audacity.

Then, eight minutes later, the text: *Boddice at the Palace – now*.

Yes, the Palace – it would be there wouldn't it, Prentice thought. Where the whole sorry-arsed saga had started. And where it would end.

The bus rattled along the road, rocked by the occasional bone-crunching jar as the driver skilfully managed to avoid avoiding the potholes in the road. Prentice stared blankly at the buildings, the tenements and high-rises, the shuttered shopfronts.

The bus passed a newsagent and Prentice read the board for the Daily Record on the pavement outside – *Massive City Centre Fire! Death Toll Mounts. No Trace Of Moon Diamond.* He turned in his seat, craning to see out the rear window, watching the sign recede in the distance.

No trace…

It suddenly slammed home; why Boddice had agreed to the meeting. It all made sense now, how easy it had been to get Boddice to show his face, to crawl out from wherever he'd been hiding last night.

Boddice thought the plan had worked. The stupid bastard actually thought Prentice had the diamond, that he'd left the others to die in the fire and made off with the stone, and here he was, calling to organise a handover. The loyal forelock-tugging servant, seeing the job through to the bitter end, no matter what. Prentice laughed. Boddice was so self-obsessed, so certain the world turned for him and him alone; the deaths of the others meant nothing to him as long as the success of his schemes was guaranteed. Why give a shit if someone fell along the way? It was all just natural selection to Boddice. Just move on. Oh, and thanks very much for the diamond. Hope it wasn't too much trouble.

Fuck him.

The bus lurched to a halt at the stop before the Palace, and Prentice scrambled down the stairs and off onto the street. The day was hot; the sun hammered down on his head as he waited for the bus to move off, causing his scalp to prickle and itch. He watched the bus lumber down the road, belching thick diesel fumes into the still heat of the morning.

He bowed his head and stared at the pavement. His shadow lay at his feet, a formless puddle of nothingness; an absence of light. Atonement and redemption were alien concepts to Prentice: as barren and meaningless as the religions they sprang from. Yet he felt them beat softly in his soul, gently insisting that what he was about to do was not only right, but necessary.

He walked down the street and round to the back of the Palace where he found an open door, the sign above it marked *Exit Only*. He stood quietly for a moment amongst the long grass, letting the sun warm his back, smelling the bitter aroma of the weeds and ferns which struggled from the baked soil in tangled, serpentine knots. He listened to the sound of his own breathing, the dry, papery rustle of his lungs; the slightness of it. The fragile ebb and flow.

'Okay,' he said aloud. He went through the door and began climbing the stairs to the auditorium. With each step he felt the familiar feeling return to him; the mantle of his persona gradually descending on him like a blanket laid over a sleeping body. Emotion and sentiment seeped from him, cooling, hardening in a dark corner of his mind. His eyes, expressionless, impassive, stared straight ahead at the steps in front of him. His heart settled, wound down to a steady pace; unhurried, constant.

Prentice reached the top of the stairway and stood at the door which led to the auditorium. His business was on the other side.

There would be no ceremony. No fuss.

He put his hand in his jacket pocket, felt the weight of the cold metal, and pushed open the door.

Boddice and McLean stood in the centre of the room. They turned in unison as Prentice strode across the floor towards them, his pace swift and unfaltering. McLean, frowning, took a single step forward before he dropped to the floor, his forehead a flowering rose, deep red oozing from the hole Prentice had put there. Boddice gaped, a frown corrugating his brow. He raised his right hand. A desperate gesture of reconciliation, or a plea for mercy? Prentice didn't wait to find out. He levelled the gun and fired a second shot, sending a bullet into Boddice's belly. Boddice's knees folded and he buckled to the floor. He moved his lips, made to say something, but Prentice stood over him and brought the gun up to Boddice's head and fired.

Boddice's body slumped where he knelt and pitched forward onto the floor.

No ceremony. No fuss.

Prentice hesitated for the smallest instant, before raising the gun to his mouth, registering the heat of the muzzle against his lips.

He knew this gun. Knew it well.

The pull weight. The break point of the trigger.

All he had to do was squeeze a little bit more.

A bit more.

A bit…

Under The Bridge

There was laughter, easy and relaxed. Clinking of glasses and cigarette smoke drifting. The girls in their summer dresses. Hot sun and the smell of spicy food. The low hum of conversation against the background city sounds. Boag watched the crowd seated at the pavement tables on Buchanan Street, envious of their casual carelessness, their safe, cosy lives. Untroubled.

Boag shifted his weight from one foot to the other, straightening his back and squinting against the sun's glare flaring from the office windows above. A couple, designer shades, sharp suits, white wine and bottled beer on the table, were staring at him. Boag could hardly blame them. He looked a state. His jacket was ripped and flayed; thin strips of cloth hanging like a leper's skin from his sleeves. His face and hands were pockmarked and spattered, little studs of congealed blood cratering his features where the molten slugs from the exploding cigar tube had tunnelled into his skin. He tried twisting his mouth into a defiant grin, let the smug bastards see he was onto them, but the fragments of metal still buried in the muscles of his face grated and ground against each other, sending shards of pain slivering through his skull. He let out an involuntary moan and stumbled, tilted off balance by the spiking hell in his head. The couple at the table turned back to each other, began whispering conspiratorially, carefully pampering their prejudices and assumptions.

Boag felt sick. The pain was one thing, but in time it would disappear. He wasn't sure he could say the same for the wounds on his face and hands...

***

After the blast in the store, he had come to lying on his back, grey clouds of smoke and dust billowing over him, ash and flakes of plaster tumbling from the ceiling above. At first he was too confused, concussed in all likelihood, to notice the stinging pinpricks on his face. As he got to his feet the pain hit him, hundreds of tiny laser-bright tines skewering through his skin, blazing points of agony, gnawing at him, devouring him. His hands jerked reflexly to his face, clawing; desperate to be rid of the white-hot torment. They, too, were covered in fresh blistering sores, blood seeping through his fingers. Boag screamed then, a guttural howl of anguish and fear. He lurched towards the wreckage of the door and scrambled out onto the fire escape and into the cool night air. Behind him, he felt the building shudder.

Boag staggered down the fire-escape stairs, careening between the railings, grabbing the metal banisters for support, before taking the last few feet in a wild swing towards the ground. He crumpled to his knees, almost fainting with the pain. But he didn't *(couldn't!)* allow himself to slip into unconsciousness – his survival instinct kicked in, deep, hard-wired neural circuits which slowly raised him to his feet again, got his legs pumping, and carried him away from the danger.

He ran like fuck.

He finally came to rest in the shadows under the Kingston Bridge, sinking to the ground behind one of the giant pillars supporting the roadway high above. As he allowed himself to be dragged down into a welcome oblivion, he became aware of a sound, a deep rumbling roar on the far edge of hearing, a distant but immense convulsion in the air. It was more than just the traffic on the bridge overhead. Much more.

***

All that had been five days ago. Since then, he'd roamed the city in a stupor, only vaguely aware of his surroundings, sleeping in the bushes by the river in Kelvingrove Park, drinking from puddles, eating leftover sandwiches and fish suppers found in bins. Twice, he'd heaved it back up, his stomach turned by the rancid, congealed remains of the food. Pain and fever dazed him, sealing him in a sweat-soaked cocoon, unable to distinguish reality from the nightmares dancing inside his head. In a graffitied tenement close he'd found a discarded copy of the *Metro* and read in disbelief of the discovery of bodies in the Palace bingo hall, unsure if he was in a delirium when he saw Boddice's name under the headline. What insanity was this? Was he the only one left?

He wandered the streets, frightened and exhausted, uncertain what to do.

Now, Boag found himself in the city centre, looking as though someone had taken a cheese grater to his face. His broken nose and cheekbone had subsided to a dull ache, but the wounds on his face had become infected, and the embedded chips of metal seemed to throb and pulse in hot waves. He needed to do something about this soon, get to a hospital, get some treatment. He could easily explain it away as an accident at a bonfire – Christ knew there were enough of them every night at various derelicts around the city, homing beacons for the vagrants and winos, the dispossessed and the crackheads.

But that was for later. Right now, he had something else to do.

A chapter to close.

Boag turned his back on the tables and shuffled down towards St Enoch Square. He walked with his head thrust forward, defiantly moving through the shoppers like an Arctic ice-breaker, the lunchtime crowds separating and parting to either side, anxious to avoid any contact with this monstrosity.

At the bottom of the street he paused. To his right, beyond the temporary barriers and the flashing yellow lights of the demolition and clear-up vehicles, Boag could see the twisted wreckage of the Bubble lying like a felled animal at the far end of the Heilanman's Umbrella. A thin haze of smoke still hung in the air, drifting lazily from under the canopy of the railway bridge. Already the city was bored by the aftermath of the fire.

A small group of onlookers were gathered at the barriers, the ruin providing little more than a temporary distraction on the way back to the office.

Boag shook his head. It hardly seemed possible he'd been in there, caught in the inferno. It seemed even less likely that he'd survived. He crossed the road and carried on through St Enoch's Square, skirting the entrance to the Underground and winding through the short back streets to emerge at the Clyde. He leaned on the railings at the edge of the pedestrian walkway. The river was a thick slab of silted sludge, dragging itself towards the sea. An earthy odour rose from the surface, the scent of hills and trees, warm fields and horses, carried down the long miles from the uplands to the centre of the city.

On his left, the old suspension footbridge swung over the river, the delicate threads of red-painted cables and ties cradling the walkway in a graceful curve which swept down from the arched sandstone pillars at either end. He smiled. It was years since he'd last crossed it. He must have been just a boy. He remembered the slight unsteadiness under his feet as the deck bounced gently with the footfalls of the pedestrians.

A sign under the archway of the pillar told him it was the *South Portland Street Bridge*. He thought of the crazed old woman in the amusement arcade. Had she mentioned that one in her rambling list? He didn't think so. He walked onto the bridge feeling in his trouser pocket for her lighter (*her* lighter; he hadn't been able to bring himself to regard it, even now, as his). It nestled, heavy and warm, amongst the oose and remnants of paper tissues which lived in the depths of the pocket. She'd said it was lucky, talismanic, but he questioned whether it had brought him any good fortune. Since he acquired the damned thing his life seemed to have gone from worse to worse still. But perhaps he was being unfair – surely luck could go either way; maybe he'd been lucky after all, but cursed rather than favoured.

The more he thought about it, the more he convinced

himself it was true. How else to describe the fact he found himself maimed and destitute, thrown into a pit of misery, yet with thirty million pounds in his inside jacket pocket? Thirty million pounds to which he had absolutely no access, no means to realise.

The Dark Side of the Moon pressed against his chest, its angular hardness like a tumour on his ribs. It had fallen from the twin's hand, whether by accident or by deliberate act he couldn't tell, and he'd watched it drop, a tiny black pellet, to the floor of the store. He'd flinched as it struck the ground, expecting it to shatter, but instead it bounced and rolled through the flames towards him, coming to rest against a disembodied mannequin head. He'd limped over to it and looked up to the Arrow far above, rooted to the spot, horrified and sickened as he watched the twins' final struggle and its awful end.

Boag wasted no time then. He stooped and swept the diamond into his fist, stuffing it into his pocket and made his run for the grand staircase to the second floor.

***

Standing in the centre of the bridge, Boag found himself breathing heavily, his legs weak and trembling, the memory of the last few days, the diamond in his pocket, both weighing him down.

This fucking diamond, this bastard lump of rock that had cost so much and was now worthless. As valuable to him as a cut-glass trinket. No-one would believe that he, Alistair Boag, had walked away from the devastation of Trusdale and Needham with the most famous item on the planet stowed in his jacket. What was the point of thirty million pounds if he couldn't even give the fucker away?

Which was why he'd come here.

He looked upriver towards Glasgow Green and the

other bridges which crossed in the near distance. Close by, a cormorant stood on a wooden pile at the edge of the water, its wings spread and drying in the sun, forming a black 'M' against the mudbanks. The river lay thick and ponderous beneath his feet. For a second he was baffled by the eddies and currents; the river seemed to be flowing backwards, *away* from the city, back towards the countryside. It was a combination of the wind and tide, or something, an illusion of return, that somehow the water would flow uphill seeking out the source, perhaps even rising back to the sky as – what? Not raindrops. Rainjumps? The idea brought a smile. He liked the possibility that things could go back to where they came from. Start again. There was a sort of comfort there, a reassurance.

Boag glanced to his right and left, made sure there was no-one else on the bridge. He reached into his jacket and brought out the Dark Side of the Moon, his fingers closing around it in a swollen fist. He didn't look at it, didn't give it a second glance.

He held his hand out over the water and opened his fingers.

There was silence.

And then, below, the softest splash.

The cormorant took to the air, wings beating furiously above the water as it flew in a wide circle to the other side of the river.

Boag could feel it. He sensed the diamond sinking, falling through the murky water, coming to rest on the black mud of the river bed which closed over it, sucking it ever deeper, the thick ooze engulfing it, smothering it.

Returning it to where it came from.

★★★

Boag turned and headed back towards the city centre. He looked at the cables suspending the deck of the bridge. The thin red strands reminded him of something, a dim and distant memory.

When he was just a kid.

He dug and dug, mining the deep core of his brain, searching for the answer.

Liquorice bootlaces. That was it. Red liquorice bootlaces. Christ, could you still even get them any more? God, he loved them when he was wee.

He laughed for the first time in days, remembering when he was young.

THE END

Acknowledgements

Thanks are due to Adrian Searle and everyone at Freight Books for making this all possible; to the excellent Russel McLean for editorial guidance, and for showing me how to cut deeply without spilling any blood; to Allan Guthrie who provided wonderful, detailed feedback on an early draft of the book; to all those friends and fellow writers who read early versions of chapters and first drafts, provided helpful comments and suggestions, and, of course, welcome encouragement.

And, finally, to Marie, for every single day.